FOR THE
LOVE OF
FRIENDS

FOR THE LOVE OF FRIENDS

a novel

SARA GOODMAN CONFINO

LAKE UNION
PUBLISHING

Text copyright © 2021 by Sara Goodman Confino
All rights reserved.

Published by Lake Union Publishing, Seattle

www.apub.com

Amazon, the Amazon logo, and Lake Union Publishing are trademarks of Amazon.com, Inc., or its affiliates.

ISBN-13: 9781542027595
ISBN-10: 1542027594

Cover design by Philip Pascuzzo

Printed in the United States of America

For Nick, Jacob, and Max

CHAPTER ONE

Sunday morning, six o'clock

A time best experienced while sleeping, preferably in your own bed and next to a loved one. Or Leonardo DiCaprio.

It is *not*, however, best experienced as I did—waking up, incredibly hungover, in an unfamiliar hotel room next to an unfamiliar sleeping man. Who, while mostly hidden by the combination of a hotel quilt and a mercifully facedown sleeping position, was likely *not* Leonardo DiCaprio.

Oh dear God, I thought, leaning over as far as I could to try to see my bedmate without actually waking him. *What (and who) did I do last night?*

Think, Lily!

Megan's engagement party. That explained the hotel. Sort of. I had been planning to stick to two drinks and drive myself the forty-five minutes home afterward. Which clearly had not worked out as intended. *But what happened?*

My eyes traveled to my cell phone on the nightstand, triggering a hazy memory of stepping onto the hotel's terrace outside the reception the previous night to answer a call. I closed my eyes, wincing. Amy had called. Repeatedly. Until I finally answered. My twenty-four-year-old little sister had gotten engaged. Which, under normal circumstances, probably doesn't seem like an excuse for getting wasted and sleeping with some random guy, though it felt like one that morning.

But I would deal with that later. First I needed to get out of that hotel room, preferably without waking my mystery bedmate.

When I was younger, I would have tried to justify my actions at the engagement party by forging an exceptionally ill-advised relationship with said bedmate. I would have snuck into the bathroom to try to salvage the tattered remains of what I had looked like before I morphed into the bridesmaid of Frankenstein, crept back into the bed, and pretended to wake up Disney-princess style, with a graceful, stretching yawn and perfect mascara. The courtship that would follow would be half-hearted on both of our ends, pursued by me solely so I could continue my day-to-day existence without feeling bad about myself for sleeping with him, and by him to keep getting effortlessly laid.

But I was thirty now, and therefore too old to lie to myself and call it honor. Or in this case, too old to lie to myself and call a one-night stand the start of a relationship. Fine, if you wanted to be picky about it, I was thirty-two and therefore *way* too old to kid myself that this was anything worth pursuing. So I slowly inched my way off the mattress without allowing it to shift. Once fully out of bed, I breathed a quick sigh of relief, then looked around the room for my clothes.

The little black dress I had worn to the party had been flung across the room's desk. It posed the next problem: the bandage-style, knockoff Hervé Léger dress had required my roommate's help to squeeze into the night before. And after a full night of drinking enough to black out, there was no way I was getting it back on without Spanx and a pair of pliers. Which left bedmate's dress shirt or suit jacket. As the odds were pretty high that I would never see this guy again (considering that I didn't even know who he was), I felt no guilt buttoning his shirt over my bra and underwear. Would I be doing a very obvious walk of shame? Yes. But again, it was six o'clock on a Sunday morning. The only people who would see me would be hotel staff and any other walk-of-shamers. I could handle this.

I quickly gathered my cell phone, keys, dress, shoes, and purse and tiptoed to the door, where I found two matching bags, one labeled "maid of honor" and one labeled "groomsman." I was Megan's maid of honor, which meant that I *would*, in fact, be seeing the bed's occupant again. Repeatedly. And in very close proximity.

Why, oh why, couldn't I have picked literally anyone else?

I had to stay and face what I had done.

I turned back to figure out my plan of attack and peered over the edge of the bed, trying to get a glimpse of the sleeping groomsman's face. But he stirred and gave a little half snore. Grabbing the maid of honor bag, I ran out of the room in a panic.

Breathing heavily, I leaned against the hallway wall. *Maybe he won't remember either,* I told myself unconvincingly. *And, worst-case scenario, there are six bridesmaids and six groomsmen. There's room to hide in that number.* I began to formulate a plan—I would give the shirt to Megan and ask her to return it to its owner. And if I could convince her to not tell me whom I had spent the night with, I couldn't act awkward around him because I wouldn't know who he was. I might just be able to survive this wedding after all.

I padded barefoot to the elevator before wedging my swollen feet into the impossibly high heels I had worn the night before. As I waited for the door to open, I studied my reflection in the mirror and rubbed desperately at my eye makeup, trying to look less like Alice Cooper. Then I pulled the ribbon off my bridesmaid swag bag and belted it around my waist in the elevator, doing my very best impression of a person who meant to look the way I did right then. Head up, eyes straight ahead, bored expression, I didn't even look around to see who could be watching me as I crossed the lobby and made my way down the too-steep-for-my-hangover marble staircase to hand the valet my parking ticket. Only when I was safely ensconced in my car, bare thighs sticking to the leather, did I allow myself a moment to rest my head against the steering wheel.

"Never again, Lily," I told myself through gritted teeth. "You're never getting that drunk again."

~

Becca was asleep on the sofa, the television quietly on Bravo, when I walked into our apartment. She had the blanket from the back of the sofa over her and had changed into yoga pants and a T-shirt, but she was still wearing her makeup from the night before. An open bottle of wine sat next to an empty glass on the coffee table.

She woke up with a small start when I shut the front door behind me. "What time is it?" she murmured sleepily.

"A little before eight," I said. "Go back to sleep."

She squinted up at me. "You look terrible."

I sighed. "Thanks, Bec."

She sat up suddenly, taking in my unconventional outfit. "That's not your shirt. How much fun did *you* have last night?" She swung her legs off the sofa and I sank down beside her.

"I don't remember."

"Always a good start. I thought you were coming home. I was waiting up for you."

"I was going to. But Amy called. She's getting married."

Becca let out a low whistle. "And she wants you in it?" I nodded and she counted on her fingers silently. "Five?" I nodded again.

"Including both my younger brother and my younger sister."

"Wow."

I leaned my head back against the wall. "I swear, Bec, if you get engaged this year and want me to be in your wedding, I will never forgive you."

"I came home alone last night and drank most of a bottle of wine myself in yoga pants, then fell asleep watching reality TV. I think you're safe." I smiled tightly. "So whose shirt is it?"

"One of the groomsmen's."

"Which one?"

"Whichever one is still sleeping it off in that hotel room."

"Wait, you saw him this morning, but you don't know who he is?"

I shook my head. "He was facing the wall. Fight or flight kicked in, and I needed to get out of there fast."

Becca started to laugh. "This kind of thing could *only* happen to you. You know that, right?"

"I know." I stood up and untied the ribbon at my waist. "I'm going to take a shower and wash the shame off. You want to get pancakes when I'm done? If I have to be in five weddings in the same year without even a boyfriend, I'm going to need all of the carbs."

CHAPTER TWO

Of course, the story of how I got here starts well before the events of Megan's engagement party. I could take the David Copperfield approach and begin with my birth, but then we would be here for way too long and you would completely lose interest before I got to the juicy stuff, like sleeping with an anonymous groomsman and going viral for being the world's worst bridesmaid. So it's probably best to start with the basics.

My name is Lily Weiss, and I am my mother's worst nightmare. In other words, I am a single, thirty-two-year-old spinster who lacks even the hint of a marital prospect and who is therefore increasingly unlikely to provide her with the grandchildren that she wants yesterday.

Or, as I like to spin it, I am a fabulous career woman who refuses to settle for anything less than true love.

Which would be an easier sell, I suppose, if my career weren't the most singularly boring job on the planet. Unique? Definitely. Well paying? Nothing lavish, but I'm doing okay. Fabulous? Absolutely freaking not.

I work as the Director of Communications at the Foundation for Scientific Technology. Capital letters theirs, not mine. Such a great title. Such a lame reality. It boils down to writing a lot of press releases for a huge science nonprofit. The foundation funds research experiments around the world, and I write about the findings of those experiments. Which sounds cool until you realize the experiments have no practical application to everyday life. Studies on marine sponge life don't exactly cure cancer.

It would probably be a total dream job if I liked science, but I don't. I majored in journalism in college because it was as far from my particle astrophysicist father's world as I could get. Don't get me wrong, I adore my dad. But he started his crusade to convince me to follow in his foot-steps as soon as I emerged from the womb, and even that early, I wasn't feeling it. For my eighth birthday, he got me a telescope and a journal to chart the stars in. That telescope sat there collecting dust while I scribbled my first story, about a pony named Chloe, in the journal.

But even majoring in journalism, I was told every time I had to write a technical article that my calling was science journalism. Apparently I have a knack for explaining complex concepts in layman's terms—maybe that's what comes from being raised in a household where neu-trinos and quarks were dinner-table conversation. And writing jobs are scarce. Writing jobs that pay enough to keep me from sleeping in my childhood bedroom and eating breakfast with my parents every morning are even scarcer. It may not be groundbreaking journalism, but my science-minded colleagues seem impressed with my ability to communicate their efforts to the rest of the world daily.

It is also the one writing job that makes my father as proud of me as he would be had I actually gone into a scientific field. And with my mother suffering the constant agony borne of knowing exactly how ineffective my dating life is at providing me with a husband, it's nice to have at least one parent's undying approval.

All of this is well and good, but it's really just background noise to get to my current predicament. Which is the weddings. All five of them.

The foundation, or FST, as it's called in the scientific community, isn't exactly a bustling hub of the young and the hip. It's full of old men who think it's perfectly acceptable to wear a tie with a short-sleeved shirt and a jean jacket with jeans. And the handful of women are basically exactly like the men, except sometimes with longer hair.

Except for Caryn.

Caryn, like myself, grew up with absolutely zero interest in science. Technically, she's the Administrative Assistant to the Director of the FST. But call her a secretary at your own peril. She runs the whole operation, largely because social skills are not exactly the strongest suit of the higher-ups here. Without her, the entire foundation would disintegrate within twenty-four hours. She also has more tolerance for people than anyone I have ever met in my life.

Our lack of interest in science was where the similarities in our career goals ended though. Caryn was still actively pursuing her MRS degree, having failed to achieve that particular title in college and somehow, inexplicably, for the seven years thereafter. Which meant that this job, for her, was a nice little marital résumé booster to show she could hold her own in an intelligent conversation and run a home and family while looking like a supermodel.

She's where the craziness began.

~

"Good morning!" Caryn trilled as she came gliding into my office.

I looked up warily. No one was that happy at nine fifteen on a Monday morning. At least no one I would voluntarily be friends with.

"Coffee?" she asked, wiggling the clear plastic, mermaid-bedecked cup that told me she had gotten my favorite iced skinny vanilla latte after her morning exercise class.

"Oh no. You want me to completely rewrite the Higgins proposal again, don't you?" Caryn didn't drink coffee—especially not mass-produced coffee from a chain. Organic juice cleanses? Yes. So if she was supporting Starbucks, whatever she wanted was going to be more than I could handle on a Monday morning. And she had bought a venti!

Caryn laughed. "Can't I just bring my friend coffee on a beautiful Monday morning?"

I glanced out the window. It was overcast and supposed to rain for most of the day. I looked back at her to see if she had finally snapped and was ready to go on a killing spree while decked out in Lilly Pulitzer and Chanel perfume, but she just stood there, smiling sweetly, her left hand holding out the coffee.

Then I saw the dazzlingly giant gemstone on that hand.

"Oh my God!" I jumped up, banging my knee and scattering papers in the process. "Caryn!"

She managed to set the cup down on my desk before I tackled her in a giant hug. "Tell me everything!"

She sank gracefully into the chair at my desk, while I grabbed the coffee like the lifeline that it was.

"Well, you know our anniversary was last night." I nodded, despite knowing nothing of the kind. They had only been dating since January and it was early July now. Was she counting month anniversaries? "So Greg took me to the restaurant where we had our first date. And I honestly didn't expect a thing." This was a bit of a stretch. She had bridal magazines in her desk. Granted, she had been hoarding those for years before she met Greg. But still. "And we ordered drinks, but the waitstaff brought a bottle of champagne instead. I looked at Greg, thinking he was going to tell them they'd brought the wrong drinks, but he wasn't at his seat, he was down on one knee." She held out her hand for me to admire the ring.

"It's perfect," I said. And it was. Which was no surprise. Caryn had honed the appearance of effortless flawlessness in absolutely all aspects of life. Sometimes I felt twinges of jealousy for how easily everything seemed to come for her, but in the seven years since she had started working at the FST, I had snuck enough peeks behind the Wizard's curtain to know there was genuine effort involved in that appearance.

Some people, like my little sister, fall backward into everything without trying. Caryn never stopped trying. I tended to fall somewhere between the two of them—I tried more than Amy did, but I couldn't reach Caryn's level of perfection even if I wanted to. Which, if I was being perfectly honest, I didn't want to. I liked being able to skip the gym when I was tired and eat refined sugars.

"When are you thinking for a wedding?" I knew the answer, but still wanted to ask the right questions. "And where? What did your mom say?"

"June. Somewhere outside, maybe by the water. But not destination. It's just too much of a strain on people. She was thrilled, obviously!"

I grinned. Caryn's news was possibly the only thing that could put a smile on my face first thing on a Monday morning.

"Will you be a bridesmaid?"

"Of course." I was genuinely flattered. She might have been my best friend at work, but we didn't exactly run in the same circles. "You didn't have to bring me coffee for *that!*"

Caryn laughed. "Let's see if you still say that after you meet the other bridesmaids."

I rolled my eyes. I hadn't met her high school friends, but I had heard the stories.

"I was in all of their weddings," she said with a small shrug. Which was totally ridiculous as reasons went, and she knew that too. Caryn's fiancé was the brother of the worst of them. Their family had more money than they knew what to do with, which explained the enormity of the rock on Caryn's finger. I never understood why Caryn was so desperate to impress this one particular group of girls, especially because Caryn herself came from money. But as a peasant, I didn't understand the ways of the extravagantly wealthy. And I knew that the fear of not living up to these other women's standards was the primary source of anxiety in her life.

"Bring it on. Just tell me I don't have to wear anything floral."

"In the *wedding?*" Caryn asked, horrified. "Oh no. Solids only for bridesmaid dresses!"

"What was I thinking?" I smiled. "I'm honored, really."

"Thank you." She hugged me. "I'm going to need you for this."

~

The next to fall was my college roommate, Sharon. Her engagement was no big surprise—in fact, she probably would have freaked out and not given him an answer if Josh had surprised her. Sharon didn't like being put on the spot. She and Josh had been living together for two years already and she knew he had the ring before he asked. "We're just going to do city hall," she confided when she called me. "I've never wanted a real wedding. I mean, you can come and all, but I don't want to do a bridal party or anything like that. You don't mind, do you?"

I assured her, quite honestly, that I did not. I would go anywhere for her, but at my age, I was past feeling that being a bridesmaid was a necessity. I was happy to do it, but would my feelings be hurt if I didn't have to wear a puffy dress and bride-selected shoes? No.

City hall was also not much of a surprise. Through the dozen-plus years of our friendship, she had been adamant that if she ever got married, her dream wedding was Rabbi Elvis in Vegas, with random witnesses off the street. Which made sense, if you knew Sharon. Not that she was the Vegas type at all, but her mother was *so* domineering and overbearing that if she knew a wedding was happening, Sharon would have zero input into any part of it.

But once there was a ring on her finger, Sharon couldn't not tell her mom, who apparently had strong opinions other than city hall.

Sharon called me in hysterics three days after the engagement phone call. "She said she'll disown me if I don't have a real wedding," she wailed. "She said I'll be dead to her. She's going to sit shiva."

"She wouldn't do that. She's bluffing."

"Have you *met* my mother? She's serious."

I sighed, having lived through many soap-operatic dramas between Sharon and her mother. Would she go through with sitting shiva? Possibly. Would she also recant as soon as the first grandchild was born? Of course. But it was a moot point because if Mrs. Meyer pushed hard enough, Sharon always caved.

"What are you going to do?" I asked, knowing the answer.

"She already booked her rabbi to marry us."

"Will he wear an Elvis costume for you at least?"

Sharon laughed and then hiccupped. "Probably not. He's like a hundred and fifty years old." She paused. "I hate to ask. I know I said you wouldn't have to be in it—"

"I'm happy to, Shar."

"You mean it?"

"Of course."

"Thank you," she sighed in relief. "I don't know how I could get through this if you said no."

~

When I met my best friend, Megan, for happy hour a few weeks later, she kept her left hand deliberately hidden when I showed up.

"I love you," I declared, sinking into the seat opposite her where a martini sat waiting for me, dirty, with extra olives, just the way I liked it. I took a long swig, needing it after the phone call I had just had with the astrophysicist who didn't think that I had accurately explained the significance of the gamma-ray burst he had been researching. "Seriously. Marry me."

"Funny you should say that." Megan's eyes twinkled as she raised her hand. "I already told Tim I would marry him."

Despite my two prior commitments, I swear that I felt nothing but joy for the girl who had been my best friend since second grade, when Amber Donovan announced the name of my crush to an entire busload of kids and Megan "accidentally" clocked her with her Snoopy lunch box. Nothing cements a friendship like hitting another kid in the face with a Charles Shultz–approved hunk of plastic complete with matching thermos.

I squealed over the ring and demanded all of the appropriate details, grinning broadly at the happiness radiating from her pores.

"I have a question for you," she said when she finished the story, pulling an exquisitely wrapped package out of a bag on the floor next to her.

"What's this?"

"Open it."

I tore into the wrapping paper and Megan laughed again, calling me vicious. Under the paper was a wooden box painted Tiffany blue with a white ribbon stripe affixed to it. *I can't say 'I do' without you*, it said in calligraphy on a card in the corner. I opened the latch and lifted the lid of the box. It contained a ring pop, a tiny bottle of champagne, Hershey's Kisses, and a pack of Essie bridal nail polishes in pale pinks. *Will you be my maid of honor?* was written in the same calligraphy inside the box's lid.

My eyes welled up. "Of course I will! How long did this take you?"

"I saw it on Pinterest forever ago—don't you ever look at my wedding board?"

What on earth is a wedding board? I asked myself, shaking my head. I was going to have to figure that out.

～

It wasn't until I was back at home that night, showing my maid of honor box to Becca, that I realized I might be a bit overextended.

"Have any of them set dates yet?" she asked.

"Megan and Caryn both did."

"Of course Megan already did." Becca wasn't a huge fan of Megan, and the feeling was mutual. They tolerated each other because of me, but Becca thought Megan was bossy and controlling, and Megan thought Becca was judgmental and snarky. I knew they were both right, but loved them for those same qualities.

"June 27."

"A June wedding, shocking."

I laughed. "Three weeks after Caryn's. And Sharon hasn't set a date yet."

"I hope it's not the same weekend as Megan's or Caryn's." The thought hadn't occurred to me yet, and I must have looked worried because Becca immediately assured me it probably wouldn't be.

"You couldn't pay me to be in three weddings in the same year," she said, shaking her head. "You're a better person than I am."

~

The combination that pushed me over the edge into a blackout-drunk night of groomsmanic debauchery came a month later. My twenty-seven-year-old brother, Jake, proposed to his twenty-five-year-old girl-friend the weekend before Megan's engagement party.

"She said yes!" he yelled into the phone as a greeting.

Jake and I weren't the closest of siblings, and I'd had no previous indication that he and his girlfriend were that serious. Granted, he lived out of state, so I had met her on exactly three occasions. And on those three occasions, I believe she said a grand combined total of nine words to me.

But Jake had pulled this particular gag before, with his college girl-friend. So I wasn't buying it this time.

"Congratulations," I said, pretending to play along. "When's the big day?"

"Probably May. We want to do a destination wedding and everything in June will be booked already."

A tiny inkling of dread began to bubble up in me—he knew too much about June weddings. But I swallowed it back down because this was how Jake operated. He had probably heard how many weddings I was already committed to from our parents and was therefore trying to build some anxiety before saying "gotcha."

"Well it's a good thing Madison doesn't like me, because I don't have the time or energy to be in another wedding."

There was a pause.

"Of course Mads likes you. We want you to be a bridesmaid."

"Ha. Is she going to be able to handle vows? I mean, she might have to say 'I do' in front of other people!"

A longer pause this time.

"Lily, you're on speaker." Jake cleared his throat. "With me and Madison."

"Hi, Lily," a quietly wounded voice said through the phone.

My stomach dropped.

"I'm a jerk," I said quickly. "Jake, I thought you were teasing me because—well—never mind! Congratulations! I'm so happy for you both! Send me a picture of the ring! I want to hear all the details!" I went into autopilot engagement-babble mode, my cheeks burning from the embarrassment of somehow getting it wrong when Jake was being serious.

When we hung up, I let out a colorful stream of expletives only somewhat related to the faux pas I had just made in insulting my future sister-in-law while she was on the line.

Was I a bad person for feeling jealous? Probably. But I doubt there's an older sister in the world who wouldn't turn a little green, be it with envy or nausea, at the realization that she was going to be in four weddings, including that of her younger brother, all without so much as the prospect of a date. They were still in their midtwenties. They could date another couple of years and be fine. What was the rush?

Jake's engagement festered in me all week. I love my little brother. I do. And it wasn't like I was ready to get married. Or like anyone had ever proposed to me. Or like I had ever been in the kind of relationship where I wanted the person to propose. I had started talking about marriage when David and I were twenty-four, but we broke up not long after that, and I hadn't been in a serious enough relationship to think about it since. The emerging details of Jake's engagement, however, combined with my mother's proud Facebook posts and completely un-self-aware comments about how happy she was to *finally* be planning a wedding made me begin to wish the entire institution had been left in the dark ages where it belonged.

~

The straw that broke the proverbial camel's back, however, came with Amy's phone call during Megan's engagement party. I felt my bag vibrate while I stood chatting with Megan's mother, but I ignored it. We were in the party room of a posh hotel, and it would have been rude to even open my bag to see who was calling. When the vibrations began again ten seconds after ceasing, I started trying to figure out how to extricate myself from the conversation, and by the fourth call, I assumed someone must have died, so I excused myself and walked onto the terrace to take the call.

"Amy? What's wrong? What happened?"

"I'm getting *married!*" she shrieked so loudly that I had to hold the phone away from my ear.

"*Not* funny, Ames," I said. This time I was confident it was a joke. In one of the marathon phone sessions I'd had that week with my mother, Amy had been on the line and she swore up and down that Jake was too young to get married, that Madison, at twenty-five—just one year older than Amy herself—was *definitely* too young to get married, and that even if Tyler proposed *tomorrow*, she would make him wait at least four more years. This seemed logical—while a year out of college now, Amy was still living with my parents, working a part-time job until she found something she actually wanted to do, and generally did not have her life together. Tyler, her boyfriend, was two years older and in law school, so while he was more centered than she was, he still seemed light-years away from being ready to tie the knot.

"That's because it's *real!* Check your text messages! I sent you a picture of the ring!"

My stomach leapt into my throat as I looked down at my phone's screen. Sure enough, there was Amy's hand, complete with chipped remnants of blue glitter nail polish, topped with an inordinately large diamond. *She should have done her nails,* I thought, unkindly.

"Isn't it gorgeous? It was his grandmother's! It doesn't fit—I have to get it sized."

I let Amy go on for a while, but I wasn't listening anymore. She was twenty-four, for God's sake! Panic began to grow in my chest as I looked back in the lighted windows of Megan's party.

"So it'll be in June," Amy was saying, "after Tyler graduates from law school. And you'll be a bridesmaid, of course."

"What?"

"Well, you're my sister! Madison will have to be in it too, I guess, right? Mom will make me include her. And we're both in hers, so I guess I have to. Jake will be one of Tyler's groomsmen. And Tyler's sister— she's twenty-seven, that's almost your age, so you'll have someone to hang out with. Oh, and Ashlee, she'll be my maid of honor. You don't mind, do you? I already asked her. I mean, I guess I can have *two* maids of honor if you really want to be one, even though that means Tyler will have to have two best men. It's too bad you're not married, because then it'd be so easy, I'd just make you my *matron* of honor—ugh, I don't have to make Madison that, do I? They'll only be married like a month when we get married, that's hardly a matron. No, she'll just be a bridesmaid. Right? Oh my God, Lily! I can't believe he proposed!"

My head was reeling, but I think I made a vaguely appropriate response of congratulations before reminding Amy that I was at Megan's engagement party and couldn't stay on the phone.

"Ooh, okay! I have to go call Jake anyway! And Grandma and Aunt Anna and so many other people! I'll call you tomorrow with all the details, okay? Bye-ee!"

I dropped my phone back in my purse and poured the remains of the drink I had been holding down my throat, then walked straight to the bar, where I ordered another. I drank that one the same way, ordered another, and remembered nothing further until waking up the following morning in a strange hotel room with an even stranger groomsman.

CHAPTER THREE

It was time to do some quick damage control. First, there was the issue of the mystery groomsman. I thought about it while I showered the morning after the party and decided it truly was best to not know which groomsman I had slept with. Curiosity killing the cat and all. And that cat probably actually died of shame from having to repeatedly face the guy she hooked up with while blind drunk. No thanks. If I didn't know who it was, I couldn't be awkward about it, nor could I develop a post-hookup rebound crush on the guy in order to justify having slept with him. Having been down that road before, I felt qualified to postulate that those relationships have an expiration date on par with that of a container of yogurt, which is far less time than a typical engagement takes, and I had zero desire to walk down the aisle at Megan's wedding with someone whom I had not only slept with, but also horrifically dated and broken up with. The only solution? Tell Megan I didn't want to know who it was and move on. I could ask after the wedding if I was still curious.

With that settled, there was the issue of keeping the details of five weddings straight. I, to put it mildly, lack major organizational skills. Caryn's and Megan's weddings would be a piece of cake on that front at least. Caryn was the most organized and highest functioning person I knew, and Megan had been planning her dream wedding for so many years that she would need almost nothing from me. Sharon's would be harder, as her disdain for all things wedding meant she would need a little hand-holding. But, I rationalized, her mother would take over the planning, and with Sharon not wanting a wedding at all, she would be pretty laid-back about the whole process. Then again, Mrs. Meyer was the opposite of laid-back, and she would be running the show. But she also probably wouldn't allow any feedback from me, so there wouldn't be much I would be expected to do anyway.

Jake's and Amy's weddings were going to cause the biggest headaches. I was definitely off on the wrong foot with Madison after the engagement phone call, and I needed to fix that. She and Jake lived in Chicago, so taking her to lunch wasn't an option, but a gift with an apology note was. And Amy—well—she was twenty-four. I figured that the odds of her and Tyler actually reaching the aisle in June were only slightly higher than the odds of me getting married to the random groomsman I had slept with. It was possible, but pretty freaking unlikely. My baby sister didn't exactly have a reputation for following through with things, and Tyler was her longest relationship, at just over a year—a year that she had spent still living with my parents. In grown-up relationship time, that took it down to maybe three months. I decided if I took her out of the equation entirely, everything else seemed far more manageable.

I can do this, I thought as I stepped out of the shower. *Just one step at a time.*

~

I had a missed call and voicemail from Megan by the time Becca and I finished breakfast. I deleted the voicemail without listening, then called her back.

"Before you say a single word," I said, cutting her greeting off, "I don't want to know who it was!"

Megan hesitated, processing. "Explain."

"Promise you won't tell me first."

"I promise nothing."

"MEGAN!"

"Ugh, fine, I won't tell you. But I want to know what happened."

I sighed. "Amy is getting married."

"Amy who?"

"My sister."

"Your sister is twelve. She's not getting married."

"Twenty-four," I said. "I agree, she probably isn't actually getting married, but she's engaged nonetheless."

"Gross. When did that happen?"

"Last night."

"Ahhh. That explains why you started mainlining chardonnay at the party."

"And that explains my hangover," I groaned. "Really? Chardonnay?"

"You drank more of it than my cousin Gina. And then you were flirting pretty hard with—"

"LALALALALA I CAN'T HEAR YOU! YOU PROMISED!"

"Geez," Megan chuckled. "You really don't remember, do you?"

"No. Did I do anything horrifying?"

"Not at the party. But I hear you have a shirt that needs to be returned."

I scrunched up my face. "He told you to get his shirt back?"

"No, he walked out of the hotel without it this morning and Tim got the story for me. I love that you made *him* do a walk of shame, too, though."

"I think it's a walk of pride when a guy does it, not shame." I paused. "Why didn't he have another shirt?"

"Because he was planning to drive home after the party before you became a factor."

I rubbed my temples. A vague recollection of holding a male arm while a disembodied voice asked a concierge if there were rooms available danced at the outskirts of my memory. "Can I give you the shirt next week and have you never speak of this again?"

Megan agreed warily. "But don't you think it'll come up? You're going to see him at the rehearsal dinner and the wedding."

"That's ten months away. It'll be old news by then."

"If you say so. Probably for the best anyway. This way you won't decide you hate him and make me rearrange the entire wedding."

Even though that was well deserved, I cringed. "See?" I said, faking a cheerful tone. "Totally responsible decision on my part."

I could practically hear Megan rolling her eyes through the phone. "You're insane. I swear, you should write a book about your life."

"Right," I said. "Lifestyles of the drunk and too old to be single. It'd be so popular."

"It would, actually."

"Yeah, and I totally want that out there for the world to see."

"Whatever." I could hear the shrug in Megan's voice. "Use a pen name. People would read it. And it'd be more interesting than what you write for work. You'd have fun."

I told Megan I would think about it, with absolutely no intention of doing so. Besides, even with a pen name, I would have to put a Sylvia Plath clause into a contract if I wrote a book about my current exploits. There was no way I could publish a book in which I didn't know whom I had slept with unless my mother was good and dead. But, with Megan's agreement to never again discuss my drunken amnesiac escapades, I could consider the subject closed for now.

CHAPTER FOUR

The rash of engagements all happened in the summer and early fall. There's something about warmer weather that apparently makes people want to commit themselves to a life of fidelity. That or engagements are contagious. Like the flu. If you don't wash your hands a lot, you might wind up sneezing and wearing a diamond. I don't pretend to understand it.

There's also apparently an unspoken rule of engagements that they're supposed to last just longer than a pregnancy would (coincidence?) and the ensuing wedding, if at all possible, is required to take place in June, or failing that, May or July.

I assume these rules are given out to all couples by the wedding deities as soon as a ring is purchased. Or they're the result of a biological urge that is activated by diamonds. Either way, having never been engaged, I didn't know either rule.

When Caryn got engaged, with eleven months to plan, I figured everything would be a piece of cake. I would have nearly a year before I actually needed to do anything for any of the weddings, and time to save money for dresses.

But once I had five weddings to plan for, I needed to buckle down and calculate how I was going to do all of this.

I estimated that each bridesmaid dress would probably cost around two hundred dollars. For five dresses, that felt ridiculous, because no one ever wears a bridesmaid dress again, no matter what the bride tells you. But over the course of nine months, I could budget a thousand dollars for dresses. Just saving a hundred and eleven dollars a month wouldn't be so bad.

Of course, there would be gifts too. So an extra hundred dollars each for that? Adding that to my current total and rounding up a little, that was one-seventy a month. And showers and bachelorette parties. The bridesmaids had to pay for those too. And bridal shower presents, which apparently didn't count as wedding presents. That was another two hundred per bride. Suddenly I was at nearly three hundred a month.

Where was I going to find three hundred extra dollars a month?

Okay, I told myself. *It's only one-fifty per paycheck. If I start bringing my lunch to work a few days a week, I can save pretty close to that.*

To make my life easier, I opened an online savings account and scheduled automatic payments to begin with my next paycheck. I could do this.

The scheduling of the actual weddings, however, meant that the following spring would be gruesome. Caryn's wedding was the first weekend in June, Megan's the final, and Sharon's mother had booked the second weekend, leaving me worried about what I would do if either of my siblings selected one of those three dates.

Thankfully, I was spared having to make such a Sophie's choice, as Amy (or, if we're being honest here, my mother) opted for the last open June weekend. Jake and Madison announced that theirs would be in the middle of May in Mexico. I confirmed to Jake that yes, I had a valid passport, and asked if Madison had gotten the flowers I sent, as I had gotten an arrival confirmation email but hadn't heard from her.

"I think so," he said. "Mads—are any of those flowers we got from Lily?" I scrunched up my nose. If she hadn't even mentioned them to him, that wasn't a good sign about my apology being accepted. "Yup. She did. Sorry, this place is starting to look like a flower shop."

I rolled my eyes. "Is Madison mad at me?"

"I don't know," he said, and then yelled away from the phone, "Hey Mads, are you mad at Lily?"

"Jake! What the hell? Stop!"

"What? She said she's not."

"Great. Thanks." *Note to self: anything you say to your brother from now on will be repeated to Madison.* But I could either stress myself out about my slipup or let it go. I chose the latter. I had made a peace offering. If she was lying to Jake about being mad at me, that was his problem, not mine.

And now I had to factor the expense of Mexico into my wedding budget, which I guessed would run me about fifteen hundred dollars for airfare and hotel. And that was in May, so I only had eight months to prepare.

Suddenly, I was at two-fifty a paycheck, five hundred a month, which, even if I prepared all my meals at home, was going to be an issue.

~

I buckled down for the month of September and lived a simple, puritanical life of sacrifice for my friends and family. I opted to pre-drink at home before I went out, downgraded to drugstore mascara, splurged on Starbucks only three days a week, packed my lunch every night before work, and made a goal of putting away five hundred dollars that first month.

Granted, my wine budget increased a bit as the brother/sister wedding whammy was taking an emotional toll in the form of phone calls and texts between my mother, myself, and Amy.

"In my day, your sister was your maid of honor. What are people going to think?"

I sighed, having had this conversation with my mother multiple times already. "It's not that weird, Mom. Especially with the age difference and all."

"I just don't understand why you won't tell her that you want to be her maid of honor."

"It's not my wedding or my place to tell her that. And if I'm being honest, I *don't* want to be."

"Of course you do."

"Mom, I'm in four other weddings. I don't need that kind of responsibility."

"You don't mind being Megan's maid of honor."

I rubbed my forehead in frustration. "If Amy wanted me to be, I would say yes. But she already asked Ashlee, and I promise that's fine."

"She may still change her mind."

"Please don't nag her about it, Mom. It's really not worth it."

She huffed, but didn't argue. "I'm just grateful that you have all of these weddings coming up."

Had I been giving her my full attention, I would have known better than to ask why, but despite frequent requests to not call me with non-emergencies at work, I was still fielding at least four calls a week from her while trying to do my job. This was her first year of retirement and she hadn't quite found her niche yet. But I was proofreading a proposal and therefore asked the question.

"It's just such a wonderful opportunity. I'm sure you'll meet someone at one of them."

And there went all attention to the proposal. For a split second, I wished I could be honest with my mother and tell her about the mystery groomsman. But while the intent would be to horrify her into stopping the constant pressure, I knew full well it would have the opposite effect; she would insist I find out who it was in order to date and/or marry him.

"Mom, I'm not trying to meet someone at one of these weddings."

"Whyever not?"

"Because it's not about me. I'm there to support my friends."

"And your friends support you, that's how it works. Everyone knows weddings are a wonderful place to meet people."

I thought back to the singles table, where I had been placed, probably at my mother's insistence, at my cousin Tina's wedding. Everyone else in my family was at the same table together, whereas my table felt like the scene from *Animal House* where they keep introducing the pledges to the same losers over and over again.

"That was probably true when you were single, but it's a little different now."

She huffed again. "I just want you to be happy."

"I *am* happy."

"Are you? You go home to an empty apartment every night and sit there alone."

My hackles rose. "Actually, I go home to my roommate, who's one of my closest friends, and either hang out with her or go out with other friends. I'm not exactly sitting in the dark working on a hope chest."

"That's not a life. You need a family. It's time."

I opened my mouth to say what I wanted to say: that my birth family was currently a great example of why I *didn't* want a family yet. I didn't want to settle down and pop out three kids in the suburbs, then nag them until they got married and had their own kids. I didn't want to be *her*.

But the words didn't come out. They never seemed to with her. Which was probably for the best. And I understood that she meant well. It wasn't that she wanted me to be *her*, she just didn't understand that there were other definitions of happiness than hers.

Besides, my generation was the first one that really was finding a different life than the previous generations had. We didn't *have* to get married and have kids in our twenties if we didn't want to. For the non-independently wealthy of us, our careers kind of had to come first if we wanted any sense of financial security before we started those families. And while my parents were still happily married, I had seen enough couples who weren't to know better than to settle for any of the guys I had met so far.

Was there a way to explain that to my mother that she could understand? No. I had tried before.

I looked at the clock. The proposal was due by the end of the day and I was only halfway through it. "Okay," I said to keep the peace and get her off the phone. "I'll try to meet someone."

"Thank you, sweetheart." She paused. "Now if you could also work on your sister about this maid of honor thing . . ."

"I'm hanging up now."

"Okay, okay, I love you."

"I love you too, Mom."

I pressed "End" and shook my head. She couldn't help herself and was never going to change.

CHAPTER FIVE

From: Caryn Donaldson [futuremrscaryngreene@gmail.com]
To: [bridesmaids]
Subject: Wedding newsletter volume 1
Date: September 24

Hi girls! Just thought I'd get a group email going so you all have each other's contact info and so you can add my new email to your address books! Of course, it'll change after the wedding to CarynDGreene@gmail.com, so you can add that as well, but I'm going to use this one until then. I'll still get emails to my old address, but I'd prefer you use this one for all wedding-related correspondence. Thanks!

Can you believe we only have a little under nine months until the wedding? There's so much to do between now and then!

I'm going dress shopping the next three Saturdays, and I thought it would be fun if you all came with me and we made a day of it! I have an appointment at three boutiques at Tyson's Corner this weekend, three in DC the weekend after, and four more in Maryland the third weekend. I'd love it if you came to all three, but just let me know what works with your schedules and I'll make sure the salons know we're coming. This is just for my dress. We'll schedule another day to go look for your dresses!

Oh, and try to keep your weekends open in May. I'd like to do the shower and bachelorette separate weekends and we'll need another weekend to figure out hair treatments, etc.

Yay! I'm so excited! Love you all!

—The future Mrs. Caryn Greene

The journalism major in me cringed at the exclamation points, but I smiled over my homemade sandwich. *This* was what made all of the scrimping and saving worth it. Seeing how excited Caryn was. Was an interim email address excessive? Yes. But I had never seen an email that screamed excitement like this in all the years I had known Caryn.

Sounds great, I replied. Just let me know what time to be there on Saturday! —L.

Her reply pinged back less than thirty seconds later. Please 'reply all' in the future. It's so much easier if everyone knows the plan!

My inbox dinged again. I'm in, a girl named Dana replied. I can go all three Saturdays! Yay! I can't wait! I'm so excited for you! What style of dress do you think you want? I love the mermaid ones, but you could pull off absolutely anything and look stunning! Do you have a Pinterest board for dresses yet?

What's up with this Pinterest thing? I wondered. *I thought it was for recipes. Should I be on there?*

An email came in from a Deanna as I was typing Pinterest into a search engine.

> Wahhhh! The nanny is off this Saturday and it's too late to switch her days. I wish I could go! I agree with Dana, I love the mermaid dresses! You've got the perfect body for one of those! Promise me you'll send me pictures of every single dress you try on! I just looked at your Pinterest board and, oh my God, you're going to be the most beautiful bride! I love every dress you've pinned! Every other bride in the world will be "Greene" with envy! I can't wait to see the dresses!
>
> Love,
> Deanna

I'll be there! the next email began. It arrived before I even finished reading Deanna's. I'm all yours until the wedding! Is Mom coming too? What about Grandma? Or is it just the bridesmaids? I love how organized you are! See you Saturday, sis! Love, Olivia.

Do these girls not work? I went to Pinterest and created an account, but didn't quite get what it was supposed to be. I would have to ask Megan. I also needed to mute my computer because the bridesmaids were starting to reply to each other's emails and the thread was giving me anxiety about how much I didn't know. What was a Kleinfeld? Why was Mia "the queen of bustling," as Deanna called her, and what did that even mean? I pictured a Victorian-style bustle, but Caryn was pretty self-conscious about her butt. She wasn't going to do anything to make it look bigger.

I grabbed my phone and texted Megan. Am I supposed to know anything about wedding dresses?

No, she replied. You get a manual on them for free with your engagement ring.

Come on, Megs.

You just get bridal magazines and learn about it that way, or you can watch Say Yes to the Dress.

What's that?

Megan sent me three eye-roll emojis, then a link to the show on TLC's website. I clicked the link and felt my eyes widen as the show began to play on my phone. There was a whole world of this stuff that I knew nothing about, apparently. My only exposure to reality TV had been Becca's obsessive watching of the Real Housewives and the Kardashians, and that was enough to turn me off of it all.

As soon as I realized Kleinfeld Bridal was the shop where the show took place, I turned it off.

I could wing this. As Caryn's sister pointed out in her email, Caryn was organized. She had to be to keep the foundation running. And her type A behavior made my life far more functional at work. Dress shopping would clearly be an in-and-out operation. The other two weekends probably wouldn't even be necessary. I just needed to ooh and aah when she put on the perfect dress and sip champagne for an afternoon. I could do that.

I ran a quick Google search of "mermaid-style wedding dresses," wondering at the intentions of the friends who had asked about them. There was only one part of her body that Caryn was self-conscious about, and it was her butt. There was no way she would wear something designed to show that off on her wedding day. No wonder she wanted me there with her. I wouldn't let them pressure her into anything she didn't like. No way, no how.

~

The line at Starbucks had been atrocious, and I admittedly left late because I wasn't sure what one wore to a bridal salon. But armed with my venti iced latte, a pair of heels with skinny black pants, and a sleeveless top, I was ready for a fun, if somewhat more glamorous than I was used to, Saturday morning. I went up the escalator to the bridal suite and was ushered into a marble-tiled room in soothing neutral shades of beige that allowed the fluffy, white dresses that lined the walls to pop. Four petite, blonde women, all looking like they were from the same cookie-cutter, country-club brunch, sat sipping champagne and cooing emphatically over Caryn, who stood on a pedestal in front of a triple-view mirror in a Cinderella-style white ball gown.

And then there was me, melting into a sweaty, brunette puddle from the heat of the parking lot, dressed in black without even a hint of anything pastel or floral to make it look like I belonged to their group.

"You made it!" Caryn said. "Lily, you'll be honest with me. What do you think of this one?"

Before I could answer, the older woman who had been holding the train of the dress dropped it and gasped, rushing to my side. "Clear liquids only around the dresses," she snapped, starting to grab the cup from my hand.

"Uh, hang on," I said, taking a huge gulp from the straw before she wrestled it away from me, holding the cup like it was full of red paint instead of a mostly melted latte.

I made a face at Caryn, who shrugged. "What do you think?" she repeated.

"It's—nice?" I said. It wasn't. A princess ball gown was fine if you were into that, but Caryn, queen of the perfectly tailored work clothes, looked uncomfortable and silly.

"It's *gorgeous*," the blonde in the pale-pink dress purred. That was honestly the only way to tell them apart. Pale pink, baby blue, mellow yellow, and dark pink, all with floral or floral-and-paisley designs. They could have all been sisters. Put Caryn in a green floral sheath dress and she would be the missing quintuplet. All angles, bones, and pin-straight blonde hair, each with at least two carats of unethically sourced diamond weighing down their left hands.

Caryn wrinkled her nose. "It's lovely. But it's not me." She turned to the simpering saleswoman. "It's too young. I'd like something a little more elegant."

"I have just the dress," she said, ushering Caryn back into the changing room.

Another salesperson arrived out of nowhere with a tray of champagne glasses and offered me one, which I took gratefully. Although at ten in the morning, I would have preferred my coffee.

I was still standing, awkwardly, with the rest of the bridesmaids not seeming to notice that I was one of them. "So, uh, hi," I said to the seated posse. "I'm Lily. I work with Caryn."

They hesitated, looking me over, then Olivia, Caryn's sister and maid of honor, introduced herself, and the rest followed suit. Caroline, Mia, and Dana had all attended the same prestigious private high school together. And Caroline, in the yellow dress, was Greg's sister.

I sat in the open chair and their conversation immediately returned to dress designers. I recognized the name Vera Wang, but beyond that, I was lost.

"Really, I don't know why she didn't plan a weekend trip to Kleinfeld's for this," Mia said. "She could have been on *Say Yes to the Dress*!"

Caroline shuddered, tilting her already surgically upturned nose even further in the air. "Kleinfeld's is so generic. And Caryn isn't tasteless enough to want to be on that."

"Of course," Mia said quickly, deferring almost apologetically to Caroline's judgment. "It would have been nice to spend a girls' weekend in New York though. The bridal salons up there are just so much more chic."

"We'll talk her into it if she doesn't find anything down here," Olivia said. "I doubt any of us would object to a weekend getaway!"

I had less than nothing to contribute, and no money left in the budget for such a trip.

Eventually Caryn emerged in the next dress, which was skintight to the knee, where it flared into a sea of feathers.

Olivia started to cry, and I commiserated. Okay, I thought crying was a little extreme, but it was heinous. It looked like a swan had exploded at the bottom of her dress. "It's just so perfect," Olivia said, her eyes glistening as she dabbed at the corners to avoid smudging her makeup. I had never seen anyone pretty cry before. Ugly cry? Sure. But Olivia actually looked *better* when she cried. It wasn't fair.

Wait, did she say it was perfect?

I looked around. The other girls were nodding in agreement, their faces cast from the same mold.

Caryn burst into laughter. "Lily, you have *no* poker face! At all!"

They all turned to me and I tried desperately to arrange my face into something resembling theirs. Unfortunately, I still had my original nose and ability to move my forehead, so that wasn't possible. I settled for trying to look like I didn't hate it.

"You don't *like* it?" Mia asked, incredulous.

"I—um—Caryn, do *you* like it?"

"You pinned one just like it," Caroline said pointedly to Caryn before she could respond. "The Versace? Remember?"

35

Caryn studied herself in the three-way mirror and shook her head. "It's beautiful. But the feathers are a little too much, I think."

"Something a bit simpler?" the saleslady asked. Caryn nodded and retreated back into the dressing room.

"I tried on something similar for my wedding," Caroline confided. "It was gorgeous of course, but I just didn't have the curves to pull it off. You need more of an hourglass figure for a dress like that."

"But not *too* curvy," Mia said. "If you're too hippy, white just isn't your friend."

"No," Caroline said in an exaggerated whisper. "Caryn would really be better off in ivory. It's more forgiving."

Guess I'm not wearing white at my wedding, I thought, horrified. No one defended Caryn, but a stormy look crossed Dana's face so quickly that I wondered if I had imagined it before it was replaced by an utterly bland expression. I took another swig of champagne. This was going to be a long day.

Caryn stepped out a few minutes later in a simple satin sheath. It was draped at the neckline to give the illusion of cleavage, which Caryn didn't really have, and looked like something Zelda Fitzgerald would have worn before diving into a fountain. I adored it.

"Do you want something that plain?" Dana asked.

"It's too basic," Olivia announced.

"You look like you're wearing a nightgown."

"A little tacky."

Caryn looked to me, and I bit the inside of my lip. I thought it was perfect. Put a long strand of pearls on her and one of those short veils that just skimmed the face, and I couldn't imagine a more elegant wedding dress. But Caryn didn't seem to be a fan, so I shook my head. The bridesmaids looked at me with the first hint of approval I had seen so far, which I realized had nothing to do with my reaction being tailored to Caryn's. They only cared if I agreed with *them*. But I just wanted

36

Caryn to feel good in her dress. And I had more of a poker face than she thought. "Too simple. I like the neckline though."

Caryn smiled reflexively at my reflection in the mirror, then retreated to the dressing room again.

We left the store around noon and went to the second bridal salon, where we sipped more champagne and Caryn seemed to try on the same nine dresses.

"Don't be discouraged," Mia said. "No one finds their dress in the first store they go to."

Dana nodded. "As long as you get it with seven months to go, you'll be fine."

"Seven months?" I asked. "Why seven months?"

"It takes that long to order a quality dress," Olivia explained. "They're made from scratch to order."

"Oh."

I suggested we break for lunch between shops two and three, but Caryn said we didn't have time between appointments. Besides, they were all doing juice cleanses and not eating solid foods right now.

"They're really wonderful for flushing the toxins out of your system," Caroline said. "And it'll help you take off those extra pounds in plenty of time for the wedding. I'll send you the info for a weight-loss specific plan."

I stared at her in absolute horror. *What extra pounds?* I wanted to ask. Were there days when I looked in the mirror and wished I could lose a few pounds? Of course. But I had never had a virtual stranger tell me that I needed to lose weight before.

I was too shocked to make a snappy comeback and instead mumbled something that sounded like "thanks" as I looked at the four bridesmaids and wondered again what exactly I was doing there. They didn't even eat! It explained their size, but it did not reassure me that they were actually human. I tried to remember seeing Caryn eat anything normal. She usually had a smoothie in disgusting shades of green and orange at lunchtime. Definitely a lot of carrot and celery sticks. But I wasn't sure I had ever seen her put a piece of office birthday cake into her mouth.

I, however, needed food and wished I had brought a snack in my purse. Not that I had the guts to eat it in front of any of them or, even worse, one of the shop assistants. If I thought the coffee thief was bad, I didn't want to know what would happen if I pulled out a sandwich. It was already two o'clock and the protein bar I had scarfed down in the car just before arriving at the first salon wasn't cutting it with all of the champagne.

"Car, I'm sorry, but I've got to bail early."

She looked surprised, but didn't ask what I had going on. "Okay," she said, leaning in to hug me. "Thank you for coming today! Will we see you next weekend?"

"It's my mom's birthday, but I'll come for as much as I can."

"Of course," she said. "Well, hopefully we find something amazing at the next store and we'll be done!"

"Send me a picture if you do?"

"I'll try. Most of the high-end salons won't let you take pictures of their gowns."

I said my goodbyes to the blondes and made my escape. When I got to my car, I turned the air conditioner up all the way and took a deep breath before I put it into reverse. *That was more intense than I expected. Are all the weddings going to be like this?*

I took quick stock of the five brides. Madison was the only wild card. I had no idea what her friends would be like because I didn't really know what she was like. When it came to my sister, I knew all of the bridesmaids. Did I like them? Absolutely not. But I could be honest with Amy at least. Megan might as well have been my sister— except one I actually wanted to spend time with. And Sharon didn't even *want* a wedding. I doubted her mother would allow us to go dress shopping—outside opinions might spoil her vision.

So this should be as bad as it got. And Caryn was fine. She didn't even mind that I bailed early. Her friends were intimidating, but Caroline seemed like the only one with a real mean streak. Yes, they were all Stepford robots, but the rest of them didn't rub it in that they were supermodel skinny with rich husbands and an innate understanding of all things wedding.

I even felt a little bad for being so judgmental about them as I waited in line at Five Guys. Whether she liked them all the time or not, they were Caryn's friends and had been for a really long time. There had to be some redeeming qualities that I just hadn't seen—probably because I was too hangry to look. Maybe I'd even learn to like them by June. No, they wouldn't eat a cheeseburger with extra pickles and an order of fries in the car on their way home today. But I also refused to feel shame for eating solid food. I saw the look on Dana's face when I suggested lunch. Diamonds may be a girl's best friend, but those Five Guys Cajun fries are a pretty close second.

CHAPTER SIX

Once I had food in my belly, though, I felt guilty. Not about the food—it was worth every bite. But Caryn had told me her friends were awful, and instead of being the honest voice of reason, I had sided with them when they didn't like a really spectacular and different dress. I wondered if Caryn *actually* hadn't loved the simple one or if she was responding to the immediate rejection from the wicked bridesmaids of the west.

Did you find anything you liked? I texted her that night. The three dots appeared to tell me she was typing, then disappeared. They reappeared, then disappeared again. You okay? I asked after that happened the fourth time.

My phone rang, with her name and picture on the screen.

"What's up?" The sound that greeted me was familiar—but not from Caryn. I had never seen her cry, not even when her last boyfriend broke up with her on the night she had thought he was going to propose. "Hey. What happened?"

It was another minute before she was composed enough to talk. "I hate wedding dresses," she said finally.

"But you love wedding dresses. What happened after I left?"

"I'm fat. And I hate my friends. And Olivia told me my mom was really hurt that I didn't bring her today, but I asked her if she wanted to come and she said she was busy."

I wanted to slap all four of those girls, and I wanted to slap myself even harder for catering to their opinions. "Caryn, you are gorgeous. And if your friends are trying to make you feel bad about how you look, they're not your friends, they're jealous assholes." She sniffled. "But seriously, though, why are they in the wedding if you don't like them?"

"It's complicated. If they aren't, then they won't speak to me anymore."

"Would that be so bad?"

"If Greg wasn't Caroline's brother, maybe not. But—" She stopped talking.

"But?" I asked gently.

She didn't respond for long enough that I checked to make sure I hadn't dropped the call. Then she sighed. "I've never told anyone this."

I waited.

"You know how my dad died when I was twelve." I did. Her mom had remarried a man who had more money than he knew what to do with about six years ago, which Caryn had exceptionally mixed feelings about. "Well, he didn't have life insurance. And he left us in a lot of debt. My mom—she—she still wanted us to fit in at school. And still go to the private school. So we faked it. A lot."

I wasn't sure where she was going with this. Who cared if she didn't have as much money as people thought? I didn't grow up rich and turned out fine. But she clearly expected a response, so I murmured, "Okay."

"I know it's not a good reason or anything, but I just—I've spent almost twenty years trying to fit in with these girls. I don't know how to stop now."

I started to tell her that you just stop. Life gets less complicated when you're not worried what the mean girls think of you. But something else dawned on me before I could get the words out.

"Caryn—do you actually love Greg?"

She started crying again. "I do. That's probably the worst part. It'd be so much easier if I were just marrying him because he has money and my kids would never have to go through what my sister and I did, but that's not it. I actually do love him. Which means Caroline is in my life forever."

I was quiet for a long time, trying to figure out the right thing to say. "What can I do to help?"

"I don't know. I just didn't feel good in any of the dresses today and they all want me to wear a mermaid dress, but I don't like how my butt looks in those and they don't care. I think they want me to look fat."

"Your butt is perfect," I told her. She started to argue, but I cut her off. "What do *you* want your dress to look like?"

She hesitated. "I liked the cut of that simple one today, but I didn't like how plain it was."

"Okay. That's a start." I gave myself a mental high five for my insight. "What would dress it up better? Lace? Beading? Feathers?"

"That feathered thing was awful."

"Thank God *you* said it."

"I looked like a bird."

"But a *really* hot bird."

I could hear the smile in her voice when she replied. "Thank you."

"You know, that could be an awesome way to put them in their place once you've picked your dress."

"What could?"

"Feathered bridesmaid dresses."

Caryn let out a choked chuckle. "Oh God. Can you imagine? But I'd be punishing you too."

"Can I drop from the ceiling in a cage and sing a song in my feathered dress?"

"Uh, Lily, have you *been* to a wedding before?"

"Of course. But that would have livened any of them up!"

Caryn finally laughed for real. "This is why I need you as a bridesmaid."

"I love you, you silly feathered goose," I told her. "Now go do something that has absolutely nothing to do with wedding dresses tonight, okay? Maybe even eat some carbs!"

"That won't solve the feeling fat in white dresses problem."

"You're right. Because that's in your head and you need a shrink for that one. Which I'm not. But if you complain that you're fat again, I'm shoving a cheeseburger in your mouth."

~

When I got off the phone, I logged into my newly created Pinterest account and found Caryn. In addition to her wedding dress board, she had boards for juice cleanses, weight loss tricks, general wedding ideas, wedding colors, wedding favors, arm-toning exercises, and bridal showers. I glanced at my reflection in the mirror over my dresser. I held up an arm and shook it, watching for inordinate jiggle. *Eh,* I thought. No one was going to mistake my body for Jennifer Aniston's, but my arms were okay. I clicked onto her wedding dresses board to see what I could find.

I scrolled for about twenty minutes trying to find something resembling what we had seen earlier, but fancier, without any luck. I did, however, notice one dress was repeated on the board. Three times, in fact. There were different pictures of the same dress, two on the same model, one on a different model. All pinned from different sources.

I wouldn't have called it a simple dress—it was covered in lace and had a sash at the waist, with a corset top that drew attention to the upper back rather than the derriere. It looked nothing like the twenties-style dress that I had loved, but I could see the appeal for Caryn. It was a slim cut through the hips, then didn't flare exactly, but wouldn't accentuate her butt.

Clicking on the image of the dress itself took me to the designer's page, and I eventually found a "where to buy" link. A salon in DC carried the designer, although it didn't say if that exact dress would be there. It was Saturday night, so the shop would be closed. Their website said they were closed on Sundays, too, so I could call first thing Monday morning. An idea began to bloom.

~

Monday morning, I waited until the shop opened at ten, then peeked around my office door to make sure Caryn was nowhere nearby before shutting my door and calling. I asked about the specific dress she had pinned three times and was told that they had it. "Great! I'll try to bring the bride by this week!"

"We offer time slots by appointment only."

"Oh. Um. When's your next available appointment?"

"We just had a cancellation for tomorrow. Otherwise the next available is a week from Thursday." I snagged the eleven o'clock appointment for the next day, only then realizing that if the dress wasn't good on her, my secret machinations would probably hurt more than they would help. But, I rationalized, if the dress *was* good, I had just freed up the next two weekends *and* made dress shopping less complicated.

~

At 10:40 the following morning, I marched into Caryn's office and told her we were going to lunch. She looked up at me, then glanced down at her diamond-encrusted watch, an engagement gift from her fiancé's parents. "It's too early for lunch."

I rolled my eyes. "You don't eat anyway. What do you care?" I came behind her desk and opened her drawer, then pulled out her purse. "Just come on. I have a surprise for you."

She looked at me warily, but stood and took her purse. "What's actually going on?"

"You'll see when we get there." I pushed her shoulders toward the door. "Come on. I have an Uber coming in three minutes."

Caryn peppered me with questions as we made our way to the Uber, but I didn't tell her what we were doing until we arrived at the salon. "I have an appointment here next weekend," she said, confused.

"Let's just try something."

"Lily, I don't want to try on more dresses today."

"Just one. For me?"

She looked upset and I wondered again if I had made a mistake doing this, but she stepped out of the car anyway. I checked us in at the front desk and a mousy-looking woman named Rita came forward and greeted Caryn. "I have your dress waiting for you," she said. "But I'm happy to pull more as well."

Caryn turned to me. "What dress? What's going on?"

"I looked at your Pinterest," I said. "You pinned the same one three times. They have it here. Let's just try that one. If it's no good, we'll go back to the office and we can do the rest of the appointments. But this one is with just me, and I'll be honest if it's not the right dress. Okay?"

She looked doubtful. "I don't even know which dress you mean."

"It's right in here," Rita said, gesturing toward a fitting room. "Can I get either of you some champagne?"

We both refused, and I sat down on the sofa outside the dressing room to wait for Caryn. She sighed, but handed me her purse and complied. Rita went in with her. That didn't seem like an enjoyable part of the experience from the previous weekend, but I had never been a big fan of stripping in front of strangers, despite my behavior at Megan's engagement party.

I scrolled through my social media feed while I waited and a text message from Megan came in. WE GOT THE HOUSE!!!!

WOOHOO! I replied. CONGRATULATIONS! She had texted me a Redfin listing a few days earlier, and I scrolled up in the conversation to see the pictures again. The house was small, but cute. The wallpaper in the dining room was a disaster, and the people who were selling it had atrocious taste—based on the sheer volume of commemorative plates, it was possible they were old enough to have died in there, necessitating the sale. But with some paint and new furniture, it had potential.

When do you move in?

We close in three weeks and will move after that!

I replied with celebratory emojis, then went back to the listing to look at the price. *Whoa. I can barely afford my rent.*

"Lily." I looked up to see Caryn mounting the block in front of the three mirrors, the dress's train in her right hand and butterfly clips holding it shut at the back.

I studied her reflection as she turned to examine the dress. "Wow," I said quietly.

"You think?"

I nodded, my eyes actually welling up. "It's perfect." It wasn't what I would have chosen for myself, but Caryn looked better than the models in the Pinterest pictures had.

She turned sideways. "It doesn't make my butt look big?"

I shook my head. "Caryn, this was made for you."

She smiled slowly. "I think—I think this is it." She turned to Rita. "Is it available in ivory?"

I looked up sharply. "What's wrong with white?" If she had heard Caroline's comment, or if Caroline had said it to her face after I left, future sister-in-law or not, I was going to murder her.

"I'm too pale," she explained. "I'll look washed out in my pictures in white."

Rita checked her tablet. "It is," she said. "Two different shades and also blush."

Caryn asked to see samples of the two shades of ivory and Rita went to find them. "I should probably keep the other appointments this weekend though," she said, still studying her reflection, unwilling to take the dress off yet.

"Why?"

"The other girls will feel left out."

I opened my mouth, about to tell her the snarky comments they had made while she was in the dressing room, but I stopped myself. That would only make her feel even more self-conscious around them. They could literally call her a cow to her face, and possibly had in the past, and she would still keep them in the wedding. "It's your call," I said finally, glad she was too engrossed with her reflection to notice the conflict that battled across my face. She wasn't wrong; I didn't have much of a poker face.

"I don't want them to hate you for going behind their backs. They can be a little—oh, you met them!" I refrained from using the word that immediately came to mind as a description. She chewed the inner corner of her bottom lip. "Maybe—maybe I shuffle the appointments so we come here first the next weekend, so I don't have to go to all those other places. It's not nice to waste their time after all, right?"

I nodded. "And hey, these places have a waiting list for weekend appointments, right?" I asked Rita, who had returned with the fabric swatches. "It'll make some other bride's day if she gets your slot. And what if you invite your mom for this weekend so she can be here when you find 'the dress.'"

"Is that weird?" Caryn asked Rita.

She smiled knowingly. "I'll pretend I've never seen you before."

Caryn dropped her shoulders in relief. I hadn't even realized how much tension she was carrying there until she lowered them. She looked at herself in the mirror again, then stepped off the pedestal to hug me. "Thank you."

I returned her hug tightly. "Of course." I paused. "Do I still get to sing in the birdcage?"

She laughed. "You can do anything you want after this."

CHAPTER SEVEN

I had a package waiting for me when I got home. I tore into it, expecting the new yoga pants I had ordered, but found a journal, brightly colored dual-tipped markers, stencils, stickers, and a gift note from Megan instead.

I know organization isn't your thing, but a bullet journal will help you keep all of the weddings straight! I already put some of my important dates in for you! XX —Meg.

Bullet journals were more Megan than me. But she had picked one that was perfect for me: it had a turquoise background with gold lettering that said, "Get Shit Done." I flipped to the first page, where she had written *Lily's wedding journal* in sparkly gold pen. Turning to June, I saw that her wedding day was filled in with rose gold, as well as her rehearsal dinner, bridal shower, and bachelorette party.

Thank you for my super cute gift, I texted her. She replied with a kissy face.

I camped out in the living room and started transcribing dates from my phone calendar into the journal. Would I actually carry a journal around with me normally? No, I was pretty digital. But the profanity on it made me like it.

Megan's first wedding dress shopping date conflicted with Caryn's appointment at the salon where we had secretly found her dress, but I figured that my behind-the-scenes work meant I could skip the fake appointment. I was supposed to go with my mother and sister on Sunday the following weekend, and I assumed I wouldn't be involved in Madison's dress shopping since they lived in Chicago. But I realized I hadn't heard anything from Sharon about dresses and decided to check in and see how she was doing.

Hey love, I texted. How's planning going? Are you looking for dresses? Can I help with anything?

I don't want to get married anymore, she responded. I called her immediately.

"What happened? I can hire someone to break Josh's kneecaps."

"No, I do want to marry Josh. I just don't want a wedding."

"Why?"

She sighed. "I went dress shopping with my mom and my sister. And the saleslady was so mean. She took away the only dress I liked."

"What do you mean the saleslady took away the dress you liked?"

"She said it wasn't good on me."

"What does she care? It's not her wedding."

"She said it wasn't good and she practically forced me out of it and then put this big puffy thing on me that she said would hide my problem areas and I started to cry." *God help the bridal salon worker who says something like that in front of me,* I thought. Yes, Sharon's mom was even harder on her about her weight than mine was, but I couldn't imagine Mrs. Meyer tolerating someone else bringing up her daughter's "problem areas."

"What did your mom say?"

"They wouldn't let her in the room with me. So I just came out and said I wanted to go home."

"That doesn't make any sense though. Why would she take a dress away from you? She works on commission!"

"Because she's mean."

"What store was it?"

Sharon named a Potomac boutique that I had passed before. I fished my laptop out of my bag and opened it. "Do you remember what the dress looked like?"

"It was white."

"Gonna need a little more info than that."

"It was satin with lace over the top part. And it was kinda A-line, but like, not a lot."

I pulled up the boutique's website, but didn't see a way to narrow that down. "Do you remember the brand?"

"Maggie something."

I googled "Maggie wedding dresses."

"Sottero? Does that sound right?"

"I think so," Sharon said.

I clicked on a few dresses. But after shopping with Caryn, something immediately caught my eye. "Uh, can I ask a stupid question? Did your mom tell the saleslady how much she was willing to spend on a dress?"

"They made us fill out a form with our upper limit on it."

"And did your mom give some ridiculous number?"

Sharon paused. "I don't know if it's ridiculous or not."

"So yes, then?"

"Why?"

"Because this brand is way cheaper than most in the store. That's probably why she didn't want you to get it."

Sharon was quiet for a minute. "Are you serious?"

"Yup," I said. "But hang on, I'm sending you a link. Was it this one?"

She put me on speaker to look at the dress. "No. I didn't see that one."

I tried again. "This one?"

"No."

"One more."

"That's it! But the saleslady said it wasn't good on me."

"How did *you* feel in it?"

She sighed. "Beautiful."

I typed the model name into Google, went to the designer's website, then clicked the where-to-buy link. "A store in Baltimore has it," I said, and gave her the name. "Go try it on there. If you still love it, get it. And if anyone says it's not good when you think it is, kick them."

Sharon hesitated again. "I don't want to go to a store again. They literally come in with you and make you take your bra off."

"I feel like you should at least get Mardi Gras beads if you have to show your boobs to someone random. Can we start a bridal shop where we give the brides beads for every dress they try on?" She finally laughed. "Do you want me to call and make you an appointment? I can come too, if you want."

"Would you?" she asked. "I didn't want to ask with how much you have going on."

"I'd love to."

"Thanks."

I smiled. I was a rock star when it came to this whole bridesmaid thing.

~

I hadn't seen Sharon's mother in nearly ten years. Partially because there was no reason to, but more by choice. Sharon and I met freshman year of college and decided to room together sophomore year. A decision that we repeated for junior and senior years as well, when we had an apartment off campus, despite her mother.

Not that her mother disapproved of me. Quite the contrary, back then at least. She heavily encouraged Sharon to spend more time with me because I was such a "good girl," which we both laughed about behind her back. I was a terrible influence on Sharon, who had never had more than a sip or two of beer before she met me. That changed quickly.

My first time experiencing the full force of Mrs. Meyer, however, was move-in day sophomore year, when she steamrolled into our dorm room and ordered us to rearrange the furniture to her liking. "Is she for real?" I mouthed to Sharon behind her mother's back. Sharon just shook her head at me to prevent me from saying anything, her eyes wide. I had never seen anything like this. Sharon, who had just as much of a mind of her own as I did when it was the two of us, turned into this meek little mouse as soon as her mother stepped into a room. It was like Sharon was a balloon and her mother was letting the air out.

When she had arranged our room to her satisfaction—including a pair of matching comforters, my own having been deemed unacceptable compared to her memory of her own college dorm room's matching state—she insisted that we accompany her to lunch, where she lectured Sharon on how to lose the freshman fifteen from the previous year. "If it sticks around for sophomore year, you'll never lose it," she warned.

The second she left, we rearranged the room the way we had discussed over the summer. Then ordered a pizza. And breadsticks.

"Dude," I said. "Your mom—"

"I know and I'm sorry. You just have to let her do her thing and then do what you want when she's gone."

"What happens when she comes to visit? I'm not redoing the room every time she pops by."

"She just wanted to walk around campus and go out for meals last year. It'll be fine."

I loved Sharon. But I now understood why her previous roommate had found someone else to live with.

Sharon's college graduation party was the last time I had seen Mrs. Meyer, and I still remembered the way she pursed her lips and said "I see," when I told her about my new job at the foundation. She expected me to go to law school or, at the very least, be writing for the *Washington Post* or *New York Times*. I wasn't even engaged to my then-boyfriend, who had visible tattoos.

But I wasn't twenty-two anymore. And at thirty-two, I didn't care in the slightest if she didn't like my job. Was I curing cancer? No. Did I love what I did? Also no. But was that any of her business? Hell no.

I arrived at the bridal salon just before Sharon and her mom and greeted them as soon as they walked in. "Lily," Diana Meyer said coolly. "I didn't realize you would be joining us today."

I looked to Sharon, who scrunched her face into a guiltily apologetic smile.

"Yup. Just invited myself along. That's how I roll."

"I see," she said. She looked around the bridal salon and turned back to Sharon. "It's not as nice as the last one we went to. Where did you find this place?"

"They had a dress I liked and wanted to try on."

"And we came all the way to Baltimore for one dress?" Her lips were pursed in a disapproving pout.

"Please," Sharon said. "I really like this dress. And if it's no good, we'll try on others."

Her mother nodded her assent, and Sharon was whisked away into a dressing room while Mrs. Meyer began browsing the shop for choices she found suitable.

Sharon came out a few minutes later, and I smiled broadly. It wasn't even that the dress was that great, it was that Sharon looked radiant in it. She looked happier than I had ever seen her.

"It's nice," her mother acquiesced. "If a bit simple."

"I like simple, Mom."

"You'll try on the other ones I picked out. Then we'll decide."

Sharon's shoulders slumped, but she agreed, then retreated into the dressing room.

While we waited, Mrs. Meyer turned her attention to me. "So," she began, looking at my left hand. "You're still single then?"

No, I'm married, I wanted to say. *But I don't wear my ring because it makes it harder to cheat and I really enjoy that.* But she had nothing resembling a sense of humor and I wasn't trying to make the next few months of dealing with her more miserable than they had to be. "Still single," I said cheerily.

"Have you tried online dating?"

"No."

"At your age, you really should."

I blinked heavily. "I'll get right on that." She opened her mouth, clearly ready to give me more unsolicited advice about how I could reverse my single status, but I was saved by Sharon exiting the dressing room in a tulle-covered disaster.

"Lovely," Mrs. Meyer said, gesturing for Sharon to stand on the pedestal before the mirror. "Something like this never goes out of style."

I tore my eyes away from the gauzy mess of a dress and looked at Sharon's face in the mirror. She looked miserable. *Say something,* I thought desperately.

Mrs. Meyer adjusted the shoulder and came around in front of Sharon. "Why do you look like that? Smile." Sharon tried, but it was a pretty pathetic attempt. Mrs. Meyer raised her eyebrows. "You want the other one then?" Sharon looked at her mother and nodded almost imperceptibly. Mrs. Meyer threw up her hands and turned to the saleslady. "I guess she's set on the first one. No one wants a mopey bride."

Sharon smiled and thanked her mother, then returned to the dressing room to put her clothes back on. "Now what on earth will we put you in?" Mrs. Meyer asked, turning to me. "It'll have to be black, I think."

"For a wedding?"

"You'll look lovely in black," she said, patting my arm. "It'll be so flattering." She looked down at my arm under her hand. "Something with sleeves, I think."

I wondered if I could get away with slipping a laxative into her cocktail at the wedding.

But for now, Sharon was happy. And that was what mattered.

CHAPTER EIGHT

I felt so good about finding dresses for both Caryn and Sharon (and surviving my encounter with Mrs. Meyer) that I decided to treat myself to my favorite salad for dinner. I asked Becca if she wanted to meet me at the restaurant, but she was at happy hour with friends from work. I texted Megan next to see if she wanted to grab dinner, but she was at her soon-to-be in-laws' house, so I called and ordered my salad to go. The fact that I would be dining alone was not lost on me after Mrs. Meyer's questions. But could I celebrate my successes with a glass of wine and an extravagant twenty-eight-dollar salad that had a crab cake in it anyway? As a Marylander, that sounded divine.

I got home, kicked off my shoes, poured my wine, pulled up my latest Netflix binge, and settled in to enjoy my overpriced salad. My phone dinged and I glanced down reflexively, then set my salad on the coffee table.

It was an email from my bank. The subject was Urgent: Overdraft.

Oh God, I thought. *That card reader at the gas station must have had a skimmer on it.*

I logged into my bank account, expecting to see that someone had bought a ninety-inch 4K TV and a Louis Vuitton purse and praying that their fraud division would be easy to deal with. *Not how I wanted to spend my evening*, I thought as the wheel spun. The page finally opened.

My mouth dropped open.

There were no weird purchases. My salad had sent my bank account twelve dollars into the red.

Meaning I had started the morning with sixteen dollars to my name.

Holy crap.

I knew my bank account was low from the auto deductions to the wedding account, but I didn't realize how bad it had gotten. And I had never overdrafted before.

My heart was racing and my mouth was dry. I quickly moved two hundred dollars out of the wedding account and into checking to cover the overdraft fee I had just incurred and pad the account a tiny bit, but that was literally the amount that I assumed I would need for a dress for one of the weddings.

Yes, I could start putting all of the wedding expenses on credit cards, but that made me nervous. I wasn't exactly a financial wizard, so I tried to limit myself to spending money that I had. And I really didn't want to spend the next decade of my life paying off these weddings. I needed to find some way to generate additional income, but other than writing about science, I didn't have any marketable skills. I couldn't fold clothes to save my life, so retail was out, and my last foray into waiting tables had ended disastrously in college when I spilled an entire pitcher of sangria on a little girl in her white first communion dress.

"How to make money writing," I typed into Google. About 1,130,000,000 results. *People* can *make money writing,* I thought, clicking on the top link. *Start a blog,* it suggested.

I paused. What would I blog about? Becca frequently said I should have a reality TV camera following me all the time because I was the only person she knew who found herself in situations like I did with the mystery groomsman. But would I actually make money off a blog about my life?

I googled "wedding blogs." About 256,000,000 hits. So that was a thing.

But would I have any friends left if I did that?

"Anonymous blogs." About 317,000,000 hits.

Okay then.

I went to my bedroom for my laptop and began researching how to make money from a blog. Basically, I just had to enable ads on my site. I would make money (granted not much unless I developed a large following) every time someone clicked on a post. It looked like it was a slow process, so I would be stuck with credit card debt in the meantime, but if I could build a following and be smart about it, this could be a light at the end of the tunnel.

~

Becca walked in a little after nine. "Whatcha doing?"

I glanced up, startled. I hadn't even heard her open the door. My salad sat long forgotten in front of me. I realized I was hungry but didn't know if crab could sit out that long, and the lettuce had started to wilt.

"Do you think anyone would read a blog if I started one?"

She sat down on the sofa and pulled a crouton off my salad, then made a face when it didn't crunch. "I mean, I would. What would you blog about?"

"Me. The weddings. My life. All of it, I guess."

"Megan would go ballistic."

I bit the inside of my lip. "Not if it was anonymous and I hid everyone's identities well."

"Why write one if it's going to be anonymous?"

I hesitated. I didn't want to admit to the overdraft from my now unappealing-looking salad. "I—I need to make some money. These weddings are expensive. And—well—I kind of need a place to vent without losing all of my friends." I hadn't realized that last part was true until I said it, but it definitely was.

"You have me."

"I know. But you're not paying me to complain about people."

She laughed. "They have people on talk shows all the time who make a living blogging. And you're funny. You'd be good at it." She stood up and stretched. "I'm gonna go change. You wanna watch something?"

I glanced up at the muted TV. I hadn't shut off my show and had let it run for the last couple hours. "No. I think I'm going to try to flesh this out."

She shrugged. "Okay. I can watch in my room."

I told her not to be silly, that I'd go work in mine, then tossed my salad, grabbed a protein bar, and camped out cross-legged on my bed with my laptop. I went to wordpress.com and created an account. **Blog title?** it prompted.

I thought for a minute, then started typing.

Bridesmania.

And I began to write.

Always the bridesmaid, but glad I'm not the bride?

    Welcome to the blog! I'm not quite sure where to start, so I'm just going to dive right in. I'm a bridesmaid in five weddings this coming summer, all taking place within the same two months.

    If it sounds like the plot of that ridiculous Katherine Heigl movie, let me stop you right there because I don't have twenty-seven friends close enough to want me in their weddings. (Does anyone? That might have been the least realistic part.) Nor am I going to fall in love with a supersexy wedding columnist who looks like James Marsden. (Okay, if James Marsden is reading this, yes, I'm single, ready, and have five weddings that I could use a date to . . . just saying. Although I don't think I'm allowed to bring a date to any of them, but that's a post for another day.)

On the contrary.

No. I have one best friend, two close friends who want me in their weddings to help deflect from horrible friends and family members, and two younger siblings who apparently don't agree with the Victorian concept that the elder sibling should be married before the younger.

I can't use their names because if my identity is revealed, I not only won't be in any weddings, I won't have any friends left. And despite the fact that I'm being snarky about them on the internet right now, I actually do love my friends.

So I'll refer to them by letters.

Bride A asked me to be in her wedding first. She's my work bestie and I adore her. Her other bridesmaids, however? I don't think they're human. And if they're cyborgs, or Stepford people, they're definitely the evil kind. But in such a NICE way.

One of them offered to send me a juice cleanse to help me lose weight before the wedding. Isn't she sweet? She's also Bride A's future sister-in-law, so I can't be rude back in person or Bride A will suffer for it. The saddest part is that Bride A told me she doesn't even like her bridesmaids, which is pretty much the saddest thing ever. So I'll play along and behave for her sake.

Bride B is lovely but has Mom-zilla (Mommy Kruger? I'm not entirely sure how naming wedding party members after horror movie icons works.) and basically asked me to be in the wedding that Mom-zilla is forcing her to have because God forbid her daughter actually have a say in her own wedding. I know I'm mixing my movie monster metaphors, but I'm going to need a bigger boat.

Bride C is like Mary Poppins—practically perfect in every way—except I hooked up with a groomsman in her wedding and I don't know which one it was. How is that possible, you may ask? Well, I'll tell you. I blacked out drunk and then snuck out of the room the next morning while he was asleep facing the wall. But I made the super-mature decision to not let Bride C tell me who the mystery man is because I can't be awkward around him if I don't know who he is.

Bride D is my brother's fiancée. At the risk of sounding like Mariah Carey, I don't know her. I'd like to. I think. But she's like twelve and basically never speaks. And I might have thought he was kidding when he told me he was engaged and made a snarky comment. While I was on speakerphone. With her. Oops. (However, in the grand scheme of Bride C and all, it wasn't THAT big of a faux pas.)

Bride E is my baby sister. She's eight years younger than me, still lives with my parents, and is walking around with her fiancé's grandmother's Tiffany diamond ring. She's twenty-four and has never held a full-time job or paid rent. Granted, there's a pretty close to zero percent chance she actually gets married, but come on. This whole situation has to be a giant troll designed to ruin my self-esteem. No one falls ass-backward into things that easily in real life, do they?

Still with me?

So why a blog? My roommate, who is thankfully NOT planning a wedding, suggested they make a reality TV show about my life. I don't do reality TV. No judgment if you do, but it's not my scene. Writing, however, is. And I figured if I could make some money off people laughing at my ridiculous existence, it would help pay off the astronomical debt I'm assuming by agreeing to be in all of these weddings. Seriously, I think getting another college degree would be cheaper!

In other words, welcome. Come for the drama, stay to laugh at my mistakes.

This is *Bridesmania.*

I proofread it and fixed a couple of typos. I felt a little guilty about trashing my siblings, especially when they had caused the least actual disruption to my life so far, outside of my own sense of failure at being significantly older than both of them and still single. Which really wasn't their fault. But Jake had ridden his bicycle into my first car when he was thirteen, severely denting it, and Amy was just plain annoying, so it was all fair play, right?

Was it any good though? Would people want to read it? I needed an outside opinion, but my three closest friends were implicated in it.

Becca would be honest.

"Hey Becks?" I called toward the living room. I heard her mute the TV.

"What's up?"

"I wrote a blog post. Will you read it and tell me if it's any good?"

"Sure." She sat down on my bed and I handed her my laptop. She nodded as she read along, smiling at the James Marsden line, chuckling about the horror movie mom names and laughing out loud at the Mariah Carey part. "Love it," she said, passing the computer back. "But what happens if one of the brides reads it?"

I tilted my head. "I mean, what are the odds that that happens?"

"Depends where you share it. Probably stay away from your social media and the big wedding websites." A grin spread across her face. "Wait. This is kind of like *The Help.* If you put something in there that the people you're trashing wouldn't want to admit to, they won't acknowledge it's you."

I was skeptical. "But I don't want to put in anything bad about my friends."

"You wouldn't, because that's not who it's being snarky about. Caryn already knows her friends are awful, Megan knows who you slept with, and Sharon knows her mom is a tyrant. But Caryn will deny up and down that it could be you because she would never admit that she said she doesn't like them, and Sharon will do the same thing because she's scared of her mom. And no guy is reading a bridesmaid blog. It's foolproof. And you don't even have to shit in their pie!"

I smiled at the reference. "Madison would probably be mortified if she read this, but I'm pretty sure she hates me anyway, so it doesn't really matter. And it's not like I know any details about her to put in the blog. And Amy doesn't read."

"I think you're fine."

"Does the title work?"

"It's perfect," Becca said. "What's your second post going to be about?"

I grinned, feeling better already. "I have so much material. Where to begin?"

CHAPTER NINE

Megan did not make my resolution to avoid the male members of her bridal party until the rehearsal dinner any easier when she and Tim moved into their new house in early October.

"It'll make the registry go so much smoother," she confided on the phone one night. "Living in an apartment, we didn't have room for anything. This way we can really pick out what we need."

"Makes sense. Do you need help moving?" I prayed she would say no.

"No." *Thank you sweet baby Jesus.* "But is your schedule clear on the twenty-first?"

"Umm," I said. "Let me look, hang on." I pulled out my bullet journal. Dress shopping with Amy the following morning, but nothing that day. "I've got nothing. What's going on?"

"Housewarming party. No gifts. Just bring yourself."

"No gifts for real, or you say no gifts and everyone shows up with one and I look like a jerk because I didn't?"

Megan laughed. "No gifts. Especially not from the bridal party. You guys are already spending enough on us this year."

The hairs on the back of my neck stood up. "The bridal party," I echoed. "So we're all invited."

"Of course." She sounded confused. "You're our best friends." Either she was doing a *really* good job of never speaking of the engagement party situation again, or in the chaos of buying a house, moving, and planning a wedding, my shame had been forgotten. I excused myself from the phone call shortly thereafter and planted myself firmly on the edge of my bed.

What did you expect? I asked myself. *Nothing is ever that easy. Just play it cool, act like it's no big deal if it comes up, and don't get drunk!* "Easier said than done," I said out loud, then sighed and walked to my closet. I couldn't afford a new dress for the housewarming party, but I wanted to look nice. Rule number one of facing down a guy you never wanted to see again is to look your very best so he at least feels that it's his loss, not yours.

~

Becca provided both the dress I wore to the party and the pep talk that got me in the door. And it helped that Megan updated her wedding website with pictures of the bridal party before the housewarming. All six groomsmen looked familiar, but I had met three of them since Megan and Tim started dating and the other three at the engagement party. None of them triggered specific memories of the later parts of the evening, and they all had similar enough coloring to prevent ruling anyone out. So while I couldn't determine whom specifically I should be avoiding, I at least knew all six potential hot potatoes' names. I couldn't imagine it getting much worse than one of them mentioning our night of debauchery and me then having to ask him his name.

"You've got this," Becca said reassuringly as I sat in my car outside Megan's new house. "And if it gets awkward, text me and I'll call you with an emergency."

I thanked her and begged her to keep her phone handy, which she promised to do. "Give me an update even if it's not awkward," she said. "And worst-case scenario, you have material for your blog!"

I laughed and hung up. So far, I had made eighty-seven cents off the blog. Not exactly a runaway success, but I only had three posts. I was afraid to post it on the WeddingWire or Weddingbee forums, even though that would generate readers, because one of the brides might see it, so my only hits so far came from Google searches.

But I hadn't written a post detailing the groomsman situation yet, so Becca was right. I could potentially get a juicy post out of this. I still hoped it would go smoothly instead though.

Before leaving the car, I typed help into a text message to her, but didn't hit send. A good offense is the best defense and all. Thus armed against future humiliation, I took a deep breath, grabbed the bottle of wine I had brought as a de facto housewarming gift just in case other people did bring them, checked the address one more time against the number on the curb, and walked up to the front door.

"I love your dress!" Megan said, hugging me in greeting. "Is it new?"

"Borrowed. But neither new nor blue."

"Come in, come in! Let me give you a quick tour!" She took the wine from me with a quick "You shouldn't have," and led me on a whirlwind tour of the house.

The doorbell rang as we were heading back down from a glimpse of the upstairs and Megan shooed me toward the kitchen, where the island was made up as a bar. "Plenty of gin and olives. Make yourself a martini."

I will not get drunk, I told myself. *No matter how much easier it would make things, I will* not *get drunk.* A glimpse around the living room showed two of the groomsmen playing a video game with Tim, while another perused the bookshelves and a fourth told a story to two of the other bridesmaids. I threw them a half-hearted wave as I crossed through the dining room, where more people were helping themselves to the platters of appetizers. I passed Megan's parents and spoke to them for a few minutes, hoping desperately that I hadn't done anything too embarrassing in front of them at the engagement party. They greeted me as warmly as ever, and, relieved, I excused myself to get a drink. *One is fine,* I rationalized.

A handful of people were seated at the kitchen table, more gathered by the back porch door off the kitchen, and two more at the bar area. I stiffened as a man behind the island looked up at me and smiled with obvious recognition. "Lily!" he said, coming around to kiss me on the cheek.

"Mark," I said, mentally thanking Megan for putting those pictures on her website. He was the best man.

"What are you drinking? White wine?"

I grimaced faintly. "No, thank you. I had enough of that the last time I saw you." Mark laughed. I grabbed the gin. "Martinis are more my style anyway." Mark reached for the shaker and the vermouth. "I can do it," I protested.

"Nah, I make a mean one. How do you take it?"

"Dirty," a voice behind me said. "Lily likes *everything* dirty." I whirled around and saw the last of the six groomsmen, Justin, grinning lasciviously at me. I hadn't needed his picture to know his name. Justin had been creepily hitting on me since I met him a year earlier at Megan's birthday party.

Empirically, Justin was attractive. He had green eyes and a nice, even smile. And he was tall—at five foot nine myself, tall was always a plus. His personality, however, quickly sapped the appeal of his physical characteristics. Especially since he tried to stick his tongue down my throat within about six minutes of meeting him. Nope. Hard pass.

Please let it be anyone *but him,* I thought desperately. But my stomach dropped as an image of his arm around me as I stumbled outside at the engagement party so he could smoke a cigarette came crashing back. I didn't remember kissing him, but I could picture his head leaning in toward mine. Not irrefutable evidence, but combined with the dirty comment, this was probably my guy. *Ugh, Lily, why?*

Mark laughed. "So *you're* the reason Megan has like seventeen jars of olives here. Makes sense now."

Deep breath. *I can have one drink an hour and be fine. Or two drinks now and none later. And then I can handle this.*

"What can I say? I like olives." I laughed nervously, turning back to Mark as he began mixing my drink. "Careful," I warned him, faking a level of gaiety I certainly didn't feel. "If it's not good, you don't get a tip!" They both laughed. *I can do this. Just act like a normal human being who hasn't slept with anyone here.*

He poured the drink and speared three olives to put in it before handing it to me. I took a sip and smiled. "I'll put a dollar in the jar. Thanks!"

"Anything for the maid of honor," he replied.

Why couldn't I have slept with that *one?* I asked myself. *Yes, he's nerdy, but he's sweet at least.*

I turned around and Justin leaned against the island, his hip touching mine. *Nope,* I thought, scanning the room, looking for salvation. Megan called my name from the living room.

"Duty calls," I said without a backward glance and catapulted myself at Megan. "What's up, Megs?"

Megan grabbed my arm and dragged me into the powder room, nearly spilling my martini on her new floors. "I'm going to kill her," she hissed.

"What? Who?"

"Claire. Tim's sister."

I mentally flipped back through the bridesmaids. Tim's sister was the tiny one with a severe case of resting bitch face. She couldn't have been more than four foot eleven, but what she lacked in size, she made up for in attitude—all of it negative. Megan had been complaining about her from the moment they met. "What did she do?"

"She just can't ever say anything nice. Like we just bought a *house*. Of course it's not perfect yet, but do you really walk into someone else's new house and start listing all the things that are wrong with it?"

"What an angry little troll," I commiserated. "Who does that? What was she even saying? The house is awesome."

Megan was blinking rapidly like she was trying not to cry. "Just harping about the carpets and the layout of the kitchen and the appliances. We're going to get new appliances after the wedding, you know."

"Aw Megs, I know. She's just jealous. Where does she live?"

Megan grabbed a tissue from the holder that perfectly matched the rest of the bathroom and started dabbing at her eyes to keep her makeup from running. "In a mansion in Potomac. New construction, of course, with a pool. Her husband's parents *bought* it for them."

I rolled my eyes. "And you're crying over what *she* thinks? Come on, how miserable does she have to be that she's living in a free house and is picking on yours?"

"It's not just that. She's so down on everything we do for the wedding too. She told me she'll only be in the wedding if she gets to pick her own dress. Like what am I supposed to say to that? It's my *wedding*. So I either have to let her decide what the bridesmaids wear, or else tell Tim his sister can't be in the wedding. What a horrible thing to do to someone."

I thought about what I had seen in my recent forays onto Caryn's Pinterest boards. "What if you give her a couple of options? Like where all the bridesmaids wear the same color but can pick from a few styles?"

Megan nodded. "I guess. It's not how I pictured it, but it's better than just having insane mismatched dresses everywhere. But what if she won't even agree to the colors?"

I planted my hands behind me and hopped up onto the bathroom counter to sit. "Then it's *her* choice to not be in the wedding. Not yours."

"But the numbers won't match."

"She's going to wear the color you pick. I promise. She's not going to pass up the chance to be in the wedding so she can say something rude to you on your actual wedding day too."

"If she makes me cry on my wedding day—"

"I'll trip her and then, oops, I stepped on her face. So sorry. Must have been the dress she picked that made her fall."

Megan laughed finally. "You can't step on my sister-in-law's face."

"If she makes you cry on your wedding day, watch me."

Megan looked in the mirror and gave her eyes a final pat with the tissue. "We should get back out there."

I nodded. "Claire's probably spreading rumors about your kitchen floor."

"She would," Megan said conspiratorially. "Thanks, Lil."

"What are maids of honor for?" I jumped off the counter, linked arms with her, and pulled the powder room door open.

"Do you want to sleep over tonight? So you can actually drink? We have the guest room all made up."

"I can't." Nor did I want to, with Justin lurking about. "I'm going dress shopping with my mother and Amy tomorrow."

Megan laughed, all trace of her earlier misery gone. "That's so cute! They're looking for a dress like she's actually getting married?"

I groaned. "It's like a toddler playing dress-up."

Megan nodded distractedly, then saw someone near the front door and called out, "Maria!" Untangling my arm from hers, she rushed off to greet her newest guest.

I looked around. I could stick to Megan's side all night, but with her running around in manic hostess mode, that didn't seem particularly appealing, even though it was the safest option. Better to mingle a bit and then make an early escape. I had a sip of my drink left. Justin wouldn't still be in the kitchen, right? I drank the last drops and decided to risk it for a second and final drink.

The room was more crowded, but I didn't see Justin, so I mixed myself a new martini. I speared as many olives as I could and walked toward the living room to see who else I knew.

Then an arm dropped heavily around my shoulder, and I looked up in revulsion at the one person whose arm I truly did not want around me. "Um," I said uncomfortably, moving out from under it. "What's up? How are you?"

"How are you?" Justin asked. "Really? That's all I get?"

"Do you want an olive?" I held up the pick from my drink.

He bent down and bit one of them, sliding it off the spear, looking up at me as he did it. I felt nauseous. That was the opposite of sexy. "It's a start. I was surprised I didn't hear from you after the engagement party."

"Oh. Uh. You were?"

He nodded, leaning in way too close. "After you just left like that without saying goodbye. We have unfinished business. And you owe me for my shirt."

Why did Amy have to get engaged on a night when I was around a guy who makes my skin crawl?

I laughed nervously. "Oh. Yeah. That. I was—I was a little drunk. I'd just gotten a call from my sister and—"

He leaned closer still, his breath sour from the beer in his hand. "I don't need excuses. I just want to know how you're going to make it up to me."

"I—um—I—" I slipped my phone out of my purse, unlocked it quickly, and hit "Send" on the message to Becca.

My phone rang seconds later.

"I—oh, wait, I have to take this," I said. "Hello?"

"Hey, Lily," Becca trilled cheerfully. "It's an emergency."

"An emergency?" I repeated for Justin's benefit. "Uh-oh. What kind of emergency?"

"Jesus. I don't know what kind. A camel bit me? How's that?"

73

I choked back a desperate laugh. "Oh—wow. That sounds—serious." I looked up at Justin. "Excuse me. Sorry!" Holding the phone to my ear, I weaved my way through the crowd and onto the deck just outside the kitchen. "Thank you, thank you, thank you," I breathed heavily into the phone.

"That didn't take long. What happened?"

"Do you have the wedding website up?" She didn't, but she typed in the address. "It was Justin. As soon as I walked in, he made some dirty comment and then he just grabbed me and asked how I was going to make it up to him for leaving without saying goodbye the morning after the engagement party. And oh my God, Bec, it was the skeeviest thing ever."

"He's not bad looking."

I made a gagging noise. "Sure. If you like date rapists. Blackout drunk doesn't equate to consent. And he made it sound like I *owed* him something." I shuddered.

"From his perspective, you *did* steal his shirt."

"He got that back."

"True. So what are you going to do? Is it too soon to leave?"

I looked at my watch. "Yeah, Megan would be upset."

"Can you say you're sick? Or that I had an emergency?"

"I doubt she'd buy that your camel bit you."

Becca laughed. "*The Mummy* was on TV. It was the best I could come up with under pressure."

I rolled my eyes. "No," I said eventually. "I'll be a big girl. I'll just do everything I can to avoid him."

"On the bright side, at least you know who you're avoiding now!"

"True. Thanks, Bec."

"Anytime. Call me back if you need another emergency because the mummy might attack me next."

I laughed and told her to stay out of his tomb. She said she made no promises and went back to her movie. Taking a sip of my martini,

I leaned against the railing of the deck, trying to make out the features of Megan and Tim's new backyard through the darkness.

"Justin still giving you trouble?" a voice asked out of the darkness.

I jumped and dropped my glass, a tinkling sound echoing below me where it shattered on the patio.

"Shit!" I exclaimed, and the owner of the voice rushed over and into focus.

"Sorry! I didn't mean to scare you!"

"You didn't *scare* me. But Megan's going to be upset I broke a glass."

He shrugged. "Eh, it gives her an excuse to register for new ones."

I squinted at him, backlit against the kitchen windows. "Alex?" I asked. He was the groomsman who had been checking out the bookcase when I arrived at the party.

He nodded. "I am sorry though. I wasn't eavesdropping. At least I wasn't trying to. I was already here when you came out."

I was still startled, but my heartbeat was starting to regulate again. "It's okay. What were you doing out here? It's cold."

He looked down. "I had an emergency of my own."

"Did your friend get bitten by a camel to save you from a total sketch ball too?"

"Um, not exactly." He hesitated. "My dad had a heart attack a few weeks ago and he was having chest pains today."

"Oh no. I'm so sorry. Is he okay?"

Alex nodded. "Yeah, but when I got a call from my sister, it freaked me out, so I came out here to take it. He's fine, but I needed a minute before I went back in. When I saw her name on the caller ID, I just thought—you know." He smiled at me tightly. "And then your poor friend was suffering from a severe camel bite, and I didn't want to interrupt."

I laughed. "I'm such an ass."

"Nah, I get it. Justin was all over you at the engagement party too."

I winced. "That was *not* my finest hour."

"Really? You're not *always* mainlining martinis and wine?" He leaned way over the deck railing pretending to look below him. "I see glass down there; I don't see any liquid."

I scrunched up my nose. "I had an excuse."

"Then? Or tonight?"

"Both. I'm blaming you for the broken glass. If you hadn't jumped out at me like something from a horror movie, I wouldn't have dropped the glass. But at the engagement party, I was—let's call it having an existential crisis."

He laughed, the corners of his eyes crinkling warmly. "An existential crisis? I think I'm going to need a judge's ruling on that one."

With an embellished sigh, I recounted the series of events that led to my fall from vermouth to chardonnay that night.

"Why didn't you just say no to being in a couple of the weddings?"

"Well, I can't to the family ones, and I had already accepted the other three when my brother and sister got engaged."

"Yeah, but it's not like you're the one getting married. Who cares if you're a bridesmaid?"

I rolled my eyes. "It doesn't work like that with girls."

"I guess not. I just have to keep Tim from doing anything too gross at the bachelor party and then show up on time in a tux."

"Lucky."

There was a pause. It wasn't uncomfortable specifically, but neither of us had anything more to say. And without a drink in my hand, I had no props to work with. I turned and peered over the railing again. "So what should we do about this broken glass situation? Clean it up or pretend we know nothing about it?"

Alex leaned back on the rail, facing the kitchen door, and smiled. "Neither. We blame Justin."

I laughed heartily. "Deal."

"Come on, let's go get you another drink so you look innocent." He started to walk away, realized I wasn't following, and turned back. A look at my face told him the reason, even in the dark. "I'll run interference for you again."

"Again?"

"God, you *were* drunk, weren't you? Yeah, I spent half of the engagement party trying to help you fend him off."

I cringed again, wishing he had spent the full party on duty, but I couldn't say that, so I thanked him.

"We'll add that to the list of my groomsman duties to average out the playing field a little. Now come on. It's cold and I don't have a jacket to give you." He held out his arm and I took it gratefully.

Justin glanced up when we walked in together, and a cloud of annoyance crossed his face, but I figured he would get over it. He had Julie, another bridesmaid, trapped against the wall in a corner of the kitchen. Her expression of distaste made it obvious that she felt like I did. If I knew her better, or hadn't already fallen prey to him myself, I might have launched a rescue mission, but it was every girl for herself right now.

"I think you're safe," Alex whispered, following my gaze.

"At least until Julie escapes. But on the plus side, she should be totally on board with blaming him for the broken glass."

Alex steepled his fingers and said "excellent" in a Mr. Burns voice, then, while facing away from the bar, grabbed a martini glass and stealthily slid it to me behind his back. "Time for a refill?" he asked loudly.

"Yes, please."

CHAPTER TEN

I wasn't hungover when I arrived at the bridal salon the following morning to shop with Amy, my mother, my grandmother, and Amy's best friend, an anemic-looking girl named Ashlee, whose vocal fry always left me feeling like she was both younger and ditzier than she actually was. I had known her since she was eleven, but she had never left much of an impression other than being a very washed-out wingwoman to my annoyingly ebullient sister. But after the first hour of dress shopping, I began to feel symptoms similar to a hangover.

"I started a dress binder," my mother announced, pulling a three-inch monstrosity out of a Lululemon tote and setting it gingerly on the shop's coffee table. It was filled with printed-out pages of wedding dresses, each stuck in a clear plastic page protector. The saleslady nodded sagely, as if this were commonplace behavior.

As my mother turned the pages, I saw the Pinterest logo repeated again and again. "Mom, did you print out Amy's whole Pinterest board?"

"Who's pinching Amy?" my grandmother asked loudly. Apparently her hearing aids had not been invited shopping with us.

My mother ignored her. "Where else would I have gotten the pictures?"

"You could have just pulled up Pinterest on your phone."

"She's new to this," my mother told the saleslady in a stage whisper. "She's never been married." I desperately missed the champagne offerings from Caryn's salons.

"I definitely want a princess gown," Amy said. "Or maybe a mermaid. Do they make a princess mermaid? Because I don't feel like I'm quite old enough to get away with a mermaid gown. They look so much better on older brides." She turned to me. "That'll be perfect when you get married."

"Why don't I just get one now?" I asked. "And I can sit around in it until I'm eighty like Miss Havisham."

"Was she that art teacher we didn't like?" Ashlee asked.

I looked at my mother, hoping for some backup, but she mouthed, "Stop it," to me instead. I leaned against the back of the armchair, crossed my arms, and stopped talking.

"What's the matter with you?" my grandmother asked. "Jealous of your sister?"

I rolled my eyes. "Absolutely not."

"Good," she said, patting my arm. "Don't get married until you find a fella who has a twinkle in his eye. That was my mistake. Your grandpa didn't. I should have held out for Frank Sinatra."

I exhaled slowly through my mouth. *Whose idea was it to bring Grandma along?* I wondered. It was excruciating enough to have to sit through this with my mom and Amy.

Eventually we were escorted to a different sofa and armchair, and thankfully offered coffee, despite the dictum of the fanciest salons. I grasped it like it contained the antidote to this whole experience—I hadn't wanted to be lectured for coming in with Starbucks again—and gave this shop an extra star in my mental ranking. The saleslady whisked Amy into a dressing room as my mother and Ashlee continued flipping through the ridiculously profligate binder and my grandmother tried to pretend she knew what was going on without her hearing aids.

I could have been invisible, so I slipped my phone out of my bag. Save me from my mother and sister, I texted Megan. My mom printed out my sister's ENTIRE Pinterest board and laminated the sheets in a binder.

Stop it, Megan replied immediately. She did not. I snapped a stealthy shot of the binder and sent it to her. So wait, she's actually pretending Amy is getting married? And they let Amy bring her pet Chihuahua into the store?

I stifled a laugh. Megan had dated Ashlee's older brother briefly in high school and was merciless. And the resemblance to a Chihuahua was somewhat striking.

Amy also said mermaid dresses are for older brides and it'd be perfect for me if I was getting married.

She's dead, Megan said. DEAD. Megan had taken an extremely targeted approach to dress shopping, in true Megan fashion. She found the handful of dresses that she wanted to try on in a single store, called them in advance, told them which dresses to have in a fitting room for her when she arrived, then went with just me and her mom, tried on four dresses and bought one. The saleslady told her she couldn't take a picture of it, but Megan told her she was buying it so she could do what she wanted, snapped a pic over her protests, and sent it to all of the bridesmaids with the caption, "Said yes to the dress, now what are you gonna wear?" It was a strapless mermaid gown with intricate beadwork on the bodice and hips. Please tell me you told her it was okay because she could wear a mermaid dress in ten years when she gets married for real?

My mom would have murdered me with her binder.

Megan sent an eye-roll emoji. Joan needs to get over it. She has two daughters, not just the teenager.

I set the phone down as Amy emerged in a dress that would require she enlist several octopi as additional bridesmaids to hold it if she planned to pee on her wedding day.

The next seven that she tried on were almost identical. My mother cried and declared her the most beautiful girl she had ever seen in each one. I debated reminding her that I was sitting there too, but I would have just gotten another reproach. So I said she looked gorgeous in all of them and tried to keep my actual opinions to a minimum.

My grandmother, on the other hand, had no such filter.

"You look like a powdered donut," she told Amy as she emerged in a dress with a colored sash. "How are you going to dance in that?"

I stifled a laugh as my mother turned on her. "Mom! I told you if you came with us you had to behave!"

"I'm just supposed to lie to my granddaughter about her wedding dress?"

"Yes!"

Amy's face fell and I felt the first real sympathy I had ever felt for her. I still didn't think for a minute this wedding was actually happening, but *she* clearly did. And my grandmother referring to her as a pastry wasn't how she envisioned dress shopping, even before my mother's impassioned, utterly unconvincing argument.

I rose and went to Amy. I was a pro at wedding dress shopping by now. "How do *you* feel in the dress, Ames?" She shook her head and I lowered mine closer to hers and spoke quietly. Not that it mattered, because my mother and grandmother were arguing too loudly to hear us. "She can't see anything anyway and she won't wear her glasses because she says they make her look old." Amy's lips turned up in a hint of a smile. Our grandmother was eighty-eight, but she was also an incorrigible flirt and the vanity was real. "How did you feel before she said that?"

"This one wasn't my favorite."

"Then who cares what she says? Go try on another." Amy nodded and went back to the dressing room, and I turned to my mother and grandmother. "You two cut it out."

My grandmother sat back in her chair and crossed her arms, a bemused smile on her face. "You hear that, Joan?" she asked my mother. "Cut it out." I wondered suddenly how much of my grandmother's hearing loss was an affectation, because I hadn't spoken loudly.

"Don't you start," my mother said to me wearily, sinking onto the sofa. "I told Amy it should be just me and her doing this. No offense, Ashlee."

I felt my hackles rising, but I bit the inside of my lip to keep from arguing with her. My mother knew how to push all of my buttons, whether she was doing it intentionally or not. Besides, I had four other weddings to deal with and would have felt no compunction whatsoever at missing this particular outing.

And I knew for a fact that *she* was the one who had insisted my grandmother be there for dress shopping, because she turned it into a dig against me during a three-way phone call. My cousins lived out of state and my mother insisted that my grandmother should be able to go wedding dress shopping for at least *one* of her granddaughters, and who knew if she would still be alive when Lily got married?

I was saved by Amy walking out in an elaborate princess dress that was much more flattering than the previous dress. "I think this is it," she said slowly, examining herself in the three-way mirror. My mother promptly burst into tears, then Ashlee, and finally Amy began to cry as well. My grandmother pursed her lips at me but said nothing.

For once, I was thankful that my mother's attention was so laser focused on Amy that she didn't notice my lack of genuine enthusiasm. But Amy was the youngest and the golden child and of course my mother was overly emotional that her baby was about to be the most beautiful bride she had ever seen.

Was I jealous, like my grandmother had asked? Not of her getting married, certainly, but yes. I was. My mother never fawned over me like this. And Amy just lived this charmed little life in which everything worked out perfectly. I was definitely jealous of her ability to do that, even if it wasn't specifically how I wanted to live my life.

As they took Amy's measurements and began the process of ordering the dress, I picked up my phone and began typing a post.

You know those cartoons where the character runs right off the cliff and doesn't start falling until he looks down?

That's my little sister. Except she never bothers to look down. Instead, she merrily skips along until she's back on solid ground, never realizing she left it in the first place.

So for her, getting married is a pretty little fairy-tale ending to her perfect romance. Which is complete bullshit because she's been with this dude for a year and has lived at home the whole time. So like, if they want to sleep together, do they have to wait until my parents aren't home? Like they're in high school? Sounds super romantic to me. (Actually, it's gross and for once I'm thrilled that my childhood bedroom is now my mom's treadmill room because if they were doing it on my old bed, I would puke.)

But I don't understand how you live your life like that. How do you not check for the ground beneath your feet? Even the coyote knew to do that, and he was such an optimist, always believing he would finally get that roadrunner. Or maybe he was just a very hungry realist with an Amazon

Prime account. But either way, I can't do that. I look down.

Which is probably why she's getting married (ostensibly—I still don't totally believe it) and I'm on my way to dying alone with a cat that will eat my face before anyone discovers me—truly a terrible fate because I hate cats. And there was that article that says they really will eat you.

But even when I try not to look down, it doesn't matter because someone always taps me on the shoulder and points out that I've run off the cliff. Remember that groomsman I hooked up with? Well, I found out which one it was, and he's the single grossest guy (Not physically. Physically he's not terrible. But he's like Jabba the Hut in a decent body.) I've ever met, and that's who I get drunk and hook up with.

Maybe being a cat lady with a half-eaten face won't be so bad after all.

I felt a little guilty putting my sister's business out there like that. But it was anonymous and, if I was being honest, it wasn't like that many people were really reading it anyway. I hit "Publish." Besides, it felt good to be writing, and it was certainly better than holding all of that annoyance in. And hey, maybe I'd break a dollar today.

CHAPTER ELEVEN

The following Tuesday, I was in line at Starbucks when I heard someone call my name from behind. I had earned my first latte from the blog (and Friday was payday, so my account was less terrifying as long as I didn't go shopping all week), so I decided to treat myself. I turned around and saw Alex, wearing a suit and waving, with three people in line between us.

I looked at him, surprised. "What are you doing here?"

"Getting coffee. What are *you* doing here? I don't think they serve martinis."

The man standing behind me snickered and the woman with a small child behind him gave me a dirty look. I glanced surreptitiously at my watch, but I wasn't running late for once, so I gestured for the people between us—rude as they were—to go ahead of me and moved back to where he stood in line.

"Cute. Very cute. I'm actually *not* an alcoholic, for the record."

"For the record," he repeated with a grin, "I didn't actually think you were. Unless you're having another—what did you call it? Existential crisis?"

I laughed and elbowed him sharply. "You're a jerk, you know that?"

"Yup. Which is why I'm *not* protecting you from Justin the next time you see him."

"Did I say jerk? I meant gem. You're a *gem*."

"That's more like it," he said. "Do you work around here? Or are you just hanging around until the nearest bar opens?"

I rolled my eyes as we moved closer in line. "Work. The Foundation for Scientific Technology."

He eyed me with surprised respect. "I didn't have you pegged as a scientist."

"Particle astrophysics. You shouldn't be so judgmental."

"Really?"

"No, I'm their head of PR. I write a lot of press releases and make really miniscule discoveries sound interesting to laypeople."

"That's still higher-tech than I would have guessed."

"What was your guess?"

He looked me up and down. "Gossip columnist. Or fashion blogger."

I burst out laughing. "Yup, that's me. In my outfit from TJ Maxx." Just the woman with the young son remained in line in front of us. "What do you do?"

"Stalk PR people for scientific organizations at coffee shops before murdering them at weddings."

"Pays well, does it? That's a nice suit."

He laughed. "I'm a lawyer. At Waters and Flynn."

"Never heard of them," I said. "But cool. They're near here?"

"Two blocks down on M."

"Ah. I'm on L Street."

"I know," he said. "We represent some of your scientists. Patent law."

"Oh—maybe I have—oh shoot—sorry, a grande skinny vanilla latte," I said, turning to the barista.

I pulled out my wallet, but Alex edged in next to me, flashing the app on his phone. "And a venti Americano." He looked down at me. "I've got this."

"Are you—I mean—okay. Thanks."

We moved aside to wait for our drinks, in a mildly awkward silence now that he had bought me a coffee.

I broke the peace first. "So do you come to this Starbucks a lot?" *Ugh.* That sounded like a pickup line. I didn't want him to think I was interested. I mean, maybe under other circumstances I could have been, but sleeping with Justin irreparably negated any potential that could have existed with the other groomsmen.

"Yeah. It's right between the Metro and work."

"Same. I'm just usually running later than this."

"So if I want to run into you again, I should be late to work?"

"Probably. Or wait until the wedding."

The barista put our drinks on the counter. Alex took them both and handed me mine. He took the hint. "Gotcha. Well, maybe I'll see you around."

I nodded, feeling a tinge of disappointment. "Yup. Thanks for the coffee."

"No problem. Have a good day, Lily."

"You too." He held the door for me, and we went our separate ways.

Good job, Lily. You meet a nice guy who buys your coffee and holds the door for you, but you can't like him because you slept with the slimy creep who is in the same wedding with both you and *the nice guy. And you wonder why you're single.*

~

I had planned on Tuesday being a one-time splurge, but I was able to justify going Wednesday because I hadn't paid for my coffee on Tuesday. Thursday—well—Thursday, maybe I was hoping I would see Alex again.

"Grande skinny vanilla latte," I told the barista absently while fishing my wallet out of my bag.

"Are you Lily?" she asked.

I looked up warily. Was I coming to this Starbucks too often? "Ye-es. Why?"

"Your coffee is already paid for. We just need to make it." She turned toward the staff making the drinks. "Lily is here!"

"What's going on?"

"Your friend paid for your drink and left you a note on the cup."

"My—do you have the right Lily?"

The barista nodded. "He said you got a grande skinny vanilla latte and that you had dark hair and eyes and a red bag."

"What did he look like?"

"She said he left you a note, which probably has his name on it, so can you do this later?" the man in line behind me asked impatiently.

I normally would have told him where he could shove his attitude, but I was too flustered. Instead I apologized reflexively and stepped toward the pickup area to wait.

"Lily," a different barista called out, and I snatched the cup before she could even set it down.

On the sleeve, in black Sharpie, all capital letters, it read, *START GETTING TO WORK ON TIME! —Alex.*

I set the cup down on an open spot at the bar by the window and snapped a picture. I sent it to Becca first. What does THIS mean???? Then I texted Caryn as well. I wanted to send it to Megan, but I didn't want to put her in the middle with Alex if I could avoid it.

That groomsman from Megan's party? Becca replied immediately. I told her yes. Ugh why are guys never that cute and sweet with me?

Is it cute and sweet or weird?

Cute and sweet. Definitely.

But what does it MEAN?

Caryn texted back. Means get to work on time so I don't have to cover for you every day. She put a winky face to show she was teasing.

He likes you, duh, Becca said.

Does he though? He didn't, like, put his phone number on it or anything.

Yeah, but he's saying he wants to see you again.

I hesitated. I can't, I wrote eventually.

Why not?

Because I already hooked up with the gross groomsman from Megan's wedding.

Would she actually care?

I thought for a minute. Megan would absolutely want me to be happy. But what would happen when it didn't work out and I suddenly had *two* groomsmen whom I had to tell Megan not to pair me with for the ceremony? And I would have two of Tim's friends I needed to avoid. It would be putting Megan in a rough spot, and I didn't want to make her choose sides. Plus, I remembered how I felt the morning after her engagement party. And how much worse I felt seeing Justin at the housewarming party. That icky feeling wouldn't just be doubled, it would grow exponentially with a second groomsman's notch on my bed. Nope. Couldn't do it.

Probably not if I really liked him. But what are the odds of it actually working out? Besides, I don't want to be the girl who got involved with two different groomsmen.

That's fair . . . So what are you going to do?

I hesitated again. Doing nothing sent a clear "not interested" message, but it would be rude to not acknowledge him, especially when he had bought me two coffees this week. And even if I wasn't interested per se, there was something about Alex that I did like. He would make an awesome friend.

I looked at the line, which had died down to only three people, then checked my watch. *Hell with it*, I thought, and got back in line.

"Do you remember the guy who bought me my coffee?" I asked when I reached the barista.

"Of course," she said. "He's in here every day."

"Can I pay for his order for tomorrow and leave him a note?"

She grinned and handed me a sleeve and a Sharpie. Her name tag said she was Taylor. "This is like *Romeo and Juliet*."

I rolled my eyes. "That makes you the nurse and means we're all dead by act five. He's just a friend."

"Wish I had a friend like that." She grinned. "He's cute."

"All yours," I said, starting to write: *Why? Being late works out well when I get free coffee for it—you're encouraging bad habits! —Lily.* *Too flirty,* I told myself, then grabbed another sleeve. Taylor smiled irritatingly and I tried again. *Never gonna happen . . . but thanks for the coffee! —Lily. Much better.* I handed it to Taylor.

"I liked the first one better," she said.

"Just friends," I said again. I paid for the coffee and left, much later for work than usual.

~

I made it until lunch before I texted Megan. What's Alex's story?

The three dots appeared immediately to show she was typing. Funny . . . he asked Tim the same thing about you the other day. What's going on there?

Nothing.

My phone rang. Megan knew me better than that.

"Tell me everything," she said.

"There isn't anything to tell. We hung out a little at your party and then I ran into him at Starbucks on Tuesday."

"Yeah, he told Tim he ran into you. And?"

I thought about leaving out the coffee note, but I hadn't encouraged anything, so there was nothing wrong with telling Megan that *he* had been flirty. Maybe. Was he being flirty?

"What are you leaving out?" She really did know me too well. I told her about the coffee cup.

"Aww, I like that. He's a good guy."

90

"What's his deal?"

"He went to high school with Tim. He's divorced. Got married a few years ago, but it didn't work out."

I recoiled slightly. Sure, I knew people who had been divorced. At thirty-two, who didn't? But I had avoided dating into that pool. Anyone who had already hit that level of commitment seemed like they were on a different plane of existence than I was. "Kids?"

"Nah."

"When did they split up?"

"Last year, I think? He was kind of out of commission while they were married, then he started trying to reconnect with people after it ended. Sounds like she was pretty controlling."

"So is he, like, hitting on me?"

Megan laughed. "Since when do you need to ask that question?"

"I don't know, this one is weird."

"*He's* a little weird. But not creepy weird. Just . . . quirky."

"I can see that," I said. "But, like . . . what now?"

"Do you want his number? I can ask Tim."

"God no!"

Megan laughed again. "Is that not how dating works anymore? I'm an old, soon-to-be-married lady. I don't know how you kids do these things nowadays."

"Dating happens entirely through coffee sleeves now. You've missed everything."

"Apparently. *Are* you interested though?"

My heart twisted a tiny little bit in my chest—not over Alex, over the question itself. I could read between the lines of the word she chose to emphasize. Megan would give her blessing *if* I were serious enough. But otherwise she didn't want to deal with the fallout and I couldn't fault her for that. We had been down a similar road before.

"No," I said quickly. Maybe too quickly. "He seems cool, but just as a friend."

I heard her sigh in relief. "Obviously I'd say go for it if you liked him. But . . . you know . . ."

"I know, Megs. I promise. Just friends." A pause. "What did he ask about me though?"

"Just what your deal was."

"What did Tim tell him?"

"That you're really easy when you switch from martinis to wine. But he already knew that."

"I'm hanging up now."

Megan laughed. "K. Text me later!"

I shook my head. She was ridiculous.

~

I wouldn't say I *rushed* to get ready for work on Friday morning, but I was mildly more conscious of the time than I typically was. Not that I wanted to get to Starbucks while Alex was still there. No, that would be way too awkward. And would probably lead to him asking me out, which I would absolutely say no to and would definitely make things *more* awkward. But I was anxious to see if I got a reply. No matter what I told Becca, it *was* cute.

I forced myself to walk slowly to the Metro and then from the stop to the Starbucks, reminding myself that I didn't actually care and that my message had been distinctly nonchalant.

I arrived a couple minutes earlier than usual, but still later than the day when I had run into Alex. I made my way through the line and got to Taylor. "Anything for me?"

She shook her head. "I told you the first message was better."

I felt a twinge of disappointment, but it was for the best. Really. There were plenty of fish in the sea who weren't off-limits.

"Grande skinny vanilla latte then," I told her. "Actually, make it a venti." I deserved a treat for behaving like a grown-up.

CHAPTER TWELVE

From: Caryn Donaldson [futuremrscaryngreene@
gmail.com]
To: [bridesmaids]
Subject: Wedding newsletter volume 2
Date: October 28

You guys! My wedding dress is officially being
made! How crazy is that?

Now, it's time to focus on YOU. I want all of
you to feel as beautiful as you did on your wedding days (or will someday, Lily!) when you stand up
there with me, so we need to find you the perfect
dresses! I've got some ideas, but I want as many
of you as possible to come shopping for them so
we can make sure we find something that flatters
everyone equally. Which shouldn't be hard, I mean
you all look like runway models anyway! How does
next Saturday look?

There was more—a lot more, actually—but I had stopped reading. The only thing "runway model"-esque about me was possibly my height. I stood a solid six inches over the rest of Caryn's Lilliputian bridesmaids. And while I felt pretty good about my pant size most days, you could probably fit one of Caryn's friends inside each leg and still have room for dessert.

I heard the chimes starting to signal a chorus of replies, but I muted my computer. I had work to do on a press release about a presentation being made at the next cosmic ray conference.

An hour later, Caryn popped her head into my office. "What's wrong?"

I looked up. I was almost finished with the draft. "Nothing. Why?"

"You didn't respond to my email."

"Oh." I clicked over to my inbox to see thirty-eight new messages. Jesus. "Sorry. I was doing the Lewis-Fielding release."

"That can wait," she said, waving a manicured hand. "Can you go dress shopping on Saturday?"

I pulled out my planner. Becca's birthday was that night and Amy wanted me to go bridesmaid dress shopping with her that Sunday. "As long as it's not too late, yes."

"We'll do early afternoon. I'm going to a barre fitness class in the morning with Caroline and Mia. Caroline swears it's why her arms look so good." I glanced at Caryn's arms and raised an eyebrow, which she ignored.

"Okay. Are you serious that you want us in nice dresses? I thought half the fun of bridesmaids was forcing us into something ugly."

"Why would I want you ruining my pictures?"

"So no huge eighties-style puffed sleeves and butt bows?"

She laughed. "Can you picture my friends dressed like that?" I tried to imagine Caroline with permed hair and fried bangs. It was a satisfying idea.

"No. But it'd be funny."

"I'm thinking pale purple. Everyone looks good in purple. And something simple and strapless and elegant. You know—something you'd totally wear again."

I tried to remember the last time I wore an elegant gown to something other than a wedding, where recycled bridesmaid dresses were beyond obvious, and the best answer I could come up with was my high school prom, fourteen years earlier. And purple? Did I even own anything purple? Granted, black was the primary color of my wardrobe, but still.

"Saturday it is."

"Great! Can you reply that in an email so everyone knows you're in? And bring a good strapless bra so we can see what the dresses will actually look like!"

I looked down at my chest and back up at Caryn's. A good strapless bra probably existed for her—but when you're a D-cup, "good strapless bra" becomes an oxymoron. "Um . . . I'll try."

~

I hopped off the Metro a stop early on my way home, determined to find a bra that got the job done. Either Bloomingdales or Lord and Taylor had to have a contraption that would hold my boobs up adequately for a wedding. I checked my bank account from the escalator at the station. This was definitely a wedding expense, as I would probably need a high-quality strapless bra for more than one of the weddings, but it was going to have to go on my credit card to be worried about later.

Two stores, eleven bras, and one saleslady who had to be forcibly removed from my dressing room after trying to adjust my breasts herself later, I had one that seemed to stay in place well enough to dance without creating the dreaded quad boob or cutting off my circulation to the point where I would suffer the loss of any vital organs. It cost a gut-wrenching ninety-eight dollars before tax and looked like it was part of a Victorian asylum restraining device rather than the pretty, lacy underthings that the girls who were less blessed in the chest were able to buy, but it would serve.

I walked back toward the Metro station. If it were warmer out, I would have walked the mile and a half home, but there was a chill in the air and the sun was setting earlier and earlier, making that option less desirable. Plus I was still in my work shoes. My phone vibrated to tell me I had a text and I looked down at it, narrowly avoiding a collision with someone exiting the Metro station while also looking at his phone.

"Lily?"

I looked up. Alex again. "What are you doing here?"

"Going home. I live two blocks that way. What are you doing here?"

"I had to grab something at Bloomingdales. I live in Bethesda."

"We're practically neighbors."

"A Metro stop apart. Us and probably fifty thousand other people in the same radius."

He smiled. "A cynic in five weddings. How's that working out?"

I grimaced and gestured toward my bag. "I just spent a hundred bucks on a strapless bra to go bridesmaid dress shopping this weekend. I think that's a pretty apt metaphor for my life right now."

"Bras cost a hundred dollars? A pack of boxers costs like ten bucks for three pairs."

"There's a tax on being female, didn't you know that?"

"Is it nice at least?" he asked, trying to peek in the bag.

I swatted his hand away. "You have to *at least* buy me dinner to get a look at my underwear."

"I'll keep that in mind." I braced myself for the dinner invitation, but he just laughed. "I'll catch you around, Lily."

~

Saturday afternoon found me strapped into the Nellie Bly straightjacket bra and stuffed into a too-small dress that wouldn't even zip over my hips, next to Caryn's sister, Olivia, whose dress fit her perfectly. While wedding dresses tended to be stocked in size ten and up to be accommodating to more brides, bridesmaid dresses were apparently as merciless as Caryn's bridesmaids.

"It's gorgeous," Olivia cooed, turning this way and that and swishing the chiffon of the evening-length skirt. "It's so flattering."

She wasn't lying. On her, it was. Even in the puke-green color that the sample came in.

On me, not so much. It had a padded bust that was detailed with ruched material designed to enhance the wearer's chest a full cup size. Which on Olivia looked great. On me? Oh dear.

Caryn looked from Olivia to me, her mouth a scowl of disappointment. This was the third one we had tried on, and Caryn's favorite by far before we put them on.

"We could try different styles for different bridesmaids," the saleslady murmured to Caryn. "One dress doesn't fit all in some cases."

I looked in the mirror and could have cried from the frustration of being made to do this.

"I—Lily, what if you try it without the bra?" Caryn asked.

"It's not going to stay up without the bra." I shook my head.

"Perhaps a minimizing bra," the saleslady suggested.

"Can we try a different dress?"

"I love this one," Caroline said. "I think you should try the minimizing bra."

I felt my jaw tightening. Earlier, she had asked why I hadn't thought to bring Spanx with me, so we could get an accurate feel for how the previous dress *could* look.

"Why don't I just get a breast reduction and solve everyone's problems?" I asked, my voice dripping sarcasm.

"Don't be silly," Caryn said. "You'd have swelling and we wouldn't have an accurate idea of your post-op size in time to order the dresses."

My eyes widened and I started sputtering that I wasn't serious, but Caryn didn't notice. "Do you have any minimizing bras she could try here?"

"No." The saleslady shook her head, eying me appraisingly. "We could try wrapping her with some fabric though." I pictured Barbra Streisand binding her chest in *Yentl*. Caryn had her head tilted and was studying my chest, as if trying to picture how that would work.

"No." I crossed my arms over my chest self-consciously. "I'm not doing that. Caryn, if I don't fit into the mold of what you want your bridesmaids to look like, I don't have to be in the wedding."

"That's a little dramatic, don't you think?" Caroline asked, hand on hip. "Are you really threatening to drop out of the wedding if you don't like the dress?"

"No, I—"

"This isn't about you. It's *Caryn's* day. You're just being selfish."

I looked to Caryn, horrified. She hadn't said anything. "Caryn, I'm not threatening at all. I'm just saying if I can't look the way you want, my feelings won't be hurt if you don't have me in the wedding." Was that true? Of course not. But I would still rather not be in the wedding than have her be miserable over how I looked in it.

"You could get a minimizing bra," Caroline said. "And maybe try a diet. We can't do anything about your height, but if you wear flats with a long dress, and we all wear heels, it won't be so bad."

I recoiled, stung. I had considered the money I'd spent on the strapless bra to be a major concession to the fact that I didn't look like Caryn's other bridesmaids, but this was too much. I opened my mouth, about to tell her to go do something that wasn't anatomically possible for her to do to herself, when I saw something interesting that made me hesitate. Dana was standing a little behind Caroline, and from that safe vantage point, she was glaring at her with the same unadulterated hatred that was probably mirrored on my face.

Oh thank God, I thought. *It's not just me.*

Bolstered by that, I started to turn back to Caroline, ready to tell her where she could shove her minimizing bra, but a quick glance at Caryn stopped me. Caroline was going to be her sister-in-law. And saying what I wanted to say would make it harder for me to stay in Caryn's life.

I took a deep breath and counted to ten.

"I'll try to find a different bra," I finally said, measuredly. "And I'm happy to wear flats. I'll even get some Spanx if I have to, but I'm not changing how I actually look."

"That's—perfect," Caryn said, clearly not knowing how to fix the situation, but also unwilling—or maybe unable—to stand up to Caroline. "Let's—let's try a different dress. Maybe—are there other styles that go with this one? We can mix and match."

"Mixing and matching is tacky," Caroline said. "Besides, the rest of us are good in the same dress, so it would just be *her* in a different one."

I balled my fists involuntarily. I had never actually been in a fight, but this might be the time to jump in the ring.

Caryn stood and put a hand on my arm, but didn't say anything.

"Maybe something a little higher cut," the saleslady suggested, flustered. "I think I have one that might work for everyone."

Caroline muttered something that sounded like "cheap," but Caryn shook her head at me and mouthed that she was sorry. My anger evaporated when I saw how sad she looked. She told me when she asked me to be in the wedding that her friends were awful. And how miserable did your life have to be when you didn't even like your friends?

"No, I am," I mouthed back. I wasn't going to say it so Caroline could hear it, however.

~

I thought the next dress made me look pregnant, but it contained my boobs better, so I no longer looked like I was channeling the ghost of Anna Nicole Smith. The other girls looked willowy and ethereal in it, and while Olivia and Caroline huffed that they liked the earlier ones better, Dana said she was happy in whatever made Caryn happy, and Caryn said it was her favorite of the dresses, which was a lie that even Caroline couldn't effectively argue against.

As I peeled it off in the dressing room, I looked at the price tag, then did a double take. Five hundred and eighty-five dollars for a dress that made me look like I had chewed Willy Wonka's gum and was turning into a gigantic blueberry? If you factored in the money I had spent on a strapless bra, then added the cost of Spanx and a minimizing bra, I'd be spending over eight hundred dollars *before shoes* on clothes for Caryn's wedding. I sat down, still in my straightjacket bra and underwear, and pulled my planner out of my bag. I could put it on a credit card, but that was *significantly* higher than the two-hundred-dollar maximum I had planned on for each bridesmaid dress. In fact, that was eighty percent of my dress budget overall. For just one wedding. I threw my clothes back on and poked my head out of the dressing room, gesturing wildly for Caryn to join me.

"What's wrong?" she asked.

"I—" I stopped myself. She looked so defeated. "Nothing. Sorry. I'm good."

"You don't hate the dress?"

I did. I hated it. But I loved Caryn and this was a stressful situation and I hadn't been any actual assistance when the whole reason she said she needed me as a bridesmaid was to help when the wicked bridesmaids of the west created scenes like this.

"It's great," I lied. "I'll totally wear it the next time I'm a guest at a wedding."

She hugged me and I mentally tallied which credit card could handle the load. "Thank you, Lily."

~

Caryn, Olivia, and Caroline had all driven together and parked on the first level of the garage, Deanna and Mia were both parked on the second level and exited the elevator in a flurry of air-kisses, leaving me alone with Dana as we rode to the third floor. I watched her from the corner of my eye as she dug through her Prada purse for her keys.

What the hell? I shrugged.

"Does Caroline *always* suck that much?" She looked at me in surprise as the elevator doors opened, as if she had forgotten I was there.

"I don't—" She stopped herself, took a deep breath, and then replied, "Yes." I started to laugh. "What's so funny?"

"You," I said. "You're a real person!" She looked confused. "I thought you were all Stepford robots." She didn't seem to get the reference. "All perfect and no emotions."

She looked down. "Oh. No."

"Sorry. It was a joke."

"No, I know."

"Why do you all put up with her if she's always like that?"

Her face was drawn when she looked back up, as though she was suddenly exhausted. "*I* don't really anymore. I try to avoid her as much as I can now. But this is for Caryn. So I'm here."

"Were you in her wedding?"

"I was."

"What was that horror show like?"

That elicited the ghost of a smile. "You don't even want to know."

"I'm just glad it's not just me."

"It's not. She's the actual worst person on the planet." Her eyes widened. "Don't tell anyone I said that."

"Your secret is safe with me." Her shoulders loosened slightly, and we stood in an awkward silence until she said she needed to get home and unlocked the nearby white Mercedes.

"I'll see you around."

Dana grinned sympathetically. "Hang in there."

"You too." I climbed into my much cheaper car and looked at my reflection in the rearview mirror. *I can do this,* I thought. Then I saw a long, gray hair, standing out among the rest of my dark strands. I named it Caroline as I clenched my teeth and yanked it out. Did she cause it? Probably not. But damn it.

CHAPTER THIRTEEN

I called Megan on my way to the bar where Becca was celebrating her birthday that night to tell her about Caroline's tirade against my perceived physical flaws.

"What a piece of work!"

"I know."

"Just seven more months and you'll never have to deal with her again. And it's really just the shower, the bachelorette party, and then the wedding itself. And there's no way people like that actually let you do any planning for the shower and bachelorette, so it'll be minimal contact."

"Great. Seven months is enough time to drop thirty pounds so I can look like they want me to."

"Are you going to do that?"

"If you're trying to tell me I have to lose weight to be in your wedding, we're not best friends anymore."

"You're perfect just as you are," she said. "Although . . . you said you'd try a minimizing bra for Caryn's?"

I took a minute before I responded. "You're not serious."

"No. I mean. I don't know. Maybe. If you're going to buy it anyway."

"Megs."

"I just—your boobs are really big. And it's going to be in a church and all."

"Are you saying my boobs are too big for God?"

"No. It's fine. We'll just make sure they're covered up in your dress."

I said okay and told her I needed to go into the bar.

"You're not mad at me, are you?"

"No. It's just been a long day." A long couple of months, actually.

"Okay. I'm sorry. I love you. We'll talk tomorrow."

"We'll talk tomorrow," I agreed and hung up.

What. The. Fuck?

I showed my ID to the bouncer, which felt superfluous. No one was going to confuse me for a teenager anymore. And the underage crowd didn't exactly do wine bars. But whatever.

"You made it!" Becca threw her arms around me. She had gone to dinner first with some friends, but I'd had to text her from dress shopping that I wouldn't make it to that part. "Did you get your dress?"

"Happy birthday! And oh God, don't ask."

"What happened?"

I gave her the short version. "Are my boobs that offensive?"

"Your boobs are awesome. They're all just jealous!"

That made some amount of sense. Megan admitted freely to being jealous of my cleavage. I was jealous of her butt. It was a tradeoff.

"No bride wants everyone staring at another girl on her wedding day."

"I guess. Today sucked though."

"Grab a drink. You'll feel better!"

I took her advice and wound up talking to Lisa, one of Becca's coworkers whom I had always liked. Becca wandered over and plopped down on the couch next to me. "You're still talking about the dress shopping?"

"Sorry. I'm being insanely boring, aren't I? I'll drink more and be entertaining."

Becca and Lisa laughed. "You're *not* boring," Lisa said.

"I keep saying her life should be a reality TV show. Did she tell you about the groomsman?"

Lisa nodded. "I'd watch."

I opened my mouth, about to tell her she could follow my exploits on my blog, then stopped myself. One glass of wine and I was about to blow my cover already? No, bad plan. I didn't know this woman. Instead I excused myself and got up to get another glass of wine. I checked my phone while I waited for the bartender to bring it. Amy had texted me six pictures of bridesmaid dresses. All of them were short and tight. At least she wouldn't have an issue with my boobs—she had a matching pair.

"Now I know you're following me," a voice said.

I looked up, recognizing the voice's owner. "Seriously? This is getting creepy."

"You're the one creeping on my territory." Alex leaned back against the bar, a glass in his hand.

"Your territory is a wine bar?"

He laughed. "No. I'm on a date. It's going really bad."

"You ditched a date to come talk to me?"

"Yeah. I told her you're an old friend." He gestured toward a girl, who was watching us with moderate hostility from a table across the room. "Wave for me."

I obliged. "She's pretty. What's wrong with her?"

"I asked her the last book she read, and she doesn't know because she doesn't read. And she said something about never trusting the mainstream media."

"Ouch. Do you need me to fake an emergency?"

"Do you have a camel with you?"

"Cute. Real cute."

"Hey, I saved you from Justin. Twice, by my count. It's the least you could do."

I opened my mouth to say he had only actually saved me once, but I had a feeling that sleeping with Justin might be more damning than being illiterate. "Fine," I said. "But we're even after this." I threw my head onto my arms on the bar and began to pretend I was weeping.

"What are you doing?" he asked.

"Pat my shoulder, then go tell her I just found out my husband is cheating on me and you have to make sure I get home okay."

"Will that work?"

"Yes. Now go tell her. With a straight face."

He left and I continued to pretend to cry. "Lily! What happened?" Becca grabbed my arm.

"Shhhh," I said. "I'm faking an emergency for Alex."

"The guy who did the coffee note?"

"The same," he said, returning. "It worked! She's leaving."

"Let me know when she's gone."

Alex waited another thirty seconds. "You're good."

I picked my head up and took a long sip of the new glass of wine in front of me. "Yes. I am. Alex, this is Becca, my roommate. It's her birthday today. Becca, this is Alex, the groomsman in Megan's wedding."

"Nice to meet you," Alex said, shaking Becca's hand. "And happy birthday. Let me get you a drink."

"No, no, it's fine," Becca said.

"He's a lawyer."

"In that case, make it a bottle."

Alex laughed. "For the birthday girl? You've got it."

"Where'd you meet her?" I asked, gesturing toward the door after Becca had left with her new glass of wine. Alex and I had both taken seats at the bar.

"At Starbucks. I wrote her a note on a cup of coffee."

"For real?"

"No. Are you always this gullible?"

I elbowed him. "Yes. I was born yesterday."

"Promise not to judge?"

"Absolutely not. Judging is what I do."

"I thought you did PR."

"For a living? Yes. But my true passion is judging others."

"I'll consider myself warned. It was a Tinder date." I cringed. "I know, I know."

"Megan said you're newly back on the dating scene."

"Asked about me, huh?"

I rolled my eyes. "She told me you asked Tim about me first."

"Maybe I did."

I put my glass of wine down. I was getting flirty and that meant it was time to stop drinking. I was not letting wine lead me into the same pit with a second groomsman just because I'd had a rough day.

Evidently he felt the same way, because he also set his glass down. We sat in silence for a minute. "What's the latest update on all the weddings?"

I put my head in my hands and groaned. "We're at the bridesmaid dress shopping stage. It's the worst."

"Why?"

"Horrible bridesmaids and body shaming."

He looked over at me. "At the risk of getting slapped for being out of line, what could they shame you about? Unless you were the one doing the shaming?"

I laughed. "Me? No. Although that would have been a great twist. When the one who thinks she's in charge of the world told me to get a minimizing bra and a pair of Spanx, I should have looked her up and down and told her to get a boob job and eat a cheeseburger."

"What's a minimizing bra? Is that what you spent all that money on?"

"God no. It's what it sounds like—it makes your boobs look smaller."

"That's a thing? How long was I out of commission for dating? What year is it? I want to go back to 1985!"

"Calm down, Marty McFly." I found myself smiling despite my day. "How long *were* you out of commission?"

"Married three years. With her for eight."

I raised my eyebrows. "That's a really long time."

"Too long, it turned out." He picked his glass back up and took a drink. We sat in silence a moment longer. "How about you? Why are you single?"

"I get married once a year and then kill the guy and drink his blood to stay young."

"Sounds about right."

I hated that question. And I'd had quite enough experience with it to be a pro at dodging it. But he didn't push, which, oddly, made me want to answer. Well, sort of answer.

"I don't know. I guess I just haven't met the right person. I don't think there's one soul mate out there. But I haven't found anyone who I've been like, hey, let me spend my life with you. And I'm *really* good at sabotaging things that aren't quite right."

"Instead of settling when they aren't. Good for you. You *should* sabotage it spectacularly when it's not right. Don't settle. Settling is bad."

"Remind me not to play *Oregon Trail* with you."

He laughed heartily. "Oh we *are* going back to 1985, apparently."

I clinked my glass to his. "To Doc Brown, wherever—and whenever—he may be."

Becca appeared at my side. "We're heading to Scotch," she said, naming another bar. "Do you want to stay longer?"

I did. Which meant I shouldn't. "No. I'm coming." I looked at Alex. "It was nice running into you. Again."

"Can I see you again?"

Yes. Say yes. "At this rate? I think that's unavoidable." I flashed him a smile and got up to leave. "See you around." I didn't turn around, but I could feel him watching me walk away.

"Smooth," Becca said as we walked out. "Teach me your ways."

"Just trying to be good. He's off-limits."

CHAPTER FOURTEEN

Amy called me at seven Sunday morning. And again two minutes later. Then three more times, until I finally answered. "What?" I asked gruffly. I had stayed out with Becca until shortly after one in the morning, when I declared defeat and went home, drunkenly mad at myself for not getting Alex's number before I left the bar. But six hours and an empty bed later, I was very glad I didn't have it.

"Did you make an appointment for today?"

"Was I supposed to?"

"Yes, it's for your dress."

I rubbed my eyes and came away with black fingers; apparently I hadn't taken my makeup off when I fell into bed. "You didn't tell me you hadn't made an appointment."

"Isn't that your job? You're the bridesmaid."

"Technically, it's your job. If you're going to delegate things to me, you have to tell me what you need me to do."

"Well, I haven't done any of this before and you're in like a million weddings, so I figured you knew what you were doing."

I sighed heavily, lacking the energy to fight with her. "Which salon are you trying to go to?" By then, I knew them all. She named a fairly low-key one with a relatively less snooty staff. "I'll call as soon as they open and see if they can squeeze us in. If they can't, I'll take the next available appointment."

"Just not on a Saturday morning. Ashlee and I started doing kick-boxing. And not Mondays. Or Tuesdays. Actually, just make sure it's a Sunday. And soon."

"Why can't Ashlee do any of this if she's your maid of honor?"

"Ashlee works a real job."

I gritted my teeth. "*I* work a real job, Amy."

"Ashlee is in finance, not some fluffy PR thing."

"I'm hanging up now."

"Okay, let me know what happens when you call the shop."

I googled the store to find out what time it opened, then set my alarm for three hours later and went back to sleep. Amy was the absolute worst and I had no idea why Tyler wanted such a mess for a wife.

~

The bridal salon agreed to squeeze us in that afternoon because we were only doing bridesmaid dresses and I mentioned that another wedding I was in had an appointment the following week. My mother, Amy, and Ashlee arrived unapologetically ten minutes later than I told them to.

Amy was unnaturally bronzed for November. "Did you go to a tanning salon?"

"God no," she said, flipping her hair over her shoulder. "That makes you look so old."

I never went tanning and could have been a stand-in if they made a new Casper movie, but it still felt like an attempted zing. "Where'd the tan come from then? Spray?"

"Nah, Tyler and I went to Mexico last weekend. Didn't you see my Insta stories?"

I didn't tell her that I deliberately never watch her Instagram stories. It isn't that I am completely uninterested in her life—although I kind of am—it is more that I can't deal with the Boomerang everything and the excessive stickering, GIFs, and random videos detailing every vapid thing she does. It is like a constant vlog of her everyday life instead of a highlight reel and is exhausting on every level.

"Must have missed it. Why'd you go to Mexico?"

"Mom didn't tell you?"

My mother was across the store already, stacking bridesmaid dresses across her arm while a saleslady hovered anxiously, offering to put them in a room for us. I tended to stop listening when she talked about Amy because it was all wedding talk now, but I didn't remember hearing anything about Mexico.

"No."

"Oh. Jake and Madison wanted us to come see the resort they booked for their wedding."

Jake had texted me a picture the previous weekend of a tropical pool surrounded by palm trees, with the caption "wedding destination" and a check mark. But I hadn't realized Amy and Tyler were invited on the trip.

"I didn't know you guys were that close."

"Jake figured it would be some good bonding time so I could get to know Madison better and he could get to know Tyler."

"Did anyone think to invite me?"

"Would you have come? It was kind of a couples thing anyway."

No, I wouldn't have gone. I didn't have the time, money, or inclination to have that much togetherness with my siblings and soon-to-be siblings-in-law. But it still stung to be excluded for the sin of being single.

I shrugged, trying to brush it off. "How was Madison?"

"She's actually really nice. Kind of shy, but we got massages and manicures and once you get a few drinks in her, she's fun!"

"So she has more personality than the wallpaper?"

Amy made a face. "You should be nicer. She's going to be our sister."

"*You* were the one who said that about her when Jake brought her home the first time!"

"Yeah, but I didn't know her then. You should make an effort to get to know her."

My mother called my name and gestured for Ashlee and me to go into the fitting rooms, which I took as a welcome excuse to exit the conversation. Lectures on social graces from a virtual toddler who still lived at home and was too immature to call and make dress-fitting appointments herself weren't good for anyone.

∽

Somewhere between the discussion of how anything short would work for everyone except me, because my legs were too long, and low-cut would be fine—oh, but not on Lily—I decided to mentally excuse myself from the conversation. After my experience the previous day, I was willing to put on whatever they wanted as long as I didn't have to pay attention to what they were saying about it.

And although I would never admit it to either of my siblings, my feelings were hurt that I hadn't even been considered for the weekend in Mexico. I mean, yes, Jake and Amy had always been closer than I was with either of them. They were only three years apart, whereas I was five and eight years older than them, respectively. They had spent a year in high school together. I had already graduated from college and was working at the foundation by that year. Everyone had always said the age difference would matter less as we got older, but instead of that happening, the two of them seemed to have suddenly bypassed me entirely and now were doing a whole level of adulting that I hadn't gotten to yet. Serious relationships, engagements, and joint vacations. What just happened?

Eventually, Amy, Ashlee, and my mother agreed on some pink chiffon disaster that I thought made me look like a piece of cotton candy, but it only cost $175, putting me somewhat back on track. For this wedding at least. So I said it was great.

"Come to dinner tonight?" my mother asked as I waited for the saleslady to return with my overburdened credit card. "Your grandmother is coming and we're getting takeout."

I agreed, mostly because it saved me a trip to see my grandmother soon. I had been so busy between work and weddings that the only time I had seen her in the last three months was when she came shopping for Amy's wedding dress.

~

Tyler and Amy dominated the conversation at dinner, prattling on happily about the many features of Jake and Madison's wedding resort.

"There are hot tubs in every room," Amy said. "And they bring you drinks all day at the pool."

"And the food was amazing," Tyler said. "You can get room service at any hour of the day or night and it's all free."

"Everything is included, so it's really a steal, all things considered."

"How much would you call a steal?" I asked. My mother shot me a look.

"Jake said it would come out to a little over two thousand a person for the weekend."

"Two thousand?" Everyone stopped to look at me. "For a weekend?"

"Well, a little more if you're not sharing a room, so probably twenty-five hundred for you, but that includes airfare," Amy said. "And all the meals and drinks. And Jake said the wedding itself costs almost nothing because the resort does most of it for free when you bring a certain number of guests. Which is great because Mom and Dad have enough on their plate with our wedding." She nudged Tyler playfully and he picked up her hand and kissed it.

"It's not exactly free when all of your guests are paying two grand apiece to be there."

"What happened to that *real* job you were bragging about?" Amy asked. "It's not like you can't afford it."

"I'm in four other weddings, too, Amy. Including yours."

"Girls, stop it," my dad said, exchanging a look across the table with my mother that immediately told me this dinner wasn't a random, spur-of-the-moment thing.

I sat back in my chair and crossed my arms defiantly, but my mind was reeling. I had only factored fifteen hundred into my wedding budget for Jake and Madison's wedding and definitely had not realized I would be paying more for being single. Not to mention I had already spent more on bridesmaid dresses alone than I had saved. An extra thousand dollars? I was going to be paying these weddings off for years at this rate.

"We actually had an idea," my mother said, hesitantly. "We were going to pitch it after dinner."

"What?" I braced for the worst.

"We'll pay for your trip," she said, then stopped.

"What do I have to do in return?"

My parents exchanged a look again. I quickly inventoried what they could have in mind versus what I would be willing to do. I doubted they would come up with anything *too* morally repugnant. "Get your grandmother there."

"What's *that* supposed to mean?" Grandma chimed in angrily. While she was as spunky as she had ever been—perhaps more so, as she had definitely lost any semblance of a filter with age—she didn't walk so well anymore since breaking a hip two years earlier. But she was still driving, despite a minor stroke, practically no reflexes, and significant hearing loss in both ears. No one wanted to ask the question of how her vision was because it was obvious the answer would be terrifying. And she was still convinced she could do everything she had done sixty years earlier, from lifting the sofa to clean under it to driving nearly five hundred miles to visit her hometown.

"You need help," my mother told her. "You can't get your own luggage to the airport, let alone deal with checking it, and you ought to be in a wheelchair to get on the plane."

"I'm *not* riding in a wheelchair like some invalid," she argued, brandishing a fork at my mother. "You act like I've never flown on an airplane, but I've been all over the world and I'll do it all again. Without help."

"Mom, don't start with this."

"Don't start with what, Joan? I'm not a child, no matter how you treat me. I don't need someone to drive Miss Daisy over here. No offense, Joan." The second "Joan" was directed at me. After thirty-two years of being her granddaughter, my grandmother still called me by my mother's name ninety percent of the time. But she had been doing that since she was in her fifties, so that alone wasn't a great indicator of declining mental agility.

I turned to my parents. "Would I have to share a room with her?"

"And what's so wrong with sharing a room with me?" I exchanged a look with Amy, who was trying not to laugh. My grandmother had absolutely no sense of modesty left. When she got a medical alert button, she raised her shirt to show it to us rather than pulling it out of her shirt. Without a bra on.

"No." My dad ignored my grandmother completely. "Your own room. Just get her to the airport, on the airplane, and to the hotel, then the reverse after the wedding."

"That's all?"

"That's all."

"Deal," I said, relief sweeping over me as I imagined the numbers on my credit card bill rolling backward. Besides, it would make great material for my blog.

"I didn't agree to this deal," my grandmother said, struggling to rise from the table.

"Do you need some help?" I asked her. She gave me a sharp look, but sat back down in her chair. "It'll be good bonding time."

"If we rent a car there, I'm driving," she said gruffly.

"There's a shuttle from the airport," my father said immediately. "You're not driving in Mexico."

"You shouldn't even be driving here," my mother added.

Grandma looked back at me. "Better to go with *you* than with *them*," she conceded.

I nodded to my parents and my mother's shoulders sagged slightly in relief, making me realize that I hadn't been the one they were worried about convincing in this deal. But Grandma and I had always done better together than my mother and I had. Or than she and my mother had, for that matter. Yes, the dynamic changed as we both got older and I didn't visit or call as often as I should, but my grandmother had always proven an ally against my mother when I needed one. And in my teen years in particular, I had needed one.

"We'll have fun," I assured her, and my mother looked at me gratefully.

CHAPTER FIFTEEN

I had finally stopped looking everywhere for Alex, brushing off the several run-ins as actual coincidence, when Taylor greeted me excitedly at Starbucks a couple of weeks later.

"He left you another note," she said when I reached the counter. I knew I should give up the morning lattes in favor of coffee at the office to save money, but it was a tough habit to break. Besides, my parents' offer to pay for my trip to Mexico had bought me enough of a financial reprieve that I could still justify the coffee. And the blog post I had written about dress shopping with Caryn and the wicked bridesmaids of the west had generated enough money for a week's worth of coffee and gotten me my first two comments. Okay, one of them was spam, but clicks were clicks.

And maybe, just maybe, a little, tiny piece of me was hoping for exactly this. "I'm not sure what it means, but I think he's asking you out."

I rolled my eyes at her and went to grab my coffee. *So I know what dinner gets me, but what do I get with lunch?*

Ugh, why does he have to be so cute about this?

"Can I leave him one back?" I asked. The line was insanely long and I didn't want to wait in it again. The guy at the front gave me an irritated look.

Taylor looked at the line and nodded. "It's on the house." She handed me a coffee sleeve and the Sharpie.

My friendship . . . I wrote back. I started to hand it to Taylor, but I snatched it back at the last second and uncapped the Sharpie again. *Text me if that sounds good,* and I wrote my phone number.

If I was being honest with myself, I didn't think I would hear from him. No guy wants to be told he's in the friend zone. It's a death sentence if you're actually interested, despite what *When Harry Met Sally* would have you believe.

But as I was walking to my apartment from the Metro that evening, I got a text message. Hey new friend, it said.

I smiled. Do you get an afternoon coffee too or did you go to Starbucks just to see what I'd replied?

The latter. I was curious.

Don't you know you're supposed to wait a solid twenty-four hours before you text someone the first time?

Why? We're friends. I don't have to play stupid games.

Good point.

So lunch? Tomorrow?

Yeah, I replied, marveling at this strange new thing I had found, where I didn't need to play games and friendship was pre-established as being all that was on the table with a guy. That sounds great.

Megan texted me a link to some bridesmaid dresses that night. She had picked a fabric and color and was going to let us choose from six different styles of dresses. I unwillingly recalled Caroline's critique that that was tacky, but I put it aside. Her country-club-bred view of weddings wasn't everyone's. Besides, Megan had her own issues with her fiancé's contentious sister, and if this would keep her calm, it was a win.

What else is going on? she asked. How was shopping with your sister?

I told her about Amy's trip to Mexico and sent her a picture of the cotton-candy dress. But I didn't mention my lunch plans with Alex.

~

"Hey," he greeted me outside the restaurant.

"Hey."

"Is this weird?"

"Nope. Friends have lunch together all the time."

"Good." He opened the door for me.

We sat at our table and perused the menus. I had been good about packing my lunch the past few months, but this wasn't a restaurant I had been to even when I still went out to lunch. "What's good here?"

"I have no idea," he admitted. "I usually just grab a sandwich from the deli next to my building."

"Which deli?"

"Goldman's."

"They have great salads there."

He grinned. "So I can expect to run into you there too?"

I shook my head. "Not anytime soon. I'm living on a shoestring budget to afford all of these weddings."

"What do you need to afford? Other than devil bras."

I grimaced. I had forgotten I was supposed to be looking for a minimizing bra. But I began ticking off expenses on my fingers. "Dresses for all five, shoes for all five, my share of the bridal shower and bachelorette parties, shower presents, wedding gifts, and everything for my brother's wedding, which is in Mexico."

He raised his eyebrows. "Guys really do have it easier than girls for weddings, huh?"

"You have no idea."

"How much does a bridesmaid dress cost?"

"The cheapest one so far was $175. The most expensive was almost $600."

"Six hundred dollars for a dress? Can you keep the tags on and return it?"

"Not a bridesmaid dress. They're custom-made in the color and fabric the bride wants."

"And you're doing all of this, why?"

"They're my friends." I might have sounded a little more defensive than I intended. "Well, and my brother and sister are two of them, so I don't have a choice there. My parents are paying for Mexico though."

"That's nice of them."

I took a sip of my water. "Kind of. I made a deal."

"What kind of deal?"

He laughed when I explained about my grandmother. "She sounds like a riot."

I shrugged. "I probably would have done it for free anyway. But they offered to pay for me, so I wasn't going to say no."

"That's fair." The waitress came to take our order. "Do you get to bring a date to them, at least?" he asked when she had gone.

"Nope. All five are strictly 'no ring, no bring.'"

"Even Tim and Megan's?"

"Wait. Are *you* allowed to bring a date?"

"They haven't said I couldn't. That's half the reason I joined Tinder. I figured I should start looking for a date for the wedding."

I shook my head. "If your invitation doesn't say 'and guest' on it, you don't get a date."

"What kind of barbaric system is this?"

"Did you let people bring dates to your wedding?"

"I have no idea. I wasn't exactly . . . involved . . . in the planning process."

"By choice or by necessity?"

"Necessity. Lauren was—is—a little intense with that stuff." He paused. "Who will save you from Justin at the wedding if you can't bring a date?"

"Hi, friend," I said with a cheeky grin.

"Walked right into that one, didn't I?"

For the Love of Friends

I kept grinning. "You asked what lunch got you, after all."

"What are friends for?" He smiled back.

~

Alex was funny. I could see why Megan called him a little weird, but we just meshed. Especially once you took sexual tension out of the equation. Not that we'd had that exactly, but once we established the mutual friend zone, I could let my guard down. With potential dates, I felt like I had to play a long game of hide the crazy, which never ended well. Apparently he was having a good time, too, because he started in surprise when he glanced at his watch.

"It's almost two," he said, shaking his head and holding up his hand to signal for the check.

"Oh crap." I didn't really care. I spent my first two years at the foundation tiptoeing around when I was late, only to eventually discover that no one *actually* cared when I showed up as long as I did my work. Which, surprisingly, made me slightly more conscientious of my timing. Some kids take the whole bowl of candy when someone leaves a "take one" sign on Halloween—not me. Being late when they weren't monitoring me felt like stealing. Of course, I was never going to be *on time*, but I was better about it overall. So I felt no guilt taking a long lunch occasionally.

"I'm late for a client meeting." The waitress brought the check and he handed her a credit card. I protested that we should split it. "My only wedding expenses are a sixth of the bachelor party costs and renting a tux—and that's *one* tux, not five. It's on me."

I didn't argue. "I had a good time," I told him, as we waited for his card to return.

He smiled. "This was fun. It's been a long time since I had a female friend."

"The wife didn't approve?"

He shook his head. "I didn't even notice her phasing them out until they were gone. I had two really close friends in college who were girls."

"Why don't you reconnect?"

"It's been too long. And I was a terrible person for letting Lauren do that."

"It happens. Speaking as someone who's been phased out by a guy friend's girlfriend before, I'd welcome hearing an 'I'm sorry.'"

He looked thoughtful. "Maybe. I'm sure I can find them on Facebook."

"You're not even still Facebook friends with them?"

Alex smiled tightly. "Lauren was—well—it wasn't worth the fight."

I put a sympathetic hand on his. "Let's do this again."

"Definitely."

~

When I eventually made my way back to my desk, still smiling, I saw I had an email from Madison—a first. It was to both Amy and me.

> Hey future sisters-in-law,
>
> Just wanted to send a quick update since you two are the only bridesmaids who aren't in town with me. I found my dress—I'm attaching a picture (Amy, it's the same one I showed you in Mexico). Bridesmaid dress shopping is a little more interesting. Amy, I ordered the one you sent me a link to for yours and it's adorable. (I found a store near me to try it on—it's too bad your wedding is after mine or I'd consider it for my shower! I know everyone says they'll wear their bridesmaid dresses again and don't, but I really will.)

Speaking of the shower, we're looking at April 17, with a bachelorette party the following weekend on April 23. I know that's not ideal for you two, so I promise it's fine if you can't make it to one or both. You'll get the official invitations later, of course, but I wanted to put it on your radar just in case. Your mom said she'll try to come out for the shower, if you want to coordinate.

And finally, dresses for you two! My sister, my cousin, and my best friend are my other brides-maids. The four of us went shopping last week-end and found a dress that should be flattering on everyone—but I want you to approve it before anyone orders. A couple of salons in your area have it, if you can get by sometime in the next couple of weeks, either together or separately, to check it out and then just let me know what you think? I'm attaching the link below, along with links to the two salons that have it.

Thanks girls!

Looking forward to hearing from you,
Madison

I clicked the link, but my phone rang before the page loaded. "Lily Weiss," I answered automatically.

"What do you think of the dress?" Amy asked by way of a greeting.

I looked back to my screen. It was a pale-yellow chiffon sheath that just hung straight down.

"I think I'm going to look like Big Bird in it."

"Right? Ugh, why *yellow*?"

I looked down at my pasty arm in the three-quarter-length-sleeved top I was wearing. "Guess we're spray tanning for Mexico."

"Great, then we'll look orange against the yellow. She can't be serious."

"I thought she was your new best friend?"

Amy ignored me. "And two separate weekends for the shower and bachelorette party? I was going to try to go, but we already went to Mexico for them."

"That one didn't sound like any great hardship."

"Lily, I work at Lululemon and Tyler has a job offer, but he's still in school now. I don't have as much money as you do."

I started to say something snarky about living off our parents, but I stopped myself. Amy was on my side here.

"Ha. You think I have money right now? Do you know how much the dress for my friend Caryn's wedding cost?"

"How much?"

"Five eighty-five."

"Shit. Is it cute at least?"

"Nope."

"Does she secretly hate you?"

I smiled. "I don't think so. She just lives on a different planet than we do sometimes."

"I know you don't like the one I picked, but I tried to keep it in a reasonable price range at least."

I had no idea she had paid attention to that. "Thank you." I didn't deny hating the dress, but I could concede that it might look sweet on someone nearly a decade younger than me. "So when do you want to go try on the dresses?"

"I could go tomorrow morning."

"I work a nine-to-five."

"Every day?" I rolled my eyes. She had never held an office job. "Gross. Okay, what about Thursday night?"

"You're on."

I typed out a reply to Madison, thanking her for keeping us in the loop and complimenting her dress. I added that I would start looking at flights and see what was doable for her shower as well. I hit "Send," hoping that my tone was conciliatory enough to make that situation less awkward.

Today was a good day, I thought, leaning back in my chair.

"Lil, did you ever finish updating the website with the HAWC write-up?" Caryn was at my door, a stack of papers in her hand.

"Ugh. No. I'll do that now." I glanced at the calendar on my wall. Just six more months until all of this was over and I could go back to having an actual life.

CHAPTER SIXTEEN

When I arrived at the bridal salon on Thursday night, Amy was already there. With our mother.

"I didn't realize you were coming," I said as she kissed my cheek.

"Amy invited me."

I gave Amy an annoyed look and mouthed, "Why?" Amy shrugged. I did not need a repeat of the "why this dress would look good on someone who isn't Lily" game today. But wasn't this whole endeavor pointless anyway? Neither Amy nor I were going to say we hated the dress and make Madison pick a different one, so what did it matter how it fit us?

"What are you going to wear, Mom?" Amy called from the dressing room. The store only had one of the dresses, so we were taking turns trying it on.

"To which wedding?"

"Jake's. I thought I'd go with you to shop for yours for mine."

"Why don't you come with me for both?"

"Ooh okay, fun!" She emerged from the dressing room in the yellow chiffon and did a little twirl. "I don't hate it." She studied her reflection in the mirror and bit her lip. "I don't *love* it, but it's fine."

I looked at her critically, studying how the dress fit her. We were built similarly, but Amy was a little thinner these days. She had been a chubby teenager and worked really hard to maintain her current weight.

But the dress was flowy without bulk and looked like it would be cool in the Mexican heat and forgiving of problem areas without necessitating Spanx. And even more thankfully, it had wide straps, so I could wear a normal bra. The color even looked good on Amy, with the remnants of her tan from Mexico.

"It looks good, Ames."

My mother was biting her lip in an unconscious imitation of Amy's face. "You don't like it?" Amy asked her.

"Who are her other bridesmaids?" my mom asked.

"She said it was her sister, her cousin, and a friend?"

"Are they bigger girls?"

I looked at her in alarm. "What?"

My mother ignored me. "It's just such a shame to hide your figure in something like that. Especially when you've worked so hard."

"I know. But it's not my wedding. It'll be fine." Mom looked unsure. Amy shrugged at me, then handed me her phone and struck a pose. "Take a picture so we can send it to Madison?"

I did, internally girding my loins for the jellyfish of a comment that was about to come my way when I put on the same forgiving dress. Amy retreated to the dressing room and emerged a couple minutes later in her jeans. "Tag, you're it."

Whatever they were discussing while I was in the fitting room was said too quietly for me to hear more than a murmur of voices. I pulled off my shirt and pants and put on the dress.

I stepped back to get as full a view as I could in the fitting-room mirror. It actually wasn't bad. Yes, the color was frightful on me, but the fit was somewhat flattering. Would I choose this dress on my own, even in a different color? No. But it was the first one any bride had picked that didn't make me feel overly self-conscious. I smiled faintly at my reflection. Yes, I would be the much older spinster sister at my brother's fabulous destination wedding in a color that didn't suit me at all. But I would still look pretty good doing it. And even my mother couldn't find a flaw with that. Actually, scratch that. This was *my* mother we were talking about.

I took a deep breath and stepped out into the shop.

My mother and Amy both tilted their heads to the same degree at the same time. *Amy* needs *to get out of that house,* I thought. *Like right now.*

"You look great!" Amy said.

My mother smiled gently. "You look lovely, Lily." I waited for the "but," and she did not disappoint. "I just wish Madison could have picked something that would look good on both of you."

Amy's shoulders sank. I gave my mother a murderous look, which she missed because she was looking at the dress, not my face. "It was good on Amy too, Mom."

"Everything looks good on Amy, of course," she said absently. "But it does nothing to show off her waist, and her waist is so small. It makes hers look the same size as yours."

My teeth clenched involuntarily. "And I'm clearly the size of a hippopotamus, so that's a problem."

"Don't take that tone," she said. "You're just a bigger girl than Amy."

I was two inches taller than her and *maybe* twenty pounds heavier soaking wet.

I wanted to tell her that she was ridiculously unfair, and it had taken me a good thirty of my thirty-two years on this earth to get past the body image issues that she had instilled in me. I wanted to tell her that *I* liked how I looked, so whatever she thought was irrelevant. I wanted to tell her that, by her standards, nothing would look good on both me *and* Amy. And I most definitely wanted to tell her to go to hell.

But you can't do that with your mom, can you? Somehow, all of those things that you want to say, that maybe you *should* say, just don't have the courage to come out of your mouth. Because it's different when it's your mom. Whatever she says cuts deeper, scars worse, and makes you feel like maybe it's actually true, even when you know it's not.

Instead, I counted to ten and bit my tongue.

Not that she noticed any of my internal struggle. In fact, she was talking to the saleswoman about whether there was any way to belt Amy's dress to make it more flattering.

Now that? *That* I could say something about.

"Mom, you can't change the dress from how Madison wants it."

She looked at me, her eyebrows raised. "None of the girls have ordered the dresses yet. So she should at least see it with a belt and see how much better it looks."

Amy's eyes were wide. She at least understood the magnitude of the faux pas my mother was committing. And even though I really didn't know her, I felt bad for Madison. Amy was the golden child and had it easier than I did, but Madison clearly hadn't grown up with a mother who didn't have boundaries. She had no clue what kind of storm was about to hit her in the form of Hurricane Joan.

I exhaled audibly. "Nope. I'm calling a foul here."

"Excuse me?"

"Don't be that mother-in-law."

Her hands were on her hips. "I'm going to be a *wonderful* mother-in-law. Madison is lucky to have someone to make sure everything looks its best."

I glanced back at Amy. *This is why you don't invite her to stuff like this,* I thought. "Mom, you have Amy's wedding to do this kind of thing. Madison gets to call the shots here. You're not in charge at this one."

"Of course I'm not *in charge*, but that doesn't mean I can't have an opinion—"

"Yes, it does. It means exactly that. Your job is to show up in a neutral-colored dress, tell Jake and Madison that you love them, and then keep your mouth closed."

Her brows came together murderously and she pointed a finger at me, which, no matter how old I got, made me feel like I was about to face major consequences for whatever infraction I had just committed. "Now you listen—"

"How did you feel when Nana told you what to do?" I asked, cutting her off. Her mouth was open like she was going to say something, but she lowered her finger.

"I'm *nothing* like Nana," she said. "That woman was a nightmare."

"Madison is shy and isn't going to argue with you. But this is *her* wedding and if you tell her how the bridesmaids should be dressed, she'll probably say okay. Then she's going to resent you. Is that what you want?"

"Why would she resent me?"

I dug desperately for an argument that would sway her and, thankfully, a light bulb went off in my head. "Remember that *New York Times* article? The one about how paternal grandparents aren't usually as close with their grandkids because of friction in the mother-in-law/daughter-in-law relationship?"

Her eyes narrowed. She had shared it on Facebook when the article first came out and emailed it to the three of us, telling Jake that he had better marry someone who would love her.

"It was true, wasn't it? We were always closer with Grandma than with Nana. And it's already going to be hard when they have kids because Jake and Madison don't live here and her parents are there. Do you really want to make it even more likely that you don't get to see their kids as much?"

She looked to Amy. "Do you agree with this?"

Amy's hand was at her mouth and she was chewing on her cuticles. She nodded almost imperceptibly.

"Fine," my mother said, throwing up her hands in defeat. "Don't ever let anyone say I don't listen. Amy, stop biting your nails." Amy dropped her hand guiltily.

"So no belts then?" the saleswoman asked.

"No," I said firmly. "I'm going to go take this off. Amy, can you tell Madison it's great?"

"Wait," Amy said. "Let me get a picture of you in it."

I turned to face her and tried to look less annoyed than I was, then returned to the dressing room to put my work clothes back on. I was starving and, the adrenaline of the confrontation gone, exhausted.

#Obsessed came the text from my sister to both me and Madison, with pictures of the two of us in the dress. Love love love it! I didn't even have Madison's phone number, but apparently Amy was in touch with her. And sensitive enough to lie about her reaction to the dress.

I looked at the pictures. Amy was radiant, her arm thrown over her head in a rapturous pose. I looked constipated, my arms at my sides, jaw clenched, a forced, fake smile on my lips that came nowhere near my eyes. *Shit.*

Are you sure? A reply came in from the number that had to be Madison's. Lily?

I pulled my shirt over my head, then typed out a reply. It's great. Honest. I only look annoyed in the pic because I was fighting with our mom. It's my favorite of the bridesmaid dresses I have so far. I realized that was an unintentional dig at Amy as soon as I said it, but I was too annoyed to care.

Fighting about the dress?

No, I lied firmly at the same time that Amy replied, Yes.

I rubbed my forehead. She meant yes, we're sure we love the dress. No, I was fighting with my mom about something else.

"Amy, don't you say a word," I said as I came out of the dressing room.

She gave me a wounded look and my mother looked up in shock. "I didn't—"

"I'm going home. I worked all day. I'll talk to you both later." I stopped at the front of the store, where the saleswoman was behind the desk. "Can I call to order when I get the go-ahead from my brother's fiancée?" She told me that was fine, and I left without a backward glance.

"What's *her* problem?" I heard my mother asking Amy before the door shut behind me.

I felt my phone vibrate with a text message as I slid behind the wheel of my car. "Amy, I swear to God," I said out loud.

But it wasn't Amy; it was Alex. Whatcha up to?

We had been texting fairly steadily since our lunch. It didn't have the all-day, everyday urgency of a budding relationship—more like the comfortable give-and-take of a friend with whom you never quite ended the conversation. I couldn't remember if I had told him I was going dress shopping tonight or not.

Attempting matricide. You?

As your lawyer, I'm going to have to advise you to refrain from texting me details of that if I'm to defend you in court.

No juror would side against me. They might even give me a medal.

In that case, let me know if you need help getting rid of the body. If I learned anything from Breaking Bad, it was to not dissolve a body in a bathtub.

I chuckled. Good to know.

The three dots appeared, then disappeared, and then reappeared. You wanna grab a drink?

There was no hesitation. I would love to grab a drink. Someplace with food preferably. I'm starving.

CHAPTER SEVENTEEN

Sharon called me the night before I was due to go bridesmaid dress shopping with her, her sister, her future sister-in-law, and her mother.

"We still on for tomorrow?" I asked. I was on my sofa, painting my nails—manicures were another casualty in the bridesmaid budget. And I still remembered Mrs. Meyer's horrified reaction to my chewed-up nails in college. If I used part of a cotton ball on a cuticle stick in acetone, I could probably clean them up enough to meet her standards—or at least to fly under her radar.

"Yeah, but . . ." she trailed off.

"But what?"

"I kind of need you to do me a favor."

"No problem. What's up?"

She paused. "I don't want you to wear black at my wedding."

"That's fine. I'm wearing purple, pink, and Big Bird–yellow for three of the others. Whatever you want me to wear will be great."

Another pause. "No—I mean—can you tell my mom you don't want to wear black?"

This time I hesitated. "Why can't *you* tell her that?"

Sharon sighed. "I did, but she just has this idea in her head of what it should look like, and she can't hear me. So will you do it?"

I groaned internally. The absolute last thing I wanted to do was pick a fight with Sharon's mom. But the only reason Sharon was having this wedding was her mother. If she needed a champion to make sure some part of it was hers, I supposed that responsibility fell to me. Her sister, the maid of honor, certainly wasn't going to do it. I had never gotten a solid read on Bethany. Was she actually her mother's little clone, agreeing with her every whim? Or was she doing what Sharon did and complying to survive? Or had it started as the latter and simply become the former? It wasn't the kind of thing you could ask someone about her sister and overbearing mother.

"Please?" she asked, when I hadn't responded.

"Okay. Is there any particular color you *do* want? If I'm going to die on the cross here, I want to make sure it's not in vain."

"I don't know. I just don't want it to look like a funeral. Other than that, I don't really care."

"What if she wants to downgrade to navy?"

"Navy? I feel like that's just as bad."

"So something light?"

"Well not white, obviously. But something—I don't know—happy?"

I wondered briefly if I could convince her to pick one of the three dresses I already had. *Now* that *would be a victory,* I thought. Then I shook my head to remove the disloyal thought. Sharon deserved her own dream wedding. Not her mother's, and certainly not my half-assed attempts to be able to afford a proper manicure again.

I grabbed a bottle of wine from the fridge and poured myself a glass after hanging up the phone. Then I looked down at my stomach. Becca walked in as I was attempting to pour the wine back into the bottle.

"Um . . . what?" she asked.

I looked up guiltily. "Do we have a funnel?"

"Why would we have a funnel?" I gestured toward the mess I was making with the wine. "You could just—I don't know—drink it?"

"I need my wits about me for tomorrow morning. And wine has calories." I looked at her. "Why are you so dressed up?"

She shot me a huge grin. "*I* have a date tonight."

"With who?"

"Will."

"Should I know who that is?"

Becca rolled her eyes. "You know, *Will* Will."

"From work?"

"The one and only."

I raised my eyebrows, impressed. Becca had had a crush on him for forever, which she had all but given up on because he never seemed to show any reciprocal interest. "How'd you swing that one?"

"I have no idea," she said giddily. "We were just talking this afternoon, and he looked at me and asked if I wanted to have dinner with him tonight."

A little voice in my head wondered if she had misunderstood and it was more like a grabbing-drinks-with-Alex kind of thing, but I told it to shut up. If anyone was due for a little happiness, it was Becca, who hadn't been on a date in the two years we had been living together and probably a while before that. She had been living with her last boyfriend until she caught him cheating on her. She hadn't quite recovered from that one yet.

"Where's he taking you?"

"Some new Asian fusion restaurant in Georgetown."

With a smile, I held out what was left in the wineglass. "Do you need this?"

She laughed. "Yes, please."

~

I stood in front of the full-length mirror on the back of my bedroom door before I went to bed and pulled up the stomach of my pajamas.

I hated that my mom was getting to me, but between her, Caryn's bridesmaids, and the sense I had that Sharon's mom wanted to put me in black because it was slimming, well—I wasn't feeling my best. Plus, not that *I* wanted to date Alex by any stretch of the imagination, but he had been a little too eager to jump into the friend zone.

I went back into the kitchen and threw away the bread, the cookies, and the bag of M&Ms that I had stashed on top of the refrigerator. If I waited until morning, I wouldn't have the willpower.

Baby steps, I told myself as I climbed into bed. I grabbed my phone off the nightstand to set my alarm early enough to make sure I didn't arrive with Helena Bonham Carter hair and saw I had a text from Alex.

Good luck tomorrow.

Thanks. Do you have anything fun going on this weekend?

Not really. Having brunch with Tim and Megan tomorrow.

Ouch. I hadn't been invited to that. I wondered if that was deliberate on Megan's part. Then again, she knew I was going bridesmaid dress shopping with Sharon, so she probably assumed I couldn't come anyway. I hadn't had time to do *anything* other than wedding stuff in forever.

Much more fun than I'll be having. The bride wants me to tell her mother that she doesn't want us to wear black.

Why doesn't she tell her mother that?

I lay back against my pillows and texted out the short version of the story.

Remember not to dissolve the body in the bathtub.

I sent a laughing emoji. You seem kinda fixated on this dissolving bodies thing. Should I be worried?

Nah, I'm more like Dexter. I have a code for my kills.

If the FBI is watching your Netflix account, you may be in trouble.

He sent back the emoji with a finger to its lips and I shook my head, feeling better. I'm going to sleep. Gotta be well rested to battle the dragon tomorrow.

You've got this, he replied.

I was smiling when I put down the phone.

~

I was *not* still smiling when I arrived at the bridal salon. But I *was* wearing my newly purchased Spanx, so come what may, less of the conversation would be about my need to drop a few pounds. I hoped.

"Good morning," I said as I got to Sharon's group.

"Hey," Sharon said, jumping up to greet me. She gestured toward the one woman I didn't know. "Elyse, this is Lily, she was my college roommate. Lily, this is Josh's sister, Elyse."

"It's nice to meet you," I said. Then I turned to Sharon's mother and sister. "And good to see you, Mrs. Meyer. Bethany."

Mrs. Meyer looked at me appraisingly and I thought I saw a glimmer of approval at my slightly slimmer physique. "Let's get started, shall we?"

Apparently she had called ahead and asked for the dresses she liked to be pulled into the dressing rooms for us before we got there. And we had three fitting rooms reserved, so we could all try on dresses at the same time and then switch. None of the dresses in my room were black and I felt my spirits rise. Maybe that had only been a suggestion and other colors were on the table after all.

I tried on the first dress—it was one I had tried for Amy already, but it had been rejected as "too old" by Amy and "too matronly" by my mother. But Goldilocks over here thought it was just right age-wise. Which I suppose spoke more to my actual age and what my mother felt my marital status should be, but whatever.

And I had to admit, as I turned this way and that in the dressing room mirror, it looked better with the Spanx under it than it had the last time I put it on.

137

But this was Mrs. Meyer we were dealing with, so I took a deep, calming breath before I exited the fitting room.

Bethany and Elyse were already out of their rooms.

Mrs. Meyer was walking around the other two girls to view the dresses from all angles. She adjusted the shoulders on her younger daughter's dress, then held a curled finger to her mouth to take me in as well.

"The one Elyse is wearing is a maybe," she said. "The rest can go back."

I looked at Sharon and cocked an eyebrow, trying to silently communicate the question, "Do *you* like these?" She shrugged her shoulders so faintly that had I not been looking for it, I wouldn't have detected any motion. But this wasn't my first rodeo, so I knew how to read her body language and returned silently to my dressing room for the next round.

The next dress was far and away my favorite of all the dresses that I had tried on for any bride. It was fitted to the waist, then had a slight flair, and a neckline that cut straight across, but angled up toward the neck from the edges. Had it been black, I would have felt like Audrey Hepburn, the irony of which was not lost on me. I twirled around for my own benefit and smiled at my reflection. This was a dress that I would actually buy to wear as a guest to a wedding. This was one I would wear again.

The lineup was already underway again when I came out. Apparently the other two girls knew to operate on the same military style of dress time that Mrs. Meyer preferred. She circled us again, a shark examining its prey.

"Lily's is a possibility. The rest aren't."

I caught a glimpse of Bethany's face before she put her mask up. Her fingers clutched the hem of the dress she was wearing, then she dropped it. Bethany loved the dress she was in. Did I love the dress I was in? Yes. Did I actually care what I wore to Sharon's wedding as long as it didn't cost as much as my dress for Caryn's? Nope.

My mouth opened involuntarily. "I'd love to try on the one Bethany is wearing too."

Bethany shook her head narrowly at me. Sharon's eyes were wide, but wary, waiting to see how her mother would respond to this small rebellion when there was a larger one brewing.

"You can do that on your time. I have a hair appointment this afternoon."

"I—"

"Next dress," she said resolutely. "Then we'll trade the good ones." I started to say something, but she fixed me with a look that stopped me.

Pick your battles, Lily. You told Sharon you would fight one for her, not her sister. I went back into the dressing room, where my next dress was possibly the worst thing I had ever put on. It was sent back, and I was instructed to put on the first dress that Elyse had and give Bethany my favorite to try on.

I was beginning to feel like I was in one of those dating shows that Becca watched, waiting to see which dress got the rose by the end of the whole ordeal, but eventually Mrs. Meyer selected a dress, then paid lip service to Sharon, asking if she agreed. Sharon did. It wasn't the one I loved, but again, not my wedding, not my say.

"So we'll be ordering three of these in black," she said to the saleslady, and Sharon looked at me imploringly.

Crap, I thought. Then I cleared my throat. Mrs. Meyer turned in surprise.

"Actually, Mrs. M., I'm not sure."

She looked at me wearily, as if this was no surprise. "Of course. You're pregnant, aren't you?" She turned to her daughter. "I told you asking someone who wasn't family to be in the wedding was a mistake."

"What? No! I'm not *pregnant*." I stared at her, horrified.

"Then what's the matter?"

"I'm just—uh—I'm not a huge fan of black."

"Since when?" She looked pointedly at me. I hadn't thought this one out. My shirt, shoes, purse, and coat were all black.

"I meant for weddings. It's—um—it's considered bad luck."

She turned to the saleswoman. "Have you ever heard of such a thing?"

"It used to be considered a faux pas, but black bridesmaid dresses are very in fashion right now," she reassured Mrs. Meyer.

"It's a bad omen—in my culture."

Her hand went to her hip. "You're half Jewish and half what again?"

"Episcopalian," I said quietly. I wouldn't quite describe either as a culture though—we had a Christmas tree but also lit Hanukkah candles. The only time I had ever set foot in a church was for a wedding on my mom's side, and my only times in synagogues were for my dad's cousins' bar mitzvahs.

"The Jewish side certainly doesn't have a taboo against black, and everyone is doing it these days. And," she enunciated each word of this next part, "it is not your wedding."

I glanced at Sharon, who was studying her fingernails. *Why am I doing this again?* Then I went for it.

"It's not yours either."

"What did you just say to me?"

"It's *Sharon's* wedding. Did you ask her what color she wanted us to wear?"

"I'm *paying* for this wedding and Sharon is *my* daughter, so this certainly is my wedding!" She turned to Sharon. "Are you going to let her speak to me this way?"

"I—"

Mrs. Meyer cut her off. "I understand that Sharon wanted you in her wedding for sentimental value, but this is completely inappropriate."

"Ask her then," I said quietly. "If Sharon says she wants black, I'll wear it and you'll never hear a peep from me about it."

Sharon looked at me, aghast, then realized her mother was watching and adjusted her face.

"Well?" Mrs. Meyer asked. "We're all waiting."

"I—" Her eyes darted to me, like a frightened animal's. "They're all so pale," she squeaked almost inaudibly. "They'll look like ghosts in black."

"So they'll go tanning."

"Maybe—maybe we could look at some lighter colors?" I felt a surge of pride. In all of the years we had been friends, I could count on one hand the number of times Sharon had actually stood up to her mom. And the wedding dress was perhaps the first time I had seen her get her own way.

But something changed in Mrs. Meyer's face. "That's what you want?" she asked, eyes narrowed.

Sharon nodded.

She turned to the saleslady. "Fine. What other colors does this dress come in?"

I looked to Sharon, who mouthed, "Thank you," behind her mother's back. I nodded and gave her a half smile, already mentally drafting a blog post about Mom-zilla.

~

I texted Alex as I left the salon. So what CAN you dissolve a body in? Asking for a friend . . .

He replied immediately. According to AMC, a plastic bin. Went that well, huh?

She asked if I was pregnant.

He sent back a shocked emoji. Meet you in the bin section at Home Depot in an hour?

Oh, so you're a full-service kind of lawyer.

Only for my favorite clients. And if you invent a new product for disposing of horrible mothers, I can help you patent it too.

What a pal.

I crossed the street toward my car feeling moderately better. I couldn't wait to peel the Spanx off, but the pregnancy comment had put me over the edge. I was going home to change and then going to the gym. Maybe if I added a couple of workouts a week, everyone would leave me alone about how I looked.

You feel like going to a movie tonight?

That felt date-like and I hesitated. Is that still a thing?

Yeah. But going alone sucks.

I've never gone alone. Not brave enough.

Really? I go alone all the time.

God, I don't even remember the last time I saw a movie in the theater. If you don't have a boyfriend, you basically never see a movie when you're an adult.

Guess I need a boyfriend, he replied with a winky face. Or we could, you know, be rebels and go as friends.

I laughed and agreed, on the condition that I got peanut M&Ms. I could do a *short* workout at the gym before the movie. You need to start slow, after all.

CHAPTER EIGHTEEN

From: Caryn Donaldson [futuremrscaryngreene@
gmail.com]
To: [bridesmaids]
Subject: Wedding newsletter volume 5
Date: December 18

We are officially in the homestretch, ladies! Less
than six months to go until I say I do!

The hard parts (for me at least ;-p) are all over!
The venue is booked, the dresses are ordered, the
photographer and makeup artists are hired, and
the menu is set. Whew! I'm tired just typing all of
that!

Now, I wanted to make you all aware of a few
dates for your collective and individual planning
purposes.

I'd like my shower to take place at least a
month, but no more than six weeks before the

wedding itself. That gives us time to update the registry before the wedding, but not so much time that we lose momentum for the big day. Which means it will need to be either the last weekend in April or the first weekend in May. I'll let you decide from there.

For the bachelorette party, it should be sometime after the shower, but not less than two weeks before the wedding. I want to be able to have a few drinks at it and still have time to completely detox so there's no trace of puffiness in my pictures—and that gives you all time to detox. I'm thinking something small and intimate, and dear God, no male nudity!

Speaking of pictures, let's talk beauty regimens. I'll let you work out the best timing for Botox and fillers with your doctors, but keep in mind that you don't want your Botox TOO close to the wedding or you'll have that dead-eye look in pictures and no one wants that. Plan your eyelash fills accordingly too. And don't forget the spray tans! They'll need to be fresh, but not so fresh that they could rub off on dresses. Also, be mindful of your keratin treatments. It's outside by the water, so we don't want frizz, but we DEFINITELY don't want that greasy, just-done hair! If you start planning it out now, maybe we could all do a spa day before the wedding and do our keratin together—it'll make it go so much quicker!

> You're the best, and I don't know how I could
> have done any of this without you!
>
> Love and kisses!
> —Caryn

I read the email again. This wasn't real, was it? She wanted us to get Botox? No, I read that part again—she was just saying *if* some of them already got it, to time it accordingly, right? I pulled out my cell phone and opened the front camera. I mean, sure, there were some faint lines on my forehead, but those weren't *wrinkles*, were they? Everyone had those. Didn't they?

Okay, Caryn didn't. Wow. Caryn got Botox? She was two years younger than me! Had I missed something? Was this a thing people our age did?

I forwarded the email to Megan, then texted her and told her to read it.

My phone rang a couple of minutes later.

"She's out of her mind," Megan said instead of a greeting.

I got up and shut my office door. "I mean—that's crazy, right?"

"Mad as a hatter. Punch me in the face if I ever get that bad."

"Gladly." I paused. "Do you get Botox?" She didn't reply. "Megs!"

"I haven't *yet*. But I'm going with Kelly next week."

I felt a twinge of jealousy mixed with my surprise. Kelly lived in Columbia, right near where Megan and Tim had moved, and based on what I had seen on social media, they had become inseparable over the last couple of months. Was she taking my place?

"Do you want to come? I can call the doctor's office and see if we can do one more."

I lifted my eyebrows experimentally, annoyed that I was an afterthought. "Do you think I *need* it?"

"God no, what's the matter with you? I'm just doing it for the wedding pictures. It'll be half worn off by then anyway."

"And eyelash extensions?"

"I mean, they look good. But they're *so* much maintenance. We can just wear fake ones for the wedding. The makeup artist will put them on. But if you're going to get them for hers, you can totally keep them for mine and it'll be fine."

Just like the minimizing bra, I thought, unkindly.

"Gotcha," I said.

"That's also so rude, telling you when the shower and bachelorette have to be. You're in four other weddings. What if the dates don't work for you?"

That hadn't occurred to me. In my relief that none of the weddings conflicted, it hadn't dawned on me that I had *ten* other parties in the weeks leading up to the weddings, which I would be expected to help plan. Some of those were going to overlap. It was just inevitable. "In that case, I doubt any of the other bridesmaids would miss me."

"But like, ask, don't tell. We don't own you."

"Megs, what am I doing in this wedding? Like seriously. I don't want to put poison in my face."

"I mean, she didn't tell you that you *had* to. She was just saying to plan it out *if* you were going to."

"Yeah, but am I going to look like an old crone next to everyone else in the pictures now?"

"No. You're going to look like a normal human being who doesn't get work done and is happy with how she looks. I'm jealous, honestly. I wish I didn't care how old I looked."

I didn't respond. There was no way she *meant* that as an insult. Megan just sometimes had foot-in-mouth disease. And I didn't think she realized how beaten down I still was about my looks by the attack of the horror-show mothers. "Thanks, I think," I said eventually. Another phone rang in the background on Megan's end.

"Ugh, I've got to go actually work. Don't change a thing—you're perfect and I love you!"

I slumped over my desk. *Wahhhhh,* I thought. I was so sick of weddings and brides and bridesmaids.

After all of the dresses had been found, my official bridesmaid duties had hit a bit of a lull, which I thought would be a well-deserved reprieve.

It wasn't.

I may have gotten a two-month break from people harping on how I looked, but my friends had all suddenly disappeared.

Oh, they were still there, physically at least. But who were these people? I literally hadn't had a single conversation with Megan, Caryn, or Sharon that didn't immediately revert back to weddings. None of them ever had time to hang out, unless I wanted to be a third wheel with their fiancés, which I really didn't, or unless I wanted to join them at bridal expos, which I was willing to do once, but had no desire to do repeatedly.

I was also getting the distinct feeling that every time I spoke, they were just waiting to transition the conversation back to their impending nuptials. There were suddenly too many "oh, speaking of [insert literally anything I said that had nothing to do with weddings here]" segues back into bridal talk for me to feel like they were actually listening.

Even Becca, who had always been ready to drop everything to grab a drink, get a pedicure, or binge-watch the latest show with me, had moved on. That date with Will had quickly been followed by second, third, and thirty-seventh dates. At the speed they were going, they were likely to have kids any day now.

Alex and I had been hanging out a decent amount, and the fact that none of my normal crew were available was good for my bank account. Caryn was always talking me into the clothes I didn't need, Megan into the restaurants I couldn't afford, and Becca into the carryout more nights than we should.

And it wasn't like the blog was earning me any real money yet. Dress shopping may have been over, but Caryn's ridiculous email missives (and the follow-ups from Caroline and her minions) had continued to provide excellent fodder. As had my mother and sister's running discussion about every wedding decision, which they felt the inexplicable need to conduct through three-way calls and group chats with me. But growing an audience was a slow process, and I was only making a few dollars per post so far.

Then again, this latest email was so out of the realm of realistic that my readers might think I was just making things up. I wondered if Caryn had *always* been this nuts and I somehow just hadn't seen it.

"Knock, knock," Caryn said, pushing the door open.

My eyes went to the notifications on my computer screen. Eighteen replies. I blinked heavily. "Hey."

"Everything okay? I didn't hear from you."

"Yeah, was just on a phone call." *Unlike the rest of your bridesmaids, I work,* I wanted to tell her. A thought dawned on me. "Are you still going to work after you get married?"

She looked taken aback. "I—well—at first, yes."

"At first?"

"Well, not when I have kids, of course."

My mother worked up until last year, when the last of her children finished college and she finally retired. My father would happily work until he was a hundred and twenty, if he lived that long, both because he loved his job and because he wouldn't last long without an excuse to leave the house. So the idea of becoming a stay-at-home mom, especially one who would probably *also* have a nanny, was foreign to me.

"Are you planning on kids soon?"

"Well not *immediately*. But probably in a year or so. I'm not getting any younger and egg quality deteriorates after thirty-five."

Was I a terrible person for debating how worthwhile it was to stay in her wedding? When we would only work together for another year or two at most? And apparently have nothing in common by then?

She shook her head. "Why do you ask, anyway?"

I tried to banish the disloyal thoughts. "No reason. Just curious."

"So, dates are okay?"

"Yeah, should be fine," I said absently. Then I thought about it. "Wait. Bachelorette *might* be a problem, depending on the weekend."

Her eyebrows didn't move, something I hadn't really realized before, but her eyes narrowed slightly. "Why?"

"My brother's wedding in Mexico is the second weekend in May." I grimaced. "Actually, the shower could be an issue too. It depends on when my brother's and sister's showers and bachelorette parties are."

"Well, if they haven't planned them yet, doesn't mine take priority?"

I set my jaw. "Imagine if it were Olivia's wedding versus mine. You have to go to the family events."

"But you're not getting married."

"I didn't mean that literally. I might be flying to Chicago with my mom and sister for my sister-in-law's shower, and I have to be at the events for my sister."

"But I asked you to be a bridesmaid first."

I mentally contrasted the reactions of Caryn and Megan, who would have said family absolutely came first (after saying that there was still a zero percent chance of Amy actually getting married).

But it wasn't worth fighting this fight when I didn't even know if there was a conflict yet. "Hopefully it'll all be fine."

She seemed mildly placated by that. "You'll need to work with the other girls to figure out shower and bachelorette. Don't let Caroline shut you out. She did that to a girl in Deanna's wedding and it wasn't pretty."

"Got it." I turned back to my computer screen, preparing to read the now twenty-two emails.

She started to say something else, but stopped herself and walked out. I breathed a sigh of relief. Where had my friend gone, and who was this psycho walking around in her skin?

The first several emails were benign enough, but then, of course, Caroline responded.

Do you have a requirement on eyelash length? And what about hair color? I was planning to get my balayage refreshed the week before the wedding, so I need to know what color you want us to have.

And then, even more ridiculously, Caryn had replied, with actual numbers of how thick the lashes should be and how long.

Was this for real?

But the last several of the messages were a different thread, started by Olivia, which didn't include Caryn. The subject was Vegas or New Orleans?

With an ever-growing sense of trepidation, I opened Olivia's original email.

And now it's our turn. Girls, we need to plan the most epic, be-all, end-all bachelorette party for Caryn! I know she said small, but come on, we all know that's not what she wants. So the question is, Vegas or New Orleans?

Vegas, Deanna replied. It's the classic bachelorette party locale.

What about Paris? Mia asked. That way we don't have to deal with all of the trashy people.

New Orleans is the perfect compromise, Caroline said, giving what was apparently the final word. My sister-in-law owns a travel agency. We'll go down May 10–13. I'll arrange everything. And I'll book my club for the shower on May 5.

Jake and Madison's wedding was May 11. On the one hand, great. I didn't have the money for a trip to New Orleans, especially not on the scale they were going to want to do it, and I definitely didn't have any desire to go on a trip with them.

But should I ask if there was an alternate weekend or just say, "Oh no, so sorry, have fun"?

There was also the issue that Caryn had *just* told me not to let them steamroll me, *and* she said she wanted a simple bachelorette party, which a three-day binge in New Orleans was not.

While I debated what to do, another email pinged in from Caroline.

> With airfare, if we do two to a room at the Ritz, it'll work out to about $1800 a person for the trip, not including spa days and all that. But we'll cover Caryn, of course, so it's actually $2200 a person and then incidentals, so plan on about $3000 total, but you'll only owe me $2200.

Three thousand dollars for three nights in New Orleans? Was that a thing? And the Ritz? She was kidding, right?

I called Megan back and hissed an outline of the latest emails to her. "Must be nice," she said.

"Nice? To ask your friends to spend three grand each on your bachelorette party?"

"Nice to be able to afford to do that."

I had assumed we would do a night of barhopping for Megan's bachelorette party. Did she want something bigger? And dear God, what if they all did?

"Do *you* want to do a trip for yours?" I asked quietly.

"I mean, I'd love it. But it's too much money. So no."

Another email pinged in and I told Megan I had to go, feeling like the world's worst friend. I wasn't spending three thousand dollars on a bender for Caryn, but I wished I had the money to do it for Megan, if that was what she wanted.

The latest email was also from Caroline. Renting the party room at her club, with catering, would run approximately a thousand dollars each, depending on how big the guest list was.

I pushed my chair back and went to Caryn's office in a panic.

"What's up?" she asked, looking at my wild-eyed face. "Are you okay?"

I sat down shakily in the chair across from her. "I—I'm sorry. I can't be in your wedding."

She blinked several times at me. "Because of the shower and bachelorette party dates?"

"No, I—Caryn, Caroline just emailed that she wants each of us to spend three thousand dollars on a trip for your bachelorette party and another thousand on your shower and I don't have the money for that."

"Did you tell Caroline that?"

"Well—no."

"Don't you think you should start there, rather than dropping out of the wedding?"

"I—" I didn't want to admit that I was too ashamed to tell Caroline I couldn't afford it. My shoulders dropped in resignation. "I can try."

"And I don't want a fancy trip. Tell them I just want something simple, like I said in my email."

"Okay," I said, my face puckered in anxiety. I got up and turned to leave.

"Oh, and Lily—"

"Yeah?"

"I can give you my doctor's name if you want a recommendation for some Botox. Just a little, to smooth those lines out."

I gritted my teeth. "Thanks. Just email it."

She smiled. "Of course."

Back at my desk, I read the most recent emails, all agreeing that the Ritz and Caroline's club would be perfect, then hit "Reply All."

> Hi everyone. Unfortunately, I'm out of town that weekend for my brother's wedding in Mexico. I also just talked to Caryn, who said she definitely doesn't want a trip—she wants to do something simple and closer to home. And is there any way to cut down on shower costs? Maybe we do the favors or flowers or the food ourselves?
>
> Let me know your ideas—I'm happy to put in as much manpower as we need!

The reply took longer than I expected—nearly half an hour passed before Caroline's email came in.

> Lily,
>
> The rest of the bridesmaids and I just had a phone conference, because frankly, we're SHOCKED that you would spoil the surprise to Caryn within minutes of the plan being hatched. What kind of person does that?
>
> We then called Caryn, who was ecstatic over the idea of a trip to New Orleans—it's her favorite place in the country, after all, so I don't know what kind of trip you told her about, but she DEFINITELY loves the idea—even though it's not a surprise anymore, thanks to you.

As for the shower, no. My club does not allow for outside food vendors or personal catering. And unless you're a professional florist or cookie designer, then no, the flowers or favors will not be an option either.

We're sorry that you won't be able to attend with us. You can Venmo me your share of the money to this email address. It will only be $1,750 for the accommodations with you not coming, but send $2,000 to cover your share of food, drink, spa, and incidentals for Caryn. And an additional $1,000 for the shower.

And in the future, please talk to us before you go running to Caryn.

Thanks,
Caroline (and the rest of the bridesmaids)

Welp. That went about how I expected. Except there was a zero percent chance that I was Venmoing Caroline three thousand dollars. And not just because I didn't have it.

I cracked my knuckles and hit "Reply All" again. I didn't work in PR for nothing. I knew how to talk to horrible people.

Dear Caroline et al,

I'm afraid I will not be paying for the party that I will not be attending. I'll make my own apologies to Caryn on that front.

As for the shower, please keep in mind that I
am working on a fixed budget. I will do my best to
chip in my share, but we may hit a point at which
I cannot go higher. I will try to rework my budget
to cover my share of the costs that you've outlined
so far.

Thank you for your understanding.
—Lily

I marched back to Caryn's office but didn't sit down this time.

She looked up warily. "Am I about to get another angry phone call over this?"

"Possibly. But I'm here to tell you that I will be unable to attend your bachelorette party. It's the weekend of my brother's wedding. And just so you hear it from me, not them, I'm also not paying two thousand dollars for a trip that I'm not going on."

"I'm sure they don't expect you to pay that."

I shrugged. "Okay. Whatever. Just be aware that when they call you, that's where I'm at." Her cell phone started buzzing on her desk. "Right on cue." I looked at it pointedly.

She sighed. "I really don't have time for all of this right now. Can't you just *try* to get along with them? For my sake?"

The phone stopped ringing, then began again. Caryn picked it up. "Hi Caroline." She nodded. "Uh-huh. Uh-huh. Actually, she's here with me right now. No, she told me that. I mean, it *is* a lot of—" She paused as Caroline cut her off. "Oh. I mean—well—let me ask her, hang on."

"If we do it the next weekend, will you come to New Orleans then?"

"No. That's my best friend's bachelorette party, and I still don't have the money."

She pursed her lips. "She said she still can't come," she said into the phone. "Look, do you want her phone number so you two can talk about this directly?"

I shook my head frantically and mouthed, *"No!"*

"Well, you need to figure it out. I'm not getting in the middle here. I can pay my own way if I have to. No, I wasn't implying that. Caroline, I'm grateful for everything you do. Yes. I know, you just want to make sure everything is perfect and I appreciate you so much for that. Lily just didn't grow up like us. It's different for her." Long pause. "Thank you. I'll talk to you soon. Love you too."

She hung up the phone and turned back to me, still standing in her doorway. "Okay, I explained," she said. I didn't hear anything that sounded like an actual explanation, unless it was the implication that I grew up poor, but okay. "But Caroline has a point too that it's not fair to ask everyone else to pay for my trip and for you to not help. So maybe if you can chip in *some*, it'll smooth things over. It doesn't have to be the full amount."

"Are you serious right now?"

She rubbed her temple. "Lily, come on. We're all adults here. There's no reason for all of the drama." She picked her phone back up. "I'm texting you both so you have each other's numbers. You can work it out yourselves."

"I don't want her having my number."

"Look, you said you'd be in my wedding. I told you what they were like and you said it was fine. Can you just stop being a drama queen and handle it?"

I was stunned into silence. A drama queen? *Me?*

"Fine," I said quietly, and left her office without another word.

CHAPTER NINETEEN

Fuck. These. Weddings.

There. I said it. Even If I'm really just shouting it into the void because like six people are reading this blog right now. But I'm ready to drop out of all of them. Literally all of them.

Bride A, which apparently stands for Asshole, went so far beyond the realm of human comprehension today that I actually don't think I want to be her friend anymore. Not only did she suggest I get Botox—literally, she told me to put poison in my face—but she also expects me to shell out two grand for her bachelorette weekend AT THE RITZ that I won't even be attending because I'll be at my brother's wedding in Mexico.

Look. I played along when she made me get a minimizing bra and Spanx. I laughed it off when she only rejected my joke about getting a breast reduction because I would be too swollen to get an accurate dress size measurement. But she is so far over the line here that she can't even SEE the line from where she's standing.

But all of that said, she's a delight compared to her future sister-in-law, who makes Regina George from *Mean Girls* look like Snow freaking White.

And Bride B? Girl, I love you, but you need to grow a pair! She literally asked ME to tell her mother that I didn't want a black bridesmaid dress (I would LOVE a black bridesmaid dress—I dress like I'm on my way to a funeral most days anyway) because she didn't have the guts to do it herself.

Technically Bride C hasn't done anything wrong. Okay, she's been a little insensitive, but that's not really anything new. But there's this groomsman who is actually kind of awesome and I can't do anything about that because of the other groomsman, so I'm over that wedding too.

Bride D—I still don't know her. But my mom made me feel fat over her bridesmaid dress, and I have to take my grandma to Mexico in order to afford to even go to that wedding. So that one is tainted now too.

And my darling little sister. Can we call a spade a spade and stop the farce now? You're not getting married. You're a child. And I can't return the dress that looks like a chewed-up piece of Bubblicious, so let's cut the crap before I have to spend more money on your make-believe wedding, please.

I have had enough!

And I'm going to . . . do absolutely nothing about it except rant in this blog that no one is read- ing because I'm too chickenshit to cut ties with any of these people.

Cool.

Any advice? Anyone reading? Is anyone alive out there?

A tiny voice in my head told me to cool down before I published this one, but I mentally gave it the finger and hit "Publish" anyway. My previous posts had been fairly benign and had gotten me almost nowhere. Go big or go home, right?

Hell with it, I thought and grabbed my coat. I was going home too. It didn't dawn on me until much later that I probably shouldn't have used my work computer to post something personal.

CHAPTER TWENTY

Early in January, my mother texted me on a Friday, asking me to come to dinner to discuss a trip to Chicago for Madison's bridal shower.

Does it HAVE to be tonight?

Why? Do you have a date or something?

I didn't. But Alex and I were planning to binge a new Netflix show that Becca said was too scary for her. Not that she was home much anymore anyway. And if she was, Will was with her. I have plans with a friend.

Can you reschedule? We need to figure out what we're doing.

I sighed and texted Alex. Can we watch tomorrow instead? Or start later tonight and finish tomorrow? My mom is demanding I be at her house for dinner to figure out going to Chicago for my brother's fiancée's bridal shower (kill me now please).

Was supposed to go on a date tomorrow, but I can cancel.

No, I don't want you to cancel for me.

Three dots. Then nothing. Then three dots again. Honestly? I was probably going to cancel anyway. Let's start the show when you get home tonight and we'll see how good it is before we decide?

Deal.

I replied to my mom. Fine, but can we make it early?

She told me to be there at six.

~

"It's important that we go," Amy was saying. "I'd be so hurt if she didn't come to mine."

"She might *not* come to yours," I cautioned. "Remember, her wedding is two weeks before the date we're talking about."

"She told me she's coming."

"Do you actually talk to her?"

Amy gave me a dirty look. "Yeah. Maybe you should too."

"Girls, stop," our mother said absently. "Amy is probably right. Lily?"

"I just—I don't really have the time or the money to drop everything and fly to Chicago for a weekend."

"She's going to be our sister."

"In-law. Calm down, Ames."

She crossed her arms. "Are you even going to come to *my* shower at this rate?"

I rolled my eyes. "I don't know, is it in Chicago?"

"Why are you being such a bitch?"

I looked at my mother, who said nothing. "Seriously?" I asked her.

"Amy, language," she said mildly.

I looked to my dad, who was extremely engaged in eating his salad and staying as far from the conversation as possible. He never publicly took my side against my mother, but he usually would against Amy when she was being ridiculous. Apparently his salad was absolutely fascinating, though, because I couldn't catch his eye.

I huffed, defeated. "I can try to find reasonable airfare. And if we share a hotel room, I can probably swing it."

"Maybe you shouldn't be in all of those weddings," Amy said, bolstered by our mother's refusal to actually check her. "Family comes first."

"Is that why Ashlee is your maid of honor?" I shot back. My mother perked up.

"Do you even *want* to be? I feel like you don't want to be in my wedding at all!"

I stood up and put my napkin on the table. "Okay. I'm outta here. Look, I said I'll go to the shower even though it's *not* easy for me to do right now, but I'm not going to sit here while you shame me about your wedding because I'm not dropping everything to be at your beck and call."

"Actually, I'm shaming you because you're making no effort to get to know Madison and it's pissing Jake off."

"Then let Jake tell me that because he hasn't said a word to me."

"When's the last time you even talked to him? He said you haven't returned his calls."

I paused. Yes, I'd missed a couple of calls from Jake, but that was like a month ago. I had figured if it was important, he would text me or at least leave a message. And then I promptly forgot about it because I had so much else on my plate with all of the brides. Was *I* the reason we didn't have much of a relationship?

When I didn't say anything, Amy continued. "I'm just saying you need to go to the shower."

"And I said I would!"

"Grudgingly! You should *want* to go."

"Some of us actually pay our own bills."

"Enough," my mom said, finally with some force. "Amy, we're going to the shower, all of us. Lily, you could make more of an effort with Madison."

"Like you did with the bridesmaid dresses?" I asked quietly, unable to hold the words in.

My mother started sputtering, and I didn't want to be there to see the steam that was about to come out of her ears. "I'm going home.

Thank you for dinner. I'll email you with airfare rates." I turned and raced out of the dining room.

My father caught me just after I went out the front door. "Lily, wait."

My shoulders slumped, but I turned around. It was freezing out and he hadn't put on a coat. I walked silently back to him and he led me into his study, where I sat in the chair across the desk from his. He closed the door behind us and sat down as well.

"I know," I said.

He raised his eyebrows. "What do you know?"

"That I'm overreacting and I shouldn't have said all that."

"That wasn't what I was going to say. I was going to ask if you're okay. You don't seem happy."

"I'm just stressed about all the weddings. And Amy's not exactly helping. Can't she stop already? We're both adults now."

He looked amused. "*You* are. We'll talk about her status if this wedding takes place and she's no longer living under my roof."

I looked at him for a moment, processing what he had just said, and then let out a small yelp of hysteric laughter.

"Never tell her I said that."

I mimed locking my lips. "Mom isn't helping either."

He sighed. "It's a good thing *you* never moved back home. I wouldn't have survived it. But your mother, as much difficulty as she has showing it sometimes, loves you to pieces." I screwed up my face in disbelief. "You're more like her than you realize."

"I think that was an insult."

"Absolutely not. But she sees herself in you and criticizes those faults. She wants you to be the perfect version of her."

"Why isn't she like that with Amy?"

"Amy's the baby. She's hard on her in different ways."

"I never see it."

"You don't live here." I didn't quite believe him. "But your biggest fan doesn't *just* provide silent moral support." He pulled his checkbook out of his drawer. "It sounds like you're struggling," he said as he wrote. "I'd like to help take away some of your stress. Consider it a loan from your own wedding account. We'll spend a little less on flowers when your day comes."

My eyes felt wet and I rose to hug him as he handed me the check. "Thank you, Dad."

"I love you, Lilypad. But uh—maybe don't tell your mother about this. It'll be our little secret."

I hugged him tighter. "I'll go apologize to Mom."

CHAPTER TWENTY-ONE

Remember in *Pride and Prejudice*, when Mr. Darcy's awful aunt is horrified that the younger sisters are "out" before the older ones are married? When did she become my favorite character? Lady Catherine has a solid point there.

I'm not saying my younger siblings need to be locked in an attic until I find a spouse, but good Lord! Forcing me to be in both of their weddings at the same time seems like the definition of cruel and unusual punishment. Can I cite the Eighth Amendment as a reason to sit these two out?

It doesn't help that my baby sister (Emphasis on baby. Doesn't she need parental permission to get married at her age?) is openly antagonizing me and has suddenly become best friends with my brother's fiancée. Who, as far as I can tell, is utterly devoid of personality. Or perhaps she has a lovely personality, but an evil sea witch stole her voice and marrying my brother is the only way to get it back. I'm not really sure yet, but my sister talks enough for two people, so I guess it evens out.

Then there's my ever-suffering mother. Poor mom. Not only is her eldest child a spinster with eggs dying off faster than you can say, "Actually, I'm only thirty-two and that's NOT too old to get married or have kids," but that spinster also lacks anything resembling prospects.

But to add insult to injury, the save-the-dates have arrived for the five weddings and two of them are addressed to me "and guest." Have you guessed which two yet?

Oh Mom, your subtlety is the stuff of legends. I wonder, if I fail to procure said dates, will she provide them for me? And will it actually be anyone good, or some random dude to whom she gives elocution lessons, *My Fair Lady*–style, to create the illusion to all her friends and neighbors that she has succeeded matrimonially with all three of her children?

I'm afraid to find out.

My mouth twitched into a smile as I reread that one. Yes, the save-the-dates for Amy's and Jake's weddings had included "and guest." But with the express caveat from my mother that it only applied if I was dating someone seriously. She would never find me a wedding date. On the contrary, I felt sure she would rather punish me for my life choices by making me go single if I wasn't in a committed relationship. But the blog version was funnier, so I kept it and hit "Publish."

It created an interesting dilemma, though, because it hadn't occurred to me that having a date at the weddings would make them far less painful. And if I *did* have a boyfriend by then, how sweet would that little getaway in Mexico be?

Okay, I had to get my grandma down there, but I would have my own room. I pictured some tall, dark, and imaginary boyfriend giving my grandma his arm as we walked through the airport together.

I shook my head, dispelling that pipe dream.

But still.

I picked up my phone and texted Alex. What's the story on Tinder?

Three dots appeared. What do you mean?

Like is it safe? Or am I going to get murdered if I use it?

IDK. Depends what you're using it for.

What are YOU using it for? As soon as I sent that, I realized I didn't want to know the answer. Dating. Just dating, I typed quickly. Just thinking since you use it and haven't been murdered yet, maybe I'd test the waters a little.

What if I'm the one doing the murdering?

You keep bringing up disposing of bodies, so I'm not ruling that out. But I feel like if you were going to kill me, you would have done it already.

Touché. Just link it to your Facebook profile so people can see you're not sketchy, and only meet people who linked it to theirs so you know you're not getting catfished. And don't give anyone your address or real phone number.

I have to link it to my Facebook? I replied with horrified face emojis. My MOM is my Facebook friend!

No one on Facebook will see Tinder stuff. It just shows potential dates that you're a real person, not a Russian troll trying to steal their identity. There was a pause. Why the sudden interest?

I can apparently bring a date to Amy's and Jake's weddings.

He sent the GIF of Katniss Everdeen volunteering as tribute.

Was he flirting? I shook my head and replied with a laughing emoji. My mom said only if I'm actually dating the person.

Do you do everything your mom says?

Don't you?

No way! I eat candy for breakfast all the time.

You do not.

Fine. Busted. I brush my teeth twice a day and always take an umbrella when it might rain.

I was smiling. I'll buy you dinner if you help me set up a profile.

That's the weirdest date request ever, but sure.

~

I started to put my phone down, then picked it back up. Amy's criticism that I hadn't made an effort with Madison or replied to Jake was still rankling me. Probably because it was deserved. But where to begin with Madison?

Ugh, I thought.

I started a new text to her. Hey future sis! Just checking in and saying hi. How's all of the wedding planning going?

I hesitated before hitting "Send." I wished I had something to ask about *other* than the wedding, but I honestly didn't know what else she liked, other than my brother, which led me to believe her taste was questionable overall. We were friends on Facebook and Instagram, but her posts were infrequent and bland. And she didn't have a Twitter, so I couldn't even see who she followed or retweeted. So with nothing else to work from, I sent the message.

The three dots appeared and she replied a minute later. Hi. I'm good. Everything seems to be coming together pretty well.

Not exactly effusive. And not much material to get a conversation going. I was contemplating what else I could say when she replied again. I hear you're coming to the shower with your mom and Amy?

Yup. Booked our tickets this week. We're looking forward to it.

Me too. She added a smiling emoji.

I thought about just telling her I wanted to get to know her, but that sounded creepy. And what on earth would I reply if someone said that to me? Was it better to just send little texts every once in a while and hope a conversation would eventually grow organically?

As I debated my next move, my phone vibrated again. But the text wasn't from Madison, it was from Jake.

Thank you was all it said.

For what?

For making an effort, you jackass.

I rolled my eyes. Yeah yeah yeah. What else is going on?

We're buying a house. I already knew that, from my mother's non-stop commentary on my siblings' lives, which, now that I thought about it, was probably why I never felt the need to talk to them.

Cool. Send me a link?

Mom told me she showed it to you already. Just say congratulations, like you're supposed to.

I started to type something snarky about how he was just fishing for compliments and rubbing it in when I was still renting, but I took a deep breath and deleted what I had written. Congratulations.

Thanks. We're excited. It's got a nice guest room if you ever want to come visit.

Okay. He didn't reply and I didn't say any more. But it was something. I made a mental note to text him the next time my mother updated me on anything major, and, feeling somewhat absolved, I put my phone down to get ready for bed.

CHAPTER TWENTY-TWO

Alex waved to me and I weaved toward his table, unwinding my scarf as I went, then sat heavily in the booth across from him. It was two weeks after we had set up my Tinder account. And an hour into my fifth Tinder date, I texted Alex to see if he wanted to meet up as soon as I could ditch the guy.

"Drink?" He had already gotten me a martini.

"Can you just get the bottle of gin and pour it directly down my throat?"

He laughed. "Went that well, huh?"

"I swear my siblings only said I could bring a date to their weddings to torture me."

"I told you I could be your date."

"And I told *you*, they said actual romantic prospects only. No 'random friends.'"

"Do they actually need to know the difference?"

"Please don't start. As much as I'd love to have you there for moral support, I don't want to lie to everyone at the weddings. Because every single person there would ask us when we were getting married."

"And you'd rather bring a random guy who you've been on a couple dates with?"

I shook my head and took another sip of my drink. "No. If I had found someone awesome, that would have been cool. But I'm done trying. I'll just go and be single and when anyone asks, I'm going to say I *was* engaged for a while, but he kept asking me when I wanted to get married, so I murdered him with a pickax." Alex laughed again. *Mental note: use that in the blog.*

For a split second, I considered telling him about the blog. Actually, I had debated telling him about it many times since I started. It would be nice to be able to share the small successes when they came. But the more anonymous I kept it, the better. And I had talked about Justin—I refused to think about the implications of why I didn't want Alex knowing about that, assuming he hadn't already heard, but I didn't.

"How was *your* date?"

He shook his head. "I cancelled it."

"Really? Why?"

"She was too—I don't know—I got the feeling that I checked all the boxes by being a lawyer, so she wanted to seal the deal immediately and lock me down. Possibly literally, in her basement."

I leaned my head on my hand, scrunched up my nose, and smiled. "Probably for the best then. You don't want to end up in a hole, putting the lotion on its skin."

"Right?" He smiled back. "Plus she's a lot younger than us. She wouldn't have even gotten a *Silence of the Lambs* joke."

"How much younger?"

"Twenty-six."

I pulled an olive out of my martini and threw it at him. "That's almost my baby sister's age, you perv."

"And your sister is getting married. It's not *that* young."

"Too young for *us.*"

"I agree. That's why I'm not in her basement hole."

"You need to get off Tinder. It's one thing if you're using it to get laid, it's another if you think you're going to find a soul mate on there."

"I know." He paused. "Are *you* using it to get laid?"

I mimed vomiting. "Uh, no. And I deleted the app before I even left the restaurant tonight."

"I never even got to swipe on you."

"Right, I assume?"

"Of course."

We both sipped our drinks, comfortable in the silence. "Mexico would have been fun though," he mused.

"Even getting my grandma down there?"

"Sure. Old ladies love me."

"She's a flirt too. You'd have your hands full."

"See? Who needs Tinder?"

I covered my face, laughing. "That's an over-sixty-year spread. Get some standards already."

"Hey, the last time I went to Cancun was my honeymoon. I'll take what I can get."

That sobered me up quickly. "I always forget you were actually *married*. You're like an *adult* adult."

He shrugged. "Not really. It was a stupid thing to do."

"Then why'd you do it?"

He took another drink, thinking. "I guess I thought it was what I was supposed to do. I was getting close to thirty and she really wanted to get married and I kind of just thought that's what people did."

"Did you love her?"

"I thought so. At first at least. But by the end, I didn't even recognize myself anymore. I was angry all the time, and she found a way to ruin anything that made me happy."

"She sounds like a blast."

"Yeah."

"What actually happened though?" He looked down. I waited, but he didn't say anything else. "You don't have to tell me if you don't want to."

He exhaled loudly. "No, I think I want to." He paused again, then continued, all the while peeling the label off his beer bottle and shredding it into a tiny pile on the table. "She really wanted us to have a baby. And I mean, yeah, I want kids. But we were fighting *all* the time and I wasn't ready, so I suggested we try going to couples therapy. She didn't want to, but she eventually agreed. So we go like six times and we get into a fight in the therapist's office about the whole kids thing, and she yells at me that it doesn't matter anyway because she stopped taking the pill a year ago and if she wasn't pregnant yet, it clearly wasn't going to happen anyway."

My eyes widened, but he still wasn't looking at me.

"And I just—I couldn't trust her after that. She had been lying to me for a year. And if she had gotten pregnant—I mean—that's forever. It's not like the little kind of lie, like when she knocked the mirror off her car and claimed she didn't know how it happened. This was—it was too big. I couldn't go back from that."

He finally looked up at me, but I didn't know what to say. Tricking someone into creating a new life was a whole other level of betrayal.

He brushed the pieces of his beer label into a napkin and balled it up. "So anyway. New subject?"

"Sure." He looked uncomfortable at having shared that much, so I reached around for something else to talk about. Anything. "Okay, new subject. Um, oh, okay, I've got one! That horrible bridesmaid in Caryn's wedding? She used the wrong 'your' in an email today!"

He smiled weakly. "What a moron."

"Right? Like how are you going to ream me out and not even use proper grammar? I will *destroy* you in a reply to that." His grin finally looked more genuine. "I need to figure out something appropriately passive-aggressive to troll her with. Maybe a mug that says 'Grammar:

the difference between knowing your shit and knowing you're shit.' I saw that online somewhere. I could send it to her."

"I thought you were overextended on your wedding budget?"

"There's *always* money to passive-aggressively mock someone horrible. Duh." I paused. "I've also heard really good things about glitter bombs."

"What's a glitter bomb?"

"You anonymously mail someone an envelope full of glitter. It gets *everywhere*. And it's cheap, so you can do it yourself. Glitter costs almost nothing."

Alex shook his head. "Remind me never to cross you."

You don't know the half of it, I thought gleefully, already planning how to mock Caroline's idiocy in the blog. But Alex was reaching into his pocket and pulling out his phone, the screen glowing.

"Hang on, it's my sister," he said, answering it. "Sam? What's up?" He held his hand over his free ear. It wasn't *loud* in the restaurant, but it wasn't super quiet either. "Wait, slow down, I can't understand you." He listened. "Oh God. Okay, which one? I'll be right there. I'm coming right now. I love you too."

He hung up and pulled his wallet from his back pocket, his face suddenly pale. "I have to go."

"What's wrong? What happened?"

"My dad—another heart attack—I have to—"

I slid out of the booth, grabbing my coat and scarf. "Which hospital?"

"Sibley."

I punched it into my phone while he threw some cash down on the table. "I'll have an Uber here in two minutes. Come on. Let's go outside." He nodded and followed me to the door. "Did she say how bad it is?"

"She doesn't know yet."

"I'm sure he'll be okay." I wasn't. This was his second, which wasn't a good sign. But, oh God, the look on Alex's face. "This is us." I gestured toward the blue sedan that pulled up to the corner.

Alex opened the door and got in, and I went around to the other side. He looked up, surprised to see me in the car. "You don't need to come."

I nodded. "Yes, I do." I turned to the driver. "We're rushing to the hospital for an emergency, so speed is good tonight."

"You've got it. Everyone okay?"

"We don't know yet."

The driver looked at our faces in the rearview mirror. "You've got a good girlfriend there," he told Alex. "Marry the ones who will come with you to the hospital."

"He'll take that into consideration," I said grimly. "But please hurry."

I picked up Alex's hand, barely realizing I was doing it, and held it in mine for the entire drive. We didn't talk.

The Uber driver dropped us at the emergency entrance, and we ran inside to the desk, where we were directed to the cardiac unit. There, in the waiting room, Alex dropped my hand, which I hadn't realized he was still holding, and embraced an older woman with a tear-stained face. I didn't need to see that she had the same eyes as Alex to know she was his mother.

"How is he? What happened?" He turned to the younger carbon copy of his mother and hugged her as well.

Sam wiped at her eyes with a tissue. "We were at dinner and he just dropped."

"What did the doctors say?"

"He's in emergency surgery right now. We don't know anything yet."

"What about the stent from last time?"

"I don't know." His mother sank back into her chair. "I don't know anything. I just told them to do whatever they needed to do."

Sam noticed me standing there and eyed me warily. "Who's she?" I felt suddenly selfish for intruding on their family crisis.

Alex flinched. "Sorry. Sam, Mom, this is my friend Lily. Lily, this is my mom, Angie, and my sister, Samantha."

Samantha shook my hand limply, apparently less irritated now that I was a friend and not more, and told me to call her Sam. His mother nodded in my general direction, but was understandably too distracted for much else.

"I'm going to see if I can get an update," Alex said, looking around for the nurses' station.

"They said they'll tell us when there's news," Sam said.

"Well I need to do *something*."

"There's nothing you can do," Angie said quietly. "Just sit. Please."

Alex sat down heavily next to his mother. I took the seat on his other side, trying to be unobtrusive. His hand was on the armrest between our chairs and I put mine over it. He turned his over to hold mine, and our fingers intertwined, which sent a small jolt of entirely inappropriate excitement down my spine.

No one spoke. My phone vibrated and I slid it discreetly out of my pocket with the hand that wasn't in Alex's. It was Becca, asking how the date went. Good, I assume, since you're not home?

Terrible, actually.

Then where are you?

I texted slowly, left-handed. At Sibley. Alex's dad had a heart attack.

Oh no! Let me know what happens.

I told her I would and slipped the phone back into my pocket. Alex looked over at the motion. "Everything okay?" he murmured. "You don't need to stay."

"I'm fine right here." I looked over to his mother and sister. "Can I get anyone anything? Water? Coffee?"

They both shook their heads. "I could use a coffee," Alex said. "I'll go."

"Stay," I told him, standing and untangling our fingers. "You don't want to be gone if the doctor comes out. I know how you take it." He nodded and leaned back in the chair, rubbing his eyes. He looked older in the harsh fluorescent lighting, and there was a hint of gray in his sideburns that I swore hadn't been there earlier.

I followed signs to the café, which was closed, but there was a vending machine that served coffee. I got a cup for Alex and paused as I passed the food machine. They had Skittles, so I got a bag for him as well. We had joked when we went to the movies that his preference was perfect because I wouldn't steal any—I maintained that the calories weren't worth it if the candy wasn't chocolate.

By the time I got back, a doctor was talking to the family. I hung back, not wanting to interrupt, but tried to catch the drift of what he was saying.

"—an excellent prognosis, assuming surgery goes well. It's a very common procedure."

"How long?"

"Probably two more hours. He only needs a single bypass because the stent is holding, so we think it should be uncomplicated."

Sam and Angie were holding on to each other, and Alex shook the doctor's hand and thanked him. I waited until he turned to leave before I returned to them and handed Alex his coffee. "What did he say?" I asked quietly.

"They're doing a bypass now. The doctor thinks he should be okay, assuming there are no complications in surgery."

"That's great!"

"Yeah." Alex sat down shakily and took a sip of the coffee. "This is horrible."

"There was only a vending machine." I held up the bag of Skittles. "But I figured these would make a decent chaser." I sat down next to him. "And I won't even steal any like you did with my M&Ms after swearing you wouldn't."

He smiled weakly. "I'm like that blood type that's a universal receiver, but with candy. I'll take any of it."

"Hospital humor, I like it."

He put his hand over mine on the armrest. "Thank you."

I laid my head on his shoulder. "Obviously, I hope there's not a next time, but anytime."

He leaned his head on mine and we sat like that for a long time.

CHAPTER
TWENTY-THREE

Sharon texted me the Tuesday after Alex's dad went into the hospital.

Do you want to go to dinner Friday night?

I hesitated. I was exhausted. I was broke. And I kind of, sort of wanted to keep my weekend open in case Alex needed me. His dad was scheduled to come home either Thursday or Friday, and I got the feeling he might need some extra support.

But Sharon *never* asked to hang out anymore. We had been inseparable in college—when you're actually friends with your roommate, you tend to do everything together. Once she moved home after graduation, though, our relationship shifted to being conducted largely through texts and social media. She always came out for my birthday, and we would grab lunch from time to time. But the asking began to feel one-sided long before she even met Josh, and I'll admit, I stopped trying so hard because of that. We still texted multiple times a week, so the conversation never ended, but sometimes she felt more like a pen pal than one of my closest friends.

So I said sure and asked where she wanted to go.

The three dots appeared and stayed for an inordinately long time, making me worry this would be some family event with her mother and that I had been invited solely to be the bearer of bad news. Again.

The message finally appeared. Yay! Wear something cute—I mean, you always look cute, but look EXTRA cute. Josh's cousin Seth just broke up with his girlfriend and you two are going to be the perfect match. He's a doctor and he's even taller than you! Just don't wear heels that are TOO tall. He's a groomsman in the wedding too so if you two hit it off, you have a date and everything. And if you get married, we'll be related!

My shoulders sank. She was still typing.

Was I opposed to being fixed up with a doctor? No, of course not. But ugh, had I reached the spinster stage where this was a thing? Yes, I had filled her in on the whole Tinder debacle, so she was just trying to help. But I still wondered if it was too late to bail and hang out with Alex instead.

Ok, I replied eventually. If Sharon noticed my lack of enthusiasm, she didn't mention it. And either way, I was happy to see her away from her mother. She turned into such a timid mouse around Mrs. Meyer, and I missed my friend.

~

I wrinkled my nose at my reflection in the elevator of my apartment building as I went down to catch my Uber to dinner. I had sent a picture of my outfit to Megan and she said it was perfect, but I wasn't so sure. What did one wear to look cute, but not desperate, when a friend decides to set her up on a date? Plus Megan seemed a little too excited about this whole situation, telling me that of course I could bring the doctor as a date to her wedding. Which was one hundred percent about Justin and I knew it.

After getting the necessary details from Sharon, I had snooped on Facebook. His profile picture was still him with a girl who I assumed was the ex, which either meant he wasn't over her or he just wasn't into social media. Neither seemed promising. He wouldn't be named *People's* Sexiest Man Alive anytime soon, but he wasn't bad-looking. And I did trust Sharon.

So with some trepidation and a little bit of nervous excitement, I touched up my lipstick before climbing out of the Uber and walked into the restaurant.

Sharon, Josh, and Doctor Seth were inside already, but still waiting to be seated. Sharon ran over and hugged me.

"I'm sorry I'm late," I said automatically.

"You're not. I told you fifteen minutes earlier than our reservation time on purpose."

I laughed. We may not hang out often anymore, but she still knew me. And that was enough to make me feel more at ease about meeting Doctor Seth. I kissed Josh on the cheek as a greeting and held out my hand to the cousin. "You must be Seth. It's nice to meet you." He nodded tensely and shook my hand, mumbling something incoherent that could have been "likewise" or could have been "I like guys," before looking away. I was *not*, I realized, the only one who wasn't totally feeling the matchmaker game.

Awesome, I thought. *Either I'm not "doctor's wife hot" or he's not over his ex.* Based on the Facebook picture, I could tell myself it was the latter. And at least I had Ubered to the restaurant, so I could drink.

Except Doctor Seth said he would just be having water when the waitress took our order, as he was on call. It looked like my martini would probably be an only child, unless he warmed up or was so boring that I decided to drink myself into oblivion.

"What kind of doctor are you?"

"Emergency." He didn't say anything else.

I glanced at Sharon. Had she already told him everything he needed to know about me or was conversation just not his strong suit? She nodded encouragingly and I sighed. "What hospital?"

"Sibley."

I opened my mouth, "And what a delightful bedside manner you must have" on the tip of my tongue. Had this been a real date, I would have said it. I was comfortable enough with who I was to recognize that a guy was either going to like me, snarky warts and all, or he wasn't. But I had seen zero evidence of a sense of humor or even a personality so far and I didn't want to make waves with Sharon's soon-to-be in-laws. So I bit my tongue and instead replied cheerily, "Oh, wow, I was just there last weekend."

He seemed mildly more interested as he looked me up and down, scanning for injuries or illnesses. "For what?"

"Oh. Not for me. My friend's dad had a heart attack and I went with him."

A nod and he checked his phone. I was dull again. Our drinks arrived and I took a long sip, then gave up and turned to Sharon. "So what's the latest with your mom?"

I didn't want Sharon to feel bad, so I hadn't told her about the phone call I received from her mother the week before, in which she ripped me apart for sending Sharon's aunts' shower invitations to the wrong aunts' houses. I asked why they couldn't just accept that it was a mistake and open each other's, which was apparently a completely irrational and unacceptable answer on my part. As soon as I got off the phone, I set her ringtone to be Darth Vader's theme music, then wrote a scathing blog post to make myself feel better.

Sharon rolled her eyes. "She's extremely focused on flowers at the moment."

"How lucky for that florist."

She pursed her lips, amused. "That poor man. He has no idea what he's in for."

"Should I warn him?"

"Eh. He's getting paid. He'll be fine. And my mom can't be the worst he's dealt with."

I sipped my drink to avoid laughing. *Oh yes she can,* I thought. "Did you pick a color scheme yet?"

"Tiffany blue and white," she said, and I smiled broadly. *Breakfast at Tiffany's* was Sharon's favorite movie, book, poster, and Halloween costume when we were in college. And while her mother's preference for black dresses would probably have been more fitting if she wanted to make that a theme, I loved that Sharon was happy with her choice.

"You could probably do some cool Tiffany's-style favors. I saw some on Pinterest."

"Since when do you use Pinterest?"

"I'm quite the expert on all things wedding these days."

Sharon looked to Seth and Josh, who were now both scrolling on their phones. She cleared her throat. "Lily is in *five* weddings this summer, including ours."

Josh read her tone and put his phone away. Seth looked up from his and saw Sharon raising her eyebrows at him. "Is that a lot?"

Sharon laughed, pleased she had gotten him to engage. "Men. Yes, that's an insane amount. But it means Lily will be a pro when it's time for her to get married."

He looked back down at his phone and I cringed. *Great. He's going to think I'm trying to marry him.* "Which hopefully won't be for a *very* long time," I added quickly. "I've had enough weddings for a while."

"But not *too* long," Sharon said. "I mean, you want kids and all."

I stood up. "I'm going to go find the ladies' room. Sharon, come with me."

"I don't—" I gave her a sharp look and she stood up. "We'll be right back."

I let her lead the way, as she had been to the restaurant before, but as soon as we were out of earshot, I grabbed her arm. "Dude, *what* are you trying to do to me here?"

"What do you mean?"

"Look, he's attractive, I'll give you that, but this guy is clearly not into it and you're talking about me getting married? You're making it sound like I've got a wedding dress on under my clothes and a tux in my purse that I'm ready to shove him into!"

Her face dropped. "I'm sorry. I hated his ex and he's actually pretty funny when he's not being all mopey. I just thought how great it would be for everyone if you two hit it off."

I felt terrible. Her intentions were good, even if the guy was a dud. "When did they break up?"

"Last weekend." I started to laugh. At least it wasn't me that was the problem.

"What?"

"And how long were they together?"

"A couple years maybe?"

I put an arm around her. "I love you for trying. But Shar, he's not over his ex yet. I could be a Victoria's Secret model and he wouldn't be into it."

She shook her head. "No, I guess not," she said sadly. "I just want you to be happy. And I didn't want someone else to snap him up. He's a really good guy, I promise."

I smiled wryly. "So not my type at all, huh?"

She laughed, having lived through several of my terrible choices in men. "No, I guess not."

"Let's go back. He's clearly not digging this, but maybe he'll be over the ex by the rehearsal dinner and then we can say we got together at your wedding." I linked arms with her as we worked our way back to the table. "Seriously, though, do you want me to send you some favor ideas?"

"I would love that."

"Will Mama Meyer approve or will I have to talk her out of something else first?"

Sharon scrunched up her nose. "I owe you forever on that one."

"Hey, I was proud. You actually stood up to her in the end."

"I was proud of myself too. It didn't occur to me that having *you* protest black was a bad plan." She gestured to my outfit.

I laughed. "Can you picture my eventual wedding? It'll look like a funeral but with better hors d'oeuvres."

"It'll happen, you know."

"Yeah. I'm *such* a catch." I flipped my hair.

Sharon stopped walking, stopping me with her. "You *are*, Lil. And when you realize that, other people will too."

I couldn't explain why, but I felt a lump in my throat. "Enough of that," I said, swatting at her gently with the back of my hand. "Let's go see if we can get Seth to answer a question with more than one word. It'll be a fun game."

~

I looked at my phone discreetly as we waited for the check. Seth had warmed up some, but not enough for me to tell if he actually had no personality or was just trying to give Mr. Darcy a run for his money at who could brood the most. But he hadn't faked getting called into work, which I counted as a win because I was at least more interesting than an evening at home crying over his ex-girlfriend.

Whatcha up to? Alex had texted about half an hour earlier.

Disappointing one of my many brides by not being remotely interested in her fiancé's cousin.

Three dots. Oh.

You okay?

Yeah. Just got home from my parents' house.

Dad okay?

The dots appeared, disappeared, and then reappeared. Yeah.

"Who are you texting?" Sharon whispered.

"Alex." She gave me a look. "What?"

She glanced over at Josh and Seth, who were looking at something on Josh's phone together, then leaned closer and whispered, "Are you sure it's not *you* who's not interested tonight?"

"Just friends. I promise."

She shrugged, then took a last sip of her wine. "Just saying."

I slid my phone back into my purse and left it there until we left the restaurant.

But once I was in my Uber home, I pulled up the conversation with Alex. He didn't usually give me one-word answers. Something was up. I'm leaving dinner now. You wanna meet up for a drink?

Nah. I don't want to go anywhere.

You want me to come to your place?

If you want. I only have beer though.

Totally not coming then.

I knew I had finally gotten a smile out of him before he even replied. Yeah yeah yeah. I asked for his address, then leaned forward and asked my driver if he minded changing the destination.

~

He was in basketball shorts and a ratty Springsteen shirt when he opened the door, a beer already in his hand. "That's a new look for you," I said, walking past him and looking around. Pretty standard boy apartment. Leather sofa. Giant TV. Not much on the walls. Bigger and nicer than my place, but that made sense because he made more money than I did. I crossed to the balcony door to check out the view.

"I'm hanging out here when the weather gets warm." I gestured to the pool in the courtyard.

"I haven't even been down there."

"We'll change that." I went to the kitchen and opened the refrigerator to grab a beer.

"Make yourself at home," he said, a hint of a smile playing across his face.

"Hey, I've been here a good ninety seconds and you hadn't offered me a drink yet. A girl's gotta do what a girl's gotta do. Opener?"

"Do you want to just look in the drawers until you find it?"

"I can."

He rolled his eyes good-naturedly, took the beer from me, and opened it with his hand. "Twist off. You don't know everything after all."

"First time for everything." I touched my bottle to his. "To your dad's health." He looked down. "He *is* okay, right?"

Alex sighed and leaned against the counter. "Yeah. He's home and seems fine, all things considered."

"Then what's wrong?"

"It just kind of hit me tonight."

"What did?"

He hesitated. "He's getting old. Like he's going to die someday. Maybe soon."

I shuddered involuntarily. Despite my often rocky relationship with my mother, I couldn't imagine life without either of my parents. But my dad was sixty-two and my mom was sixty. Yes, my grandma was still going strong, but she was my only remaining grandparent. And my dad's father died younger than he was now, before I was born.

I had really only contemplated their mortality as an adult once, at my other grandmother's funeral. It was the only time I had seen my father cry. And I realized, as I sat next to him, my mother on his other side, each of us holding one of his hands, that one day I would be in his position. It was a thought I tried to suppress as much as I could, telling myself my mother would live to be at least a hundred just in case I gave her a late grandchild, and my dad—well—he biked a lot and was in really good shape. Better than I was. He would be okay because I needed him to be. Right?

Two heart attacks though—that didn't bode well. And I couldn't lie and say it did.

"I'm sorry," I said finally. "I wish I had some awesome answer or a magic wand I could wave to fix that, but I don't."

"I know. And it happens to us all eventually."

"Unless we become vampires and make our parents vampires too."

He shook his head and chuckled. "What is *wrong* with you?"

I hopped up onto the kitchen counter next to him. "So much."

"Clearly. Your butt is where I prepare food right now."

"Hey, you said to make myself at home."

"Remind me not to eat anything you've cooked if this is how you are at home."

"That is *so* cute."

"What is?"

"You thinking I can cook."

Alex shook his head. "You're a mess."

I jumped down from the counter and cocked a finger at him. "Yes. But I am a mess who knows how to make you feel better. You wanna go watch a documentary about a murderer?"

He looked at me askance. "That's supposed to make me feel better?"

"Totally. You're always talking about how to properly dispose of bodies whenever I say I'm going to kill someone." He laughed. "You in?"

The corners of his eyes crinkled warmly, and I couldn't help but smile back. "Yeah. I'm in."

"Good."

CHAPTER TWENTY-FOUR

From: Caroline Morgan [MrsMorgantoyou@gmail.com]
To: [bridesmaids]
Subject: Bridal shower and bachelorette updates
Date: March 1

We're just over three months away from Caryn's big day, which means it's time to make sure everything is perfect for our celebrations of the bride.

The shower is set for May 5 at Kenwood. I'm having everything done in-house, so all you need to bring is your lovely selves.

For the bachelorette weekend, I understand that Olivia and Dana said they would prefer to stay at a different hotel instead of the Ritz because the other hotel has a rooftop pool and bar. However, the fitness room there is basically a treadmill in a dungeon (I'm attaching pictures for comparison) and to do that to Caryn just weeks before her wedding would be cruel. You two can plan your own separate trip if you want, but this weekend is about Caryn. Not to mention, we don't want a repeat of the sunburn you got before Mia's wedding, do we, Dana?

As for the itinerary itself, I've only booked a loose outline of activities, so we have plenty of flexibility. We have reservations for dinner for all three nights, a spa day, an "aphrodisiac tour," reservations at a few boutiques, three fitness classes, and a party bus each night. But the rest is wide open! I also hired a photographer to document the whole experience for us, of course, so plan to look your best!

Finally (and I HATE to bring this up), I'd like to remind you that not everyone has paid yet. The total cost for the bachelorette weekend has increased to $3,000 each for those of us who are going, unless, like Lily, you've chosen to make other arrangements.

Ta ta for now!
—Caroline

I rubbed the base of my neck where it met my shoulders. Who *was* this crazy person? Admittedly, I felt mildly better now that she was roasting Olivia, but I felt for Dana after our conversation in the parking garage. Did Caroline actually have friends? Or just people who were too terrified of her to speak up?

But unfortunately, she had left a detail out, and it was one that I needed to know. I waited a half hour, hoping someone else would ask the question, but when no one did I finally wrote to her, being sure to reply all.

Sounds like you've got everything under control!
But what time is the shower?

Thanks!
—Lily

She shot back an immediate answer saying only 3:00 PM. I entered it in my calendar, noting that the rest of that weekend was blissfully wide open, although I was sure that would change. And with the wedding in Mexico the following weekend, I wouldn't have much of a reprieve before the next round of chaos.

Not that I'd had anything that felt even mildly like a break since the engagements began, anyway. Trying to juggle the details of all five weddings was exhausting and would have destroyed any social life I had—if I still had the money or friends to have one. And the blog, while therapeutic, also took more time and energy than I expected, especially as I got better at it. Building an audience meant responding to comments and pingbacks, finding other bloggers to network with, and posting links to it anonymously in places where I felt confident my brides wouldn't be looking. The writing part was great. The rest was tedious, especially between work and weddings. But every time I got a new follower or comment, it felt a little more worth it.

And at least Megan's was the only shower at which I was expected to do a significant amount of the planning, and the only other bridesmaid with strong opinions was Claire, Tim's sister. Early in the process, she volunteered to host the shower at her house, which, while far away from Megan's new home in Columbia, looked nice, if bland, from the pictures Claire sent. And certainly cheaper than renting a venue, so I agreed.

Unfortunately, that meant she thought she was in charge. The day after Caroline's missive, I found myself driving out to Potomac to meet with Claire and the rest of the bridesmaids for a "planning sesh."

Claire's au pair opened the door to her McMansion. "Welcome," Claire said expansively, coming into the foyer from a room in the back of the house. "The rest of the girls are already here, of course."

I glanced discreetly at my wrist. I was literally two minutes late. This was a punctuality miracle for me and someone should be putting a medal around my neck, not passive-aggressively telling me I was late.

She escorted me to the living room, the long way, I realized, as we passed through every other room on the first floor to get there.

Jennifer, Kelly, and Julie were sitting together on one sofa, Chrissy was on the loveseat, and an older woman I had never seen before was in one of the two armchairs. Claire immediately arranged herself in the second armchair, which felt rude, as I was still standing, but she clearly wanted that particular chair—it was higher than the rest and arranged so it was facing the group. I said hello and then took the remaining seat next to Chrissy.

"As I was telling the other girls," she said, expressly to me, "I asked Donna to be here today. Donna is *the* premier party planner in the DC area."

I was ninety percent sure that wasn't true, or else Caryn and her cronies would be using her, plus her Louis Vuitton Neverfull bag, sitting next to her on the floor, would be real if that were the case—and it wasn't. Donna smiled graciously and nodded.

"The shower will be outside, of course," Claire said. "We'll open the pool early. Not that anyone will swim, but it's just so much more festive when there's a pool."

"Do we have a backup plan?" I asked. Claire looked at me in annoyance. "The weather is so iffy in the spring. It could be ninety-four degrees or forty and raining."

"We'll have a tent," Donna said reassuringly.

"A tent isn't much help if it's freezing out."

Claire opened her mouth to speak, but Donna responded first. "If the forecast is bad, I'll rent space heaters."

I nodded. "Okay." The au pair entered with a tray of hors d'oeuvres and I wondered who was watching Claire's daughter.

I kept my opinions to myself while Claire and Donna went through a rundown of the decorations, but I spoke up at the suggested menu. "No mini crab cakes."

"Excuse me?"

"Megan is allergic to shellfish."

"What kind of Marylander is allergic to crab?" Claire laughed. "Is that even a real thing?"

"It is, and she's allergic."

"Is it an airborne allergy? Will she die if she's in the same room as them?"

"No."

"Well then she can just not eat the crab cakes."

"It's *her* shower. Don't serve foods she can't eat."

Kelly and Jennifer nodded in agreement, but no one said anything. Claire stared at me and I realized that Caroline would probably be Claire's personal lord and savior. Caroline was everything Claire wished she could be—actually rich, able to shut people down effortlessly to get her way. Instead she was a bratty gnome who was being mean to her future sister-in-law out of—what, exactly? Jealousy? Pettiness? Had her husband's sister been mean to her and she thought this was how it was supposed to go? I had no idea. But I was the maid of honor, and this wasn't going to fly.

Claire was still trying to formulate her next move, but I turned to Donna. "Scratch the crab cakes."

Donna glanced at Claire, then back at me. She crossed them off the legal pad on her lap with a long motion.

"Any other shellfish on the menu?" Donna shook her head, not even looking at Claire, who was silently fuming. "Good. What's next on the agenda?"

~

By the time I left Claire's house, I knew I had made an enemy. Which perhaps I would have cared about if Megan liked her, but she didn't. So instead of worrying about it, I was planning the blog I would write.

> Remember Mini-Me from *Austin Powers*? Well I just met the wickedest of the wicked bridesmaids' Mini-Me. I'd say I should get the two of them together, but that would be a disaster. Partially because the wickedest bridesmaid would eat Mini-Me for lunch (then spit her out, of course, because the wicked bridesmaids of the west don't actually eat or digest food—pretty sure they survive on the consumption of human souls alone), and then how would I explain to Bride C's fiancé that I was responsible for his sister's disappearance? If he hasn't been reading the blog, I'm not sure saying that an evil bridesmaid chewed her up and spit her out like a shark does a surfer would mean anything.
>
> It was uncanny, however, how much like a dollar-store version of a wicked bridesmaid of the west she was, with her Costco appetizers and her knock-off-purse-toting party planner. Granted, she didn't grow up ridiculously rich, like the wicked bridesmaids did, which, if *The Great Gatsby* taught me anything, explains the difference in their behavior,

old sport. The evil bridesmaids would never invite me to their houses to show off their green dock lights, because they don't care what I think—I clearly don't have enough taste (or money) to appreciate their belongings without salivating over them.

But this chick had the nerve, at Bride C's house-warming party, to critique the house that Bride C and her fiancé bought when Mini-Me's in-laws bought them their house. You don't even OWN the glass house you're throwing stones from, sister. Knock that off!

In other news, the queen of the evil brides-maids snapped at other bridesmaids in an email! I felt a small amount of sympathy, but was mostly shoveling popcorn in my mouth while I watched all the drama. She then, of course, came after me, but could there be a rebellion brewing amongst the wicked bridesmaids? I'm twisting my hair into Princess Leia buns just thinking about the idea.

May the bridesmaid force be with you!

Alex texted me just after I hit "Publish," with a picture of him holding two ties up to his neck. Which one?

The blue. Better with your eyes.

Does it go with what you're wearing? He had a benefit for work that night and I had agreed to go as his date.

I made a face. You were married too long. We're not framing pictures from tonight to put on the mantle.

Good point.

I still need to do my hair, so I'm gonna go shower. I'll see you at six.
He sent a thumbs-up emoji.

~

"You look beautiful," Alex said when he picked me up. I twirled for full
effect. It was the only event all year where I could wear a cocktail dress of
my own choosing, even if it was a few years old. And, though I would never
admit it to Caroline, with the Spanx that Caryn had guilt-tripped me into
buying, I felt *really* good in it. Was the underwear remotely sexy? No. But
it wasn't like my dress was coming off until I was alone, so who cared?

I straightened his tie. "You clean up well too." He wore a suit to
work every day, but this was a nicer one. His hair was freshly trimmed,
and he had shaved off the little bit of stubble he usually kept, the after-
shave smell lingering alluringly.

"Shall we?" he asked, offering his arm. I took it and we went to the car.

The benefit was at the same hotel where Sharon was getting married. I had originally suggested Metroing so we could drink, but Alex
said he wasn't having more than a drink or two at a work event. Mildly
shamed, I agreed to stick to that plan as well.

"Just don't get engagement-party drunk and you're fine," he said. I
elbowed him playfully. His face grew more serious. "Are you ready for
everyone to assume we're together?"

"Does it help you career-wise if I say we are?"

"It's not the fifties. They know I'm divorced. They're just going to
make assumptions when they see us."

"In that case, let's tell everyone I'm your sister and then make out
all night."

"Oh okay, good, that'll go over well." I laughed. "Don't be *too* much
of a jerk please," he said.

"I'll be like Goldilocks. Just right."

196

He brushed a hair off my forehead. "She was breaking and entering. It was the baby bear whose stuff was just right."

"I said what I said."

~

After the dinner part of the evening ended, I turned to Alex and said, "Thirty-six."

"Thirty-six what?"

"Thirty-six people asked how long we've been dating."

"And what did you say the latter thirty-five times to that?" He knew me well.

"That we've been together since high school, and I was really upset when you and my sister wife split up so we're looking for someone new to add to our marriage."

He covered his eyes with a hand. "Seriously?"

I rolled my eyes. "No. I said a few months to everyone."

"Excellent. Want to keep up the lie and dance?" I looked to the dance floor, where about a dozen couples were dancing, and made a face. "Come on," he said. "It's good practice for Tim and Megan's wedding."

I agreed and followed him out to the floor. "It's weird," I said, as we swayed to the music. "I've never once referred to them as 'Tim and Megan.' It's 'Megan and Tim' to me. Is it always like that with the person you knew first?"

He thought for a minute. "I think so."

"What happens if you've known both people an equal length of time?"

"Maybe that's when they get one of those celeb nicknames like Brangelina."

"I guess. So we'd be Lily and Alex to my friends and Alex and Lily to yours?"

"And Ally to the people who knew us the same amount of time. Or Lilex."

I laughed. "Lilex sounds like a knockoff watch brand. Ally it is."

We danced without talking for a couple of minutes. I was glad he would be at Megan's wedding with me. Going completely dateless to four of them was going to be rough. And I thought, for the millionth time, about lying to my family and saying Alex was my boyfriend.

The idea had some appeal to it. It would mean having a date to Jake's and Amy's weddings and being an awkward single only at Caryn's and Sharon's. Yeah, we would get asked when we were getting married, but we could play along with that. Help getting my grandma to Mexico would be useful as well. She *was* a handful.

I pulled back slightly to look at him. There was no denying that he was handsome. I mean, he wasn't a Hemsworth, but who, other than the Hemsworths, was? He was already the first person I texted most mornings and the last person I texted at night. Did it *have* to be fake? What would it be like to kiss him?

He caught me looking at him. "What are you thinking?" he asked warily.

"Nothing." I shook my head, more at myself than at him. What a dumb idea. He wasn't into me like that anyway. Plus, Megan would murder me.

I glanced over his shoulder at the movement I saw back at the tables. "Ooh, dessert time!" I took the hand that had been in mine to dance and pulled him back toward the table, away from the dance floor of dangerous plans.

CHAPTER TWENTY-FIVE

March came to an end, flouting the "in like a lion, out like a lamb" cliché, as it does so often in DC, and ushered in a minor April snowstorm that left my mother in fits about our trip to Chicago for Madison's bridal shower.

"We're not leaving for another week," I told her on a three-way call with Amy. "It won't still be snowing by then."

"What if it's snowing in Chicago? It's colder up there."

"They know how to deal with snow in Chicago. Remember when Obama called us snow wimps? You're giving him more material."

My mother harrumphed at that. "It'll be fine, Mom," Amy said soothingly. "And worst-case scenario, at least it won't snow next month when we go to the actual wedding."

"It would be just our luck to get stranded in Chicago, when we have so much to do," she said. "Maybe we shouldn't go."

I rolled my eyes. "Mom, we booked the tickets. We're going."

"Well of course we're going," she said, as if she hadn't just suggested not going. "I'm just saying, is all."

"Okay, I'm going to go pack."

"Wait," Amy said. "Are you bringing your flat iron? If you're bringing yours, I won't bother bringing mine."

"Oh, good, I need one too," my mother said. "That's perfect. Lily, you'll bring yours."

"Want me to bring a communal hairbrush too?"

My sarcasm was lost on them. "Do you have a good one?" Amy asked.

"I'm hanging up now."

~

Dearest blog readers, I have made some terrible decisions in my day. Sleeping with that groomsman. Agreeing to be in Bride A's wedding. Not running for the hills when I met Bride B's mom a dozen years ago. Overplucking my eyebrows in the early 2000s (seriously, when do those hairs grow back???).

But this? Oh, this is a whole new circle of hell that I have descended into. I am sharing a hotel room for two nights with my mother and baby sister.

I'm fully aware that that doesn't sound so bad. I'm sure there are people out there who would LOVE to spend a weekend in Chicago with the two of them. Would they feel the same way after the two days were over? Sure—if they belong in Azkaban. Remember Helena Bonham Carter's wanted poster? That's me, right now. Hair and all.

Because my little sister left my flat iron on and now it's dead.

Note: She has a better flat iron than I do, but she didn't want to bring hers, so I was instructed to bring mine. Now I have none.

Of course, I've traveled with her before, albeit not in several years, so I planned ahead. I packed twice as many outfits as I needed, knowing she would take at least one. (My first choice for future sister-in-law's bridal shower? Little sis looked lovely in it. Almost as lovely as the clothes' owner would have looked. But by the time I got out of the shower, she was already in my outfit and "It would take too long to change, so couldn't I just wear something else?")

And to add insult to injury, my mother didn't pack any makeup because "Yours always looks so nice. You can just do mine." You may have birthed me, but that doesn't mean I want to share a mascara wand with you. That's how you get pinkeye.

Blah blah blah, the shower was lovely and all, even if I looked like someone pieced me together from Goodwill.

And even bigger shocker—you know how my future sister-in-law doesn't speak? I may have solved the mystery because her mother NEVER STOPS. Oh my. I felt like she was taking a medical history and worried that I was going to have to provide a urine sample. Maybe future sister-in-law never got a chance to speak growing up and doesn't know how?

Gotta go, though—I'm extremely worried that if I take my eyes off my toothbrush, one of them will use that next.

To be fair, my mother had forgotten her makeup and was in hysterics, so I offered my services. And Amy had *always* stolen my clothes, so I was entirely prepared with an equally cute backup outfit, knowing she would take one of mine rather than wear her own clothes.

Madison was really happy that we made the effort to come to the shower—granted, we heard that through Jake, who wrapped me in a bear hug before giving me shit about taking time out of my busy schedule to do something for my family, and through her mother, who knew a shocking amount about me before I opened my mouth in an attempt to get a word in edgewise. Apparently Jake talked about me with some frequency, which made me feel like a jerk—I wasn't sure some of my friends even knew his name.

But the whole truth didn't play as well, and I felt like taking some creative license.

The blog was slowly picking up steam, thanks to my efforts at networking. I was up to fifty-eight followers and usually added one or two with each post now. But more importantly, I was excited about writing for the first time since college, when I was on the campus newspaper staff. The only writing I had done since then was for the foundation, and it was refreshing to write something that I so thoroughly enjoyed. And strangers on the internet were appreciating what I was writing, too, which was quite the ego boost.

Unfortunately, having an audience also wiped away any sense of decency that I had in mocking others. But, as I rationalized it to myself, with fifty-eight followers, the odds of the guilty parties ever seeing what I wrote about them were miniscule at best. And maybe if they weren't being so toxic, I wouldn't have written about them in the first place.

Plus the flat iron really was a point of contention. Amy swore she turned it off, yet it somehow stopped working between her using it before the bridal shower and that evening when I tried to touch up my hair before dinner. To stop the bickering, my mother finally snapped at us, "If it's that big of a deal, I'll buy you a new flat iron! Why can't you two get along?"

Going to kill them, I texted Megan from the bed I was sharing with Amy after we shut out the light.

She didn't reply. That was happening more and more frequently these days. Was it wedding stress or living with Tim or just us growing apart? I didn't know.

Thank God for Alex. I copied my text to Megan and sent it to him.

Chicago is a good place for that, he said. What'd they do? I explained the clothes and flat iron debacles. Why didn't you just say no?

I rolled my eyes. Doesn't make a difference when I do.

Have you actually tried it? Or if they say to bring your flat iron so they don't have to bring theirs, just don't bring one.

Isn't that totally passive-aggressive?

Says the girl who told me there's always money to passive-aggressively troll someone? No, if you actually say the word "no" to them and then follow through, that's the exact opposite of passive-aggressive.

But it's my mom and sister.

Even better. They need tough love from someone who actually loves them.

Do I though?

Yes. Now go to bed and don't add to Chicago's murder stats.

Okay, okay. Good night.

"Who are you texting?" Amy whispered over our mother's snores.

"A friend."

"You smile like that for all your friends?"

"Yes," I said defensively, setting my phone down.

"Oka-ay," she murmured.

I waited a moment, listening to our mother's half starts and then resumptions of the noise she was making.

"How are we going to sleep over that?"

"Right? How does *Dad* sleep every night?"

"He must be used to it by now."

"Thank God Tyler doesn't snore."

We didn't speak for another minute or two, and I thought about what Alex had said. "Hey Ames?"

"Yeah?"

"Can you please ask before you take my clothes? I don't actually mind lending you stuff if you ask first. But today sucked."

"I'm sorry," she whispered, surprising me. "I was just trying your outfit on and then Mom said it was so much better than what I brought. I didn't think you'd mind."

I seldom saw my mother critique Amy in the same way she did me, but I thought back to my dad's comment that she was hard on Amy in different ways. And I wondered if Amy saw how often she did it to me, or if we both thought we were the only one. *How much of the tension between us is because of her?*

And was she just doing what she had learned as a kid? My mother and her sister competed over absolutely everything. And my cousin, who was six months younger than me, was married, with her second baby on the way, which was probably part of why my mom was so upset that I was still single. It meant Anna was winning the Joan and Anna battle royale for sibling superiority. But Anna's youngest was still single, so Amy's impending wedding gave my mother a leg up, hence the current favoritism—at least as I saw it.

I wondered if it was something genetic and if I was destined to do the same thing to my eventual kids. My grandmother, as accepting as she was of me, picked my mother apart pretty regularly. And while my mother said she had learned to ignore her, I had seen her change her hairstyle after a comment from my grandma. Or remove an outfit from circulation entirely.

Maybe none of us had it easy.

But maybe being more aware of how we treated each other could help break the cycle.

"Thanks," I told her, and I reached across the queen bed and squeezed her arm.

My last thought as I rolled over to go to sleep was to be relieved I hadn't kissed Alex at his company benefit. I needed him too much.

CHAPTER TWENTY-SIX

The morning of Caryn's shower was the first, and only, time I ever mentally thanked Caroline for anything. Because of the shower's start time, I got to sleep gloriously late and wake up with a luxurious stretch and birds bringing me my breakfast.

Okay, maybe not the birds.

But I did sleep in and drink a cup of coffee out on the balcony, the first time it had been nice enough to do that all year. In the DC area, you tend to get about three days of true spring between winter, second winter, fake summer, monsoon season, third winter, and then swampy summer. And because it was shaping up to be one of the few true spring days, I used my free time to go for a run.

By the time I had eaten a light lunch and cleaned myself up, I felt ready to conquer the bridal shower, wicked bridesmaids of the west and all. I put on my first-ever piece of Lilly Pulitzer clothing (okay, so it was bought secondhand off Poshmark and was a few years old, but I couldn't afford a new one and this was the only time I would ever actually wear it) and a pair of wedges and set off for the country club with my professionally wrapped gift in tow. I was even early—I knew Caroline was lying about not needing help setting up.

I gave my hair a last brush and touched up my lipstick before I handed the valet my keys and walked confidently inside.

A quick check of my watch told me it was two thirty, but there was already a sign in the lobby pointing to the Donaldson-Greene Bridal Shower. *Perfect,* I thought, bypassing the front desk.

The gift blocked much of my view. I had gone with a registry vase that was just barely out of my price range, and the box was enormous, especially festooned with the multiple bows and spiraling ribbons that belied a talent far beyond my wrapping abilities.

I pushed through the glass-paneled door into the room where the shower would be held and stopped cold.

Busboys buzzed around the room, piling half-empty glasses and plates into bins, throwing away discarded napkins and wrapping paper, and pulling down decorations.

Setting the gift down, I checked my watch. Then I pulled out my phone and checked the time against that. Both read the same: 2:32.

They must be cleaning up from an earlier shower, I thought. *I'm still early.*

But there were bags of personalized cookies on the table closest to me, and I could see, even from the doorway, that they said "Caryn" against a pale-green background for a play on her new last name.

I felt sick.

How could I have messed this up? I did literally nothing all day and actually *bought* a dress to fit in. I knew that missing the bachelorette weekend upset Caryn, so it was incredibly important to me that I not make waves for her shower. Hot tears pricked at my eyes as I picked up the present and left the room. In the hall, I set it down again and pulled my phone back out, searching my emails for the one from Caroline that said the time.

I found it—3:00 p.m. I reread it, noticing suddenly that it had gone only to me, not to all of the other bridesmaids. And I realized, with a sense of foreboding, that that omission wasn't because the other bridesmaids already knew the time.

She didn't want them to see that she had just deliberately told me the wrong time.

My hands started shaking as I considered the implications of what she had done. Caryn was never going to forgive me. Which, okay, if she knew what I had been saying about her on the internet, I could understand, but she didn't. Caroline did this to me entirely because she didn't like me and knew she could get away with it. There was no way she would own it, even if I told Caryn everything.

"You're late," a coolly amused voice said. I looked up to see Caroline smirking. "Caryn was upset."

My fists balled involuntarily. "How could you do that? Like, I expect you to do that kind of thing to *me*, but how could you do that to *her*?"

"I don't know *what* you mean." She brushed past me to go into the party room, but I grabbed her arm. "Take your hand off me!"

I dropped her arm. "I have the email! You told me it was at three!"

"Interesting. I have an email too, telling you it was at twelve." She looked me up and down. "How old is that dress anyway?"

"I'm showing her the email. I'm not letting you get away with this."

She shrugged. "I already showed her the one telling you the time. With all of your email addresses on it."

"What does that even mean? You faked an email to make me look bad? Don't you have anything else going on in your life?"

She colored slightly. "Oh, you are not even a thought in my mind. I just didn't want you showing up in your yard-sale dress and ruining Caryn's day. She doesn't need you. She has me. And we're going to be family now. You're nothing."

I just looked at her, too angry to speak. Finally, voice shaking, I said, "This isn't over."

"Oh, but it is. Besides"—a cruel smile crept across her lips—"I don't think Caryn still wants you in the wedding after this. You can go back to your tacky little life now." She walked back into the party room and started ordering the busboys around. I debated hurling the heavy crystal vase at her head, but she was the type who would sue for assault.

Shoulders slumping in defeat, I left. The wait for the valet felt interminable; I just wanted to get out of there. Eventually, he pulled my six-year-old Hyundai Elantra around the loop in front and had the grace not to mention that it was probably the least expensive car he had ever driven there.

I threw the present in the trunk and climbed in, feeling lower than I had since the morning after Megan's engagement party.

A car pulled in behind mine, so I put it into drive, barely recognizing where I was going.

When I came to a stop, I was in front of Megan's old apartment building. But Megan didn't live there anymore—she had moved to Columbia, forty-five minutes away. Muscle memory had just taken me there, craving the comfort of my best friend. I put my head down on the steering wheel and started to cry.

When my tears had slowed and my breathing calmed, I called Megan. I knew I needed to apologize to Caryn, but I didn't know how to start. Megan would know what to do.

She answered on the third ring. "What's up? Aren't you at the shower?" The background was noisy, people talking and laughing, glasses and silverware clinking.

I started to tell her what happened, but she stopped me. "Hang on, it's loud here. Let me find a quieter spot." She moved away from the noise. "Sorry, we're out with some new friends in Baltimore for drinks by the water since it's so nice out today."

I hadn't seen Megan in a couple of months. Yes, I had been busy with wedding stuff pretty often, but she hadn't invited me to her house since January. She was building a whole new life, and I wasn't in it.

"Start over. What happened?"

I gave her the short version, not wanting to keep her from her new friends and also worried she would just cut me off if I spent too long explaining.

"You have to tell her."

"But Caroline already showed her this fake email."

"So? She needs to know."

"She's not going to believe me."

"Then is she really your friend in the first place?"

Are you *anymore?* I wanted to ask. *Because I still need you and you're never there.*

"Look," she continued. "If someone was doing that in *my* wedding, I would want to know."

"Yeah."

"I know that 'yeah.' You're not going to tell her, are you?"

"It's not going to help. She's already mad at me for not going to the bachelorette party and not paying my share."

"Then she's being unreasonable. You have your brother's wedding that weekend. And no one spends that kind of money on a trip they're not even *going* on."

"I think she's going to kick me out of her wedding. Caroline hinted at it."

"Is that *such* a terrible thing? Be honest."

"It'd be so awkward at work."

"Yeah, for *her*. She's got to see *you* every day if she does that, not the other way around. You've got this."

"Thanks, Megs."

"Listen, I've got to go back in. Call me later, okay?"

I said I would, but we both knew that I wouldn't because we were done talking for the day. Which wasn't how it used to be, but Megan had a new life now. And I didn't.

CHAPTER
TWENTY-SEVEN

I sat down at my computer when I got home, but the words wouldn't come. I needed to know how it turned out first. And as much of a relief as it might be to not be in the wedding anymore, especially with a keratin treatment and fake eyelashes still on the docket of things that I had to sit through (and pay for), I wasn't ready to write Caryn off as a friend.

However awful she had been these past months, it didn't cancel out the seven previous years of friendship. She had kept me sane at work when I was bored silly by the content of the press releases. Touched up my hair and makeup when I went on television. Helped me prepare for interviews with the press by going over questions they were likely to ask. Commiserated when I had to deal with scientists who lacked even basic social skills. If our friendship was the sum of its parts, yes, her behavior since gaining that diamond on her left hand had detracted from the overall equation, but we were still very much in the positive column.

I bit the inside of my lip and called her. When she didn't answer, I left a voicemail saying that I was so sorry and to please call me.

She didn't.

~

When I woke up Monday morning and saw I had neither a call nor a text from her, I felt a twinge of annoyance. What if I had been in a car accident and was lying in a hospital bed and *that* was why I had missed her shower? She really wasn't going to call me back to find out what happened?

By the time I got on the Metro, that annoyance had morphed into dread. She was *really* mad if she didn't even care if I was dying in a hospital bed. And I didn't know what to do—should I tell her what Caroline did and risk her not believing me? Or just act like, *Oh no! Ditzy Lily screwed something up again! Please don't hate me?*

Maybe I should just quit instead of facing her again. No, I wasn't making real money off the blog, but there had to be *some* other writing job that would pay the bills. I didn't *like* my job anyway, I rationalized to myself. So maybe if I just didn't go back, I could find something that I actually enjoyed doing and it wouldn't have to be about never seeing her again.

Just get there, I told myself. *Take your cues from her.*

Morning, Alex texted me just before I got to Starbucks. When he asked about the shower the previous night, I hadn't gone into detail. Just said Caroline was a nightmare and left it at that. So he didn't know I was a wreck today.

Hey.

Left you something at Starbucks. You seemed a little down last night.

How did he know that from a couple of texts? You're the best.

I know.

I cut the line and waved to Taylor, who pointed toward the pickup counter. The weather had flip-flopped back to cold after the previous day's sunshine and warmth, so it was a hot coffee, not iced. *Seven more weeks and you'll be done with weddings. You've got this! —A* was scrawled on the sleeve.

Bolstered by the knowledge that one person was still there for me, I steeled myself to see Caryn and walked the remaining three blocks to the foundation.

She looked up, annoyed, when I came into her office. Not that her eyebrows actually rose anymore, but she looked at me expectantly nonetheless.

"Caryn, I'm so sorry."

"Yeah. You said that in your voicemail."

"I—"

"You could have at least told me you weren't coming. When you realized you screwed up."

"I didn't realize I screwed up until I got there at two thirty—"

"Caroline showed me the email *and* the text messages, Lily. You can cut the crap."

"What text messages?"

"She texted asking where you were and you said you thought it was at three."

I was stunned into silence. "And the messages were from me?" I asked quietly.

"Unless she's got another Lily Weiss in her phone who was supposed to be at my shower." She crossed her arms.

Caroline was better than I had given her credit for. She must have changed someone else's contact in her phone to say my name and gotten them to send a fake text from me. And there was a zero percent chance that Caryn was going to believe that was what happened because what kind of crazy person *does* something like that?

You've got this, Alex had said. I nodded to myself.

"We must have crossed wires at some point," I said.

"How's that?"

"I emailed her when she was talking about shower stuff and asked what time it was, and she told me three."

"She showed me the email—"

213

"There was another email. And I don't know what happened, maybe autocorrect added the one and the two for the twelve and said three but . . ." I pulled up the email on my phone and showed it to her. "And if you scroll, you can see that that was in response to my question of what time the shower was."

"So why didn't you ask, if there were two different time emails?"

"I must have missed the one that said twelve. Caryn, I'm really sorry, but it was an honest mistake." She looked unsure. "I got there at two thirty to help set up and they were already cleaning up. I was devastated. I bought a Lilly Pulitzer dress to wear to it and everything. So I'd fit in."

This finally elicited the ghost of a smile. "You? In Lilly Pulitzer?" I gestured for her to give me my phone back, and I pulled up the selfie I had taken in front of the mirror before leaving for the shower.

"Is that vintage?"

"Look, the point is I really did try and I'm so sorry that I screwed it up. I have a present for you, too, but it's too big to bring on the Metro."

"It was really awkward trying to explain to everyone why one of my bridesmaids was MIA."

"I know. I'll make it up to you, I promise. I don't know how yet, but I will."

"Will you wear the Lilly dress to work?"

"Will that make you feel better?"

She shrugged slightly. "Maybe a little. It'll be funny either way."

"Then I'll do it." I got up to leave. "Thank you for being so understanding."

"Just don't screw up the time for the actual wedding. I know you've got a lot on your plate, but I should matter too."

"Unless it's wrong on the invitation, we're good," I promised and went back to my office.

I wrote a blog about Caroline before I did any work. The fake text messages were a whole new level of psychotic. But one thing she had said kept coming back to me. She said Caryn didn't need me now because she had her. Was *that* what this whole thing was about? She just needed to be number one in Caryn's life? Was she making her brother's life miserable too? Or did she sense that Caryn had been trying to impress her for most of their lives and didn't want to lose her little minion to a less fawning friend?

After I hit "Publish," I leaned back in my chair. It was just after ten thirty and I hadn't done anything remotely productive. Who had time to work with all of this pettiness? But before I dug into my work emails, I texted Alex. Thanks for the coffee. Drinks after work? You won't BELIEVE the story I have for you.

CHAPTER TWENTY-EIGHT

Not that I had time to dwell on Caroline's backstabbing. As much as she claimed she wasn't thinking about me, I truly didn't have time to waste on her after I got it out of my system by blogging. Jake and Madison's wedding was the following weekend and I needed to get ready for Mexico.

I was briefly jealous of my parents, who were spending four days there before the wedding and three days after—they were getting an actual vacation. I, on the other hand, would fly down on Friday, go to the wedding on Saturday, and then go home on Sunday. According to Amy, I wouldn't even have time to lie by the pool while a bronzed cabana boy brought me drinks.

"You should stay a few more days," she said. "Tyler and I are making it a mini pre-honeymoon."

"Didn't you already get one of those when you went to check out the resort with Jake?"

She shrugged. "I mean, Mom and Dad are paying, so I wasn't going to say no. Plus I can get a little color, so the yellow dress won't be as bad."

My mouth dropped open. They had said they would pay for my trip *if* I brought Grandma. Amy was getting a free vacation with her fiancé and didn't have to do anything but show up and not get sunburned before her wedding?

Sputtering with the unfairness of it, I called my mother.

"You should have told us you wanted to stay longer," she said. "I don't think your grandma would mind, but I thought you would need to get back to work. Amy's job isn't exactly essential."

"Well, I want to stay longer."

"It's too late now. The flights and hotel rooms have already been booked."

I spent the day fuming at my mother and sister, then did my best to shrug it off. I was still getting a free trip to Mexico after all. And if nothing else, my grandmother would provide fabulous blog material.

~

"This is stupid," Grandma grumbled as she opened her door for me. "I don't need a babysitter."

"I'm not your babysitter," I said good-naturedly. "I'm just your travel buddy today."

"I don't need a travel buddy."

"Well you've got one. And I'm your eldest grandchild, so how about we just enjoy the time together."

"Don't patronize me, Joan."

"Lily."

"I know your name, Joan."

"It's Lily, but okay. Do you have everything packed?"

"Of course I do. I'm not a child!"

"Do you have your passport?"

"What do I need a passport for?" This was going to be a long day.

"You need one for Mexico," I said measuredly. "Do you have a valid one?"

"I've never needed a passport to go to Mexico in my life."

"Have you ever been to Mexico?"

"No."

I discreetly pulled my phone out and texted my mother, who was already in Mexico. Mom, she doesn't have a passport.

"Okay, but do you *have* a passport?" I asked my grandmother again.

"What do I need a passport for?"

My phone dinged back. It's upstairs, in her top right dresser drawer. I took her to get it renewed myself.

"Mom said it's in your top dresser drawer. Do you want me to go get it?"

"It's already in my purse. Why are you being so dramatic, Joan?"

I bit the inside of my bottom lip. I was being underpaid, apparently. But the abundance of free booze once we got there would be a welcome reprieve.

"Great," I said with false cheerfulness. "I'll just put your suitcase in the car and we'll be on our way."

I figured an Uber would be the best way to get to the airport because the driver could drop us right at the terminal and I could put my grandmother directly into a wheelchair, so that was how I had gotten to her house as well.

"Where's your car? Who's driving?"

"This is an Uber. It's like a taxi."

"Oh. But we can't leave yet."

"Why not?"

"Ken and Louise are coming with us." Louise had been my grandmother's best friend since my mother was a baby. Ken was her second husband, and he had been pals with my grandfather before he passed. While I had known them my whole life, I hadn't realized they were invited to the wedding, let alone coming with us.

"Since when?"

"I told them we could give them a ride to the airport."

I looked at the Uber, which was a CR-V. It would probably hold all of the luggage, but we would be extremely squished in the backseat. "Did you think maybe you should have let me know that?"

She shrugged. *My Uber rating is about to drop off the charts,* I thought despairingly. I went to the driver's window and tried to explain the situation. She couldn't have been nicer, but she also didn't fully understand what kind of craziness was about to occur in her car.

Ken's Cadillac careened into view and came to a crooked stop on the street outside my grandmother's house. "Hello, Lily," Louise waved cheerfully. "Who's ready to go to Mexico?" She pulled a rainbow-colored sombrero out of the backseat and put it on her head.

My eyes widened. *Holy hell. My blog readers are never, ever going to believe this is real.*

We crammed the luggage into the trunk and Ken sat in the front seat. As the youngest member of our traveling party, I was wedged into the backseat between my grandmother and Louise, who proceeded to grill our Uber driver about her family, education, marital status, and why she didn't yet have children. We would have to take a taxi back home because there was no chance any Uber driver would ever pick me up again.

I texted my father this time. In the Uber on the way to the airport. She told Ken and Louise they could come with us.

My father sent back a face-palm emoji. At least they'll keep her distracted on the plane. I'll have a drink waiting for you when you get here.

My phone dinged again. Have a great trip, Alex wrote.

I am in hell. I know I deserve it, but oh dear God.

What's wrong?

I explained the situation and he replied with crying-laughing emojis. Please get a picture of the sombrero. Will she let you take a selfie in it? It was on Louise's lap, which meant it was half on mine, so I snapped a surreptitious picture of it. Not that it mattered. Louise was deep in conversation with the Uber driver about her hysterectomy.

When we eventually arrived at the airport, I helped everyone get their bags out of the car and then went back to the Uber driver. "I am so, so sorry about this."

"You're lucky you still have your grandma," she said. "She was nice."

I wasn't sure she meant the same woman that I knew, but I thanked her anyway.

We got my grandmother to her pre-reserved wheelchair inside the terminal, and I was pleased to find that it came with a porter to push her. "This is silly," she told the porter. "I can walk just fine."

"Happy to do it, ma'am," he said.

"Here, Evelyn, will you hold my sombrero since you're in the chair?"

"Why don't you just wear it?" my grandmother asked Louise.

"Inside?"

"It's vacation!"

"True," she said, putting it on. "We'll have to get you one down there too."

"Where's Ken's?"

"He's so vain about his hair, he won't wear it."

I looked at Ken's thin, gray hair. But at least he still had hair, which was worth showing off at his age.

"Let's get our bags checked and go through security, then you two can worry about hats." I guided them toward the check-in desk.

Checking the bags was easy. Security was a different matter. "What's taking so long?" my grandmother asked.

"You have to take off your shoes and take all of the liquids out of your bag," I explained. "It means security takes longer."

"I'm not taking off my shoes."

"Everyone does. It's the law now."

"Since when?"

I outlined the brief history of terrorism to my grandmother and her friends, who apparently were last frequent fliers in the 1960s. I prayed none of them tried to smoke on the airplane.

"I have to take off my shoes because they think I have a bomb?"

"Shh, Grandma, you're not supposed to say 'bomb' at the airport."

"Now I know you're making this up, Joan. I'll prove it to you. Bomb bomb bomb bomb bomb!" She looked at me defiantly. "What are they going to do? Arrest me?"

"Yes," I said through gritted teeth. "They are. So please just stop."

"You're so serious." She turned to Louise. "How did I wind up with such a serious grandchild?"

"I couldn't tell you," Louise said mildly. "But my Billy is the same way." "Her Billy" was a thirty-eight-year-old proctologist who had gone by William since he was nine.

Louise and Ken removed their shoes when it was time. My grandmother didn't. And because she was in a wheelchair, no one said a word. She smirked at me triumphantly. I just shook my head and went to get a gigantic coffee as soon as I had deposited the three of them at our gate.

We had almost an hour left until takeoff. Armed with enough caffeine to face the elderly again, I started drafting a blog post from my phone.

This is gold, I thought as I typed. *Everyone will think it's fiction, but damn, it's good material.*

I proofread quickly and posted it, just before they started preboarding.

My father was right about the benefits of having Ken and Louise on the plane. The three of them sat in a row together, leaving me twenty-two glorious inches of aisle freedom. And because none of them would willingly wear their hearing aids or admit that they couldn't hear without them, conversation across that great divide proved futile.

I put in my earphones, pulled out my Kindle, and for the first time in weeks felt myself begin to relax.

~

When the time came to fill out the paperwork for entering Mexico, I leaned across the aisle and told my grandmother I would fill hers out for her. "Thank you, Joanie," she said. "Your grandfather always did that."

"No problem, Grandma." I had given up correcting her on my name. I filled in the necessary information, and as soon as we had landed, I turned airplane mode off on my phone.

It took a minute to connect to the Mexican LTE signal. When it finally did, I began downloading my emails. There were thirty-two of them to my personal account.

Oh God, I thought. *What fresh hell is going on with the wicked bridesmaids of the west now?*

But none of them were about Caryn's shower or bachelorette party. Instead there were seventeen likes on the blog post, and nine comments and six new followers on my blog.

I felt a rush of nervous excitement. The highest number of comments I had gotten on a post so far was four, and that had taken almost two weeks to accomplish. I scrolled through.

"Hysterical!"

"Oh my God, please update this with more."

"Is this for real? Which airport just let her through security like that?"

"Can your grandma be my friend? I want to be exactly like her."

"Why do I need a passport? Classic!"

And so on.

I checked the blog stats and saw a lot of the new traffic was coming from social media sites, which meant people had started sharing it with their friends. I smiled broadly as another email came in.

Not that I could bask in that glory for long, because getting my grandmother and her friends through customs proved challenging, as Ken and Louise were stopped for discrepancies on their customs forms.

"Here," Louise said to my grandmother. "Just take my purse through for me. I'll be out in a minute."

We're going to Mexican prison, I thought, handing Louise back her bag.

"What's wrong with you?" my grandmother asked. "I carry stuff for other people all the time."

"Through customs?"

"Sure."

I pressed my fingers to my temples to fight the emerging stress headache and then pushed her wheelchair to the other side to wait. *Hopefully the resort has massages. I'll charge it to the room. My parents owe me.*

~

"That's a mistake," I told the man at the front desk. "We have two separate rooms."

He checked his computer screen again, and then gestured for a woman to come over.

"What seems to be the problem?" she asked in lightly accented English.

"My grandmother and I are supposed to have separate rooms."

The woman checked the computer screen and tapped the keyboard a few times. "No," she said. "It says right here that you're booked into a junior king suite together."

"All set?" my grandmother asked, wandering back over. She already had some kind of tropical drink with six pieces of fruit stacked on a skewer and a straw with an umbrella.

"No," I said, then turned back to the woman behind the desk. "You need to fix this. We need two separate rooms."

"Oh," Grandma said. "I called the agent and said I was rooming with you."

223

"You did what?"

"Why should we pay for two rooms? It's not like you have a date." She took a sip of her drink. "If you want to bring a man back to the room, just tell me and I'll go to the pool or Ken and Louise's room for a bit." My mouth dropped open in shock. "What? We're on vacation."

"We need two rooms," I said to the desk clerk, who had the good sense to wipe the look of enjoyment off her face.

"Everything is booked, I'm afraid. We have eight weddings and three anniversary parties this weekend."

My grandmother smiled at me. "Hi, roomie."

Well, dear readers, I have hit rock bottom. I am no longer dateless at my younger brother's tropical destination wedding. Instead, my date is my eighty-eight-year-old grandmother, who cancelled her reservation for a separate room without telling me.

As I write this, she is sitting naked in a heart-shaped hot tub in our room, drinking some kind of daiquiri (her third!), and watching a telenovela with English subtitles. I was called a prude for asking if she could please put her bathing suit on. The room has a single king-size bed and a foldout sofa, which she told me I was a fool for planning to sleep on instead of sharing the bed with her because it would destroy my back. And by the way, she sleeps in the nude too.

Sofa bed it is.

And because it wouldn't truly be rock bottom without the implication of my promiscuity in front of random strangers, she told me at the reception desk to just let her know (Via sock on the door, maybe? Apparently my grandmother is cooler than I am too. Another dagger to the heart!) if I wanted to bring a gentleman caller back to the room for a visit and she would make herself scarce. Which brings me to my next greatest fear: that I will return from the rehearsal dinner tonight to one of her compression socks on the door.

At which point will all of Mexico's great tequila wash that vision from my eyes?

Stay tuned. I'm sure saying "I've hit rock bottom" is the same as saying, "I'll be right back" in a horror movie and something inherently worse is about to happen.

"Joan!" my grandmother called to me from the hot tub. I had taken my laptop out to the balcony to write a new post as soon as she began stripping to climb into the tub. "Can you call room service? I need another dirty monkey."

She's requesting another drink, I wrote. So I have to sign off. Wish me luck!

I hit "Publish," then told her I would.

Ah, so your grandma has reached the stage of life where she doesn't give a fuck, Alex texted when I told him what was going on.

Less than zero fucks given. But she told me to just let her know if I want to bring a guy back and she'll go hang out by the pool.

He replied with three crying-laughing emojis.

I should have just lied and said you and I were together so I wouldn't have to come to this alone, I said.

The three dots appeared to show he was typing, then they disappeared. The delay was long enough that I wondered if I shouldn't have said that. The connotation of us sharing a room in Mexico could have been less than platonic, after all.

Next time, he finally wrote.

Next time one of my siblings gets married in Mexico?

Yeah.

You're so helpful right now.

He replied with a winking face, which seemed to end the conversation. If I misspoke, I misspoke. I couldn't deal with more drama, not with the rehearsal dinner that night and wedding the next day.

CHAPTER
TWENTY-NINE

I yawned as the stylist curled my hair around the wand. My mother apparently inherited her tendency to snore from her mother, and the snores had continued until five, when my grandmother woke to do her "calisthenics," which as far as I could tell consisted of her standing on the balcony in a bathrobe and drinking a cup of black coffee that she brewed next to my head on the pullout sofa. Not the restful night's sleep at an all-inclusive resort in Mexico that I had envisioned, but I was glad she had put on the robe.

And at least they had a real coffee bar at the resort. It wasn't Starbucks, but it *was* an iced latte with vanilla. I took another sip and wondered if room service delivered refills to the resort's salon as well.

I had hardly even seen the bride. She said a quick hello at the rehearsal dinner the night before, but that was it. She seemed a bit more effusive with her family and friends, but I only witnessed that from afar.

She looked really happy, though, across the salon, as a makeup artist shellacked her final product into place. Truly, genuinely happy. You watch all of these movies and TV shows where the bride is nervous or crying before her wedding and you forget that this look of pure happiness is how it's supposed to be. *I should use that,* I thought, pulling out my phone.

I opened the WordPress app to start a new post, then paused. I had a hundred and seventeen notifications.

That couldn't be right. I clicked over to the notifications tab—thirty-nine likes on the post from the previous day about my grandmother, forty-two on the one about sharing a room with her, nineteen new followers to my blog, and seventeen comments.

Excitement prickled along my spine as I scrolled through the comments.

"This is fake, right?"

"It's like a train wreck and I can't look away."

"Girl! Your grandma is gonna kill you if she reads this!" (I'll admit, that one gave me pause. Then again, my grandmother's grasp of the internet was tenuous at best—she thought it was called "the Google." And I couldn't see her trolling wedding blogs in her spare time.)

"You seriously say everything I wish I could about being in a wedding."

"LMAOOOOOOO."

"If you come home to a sock on that door, I'm going to die."

"What happens to grandma in Mexico stays in Mexico . . ."

"Yaaaaas girl, keep that snark coming!"

"Imma sit right here and wait to see what granny does next." With a GIF of Michael Jackson eating popcorn.

I realized I was grinning broadly and looked around surreptitiously to make sure no one had noticed. The only one looking at me was my grandmother, and her eyes narrowed as she pursed her lips. I felt a wave of guilt. Did she know somehow? Had she gone through my phone while I was in the shower?

She sipped more of her mimosa, and I laughed off the thought. My grandmother's iPhone was the last one in existence without a passcode because she had locked her previous phone for 556 days trying to figure it out. There was no way she had gotten into mine.

Another notification came in, and I smiled again, clicking over to the new post tab.

You forget that a wedding is actually about being happy, I started, then stopped. I had followers now. People who would get notifications when I posted something. Would they stick around if I wrote a sweet post? No way. They came for the snark, and it was my job to deliver.

I glanced back at Madison. Her makeup done, she had come to sit next to my grandmother, saying something that looked ridiculously genuine. But was there anything to say about Madison that was snarky? She was . . . sweet. Not simperingly, sickeningly so, but just a nice Midwestern girl without an ounce of my sardonic humor.

I couldn't annihilate her on the internet.

But the blog wasn't really about the brides. It was about me and my experiences in their weddings. They were supporting cast at best. I hadn't realized that before, and it was empowering because it was the first thing all year that had been about me, not them.

I was still thinking about what I would write when they called me to get my makeup done. And by the time I was finished, we had to do photos and then go to the wedding itself, so I was out of time. *I can sneak away for a little during the reception,* I thought. After I walked down the aisle in my yellow dress, my job was done until it was time to get my grandma on the plane back home. And Ken and Louise, apparently, as they would be on our return flight and sharing our Uber back to my grandmother's house as well.

I felt a twinge of legitimate envy watching the ceremony. Jake was grinning ear to ear while he waited for Madison to come down the aisle, and I was close enough to hear him tell her that she was "so beautiful" when she reached him. He held her hand through the ceremony, and I saw my mother crying unabashedly during their vows, when he promised to love her unconditionally for the rest of their lives.

My mother had never shed tears of joy over me. Of anxiety, irritation, and anger? Sure. But joyous tears? And the way Jake and Madison looked at each other—they could have been the only ones there. No one had ever looked at me like that. Here I was, five years older than Jake, and he had found this level of happiness that I didn't think I was capable of. What was wrong with me?

Then it was over. Jake stomped on a cloth-wrapped glass, despite having an otherwise nondenominational ceremony, everyone cheered, and it was time for more pictures, then the cocktail hour.

I got a glass of champagne and set it on a table to check my phone for more notifications. There were twelve. I was reading the comments when my grandmother sidled up to me, another slushy, tropical drink in her hand.

"Who's the fella?"

I looked up in shock. I hadn't seen her coming and had no idea what she was talking about. "What?"

"I saw you smiling at that phone. So who is he?"

"No one."

She poked me in the ribs with a bony finger. "Don't you lie to me, Joanie. I've known you your whole life."

"Lily, Grandma. And no guy. I was just reading something—funny."

She gave me a sly look that told me she didn't believe a word I said. "Don't drag me all the way to a foreign country for your wedding, please. I'm too old and it's too hot."

I sighed. "I promise, I'm not getting married. Probably ever, at this rate."

"Is it a girl then?" My mouth dropped open. "What? It's legal now. No one said you had to marry a boy."

"Grandma!"

"Just promise me it'll be closer to home."

I closed my eyes and counted to ten. "Okay. First of all, I'm straight. Second, I'm single. Third, I have zero marital prospects on the horizon."

She shook her head and made a tsk-tsk noise. "We'll fix that, Joan," she said, patting my arm reassuringly. Then she called to Louise and made her way to her friend as fast as her bad hip would allow.

That woman is going to be the death of me, I thought, drinking the rest of my champagne and going back to my phone.

Jake and Madison had a sweetheart table, so I was seated with Amy, Tyler, my parents, my grandmother, and my aunt and uncle for the meal and toasts, which felt agonizingly slow. I just wanted to find a place to camp out and write a post about what my grandmother had just said, but with my mother's eyes on me every time I pulled out my phone, that was proving difficult.

I felt a buzz while Madison's sister was giving her maid of honor speech, and I glanced down at my phone next to my leg on the seat.

How drunk is Grandma? Alex asked.

She asked me if I was a lesbian and said she was cool with it as long as my wedding is in a cooler climate and closer to home.

He sent laughing emojis. How's the wedding otherwise?

Well . . . I look like Big Bird in my dress, but my brother seems really happy. So a success?

And no Justin, so it's already a step up from Tim and Megan's, right?

Depends if there's an old lady knee-high on the doorknob when I get back to my room tonight.

Keep me posted. He sent a GIF of the scene from *Grease* with the guys saying, "Tell me more, tell me more."

You are such a nerd, you know that?

Did you laugh?

Well, yeah.

Then who's the real nerd?

My mother elbowed me. People were clapping and I was still on my phone. "Sorry," I whispered.

"It's your brother's wedding. Put the phone away," she hissed out of the side of her mouth. I slipped it under my leg.

After what felt like an eternity, the dancing began. My parents were on the dance floor, as were Amy and Tyler, and my grandmother had left the table, so I felt safe to start typing a post.

I was mulling over where to begin when my grandmother appeared in front of me, holding the arm of a handsome man.

Oh God. It's happening, I thought in horror, looking up at the guy. *What could possibly be in this for him? He's my age at most! What a creep!*

"I have a present for you," she said, grinning. "This is Andrew, and he's single."

I looked at her in alarm. "Grandma!"

She ignored me. "Andrew, darling, this is my granddaughter Lily."

"Hey," he said amiably. He looked vaguely familiar, which hopefully did not mean he was a second cousin. And she got my name right for once.

"I'll leave you two to get better acquainted," my grandmother said with a wink. "And remember, just let me know if you need the room tonight!"

I wanted to crawl under my chair.

"Would you like to dance?" Andrew asked.

I had less than no desire to dance with some random dude at my brother's wedding. Especially with some random dude whom my grandmother had coerced into asking me. But she was standing about four feet from us, nodding and making a shooing motion with her hands. And saying yes to one dance would (hopefully) get her to drop the subject and therefore help me survive until we got home the following evening.

"Uh, sure," I said, dropping my phone into my purse.

We got to the dance floor and Andrew put his arm around my waist. "So are you friends with Jake?" I asked.

He gave me a funny look. "You don't remember me?"

I looked at him more carefully. "Should I?"

"I'm crushed," he said, smiling. "I was so in love with you."

I shook my head. "I'm sorry, I—"

"Andrew MacKenzie?"

My eyes widened. "*Andy* MacKenzie?"

He shrugged. "It's Andrew now. But you can call me Andy if you want."

I used to babysit for him when I was fourteen and he was eight. Meaning he was now—I did the math quickly in my head—twenty-six. And I had been his babysitter. Nope. Absolutely not. I dropped his hand and backed away a step.

"What's wrong?"

"I'm sorry. Too weird for me."

"What is?"

I gestured to the space between us. "This."

"Dancing?"

"My grandma—trying to set me up with someone I babysat for."

"That was almost twenty years ago. We're both adults now."

"Look, Andy, I'm sure you're great and all. But no amount of adult erases that. I could be eighty-six and you could be eighty and it'd still be gross."

He shrugged again. "Your loss. Your grandma made you sound pretty desperate."

"Okay," I said. "Thanks. Bye. Have a nice life." I dashed back to the table, snatched up my purse, and ran out of the terraced area where the party was.

I found a set of cushioned wicker sofas encircling an empty firepit just around the corner and collapsed onto one, both grossed out and hurt that he had called me desperate.

I hated everyone at that stupid wedding. I hated Jake and Madison for making me come here, where I was forced to share a room with my grandmother and then exposed to ridicule like this. I didn't stop mattering just because I was thirty-two and single and they were younger and getting married.

233

I pulled my phone out, and I didn't hold back. When I was done, I didn't even proofread it, I just hit "Publish," then closed my eyes to regain my composure. The blog was cathartic that way. By the time I published it, I had flushed most of the anger and shame out of my system. I would be expected to rejoin the party with a smile on my face and, having just eviscerated them anonymously on the internet, I could do that.

On my way back into the party, I stopped in the bathroom to do a makeup touch-up. The sun had set, so the lighting was forgiving, but I didn't want to look like anything was amiss for pictures.

Madison was in there with her sister and two friends, who were giggling about having just held her dress so she could pee.

"Lily," she greeted me warmly, coming over and taking my hands in hers. I started in surprise, mixed with a little guilt. "Amy told me what happened with your room and I wanted to apologize—I had no idea about the mix-up."

I shook my head. "My grandma called the agent and told them she was rooming with me. It wasn't anyone else's fault."

"But we could have rearranged some of my friends and found a room for you. I'm sure we still can for tonight if you want?"

"That's—kind—of you. But no. She'd be offended if I did that. And it's just one more night of her snoring."

"Thank you for putting up with the inconvenience to be here. It means so much to me. And to Jake, although he'd never say it, of course."

"Of course."

"We'd love it if you'd come to Chicago to visit us sometime."

"I—uh—sure. After all these weddings. Maybe."

Madison's mother walked into the bathroom, looking for her, and told her that one of her uncles wanted to dance with her. Madison excused herself and her friends went with her, leaving me alone in the bathroom, where I gripped the sink and stared at myself in the mirror.

She's nice, I thought. And at least I hadn't trashed her specifically in the blog. Mostly because I had absolutely nothing to say about her. But I still felt guilty. Here she was inviting me to come visit her, when I had made absolutely no effort to get to know her. What was wrong with me?

I left the bathroom and grabbed another glass of champagne, which I promptly downed.

~

I woke up in pain. My head hurt, which I assumed was the champagne, but so did my arms, shoulders, and neck.

"Good morning," my grandmother said, observing me from the room's chaise lounge, a glass of orange juice in her hand. I cringed and sat up, rubbing my forehead.

"Everything hurts."

"I should say so. That's quite a sunburn you got."

I looked down at my arms in alarm. They were bright red, with pale stripes where my dress had been. It hadn't occurred to me to put sunscreen on for the ceremony, which was outside, as were the pictures and reception. "Oh no," I said weakly, sinking back down against the pillows. "Caryn is going to murder me."

"Who's Caryn?"

"Not my girlfriend, if that's what you're asking. She's getting married in three weeks and I'm a bridesmaid in her wedding and she was very clear about no tan lines."

"I don't think that's within her control anymore," my grandmother said wryly. She held out her glass to offer me a sip. "Hair of the dog?"

Apparently it wasn't just orange juice in her cup. I shook my head, which I instantly regretted, and hoped a little booze would make her more docile for the trip home, rather than more belligerent. Then I went to take a very cool shower.

~

I read through the latest notifications on my blog over breakfast. There were a lot of them. I was finally picking up some steam and would hopefully be generating some revenue from it too. One person even commented that I should be writing a book. *Well, that's an idea,* I thought. Not now, of course. But someday. Maybe.

I looked around the table at my family. Everyone looked as queasy as I did, and mine was far from the only sunburn. Amy burst into tears when my grandmother told her she looked like a lobster.

"What are you so upset about? You have more than a month until your wedding. You won't be burned by then," my grandmother said, throwing up her hands as my mother comforted Amy. She turned to me. "This is why you're so much more fun, Joan. You can take a joke."

My father caught my eye, clearly holding in a laugh. "Yeah, Joan," he said, chuckling.

I glared at him over my coffee, then went back to my phone.

Alex texted me while I was reading comments. So? Sock or no sock?

No sock. But she tried to fix me up with a kid I BABYSAT for.

Nice. Did it work?

I responded with a puking emoji.

Guess that's a no then. What time do you get home today?

Five.

Wanna grab a drink to decompress?

No more drinks! I sent the emoji with the girl holding her arms across her face in an X shape.

He sent a laughing emoji. Oh, all-inclusive resorts. You've claimed another victim.

Dinner instead? I have no food at my apartment.

Sure. Text me when you land.

236

CHAPTER THIRTY

With Jake and Madison's wedding done, I entered the homestretch of the final six weeks until Megan's wedding.

The next event was Megan's bridal shower and bachelorette party on the Saturday after Jake's wedding. My sunburn began to fade to tan, and I spent an inordinate amount of time googling natural-looking self-tanners to fill in the white spots before Caryn's wedding. I couldn't afford another screwup there.

The shower went smoothly. I arrived two hours early to help set everything up with the rest of the bridesmaids, and the weather cooperated enough to allow us to congregate on the patio by the newly opened pool. I wore carefully applied SPF 70 on my tanned areas and nothing on the white lines to try to even everything out naturally.

"What's this?" Megan asked when she got to my gift. Claire and her husband had bought a present together, and the rest of the bridesmaids chipped in to buy from the registry, but I had done my own thing.

"Open it," I told her.

It was a giant basket filled with mementos of our years of friendship, but designed to help her transition to the next stage of her life. I gave her framed pictures, along with matching empty frames to be filled with pictures from the wedding. A mug with a picture of the two of us together on it with the text "Sisters before Misters." Three wineglasses, labeled "Mr.," "Mrs.," and "Third Wheel." And finally, at the bottom of the basket, a gift-wrapped Snoopy lunch box—the clone of hers from second grade—that I bought off eBay. I had tied a gift tag to the handle and written on it, *For an eventual daughter, when she needs to find a lifelong best friend.*

Megan cried and enveloped me in a huge hug, making all of the drama feel insignificant.

~

Megan's bachelorette party was that night, concurrent with Tim's bachelor party. We were going out to dinner and then dancing. The bachelor party, according to Megan, was just poker night with the boys.

Alex had told a different story over dinner when I got back from Mexico, however. Tim hadn't lied to Megan; he thought poker night was the plan. Except no one was actually going to Mark's house for poker—they were going to a strip club in Baltimore.

"Gross."

Alex shrugged. "It's what you do."

"Okay, but now that I know, what do I tell Megan?"

"You can't tell her."

"You're putting me in a bad spot. Plus I have no filter when I'm drinking."

"You don't really have one when you're sober."

"Thanks."

"Just don't say anything. She won't ask you if you know different."

"And if she does?"

"If she does, it's up to you. Just don't bring it up. Please."

Armed with that knowledge, I texted Alex when my Uber pulled up at the restaurant. Be good tonight.

Who me? he asked, followed by the halo emoji.

You AND Tim please.

Will do. You be good too.

I rolled my eyes. I planned to stay relatively sober. *Not my night,* I reminded myself as I stepped out of the car.

Yeah, yeah, yeah, I replied. Heading into dinner now. Have fun. Just not TOO much!

You too.

Dinner was a little strained, because Claire very vocally resented having both parties on the same day because she had to clean between them and couldn't rest. And the bachelor party being at the same time meant that she couldn't stay out late—her husband insisted on going to the bachelor party and the au pair had been on duty all day during the shower. But at least everyone loosened up once she left to go put her daughter to bed after dinner and we got to the first club.

~

I was hot, but having fun. My hair was frizzy from the DC humidity and I was sure my makeup was a mess after three hours of dancing, but the bachelorette party seemed successful. Megan was happily drunk, but not sloppy, and I kept plying her with water to make sure she wouldn't feel too horrible in the morning.

When my phone rang shortly after midnight and Alex's name popped up on the caller ID, I laughed. "Who's drunk dialing you?" Megan asked. She grabbed my phone. "Alex!" she shouted, sliding the icon to answer it. "How's poker night? Is Tim behaving?"

My eyes widened. I really hoped there wasn't a lot of background noise wherever Alex was calling from.

"I can't hear him," she said, handing the phone back to me. "It's too loud in here."

I held the phone to my ear. "Alex?" She was right, I couldn't understand what he was saying, but his tone wasn't happy. "Hang on, let me go outside."

I made my way through the crowd and down the stairs to the street, walked a little farther to get away from the smokers, then tried again. "What's wrong?"

"I did something stupid," he said quickly.

I felt a strange sense of dread. Better him doing something stupid than Tim though. And it wasn't like I had any right to care if he hooked up with a stripper.

"What did you do?"

"I told Justin we're sleeping together."

"You did what?"

"Okay, listen, I know it sounds bad." His words were slightly slurred. "But I figured it was better than the alternative."

"What's the alternative?"

"He was bragging about how he was going to—sleep with you—at the wedding."

Had I actually been drinking, I probably would have vomited at that point.

"He—what?"

"He was telling everyone, and he was saying how bad you wanted him at the engagement party, and I just—I didn't say we were together exactly, just that we'd been hooking up for a while now. I didn't think you'd want him saying that to everyone. Or worse, actually trying to do it at the wedding."

"I mean—I don't—but wasn't there anything else you could have said?"

"It was that or punch him."

"Ha. Couldn't you do both?"

He ignored my joke. "But okay, so he didn't believe me."

"Why wouldn't he believe you?"

"Right? It's not so unbelievable. But anyway, I—the first thing I could think of as proof was our text-message chain. Like it didn't have anything bad, but it showed that we talk a lot, like every day, so I

240

showed him that and the part about being good tonight convinced him, I think, but I thought you should know."

"Thank you. Both for doing that and for telling me."

"You're not mad?"

"That Justin won't be trying to—ew, seriously, that's too gross to even say. No, I'm not mad."

"He'll probably make comments about us at the wedding though, so you needed to know."

"It's fine, I can pretend it's true."

Alex started to say something else but stopped himself.

"What?"

"Nothing," he said. "I should go back in."

"Me too. Can *I* punch him when I see him?"

I could hear the smile in his voice. "As your lawyer, I'd advise against that."

"And as my fake boyfriend?"

"Go for it."

"Great. I'll talk to you later."

"Lily?"

"Yeah."

"I really am sorry."

I rubbed my temples after hanging up. Fucking Justin. It wasn't bad enough that I hooked up with him once? He had to tell everyone I was going to do it again?

I took a deep breath and went back inside, where Megan immediately grabbed my wrist in a death grasp. "You're sleeping with Alex?" she hissed.

"What?"

"Tim just texted me that Alex told everyone that you two are, like, together. What the hell, Lily?"

I peeled her fingers off my wrist and rubbed it where her nails had dug in. "I'm not sleeping with Alex. Or anyone, actually."

"Then what was he talking about? And why was Alex calling you just now?"

"We're friends. Justin was telling everyone he plans to hook up with me at the wedding, so Alex said that so he'd stop." I could tell she didn't believe me. "Honest. I'd tell you if something was going on."

She scrutinized my face a minute longer, then sighed in relief. "Good. I mean, I want you to be happy and all. But I can't deal with that drama at my wedding."

"It wouldn't be drama," I said quietly.

"No offense, Lily, but it's you. You know you can't handle anything that's actually good without sabotaging it, and Alex is one of Tim's oldest friends. He's not going anywhere just because you decide you don't like him anymore. This isn't like when we were younger and I could hate a guy just because you did."

My lower lip trembled, and I blinked rapidly to keep from crying. "I—"

"Don't get upset. I'm not trying to be mean. You just don't do relationships, so it's for the best if you aren't sleeping with my husband's friends. That's all. Come on. Let's get another drink."

I let her pull me back toward the bar, but when she rejoined the rest of her friends, I pulled out my phone and pretended to answer a text.

"I need to go," I told her.

"Because of what I said?"

"No," I lied. "Amy is having an emergency about Tyler."

"Is she okay?"

"Yeah, I'm sure it'll be fine, but—I need to go."

"Okay," Megan said, pulling me in for a hug that I didn't return. "Call me tomorrow."

~

242

I made it to the sidewalk before I began crying in earnest, then I clung to a lightpost for dear life while I tried to get myself under control enough to walk to the Metro. I swallowed a huge lump and began walking, just needing to get home.

Becca wasn't at the apartment—it seemed like she never was anymore. I wished she were there. I needed someone to commiserate with, someone who understood.

I considered calling Alex back, but I didn't want to interrupt Tim's bachelor party any more than I already had, without even being there.

Megan's comment wasn't remotely fair—I had practically been a nun since her engagement party. A nun who cursed and drank, but men-wise, I had been so good. Yet enough of Megan's comment rang true to scare me. I had found something good with Alex, even if it was platonic. And calling him now would lead to his coming over, which would lead to me sabotaging everything, just because Megan hurt my feelings.

I sank onto the couch, kicked off my shoes, and curled up in the fetal position.

I'd had relationships, of course. Just nothing lasting beyond six months. Not since David, when I was twenty-four. I realized with a shudder that that had somehow been eight years ago. I was Amy's age when we were together.

I wouldn't say David broke me, because that gave him too much credit, and the reality was that he had just never been that invested. Instead, I broke myself over him. He could waltz through my door at that exact moment, and I would, without question, tell him to get out. I didn't want him anymore. I probably never actually wanted *him*. He was just so perfect on paper that I fell in love with the idea of him, not the reality. And he was such a coward in dumping me that he couldn't admit that he just didn't care. Instead it was all about how he needed to work on himself, but knew I was "the one" for him when he eventually got there. And idiot me believed him.

Three years later, Facebook told me he was married. To a blonde who resembled the rat from the Muppets and who commented on all of his posts about how funny he was. Spoiler alert: he wasn't that funny. And he had two kids now and had lost most of his hair. Not that I still Facebook-stalked him. Well, not more than once or twice a year at most.

And since then, I had just been working under the assumption that anything that seemed too good to be true, well, was.

So was Megan wrong? No. Especially considering that I met David through her. He had been her friend in college. And when we broke up, she chose me without hesitation, ending that friendship. With eight years of distance from the situation, I realized that must have been harder than it looked to me at the time.

But Megan also didn't realize that I now understood what I had done by building an effigy of David instead of looking at the real person. Or how much growth it took to sneak out of the hotel room after her engagement party instead of trying to form a meaningless relationship with Justin to validate my mistake—a relationship that I would then have to intentionally sabotage because Justin was the absolute worst.

Hell, a few months earlier, I would have definitely called Alex and asked him to come over, ostensibly to prove Megan wrong, but in reality to do exactly what she had accused me of.

Instead, I took a long shower, the water as hot as I could stand it, and got into bed. There I lay awake, staring at the ceiling, wishing I had managed a different trajectory eight years earlier instead of taking David at his word. Because Megan was wrong about one thing: I didn't sabotage relationships, I sabotaged myself. There was a big difference.

CHAPTER THIRTY-ONE

I woke up sad, but clear-headed, to an apology text from Alex.

I'm so, so sorry. It had come in around four in the morning.

I smiled grimly. At least he was sweet about it. Even if the fallout sucked. I sent a reply, figuring he had to still be asleep. So how was I last night? Since we're apparently a thing now . . .

But he replied immediately. Amazing. How was I?

You got too drunk and passed out.

Ouch. I probably deserve that one.

It's okay, we made up this morning.

Oh good. I'd hate to think we were fighting because I got too drunk. Did you?

Nah, the Justin thing sobered me up real quick. You?

My sister called me having a meltdown right after I got off with you, so I bailed early, I lied. Best to keep the story consistent since Tim apparently told Megan everything.

Hope everything's okay.

It is. I hesitated, then added more. Megan is mad at me though. Tim told her that we were sleeping together and she didn't like that.

Did you tell her the truth?

Yeah. Sucked anyway.

I'm sorry, he said again. Three dots appeared, then disappeared. Apology brunch today?

Absolutely nothing sounded better than a mimosa and some French toast with Alex. I wish. Today is salon day with the evil bridesmaids.

Gross. How long will all of that take?

Forever, apparently. Caryn said a keratin treatment takes three hours and then I can't wash my hair for three days, and the eyelashes will take about an hour too. No idea if they can do the eyelashes while my hair is getting done.

And what's the point of all this?

That was a really good question. It was the compromise I reached when I couldn't go to Caryn's bachelorette weekend extravaganza in New Orleans. And I was still meekly hiding the tan lines that I hadn't completely fixed from Mexico, so a flat-out refusal to get my hair straightened and eyelashes extended wasn't worth the drama, even if it would save me something like five hundred dollars.

On the plus side, I wouldn't have to wear fake lashes in the remaining four weddings, and my hair wouldn't frizz. There were worse beauty procedures that you could go through in DC in the summer.

Salvaging that friendship, I said eventually. And beauty of course. I sent the hair-flip emoji.

He replied with an eye-roll emoji. Try not to stab anyone with a pair of hair cutting scissors.

I grinned.

～

I wasn't grinning anymore at the salon.

"Wait, what?" I asked Caryn.

She sighed. "I said it in the last newsletter email."

"You did not tell me I had to dye my hair a different color." The stylist had separated pieces of my hair for what I assumed was the keratin treatment, then left and come back with foils and dye. "Is that the keratin?" I asked suspiciously. She told me it was the highlights because they do color before keratin. When I said I wasn't dyeing my hair, she said she was just doing what the bride told her. I jumped up and charged over to Caryn's seat to straighten out the misunderstanding.

"It's not a completely different color, just some balayage highlights to soften how dark your hair is."

"I like how dark my hair is."

Caryn threw her arms up in an exasperated gesture that I had come to know all too well. "You're the only one with dark hair. I don't want you to be the one who stands out the most in the pictures!"

"Caryn, you're going to be wearing a wedding dress. No one is going to notice my hair color."

"Then what's the big deal if you change it a little?" she asked, arms crossed. I looked behind her at the other bridesmaids, who were all there for touch-ups only. Caroline smirked.

"So basically, you want me in your wedding as long as I look exactly like them"—I gestured over her shoulder—"and nothing like me."

"Fat chance of that happening." Caroline snickered loudly enough that she meant to be heard, though she would deny it if I said anything. Dana looked at me sympathetically. Caryn didn't reply.

I bit the inside of my lip. Hard. And for the approximately nine-hundredth time, I debated just telling her I was done and walking away. But if I did that, she would never forgive me.

"Fine," I said through gritted teeth. "As long as it's just highlights, not a full color change."

"If you'd read the email . . ." Caryn said, but I walked away and went back to the stylist's chair.

"Subtle," I warned her. "Or I'm going on Yelp."

~

By the time I left the salon five hours later, I didn't recognize the reflection of the girl in the mirror behind the checkout desk. The highlights were subtle by the stylist's definition, but still more blonde than my hair had ever been before. My hair was stick-straight, with strict instructions not to let it "bend" or get wet for seventy-two hours, and I looked like a Kewpie doll with the eyelashes. If it wouldn't have ruined them, I would have been shedding some angry tears.

I went home and sat down in front of my laptop.

> Bridezilla A just attacked me at a salon.

> No, like actual assault.

> As I sat docilely in her stylist's chair (cheating on my own stylist, no less) like a lamb waiting for the slaughter—or in this case, the keratin treatment to destroy the natural beachy waves that are the envy of so many people—the stylist, at the bride's request, began dyeing my dark hair blonde.

> Naturally, I protested, only to be told that if I had read Bridezilla's latest email missive about the wedding (forgive me, dear Bridezilla, but your "wedding newsletters" have gotten longer than a CVS receipt and I believe you're up to number fifty-seven—no joke!), I would have known that my hair was about to change color. Because apparently not reading it is the same as giving consent? I didn't even click an "I agree" box after not reading it, like I do with Apple notifications!

248

So let's see, for this wedding alone, I have: lost seven pounds (not from actually trying, mind you, but from not being allowed to eat when I'm around the Bridezilla and her evil minions and the added stress of having to actually interact with these people), become a straight-haired blonde, and now have gigantic eyelashes obscuring the top part of my vision. Is it legal to drive with these on? I feel like giant space spiders are invading every time I blink.

If this is how you live your daily life, more power to you. But to force it on others for the sake of "not ruining the pictures" is beyond absurd. Hasn't she heard of Photoshop?

I did, however, stand my ground on the Botox issue. So I'm ruining the pictures anyway by being the only bridesmaid whose face still moves as nature intended. In fact, to fix that faux pas, I may hire someone to Photoshop the wedding pictures— not to fix my face, but to fix the bridesmaids of Frankenstein so they look like actual people, not genetically modified Barbie dolls.

Mom-zilla's daughter's wedding is the weekend after this one. What's going to happen when she sees my new look? Will Mom-zilla battle Bridezilla? And if so, can I sell tickets to recoup some of the fortune that I just paid to look like anyone but myself?

Feeling better, I hit "Publish." Then I took a selfie and sent it to Megan. This happened.

She called me immediately. "That's a filter, right?"

"Nope. Caryn dyed my hair."

"Are you kidding me?"

"Nope."

"That's so disrespectful."

"I know."

"I mean, you have three more weddings coming up. She's not the only one who wants her bridesmaids to look a certain way."

My mouth dropped open. "What?" I asked quietly.

"You've still got a month before mine so you have plenty of time to dye it back without totally frying your hair. But like, it would have been nice if she'd consulted with some of us. What's your sister going to say?"

It took me a minute before I could respond. "I'm getting another call," I said finally, copping out. "I've got to go."

"Okay, love you. The eyelashes are great, by the way! Talk later."

Did I have any normal friends left? Or did weddings turn everyone into unrecognizable zombies who fed on bridesmaids instead of brains?

I heard the front door to the apartment open and Becca called my name. "I'm just grabbing some clothes," she called from the living room, the sound of her voice moving closer. She stopped in the doorway to my room. "Oh. You're home. What did you do to your hair?" I looked up. "Are you wearing fake lashes?"

"Caryn had a bridesmaid salon day to get ready for the wedding."

"Isn't her wedding not for two weeks?"

"They chemically straightened my hair. I can't wash it for three days, so it'll be perfect by then. And the lashes last a month."

"How much did all of that cost?"

I shook my head. "You don't even want to know."

"Wow," she said, flopping down on my bed. "I know I haven't seen you much lately, but I didn't expect you to look like a completely different person."

"Yeah. I didn't either when I woke up this morning." I looked her over. "You look good."

She smiled. "I'm sorry I've been so MIA."

"Don't be. Things going well?"

"Oh my God, Lily, you have no idea. Will is amazing."

"I'm happy for you."

"It still doesn't feel real. Like, wasn't I the yoga pants queen a couple months ago?"

"You certainly were."

She reached across the divide and grabbed my hand. "It'll happen for you too, you know. When you're not expecting it."

"Well, I've got a gross guy who I've already slept with telling everyone he's going to hook up with me at the wedding—possibly right on the dance floor, I don't have all the details—and a fake boyfriend defending my honor, so I think I've got enough on my plate without dating right now. But thanks."

"Blog about it," she said. "You always have the best stories."

"Just did. You can read all about it."

She grinned. "Can't wait."

CHAPTER THIRTY-TWO

My baby sister's bachelorette party. Five words, endless degradation. When a thirty-two-year-old woman is forced to don a bedazzled "bridesmaid" shirt, candy necklace, and condom belt and walk around with penis straws, it certainly lacks the appeal that it may have for the twenty-four-year-old bride and her posse of barely legal friends.

Yet this is the situation I find myself forced into tonight. The bridesmaids and I have rented a hotel room, decorated it with a penis piñata (filled with condoms and penis-shaped lollipops, the former of which I was forced to buy in bulk), and set up the party with penis glasses and a penis-shaped cake. I have truly reached the point where if I see another penis, even a real one, I will run screaming. But isn't that how most married women feel? Watch out, baby sis, you'll be tired of them soon enough.

Whereas I, still woefully single, am probably pushing my impending spinsterhood further and further toward permanency by wearing what I am currently wearing. Not that I'm expecting to pick up guys at my sister's bachelorette party, but as my grandmother pointed out, it would be nice to have a date to all of these weddings.* Even if that means I do, in fact, eventually have to look at another penis.

*Of course, thanks to "no ring, no bring," I'm not allowed to bring dates to these weddings anyway. It's barbaric, really, and lets all those groomsmen think they have a chance. So many more penises that I don't want to see!

I would post a picture of this hideousness, but then my anonymity would be destroyed, as would my relationship with all five brides. So I'm sorry, dear readers, you'll have to use your imaginations.

Meanwhile I will probably spend my evening using the endless supply of ponytail holders on my wrist to keep the twenty-four-year-olds' hair out of their faces while they puke up the ridiculous amount of Fireball they have already started consuming.

Wish me luck! I'm going to need it . . .

I hit "Publish" and slid my phone into my back pocket. Then I sighed and looked in the hotel mirror again. I looked like a moron.

Ashlee had joined me at the hotel to help set up and made the condom belts for the bridal party. She thought they were cute.

My phone vibrated. That was fast, I thought, assuming I had already gotten my first comment. But it was a text from Alex. Have fun tonight! with an eggplant emoji and a puking face. I laughed.

I'm wearing a bedazzled tank top and a belt made out of condoms, I replied. And I just hung a penis piñata from a hotel room ceiling.

Penis piñata? Pics or it didn't happen!

I snapped a picture of myself in the mirror with the piñata visible in the background, miming shooting myself in the head with my free hand and hit "Send." Things I never thought I'd say before this year: I'm sick of penis cake.

Alex replied with the crying-laughing emoji and That condom belt is H-O-T.

Shrieks of laughter started filtering through the closed hotel room door. Ugh, I wrote. Amy and her Brownie troop are here. Gotta go.

Have fun, he said again. I pocketed my phone and opened the door to let the girls in—Amy, three bridesmaids, and six other friends, two of whom I had known since they were babies, which was approximately five minutes ago. Four others had been her friends since high school. I had met them, but I had already been out of college by the time Amy started high school. One was Madison, freshly tanned from her "first honeymoon," as they were calling their week at the resort in Mexico after the wedding. They would take their "real honeymoon" later in the summer in Greece. Apparently my brother's job paid much better than mine. The other two girls I had seen at Amy's shower that morning but couldn't have greeted by name if my life depended on it.

"Lily!" Amy screamed, hugging me like she hadn't seen me earlier that morning. She had a bottle of champagne in her left hand. "Look what Grandma gave me for tonight!" She spun around, taking in all of the decorations in the hotel room. "Oh my God, you guys! I'm going to cry! I love it!" She ran over to the penis piñata. "Quick, someone take my picture!" She opened her mouth very wide next to it, while three girls snapped pictures of her. I tried not to roll my eyes.

Once she had selected her favorite of the pictures, sent it to herself, and uploaded it to both her Instagram and Snapchat stories, she declared it was time for a drink. I peeked at my watch and saw it was only eight thirty. I was in for a long night.

"Does anyone have a corkscrew?" she asked, holding up the bottle of champagne and pulling the foil off the top.

"I do!" Ashlee pulled one out of her monogrammed "Maid of Honor" bag. "A maid of honor is always prepared." Ashlee grabbed the champagne bottle and opened her corkscrew as the girls grabbed glasses and chattered excitedly.

"Whoa!" I rushed to Ashlee's side. "You don't open champagne with a corkscrew."

"You don't?"

I sighed again and looked around the room, then took the bottle from Ashlee, told the girls to have their glasses ready, and expertly opened it, wondering what would have happened had there not been a responsible adult there. I poured a few drops in all of the plastic "bachelorette" cups that were shoved toward me.

"To Amy," Ashlee declared. "The future Mrs. Gilchrist."

"To Amy," everyone echoed.

"Now let's get drunk!" Amy yelled, and the ensuing shrieks made me worry we were going to have a hotel noise complaint on our hands very soon.

~

By the time we left for the first bar, I had a splitting headache and had already begun to debate whether Excedrin was a better choice than drinking. But I figured it would be less intense once we were out of that hotel room. Besides, we were going to a bar in Adams Morgan that I used to love hanging out at. Granted, that was when I was Amy's age, but it would be fun to go back to one of my old haunts, right?

No.

They say you can't go home again. Well, they lie. You can go home. Going home is fine. Your mom may nag you about being single, but at least she'll cook for you and feign concern while bemoaning your failure to produce grandchildren. You can totally go home.

What you cannot do, under any circumstances, is return to your favorite bar after not having gone for the last six years. Because the same people are still there. No, not the *exact* same people, because the exact same people are now your age and probably home with their spouses, babies, and dogs. But the same generic, midtwenties crowd is absolutely still there and suddenly you're the oldest person in the room other than three creepy guys, one of the bouncers, and the dude who is clearly the owner. But unlike the other geriatrics in the room, I was wearing a belt made out of condoms.

And in the time it took for me to get myself a single drink, one of the girls had begun making out with someone in a corner, another was sobbing at a table, and Amy had some guy nibbling on her candy necklace. *Not my circus,* I told myself, taking a sip of my martini. *Not my monkeys.*

I made a face. This was a terrible martini. Of course, when I still drank here, I didn't drink martinis.

Screw it, I thought, drinking the rest in one long gulp. *If you can't beat 'em, join 'em.*

I turned around and ordered two shots of Jägermeister. Never a good idea, but maybe being drunk was the way to survive this night. The bartender poured the shots and slid them to me. I took both over to Amy. Half of her candy necklace was missing as she giggled with the guy who had eaten it. *Maybe Megan was right and she's not going to make it to the aisle.*

"Come on Ames, it's shot time," I said, elbowing past the candy fiend.

"You take shots?"

I rolled my eyes. "Since you were in the third grade. Come on. I'm doing one with you."

She took the shot glass, clinked glasses with mine, and threw the drink down her throat. "Ugh! What *is* that?"

I looked at her like she was an alien. "Jäger."

"People still drink that?"

I took a deep breath. "Yes. That's what we always did shots of."

She pouted slightly. "I need some Fireball to get that taste out of my mouth!" As if by magic, two other bridesmaids appeared with shot glasses of the cinnamon liquor she had requested.

My phone buzzed, and I pulled it out to avoid choking the bride. While it may be rude to look at your phone while you're out, it's still more polite than publicly killing your sister. It was a text from Alex. How goes it?

Sweet baby Jesus, I wrote back. Save me from these children who don't even know what Jäger is.

So teach them! Isn't that your job in this wedding?

I tried. Amy demanded a shot of Fireball immediately after. Did that even exist when we were young?

I think we drank Goldschlager to feel fancy when we wanted something with cinnamon in it back in our day.

I have never felt this old in my life.

Lol. You're what? 31?

32.

Ahh, I see, Alex replied. You're ancient. With a granny emoji.

I laughed out loud, then jumped as someone sidled up next to me. "What's so funny, bridesmaid?" the sidler asked. "Texting your boyfriend?"

I turned to size him up. Way too young for me, of course, but cute. And there was no harm in flirting a little. "No. No boyfriend. Just a friend who agrees it's ridiculous to wear a condom belt when your sister gets married."

He nodded at Amy's veil. "That's your sister?"

"Yup."

"Nice. I'm Kevin."

"Lily."

"Can I buy you a drink, Lily?" I agreed and he ordered another terrible martini for me and a Bud Light for himself. The drinks came and he paid cash, then clinked his glass against mine. "Cheers."

I scanned the room quickly. Crying girl was dancing with some guy, making-out girl was still making out, and Amy was laughing with a bunch of her friends, drinking their drinks through penis straws. Everything was under control. I could relax. "So Kevin," I mused. "What do you do?"

"I'm an intern on Capitol Hill," he said confidently. This was clearly a line that got him girls. "Still deciding if I want to go the lobbyist route or eventually run for office myself. What about you?"

"PR at the Foundation for Scientific Technology."

"That's cool. How long have you been there?"

I knew the truth about my age would shock him, but I did not give the tiniest of rat's asses what this kid thought. "Ten years. I started straight out of college."

"Ten years?" he repeated. "I can't imagine doing anything for ten years." He leaned in closer. "But that's what I like about you older women. You know what you want. I always learn a thing or two when I sleep with someone so much older."

I reeled like he had slapped me. "Have fun with that," I said and started to walk away.

"Baby, don't go," he said, grabbing my arm.

I turned around and got right in his face. "Fine, you want to learn something from an older woman? First lesson: don't call a woman old. Second lesson: don't assume you're sleeping with anyone. And third lesson: don't *ever* touch me." His eyes widened and he dropped my arm. I stormed off, leaving my drink on the bar, and only realized as I got to the doorway how much more effective it would have been if I had thrown it in his face. You don't get enough opportunities to do that in real life, so you should always take them when they come.

I went outside to where the smokers had been banished and sincerely debated just going home. Yes, it would be rude because Amy was my sister, but honestly, she didn't actually care if I was there. As the semi-responsible adult, however, I needed to make sure she made it home okay. And to survive until the end of the night, I needed a buddy.

So I called Alex.

He answered on the third ring. "What's wrong?"

"Are you home?"

"Yeah, why?"

"Do you mind coming out to Adams Morgan? I need reinforcements."

Alex laughed. "Sure. Let me just change and get an Uber. Be there in like half an hour?"

"I owe you. Big time."

He laughed again. "You can pay me in jumbo slice and leftover cake."

"Deal."

～

I had a beer waiting for him when he got there and greeted him with it as soon as he walked in. He looked me over, but refrained from commenting on my newly blonde hair, probably because I had been complaining about it nonstop in texts. "Nice belt."

I looked down. I had forgotten I still had the condom belt on. I yanked it off and dropped it in the trash.

"Now that's just a waste. You could hand them out to all of the people who are about to make terrible decisions tonight."

"The maid of honor made them by hooking the packages together with safety pins."

Alex shook his head. "Not the sharpest knife in the drawer, I'm guessing."

"She's not even a knife. She might be a spoon."

"I'm sure she's a very sharp spoon." He looked around. "I haven't been here since before I was married."

"You weren't allowed out when you were married?"

"If I was a good boy, I could go to the movies." He rolled his eyes at me. "You don't still come to places like this, do you?"

"God no."

A bar-top table opened up and we looked at each other, then made our way over. The two seats were pulled next to each other, providing a clear view of the rest of the bar. "We're officially the oldest people here," Alex said.

"Except that guy, who I think owns it."

"Nah, he's a narc."

I laughed. "Oh God, we're old."

He gestured with his beer. "So I'm guessing your sister is the one in the veil."

"Yup. That's Amy."

"And the guy eating candy off her neck? Not your future brother-in-law?"

"Nope. Total stranger. Super classy."

"Definitely runs in the family."

I leaned my head on his shoulder. "I missed you." Between the shower, the bachelorette party, Caryn's salon mess, and trying to keep my head above water at work, I hadn't seen him in person since the night I got back from Mexico.

He leaned his head on mine. "I'm here now," he said quietly. "This seems pretty under control."

"Who's this?" Amy was suddenly at our table, a drink in one hand, the other on her hip. "Lily, do you have a secret boyfriend?"

I picked my head up, annoyed, the moment gone. "No. This is Alex."

"Amy," she said, sticking out her hand. "I've heard absolutely nothing about you."

Alex laughed. "I'm crushed. I've heard all about you."

"Don't believe a word Lily tells you. I'm delightful."

"Funny, she told me you're delightful. I guess that's wrong."

"She did not."

"Did."

Amy turned to me. "I like him. Where have you been hiding him? He's cute too."

"We're just friends, Amy."

"So, friend, what do you do?"

"I'm a lawyer."

Amy raised her eyebrows at me. "Single?"

"Divorced."

"Kids?"

"No."

"And you're not dating my sister because—?"

"I'm gay."

"Oh my God, I'm so sorry—I didn't mean—"

"He's not gay. We're just friends."

Amy made a face at me. "I need another drink," she said, downing the rest of hers and handing me the empty glass. "Will you get me one?"

I glared at her, but got up to comply. Amy slid comfortably into my seat. "So, Alex," she began. I made my way to the bar.

The crowd had begun to pick up. I had forgotten that the under-thirties didn't even leave their houses until eleven and anything before midnight was early. It took much longer to get the bartender's attention, so I ordered another drink for myself and another beer for Alex as well while I was there.

By the time I made it back to the table, Alex was smiling at my sister. "You're welcome," she said when I handed her the drink.

"Thank you is the traditional response."

"I'll let Alex tell you," she said sweetly, giving me a wet kiss on the cheek. "Back to my party! It was nice to meet you!"

"Tell me what?"

He laughed. "Your sister invited me to her wedding. As your date."

I blinked rapidly. "She did what now?" He shrugged. "My mother is going to have a field day with this one."

"I told her my answer depended entirely on you."

"Do you want to go?"

"Do you want me to?"

"I asked you first."

He shrugged again. "Could be good practice for Tim and Megan's. And it will keep your older relatives from asking why you're still single."

He had a point. "Okay," I said, feeling a twinge of something other than dread about my sister's wedding for the first time since it was announced.

"It's a date," he said, clinking his glass against mine.

CHAPTER
THIRTY-THREE

When the evening devolved, it devolved quickly.

Ashlee came to find me, her hair disheveled and her face green. "Kayla, Taylor, and Fiona are all throwing up," she said.

I shook my ponytail holder–covered wrist at Alex. "Duty calls."

"Gross. I'll sit this one out."

"Keep your phone handy. I might need help getting Ubers."

"Will do."

I followed Ashlee and handed her a ponytail holder just in time for her to vomit into the sink. I did not miss this phase of young adulthood.

Madison seemed to be running the show in the bathroom, switching from stall to stall, holding girls' hair. "Here," I said, handing her three ponytail holders.

She looked at me gratefully, a slight sheen of sweat shining on her forehead, and then began tying up a girl's hair for her.

Taylor flushed the toilet and exited the stall. "I feel better," she announced. "I'm going to get another drink."

"Nope," I told her cheerfully, steering her toward the wall, away from the door. "You're done."

Ashlee seemed much more composed after she threw up, and I suspected her nausea was more from the smell of vomit in the bathroom than from too much alcohol.

I realized Amy was nowhere to be found. "Has anyone seen my sister?" Ashlee and Madison exchanged a look. "What?"

"She was talking to some guy," Madison said, and Ashlee shot her a murderous look.

My shoulders dropped. *Not now, Amy,* I thought despairingly. I knew my little sister had inherited some of my self-sabotaging ways, but she was within three weeks of the altar.

"Where?" I asked.

"The booths by the dance floor," Madison said.

"Round everyone up," I told her. "We're heading back to the hotel. I'll get Amy."

I made a beeline for the booths. But when I got there, I found Alex sitting next to Amy, the guy who had been eating candy off Amy's necklace across from them.

"What are you doing, Alex?" Amy slurred.

"Being a cockblock," he responded matter-of-factly. "You'll thank me tomorrow."

She punched him lightly on the arm. "You're so silly. I'm not doing anything wrong. Am I, Luke?"

Luke looked none too pleased with Alex or his declared intentions.

"Come on, Ames, time to go," I said, planting my hands on the table and leaning directly into her sightline.

"What time is it?"

"Last call."

"No it's not," Luke said, checking his phone.

"It is for us," I said firmly. Alex stood and offered Amy his hand.

"I wasn't doing anything wrong," Amy said again, petulantly, but she took Alex's hand and stood.

I put an arm around her waist. "You only say that when you are, in fact, doing something wrong. Don't forget, I've known you since you were born."

Amy pouted, then burst into tears. "I really wasn't though. I love Tyler. I wouldn't mess that up."

Alex gave me a look and tilted his head toward the door. I nodded.

Madison and Ashlee were crowded at the entrance with the rest of the girls. Two were sitting on the floor, looking like they might throw up again. "I'll see if I can grab a couple of trash bags from the bar," Alex said, surveying the situation. "How many Ubers do we need?"

I counted the girls. "Two regulars and an XL. I'll order the XL, you do one, and Madison, can you do the third?"

She nodded and pulled out her phone.

"Let's get everyone outside to wait. The fresh air will help."

Amy was crying onto Ashlee's shoulder, and I counted the girls again. We had left no man behind.

Madison took the first batch of girls in her Uber, Alex took the second, and I brought up the rear with the last of us. No one threw up in mine at least, and I helped the four drunk girls into the elevator and up to our suite.

Alex opened the door for us, his eyes wide. "This sounds like it would be every guy's dream. But get me out of here, please."

I laughed. "Can you hang out a few more minutes?"

"Now that you're here, yes."

"Thank you."

I helped the drunkest two girls into their pajamas, gave everyone a bottle of water, and told them to brush their teeth.

"Thanks, Mom," Amy said, her tears completely forgotten.

I rolled my eyes. "Wash your makeup off too. The last thing you need is your skin breaking out before the wedding."

I found Madison. "Do you think it's okay if I bail? I've had enough for one night."

"Definitely. I can handle it from here."

"Thanks." I kissed her on the cheek. "Sis."

She smiled broadly, and I thought about her invitation to come visit her and Jake. It might be nice to get to know her. And she was far less of a mess than Amy.

I grabbed my bag and headed to the door, where Alex was standing, watching me in awe.

"Is this what all bachelorette parties are like?"

"God no. This is what happens when little kids get married." I checked the time on my cell phone. "Do you think the hotel bar is still open?"

"Only one way to find out," he said, taking my bag from me.

~

The bar was open, and nearly empty, except for a couple of midfifties guys in suits at a table. Alex and I sat at the bar.

"A Stella and a martini," he ordered. "Extra olives."

"At least they can probably actually make one here," I said. "The martinis at that bar tonight were the worst I've ever had."

"Anything beyond a shot is probably out of their wheelhouse."

"And when you're Amy's age, you don't know better anyway."

Our drinks arrived. "What should we toast to?" Alex asked.

I thought briefly. "To Amy. The only bride to actually allow me to bring a date to her wedding."

Alex smiled and clinked my glass. "Technically, I can be your unofficial date to Tim and Megan's too."

"Well you kind of have to be now, since you told everyone we're together."

"I can tell them we broke up and let Justin know you're available?"

"Why? Do you hate me?"

He smiled again. "No. I definitely don't hate you."

"Then don't tell Justin anything of the sort. I still can't believe that sleazebag was going around saying that."

"I swear I almost hit him."

"I still might do it myself in a couple weeks. What does Tim see in him?"

"He's—he's fun in that bro way. Until he's telling everyone he's going to sleep with your best friend."

I leaned back, surprised. "I'm your best friend?"

He looked at me carefully with an expression I hadn't seen before. "Well. Yeah. I think you kind of are now."

I didn't respond immediately. Megan had been my official best friend since second grade, of course. Caryn, as much as I didn't like her at the moment, had the title of "work best friend." But Megan had been pretty MIA lately. And her requirement that I stay away from Tim's friends romantically rankled me. No, I wasn't demoting her, or Caryn for that matter, but maybe—maybe Alex had grown into a different type of best friend. I hadn't even sent Megan a picture of my ridiculous bridesmaid getup. Or texted her all evening. And she wouldn't have dropped everything to come help me with Amy.

I realized I hadn't replied and needed to say something. "I—I hadn't put a label on it. But yeah, I think you're one of my best friends too."

His shoulders loosened in relief. "Are we supposed to get those matching heart necklaces now? My sister always got those."

"Tattoos," I said sagely. "That's how millennials say 'I love you.'"

He started to say something, but stopped himself and took another sip of his beer. "I think they're getting ready to close up." He put some money down on the bar. "I'll take you home."

"Your place is closer. We can just share an Uber there, and I'll take it the rest of the way." He gave me a look. "Fine, I won't argue."

"That's a first," he said.

I nudged him with my shoulder. "You're one to talk."

"I'm a lawyer. I get paid to argue."

"Calm down there, Atticus Finch. You get paid to help people copyright stuff."

"Oh good, you *are* feeling okay."

"Smart-ass." He cocked his head toward the exit and I nodded. He held the door for me, and we waited under the hotel's awning for the Uber to arrive as a cool mist began to dampen the pavement.

~

"Thank you for coming tonight," I said as the Uber driver pulled up to my apartment building. "I couldn't have done this without you."

"Yes, you could have. You're much less of a mess than you think."

I huffed good-naturedly. "Who says I'm a mess?" He started to answer, but I cut him off. "Don't. Even I can't say that with a straight face."

"I'll walk you up."

"You don't need to, it's right here. And I'm not drunk."

"I know, but I want to."

I shrugged, and he told the Uber driver he would be right back.

We walked the few feet to the door. "Safe and sound," I said.

"I know. I just needed to work up my nerve."

"Your nerve? To do what?"

"This," he said, leaning in and kissing me.

Deep down, I think I had known how I felt ever since Megan's housewarming party. Somewhere, buried beneath layers and layers of denial and scar tissue from the wound I had created with David and my own hardheaded sense of self-preservation, I knew that Alex was more than a friend. Because that feeling didn't just magically appear when he kissed me. It was more like it had been there since the beginning and had finally broken free.

And because it had always been there, it didn't take long for me to get over my surprise and kiss him back. Hungrily. Greedily. Like he was the oxygen I needed to survive, because right then, he was.

He pulled back slightly—it must have been him, because I know it wasn't me—and smiled, touching a finger to my cheek so gently that it sent a shiver of anticipation down my spine.

I opened my mouth to tell him to come upstairs. To get rid of the Uber driver and be mine. But Megan's words came back to me. And while I couldn't imagine a scenario in which I would stop liking Alex, there were a million where he stopped liking me. Like when he inevitably found out about Justin—which would probably happen at the wedding. *I can't deal with that drama at my wedding,* Megan had said. But it wasn't just her comment—I had ruined this one before it even began. And while I wasn't exactly in the running to be named bridesmaid of the year, I had one thing within my control: I could avoid sleeping with a second groomsman in my best friend's wedding.

"I can't," I said, my face contorting from the pain of admitting that. "I—I want to, but I can't."

"Yes, you can," Alex said, taking my hands. "Lily, there's nothing keeping us apart. I know Megan didn't like it when she thought we were just sleeping together, but she'd get over it if we were serious."

I shook my head and pulled my hands away, starting to cry. "I'm sorry. I want to, but I can't do this."

Alex was saying my name, but I had to get away. I dug in my purse until I found my key fob and waved it blindly at the locking mechanism to open the door. I ran past him into the building, half praying he would follow me, half praying he wouldn't. I turned, just in time to get a glimpse of his bewildered and hurt face as the door closed behind me, then I sank down on the tattered sofa in the lobby and cried until I had no tears left.

At some point, I left the lobby and made my way upstairs to my apartment, which was devoid of Becca, as it had been ever since she started dating Will. I kicked off my shoes by the door and padded bare-foot to my bedroom, planning to go right to bed. But my open laptop caught my eye and I stopped.

The blog was so therapeutic. I could hide behind the anonymity of the internet to say what I truly felt, without worrying that I was offending anyone or hurting anyone's feelings. It was the one place where I could actually pour out all of the pain I was feeling and maybe—maybe feel a little less bereft.

I sat down, having no idea where to begin. But my fingers knew what to do.

I just did the hardest thing I've ever had to do and made the biggest sacrifice I've ever made in the name of friendship. Bride C, my lifelong best friend, told me last weekend that I couldn't date her fiancé's friends. Which sounds both petty on her part and like a no-brainer on mine, but matters of the heart are never that simple.

It's actually not petty of her. She's not wrong. I have the world's worst relationship track record. I could give you all the sob story about the one who got away from my youth, but the reality is that I did all of this to myself. I fell in love with an idea that didn't exist and stayed fixated on that idea for a really long time, sabotaging anything that could have been a relationship along the way because it wasn't that.

But this time, I met someone real. Someone funny, and charming, and sweet, and kind, and wonderful. Someone who, against all odds, sees me. Likes me. The real me. Not the internet persona, not the shined-up penny version I present to most of the world, but me, flaws and all, and still wants what he sees.

So what's the problem?

I got ridiculously drunk and slept with the most repulsive, former-frat boy meathead I could find—who happens to be a groomsman in Bride C's wedding.

Did I mention Perfect Guy is also a groomsman in Bride C's wedding?

Bride C knows I slept with the horrible one, which is why she told me to stay out of her fiancé's circle of friends for future dalliances. So you see, dear reader, she's not wrong to make that demand of me. I've already been there, made that mistake, and she's perfectly right to not want me to have slept with two of her husband's best friends before her wedding.

Especially with my history of screwing everything (and apparently everyone) up.

So when Perfect Guy kissed me tonight after being his perfect self and helping me manage the girls at my sister's bachelorette party (and even preventing my idiot sister from doing something with a random dude that would probably call off the whole wedding), I realized three undeniable truths.

I am head-over-heels crazy about this guy.

I already ruined it by sleeping with the repulsive guy.

And if I follow my heart, I'll lose both of my best friends (Did I mention he told me I'm his best friend tonight? How is he so perfect?) when he finds out what I did and it falls apart.

I did the right thing tonight. Even though it hurt like hell and cost me the best guy who will ever be interested in me, both as a friend and as more.

But I kept my word to my other best friend, and I didn't hook up with two groomsmen in her wedding.

Lowest bar ever? Met.

And the worst part is, unlike pretty much everything else from this crazy, messed-up year of weddings, this is all my fault.

Side note: I really hope tears don't ruin eyelash extensions, because if they do, I just screwed up yet another wedding.

Not my best writing, but it was such a convoluted story to tell. And just putting it out there made me feel better because there was no one I could talk to about it all. Not Megan, not Alex, not Caryn, and not Becca, who would probably be moving out soon at this rate.

I hit "Publish," and then closed my laptop.

I got up mechanically and washed my makeup off, then changed into pajamas. I was on such thin ice with Caryn, and God knew she would take any blemishes as an intentional sabotage of her pictures next weekend, so leaving the makeup on was not an option.

On my way to bed, I checked my phone to see if there was anything from Alex—there wasn't—and did something I never did. I turned my phone all the way off. No alarms, no texts to wake me up. Nothing. I wanted to sleep for as long as my body would let me.

I climbed into bed and lay there staring at the ceiling for a long time as I thought about where I had gone wrong, and wishing, desperately, that I could turn back the clock and avoid Justin entirely.

Eventually, I fell asleep. And if I dreamed, I mercifully remembered none of it.

CHAPTER

THIRTY-FOUR

I woke up at some point and drank some water, then went back to bed. I woke up again to pee, drank more water, ate a protein bar, then went back to sleep.

When I woke up for real, my eyes felt puffy and swollen, and the whole situation with Alex came flooding back to me. I sighed, swinging my legs out of bed, and went to take a shower. I didn't want to turn on my phone yet because I knew there would be nothing from him.

After my shower, I pulled on a pair of yoga pants, a sports bra, and an old University of Maryland T-shirt that had seen better days, and I ate a yogurt. The clock on the microwave said it was almost noon, which wasn't so bad, all things considered, but because it was Memorial Day weekend, that meant I had a long day and a half in front of me to fill on my own.

I should check on Amy, I thought. Maybe she needed help with something for the wedding, and that would take my mind off everything. And I hadn't been as kind as I should have been the previous night. Or at her shower. Or in the previous year, for that matter. I honestly didn't know if Caryn and I would still be on speaking terms after her wedding, and Megan was fading fast as well. I may not have always liked Amy, but she would always be there, so the least I could do was treat her like a human being.

Of course, calling her also meant I would have to tell her Alex wasn't coming to the wedding, but if I was lucky, she wouldn't remember that she had invited him in the first place.

With a distinct feeling of dread, hoping there would be something from Alex saying I was still his best friend, but knowing that there wouldn't, I picked up my phone and held the power button.

It buzzed relentlessly in my hand, notifications filling the screen.

Voicemails and missed calls from Megan, Caryn, Amy, Sharon, Megan again, Becca, Megan again, Jake, Sharon again, Becca again, my mother, a cousin I hadn't talked to in ages, and a couple of numbers I didn't recognize.

The emails were still loading: 250, no, 300, no, 487, no, 726 new emails.

What on earth? I looked at the calendar icon. It wasn't Sunday. I had slept for close to thirty-two hours. Which thankfully didn't matter because of the holiday. But still. What was going on?

The text messages came clanging in as well.

I clicked Megan's thread first.

Are you kidding me?

Jesus Lily

You started a fucking blog?

What were you thinking?

I don't even know what to say to you right now

Are you really not even going to answer me?

The blog. Oh God. The blog.

I dashed across the room to my laptop and flipped it open, my heart racing. My name wasn't anywhere on it, so Megan must have stumbled on it randomly and figured out it was me. Of course she would be able to tell that I wrote it; she knew me so well.

I refreshed my blog dashboard page. When I saw the number of hits, I closed my eyes, assuming I would see the real number when I opened them. In the thirty-two hours since I had hit "Publish," the blog had amassed over a million new views.

"What the hell?" I exhaled.

"Lily?" Becca called, the door opening. I didn't move from my computer screen.

She came to my doorway. "Where have you been? I've been calling you."

I looked up at her, my eyes wide. "I—turned off my phone. After the party."

"Jesus," she said, sinking down onto my bed. "When did you get back online?"

"Just—now."

"So you don't know?"

"What happened?"

Becca typed something on her phone and handed it to me. "Buzzfeed," she said. "You went viral."

"I—what?" I took the phone from her. A Buzzfeed headline read, **World's Worst Bridesmaid Hilariously Blogs about Her Five Bridezillas**. It was typical Buzzfeed-style writing, an author detailing her favorite parts of my snarkiness with screenshots highlighting specific passages.

I skimmed through it. The last paragraph had what I needed to know.

> And while I can't one hundred percent confirm who the bridesmaid from hell is, a recurring IP address where posts and comments from the blog's owner originated is registered to the Foundation for Scientific Technology. I did a little social media sleuth work (or stalking, call it what you will—it wasn't hard; there are only three women under

fifty who work there) and it looks like FST's Public Relations Director, Lily Weiss, is, in fact, listed on five different wedding websites as a bridesmaid, including her brother's, her sister's, and three friends, one of whom is a coworker. If that's not a smoking gun, I don't know what is.

*Note: Messages to Ms. Weiss have gone unanswered so far. We'll update this post when we hear back from her.

Fuck.

I looked up at Becca. "Is it too late to deny it?"

She grimaced. "If you'd seen it early enough, maybe you could have. But I think everyone and their mother has seen this post by now. It's all over my Facebook and Twitter timelines."

The room started spinning and I thought I might throw up, but I closed my eyes and waited for the spell to pass.

"I don't think I'm in any weddings anymore, am I?"

"I don't know."

I put my head in my hands. "I don't even know where to start dealing with this. Should I take the blog down?"

"Honestly? I don't think that would do much. It's already been screenshotted everywhere." She paused. "I got worried when you weren't answering your phone. I thought—I don't know."

I reassured her that I wasn't about to do anything stupid and thanked her for being probably the only friend I had left.

"It's not—I mean, it's not *that* bad."

"Thanks, Bec."

"No, I mean, you didn't actually say anything that bad about Megan. Or Madison. Or Sharon—well, I mean, you did about her mom, but not about her. And Caryn's were mostly fine until the last few; it was more about her friends and they already hated you."

I thought about what I had said about Caryn after the hair and eyelashes debacle. And about Sharon's mother. And Amy. Oh God. I hadn't held back about Amy. Did I say she had been flirting with someone else at her bachelorette party? I couldn't remember now.

I took a deep breath and exhaled through my mouth, trying to fight off the impending panic attack.

Becca excused herself when I said I needed to go through my voicemails, and I climbed back into bed to listen.

The first one was from Megan. "I don't even know what to say right now. You just—you put my business out there in a blog? What were you thinking? Don't call me back yet, I don't think I'm ready to talk to you."

Could have been worse, all things considered.

Caryn's was next and her voice quivered with anger. "How could you do this to me the week before my wedding? Everyone is mad at *me* because you published what I said about them! What kind of person does that?"

Amy didn't leave a message. She clearly listened to my outgoing greeting and then hung up instead of saying anything.

Sharon's message was hard to hear through her tears, but what I could make out was: "Tell me that wasn't you. My mom is mortified. I'm mortified. I told her it couldn't actually be you and that you're going to sue Buzzfeed. Just—tell me you didn't do that. You didn't say that."

Megan's second message began slightly more measuredly. "I appreciate that you didn't sleep with Alex," she began. "But is that really what you think of me? I come across like such a raging bitch and you don't even begin to address that you might have done anything wrong in this situation? You aren't exactly a saint here. Plus Tim's sister says she's not going to be in the wedding anymore if you are, which maybe I should thank you for, but it's still a mess I have to clean up. And seriously? Why haven't you called me back?"

I took the phone away from my ear and switched to the text messages.

Becca had texted asking where I was, but I skipped over that thread. There was one message from Alex. My heart in my throat, I clicked it.

After all of this, you slept with Justin? You got a couple things wrong though: I'm not perfect, and I definitely don't know who you are.

A sob rose up in my throat. I deserved everything I got from my friends and then some, but this? Alex was the last person I wanted to hurt and now—well, now he was gone.

But oh God, he wasn't. I still had to see all of these people again. Assuming any of them still wanted me at their weddings, let alone in them.

I went back to my computer. There had to be an option to delete the blog. There it was, under settings. I clicked "Delete Blog" and got a prompt asking me to type in my password to confirm the deletion. I hesitated a moment—the text in the box said this was permanent and the material could not be recovered if I deleted it.

I had enjoyed the blog more than any other hobby I had ever picked up. True, I was the worst version of myself on there, but I was also writing. Really writing. For the first time since college. And it had felt like—like I had found myself for the first time. Even if I was being horrible, just the act of putting those words into the world had been a rebirth of sorts. Could I really just throw that all away?

Yes, it needed to be done. And it needed to be done before I could apologize to anyone. Before I even listened to the rest of the messages. I typed my password and kissed my first attempt at personal writing in more than a decade goodbye.

I picked my phone back up, then put it down without unlocking it. Instead I opened my email on my laptop, letting the now 1,963 emails download. Most were comments on the blog. I skimmed through a couple dozen, which were split pretty evenly between encouraging responses, similar horror stories, or compliments on my humor or writing, and negative responses. The negative half were more in the vein of what I deserved, wondering why anyone liked me enough to want me in their weddings in the first place. I concurred wholeheartedly.

When I filtered out the WordPress notifications, there were two from Buzzfeed writers, one from someone at AOL News (which I didn't know was still a thing), and one from a *Washington Post* reporter trying to confirm my identity as the author of the blog. That last one scared me. A lot. If Buzzfeed figured out who I was because I posted from work, this could have negative splash-back there. Could I get fired? I was supposed to represent the public image of the foundation, and my own public image had just gone viral for all the wrong reasons. I didn't imagine that going over well. And while yes, I had contemplated quitting over Caryn, I hadn't been serious. How would I pay my rent? I put my head in my hands again and tried to get my breathing under control.

What had I done?

~

The worst of the voicemails was my mother's. "I don't even know what to say to you. How could you do this to your brother and sister and to me? Your grandmother saw what you wrote about her. And about that—man—who you—your father read that. Is this who I raised? What am I supposed to tell people? Amy is saying she doesn't want you in her wedding and how will we explain that? I don't know what to say."

There's something about a mother's disappointment that cuts you to the bone, no matter how old you are. That's not to say I wasn't used to disappointing her, but I wanted to crawl into a hole to live out the rest of my days among the grubworms when she told me my father had read the post about Justin. And when she mentioned my grandmother, I realized I had to start an actual list of people I had wronged. Because she hadn't even crossed my mind. Granted, if I lost my job, I was about to have nothing but time to make it up to them and would probably wind up moving in with my grandma because there was no way my mother would take me now. Grandma, well, she would probably get over it.

Jake's voicemail was concise, at least. "Madison has been crying for an hour. Why can't you just be a normal sister and make her feel welcome? I can't believe how selfish you are."

I grabbed a notepad and started my apology list. Caryn had probably gotten the worst of it in the blog and I was sure her friends were giving her holy hell, so she belonged at the top. Then I wrote Amy's name above hers. I had forgotten to check if I had called her out about that Luke guy before hitting "Delete," but if I had, that was actually the worst. Sharon was next, then Jake and Madison. Megan came fifth. She would forgive me no matter what, in the end. Then, after I had made amends with all of the brides, next up were my mother, my grandmother, and my father. I didn't even write Alex's name on the list. I was beyond salvation there.

It was one o'clock, and I had a lot of work ahead of me.

I tried Amy's cell phone. She let it ring twice and then sent it to voicemail. I pressed the call button again. Same result. She picked up the third time, however. "What, Lily?"

"Don't hang up," I said quickly. "Amy, I'm so, so sorry."

She didn't say anything for a moment. "Is that all?"

"No. I didn't have any right to—"

"No, you didn't have any right! If you hated me that much, you didn't have to be in my wedding at all!"

I hesitated. "I don't hate you, Ames. If anything, I think I'm jealous. Everything always comes so easy to you."

"Nothing comes easy to me! I'm working a part-time job and lived at home until two weeks ago! I took five years to graduate college and can't find an actual career. You walked out of college into a job, you never had to move back home, and all anyone does is talk about how successful you are. But me? No one has ever said anything like that about me. I'm the screw-up baby sister. And God forbid one good thing happens—I find a great guy—and you try to ruin that just because I was talking to someone I knew in college?"

"I didn't try to ruin—"

"Then why would you say that on the internet, Lily? Do you know how hard that was to explain to Tyler?"

"I'm sorry," I repeated. "I can talk to Tyler and explain it wasn't like that."

"I already talked to Tyler. He loves me, and he trusts me. Which is way more than I can say for you."

"I—" I took a deep breath. "I'm not going to make any excuses. I was wrong. What can I do to make this right?"

"I don't know," Amy said. "It's not my job to tell you how to fix it when you mess up. You have to figure that out."

I paused, taken aback. Of all the people to hit me with that truth bomb, she was the last one I would have expected. Which just showed how wrong I had been all along.

"Do you want me to drop out of the wedding?" I asked quietly. "I will if it's what you want."

She hesitated. "No. I want you to be my big sister and be happy for me, which you haven't done yet."

I felt my shoulders slump. She was right. Not once in this whole crazy year had I taken a moment to be happy that my little sister was happy. I said she was too young, and I said I didn't think she would actually get as far as a wedding, let alone spending her life with someone, and I was snarky about much of it, even to her face. And if what she said earlier was true, about thinking everything came so easily to me—wow.

"You're right. And I'm so sorry. I got so wrapped up in feeling like the victim because I was in so many weddings and am so much older and have no prospect of getting married anytime soon that I didn't think about what was actually important." She didn't say anything. "You. Being happy. That's what's important. If that wasn't clear. Because you're my sister, and I love you, and—I—I—" Tears were flowing down my cheeks and I trailed off, unable to say more.

Amy let me cry for a couple of minutes, and I heard her sniffle. "I love you too. I still hate you right now, but I love you. Don't you know how jealous I always was of you? You were off living this glamorous life and you didn't need any guy to make you whole. I—I don't know who I am if I'm not with someone. And that's scary because I love Tyler so much and what if it doesn't work out? You, at least, know how to be on your own."

"Not entirely by choice," I admitted quietly. "I want to find all of that. I just—can't."

"What about that Alex guy?"

"He—well, he saw the blog too."

"And—?"

I sniffed hard, trying not to lose it completely. "No, that's done now."

"I'm sorry," Amy said.

"Me too."

"You know what could start making it up to me?"

"What?"

"Let me be there when you explain this to Grandma. I'm dying to know what she says about the sleeping-with-that-other-groomsman thing after the post you did about her at Jake's wedding."

I laughed through my tears. "Okay."

"I'm not serious—well, a little. Just tell me what she says."

"I will."

"Lily?"

"Yeah?"

"It was good. I mean, not the parts where you made fun of me. But the writing was really good."

I thanked her and got off the phone before I started to cry in earnest again. I wasn't even sure which part I was crying over anymore, but I cried harder than I had after telling Alex I couldn't be with him.

CHAPTER THIRTY-FIVE

I tried calling Caryn, but she sent me to voicemail each time. Eventually, I left her a message. "It's Lily. Please call me back. I want to apologize and figure out how to make this right. I—I'm really sorry. Please call me."

If she didn't call back, I didn't know how I was going to face her at work on Tuesday. And it didn't help not knowing if it would be my last day. I had spent ten years at the foundation; my résumé was pretty dusty.

I looked at Megan's name on my list and considered letting her jump the line. She should be one of the easier calls, but I hesitated. I wasn't ready to talk to her. Was I in the wrong? Absolutely. But I had also just made a huge sacrifice for her, bigger than any I had ever made in my life. And the fact that none of her messages acknowledged that beyond saying she was glad that I hadn't slept with Alex—did she even read the post? It was never about sleeping with him. I mean, yes, that probably would have happened if I hadn't said no, but this wasn't a hookup.

I felt terrible about hurting her, but I also felt terrible that she didn't realize she had hurt me. And I couldn't talk to her until I could make the conversation not be about me losing one of the most important people in my life because I was trying to do right by her. Which I couldn't do yet.

No. It was better to go in order. It was time to call Sharon. With the exception of saying she needed to be brave enough to stand up to her mom, I didn't think my posts about her were that bad. I mean, I was saying what she wished she had the courage to say to her mother. But her tear-filled voicemail told me that her mother was going to make her life miserable over this, and that was my fault.

"It wasn't you, right?" she said by way of a greeting.

I paused. "No. It was me."

There was a sharp intake of breath past her teeth. "I see," she said, echoing her mother's censure of choice. A tiny piece of my heart that hadn't yet shattered fell apart. Despite it all, Sharon still wanted to please her mother, even if doing so meant becoming her.

"I'm so, so sorry." She was silent. "I never wanted to hurt you—please know that. The whole thing started because of Caryn's friends, but without the context of the five weddings, it didn't make sense why I was so—God, I don't even know—jaded? Cynical?"

"Mean?" she supplied.

"Yes. Mean too." The Buzzfeed post said I might just be the snarkiest person in the world, which I hoped was hyperbolic. "But I tried to focus on the people who were making my life difficult, and you never once did that."

"Lily, you called my mother a Japanese horror monster and said her skin was pulled so tight from plastic surgery that you were worried it would split open during the wedding and all of the demons inside her would come spilling out."

Crap. I did say that, didn't I?

But Sharon wasn't done. "Not to mention you called me spineless when it came to her and said I would throw myself off a bridge if she told me to."

"I didn't say 'spineless,' but—I mean, you didn't even want this wedding."

The next thing she said was so quiet that I almost couldn't hear it. "I did, actually."

"You told me you wanted to elope and your mother was forcing you to have a wedding."

I heard her start to cry. Which didn't mean she was upset; Sharon cried when she was angry instead of yelling. "She 'forced' me because I wasn't brave enough to do it if she didn't push me. I've been in therapy for eight years to deal with my social anxiety issues, and I said I wanted to elope because I didn't think anyone would actually come if I had a real wedding."

"I—didn't know any of that."

"Of course you didn't. I hide it. Not that you ever asked if I was okay when I didn't go out to things. You just stopped inviting me."

I stopped inviting her because she always said no. She was busy, or tired, or had other plans. But wasn't that the hallmark of social anxiety? Struggling to say yes to social outings?

Sharon and I had lived together for two years. She usually went out when I did in college, but she almost always had a drink or two at home first. But after college, she moved home to save money for a couple years, and I moved to Bethesda, first with Megan, then with Becca, when Megan switched jobs and wanted to move farther north. When Sharon stopped coming out, I just assumed her mother was exerting her domineering force over Sharon's social life and that I had been cut out.

If that wasn't the case—what had I just done to my friend?

"So you—wanted the big wedding with the white dress and the whole nine yards?"

"Yes. I want to get to do everything that everyone else does too."

"But you always said—"

"I didn't think anyone would want to marry me, so I pretended I didn't want any of it."

I stopped again. Did I think anyone would ever want to marry me? Well, not today, obviously, but I always assumed it would happen some- day. Kids too, even though my mother might be right that at thirty-two, perhaps I was cutting it close on that one. I joked that I would be a crazy cat lady who hated cats, but I never for a moment thought I was truly destined to be alone.

I was quiet and humbled when I replied. "I'm sorry, Sharon."

She was still crying, but the tone had changed. "I don't think that's enough."

I started to ask what I could do, but Amy's words rang in my ears. "I know. And I'll do whatever I need to do to make this right."

"I don't know if you can. How am I supposed to make my mother look at you in all of my wedding pictures, knowing what you said about her?"

"I don't know."

"I don't either."

There was a long pause. "Do you want me to not be in your wed- ding anymore?"

Another pause. "I have to think about it."

"Okay," I said quietly. "I'll do whatever you want. And I really am sorry."

I wasn't crying when I hung up the phone—I honestly didn't know if my eyes were capable of producing more tears. But I was shaken to the core. What kind of friend was I? What kind of person?

It had never once occurred to me to stop and look at Sharon's behavior through any lens other than my own. I thought, after knowing her for so many years, that Sharon was like me. Which, saying that now, sounded like an insult. But I thought all of my friends were like me. I couldn't fathom why Caryn cared what Caroline thought, even after she told me about the circumstances of her dad's death, because *I* didn't care about money or social status. I thought Megan was being unreasonable about Alex, but I hadn't once let her know how I felt about him. She wasn't a mind reader any more than I was.

Buzzfeed was wrong. I wasn't the snarkiest person in the world. I was just one of the least self-aware. I thought everyone else was the problem, but it had been me all along. Okay, not *entirely* me. Caryn's physical demands had gotten ridiculous, and Megan was probably the most like me in that she wasn't exactly examining my motives either.

But one thing was certain. In making the blog about me, I had proven I didn't deserve the position any of my friends or siblings had elevated me to by asking me to be in their weddings.

No wonder I'm alone, I thought.

I shook my head. I wasn't going to be able to fix everything. That much was obvious. Sharon and Caryn would probably never speak to me again, and they'd be entirely right not to. But my family would have to get over it eventually.

At least I hoped they would.

Phone calls in which my brother conveyed information from me to Madison had historically not worked in my favor. Jake and Madison were leaving the following day to go back to Chicago until Amy's wedding, so I decided to kill several birds with one stone and just show up at my parents' house to beg forgiveness from everyone at once.

CHAPTER THIRTY-SIX

My apartment was only about twenty minutes away from my childhood home, which, on the drive that day, felt metaphorical for how far I *hadn't* come from childhood. When you're a kid, you think you'll know how to do everything once you're an adult. But I must have screwed up somewhere along the way because Amy was the only one actually speaking to me, and I was driving to my parents' house to apologize for being the biggest jerk on the planet. Not to mention the distinct possibility that I would need Amy's recently vacated room, depending on how things played out at work.

I parked in the driveway next to Jake's rental car and took a moment to steel myself. I reached for the doorknob to let myself in—I had never knocked at my parents' house unless I had forgotten my key—but this wasn't a normal visit. So I removed my hand and pushed the doorbell, then waited.

My father opened the door, his glasses absentmindedly far down his nose. "Lily?" he asked, pushing the glasses up. "What are you doing here? And why did you ring the bell?"

"I didn't think I should just walk into the arena unannounced. The lions should know I'm coming."

He patted my shoulder and gestured for me to come in. "It's not as bad as all that. Your mother—well—you know how she gets. Everything is the end of the world. Until the next big crisis, at which point that's the end of the world. Hopefully the florist screws up something for Amy's wedding and she'll forget all about this."

My eyes welled up in gratitude. He patted me again awkwardly. "I'm sorry you had to see all that though," I said. "I never would have said as much if I thought people would know it was me—it wasn't all true, you know."

He shook his head. "I didn't read a word. I'm just going off what your mother told me."

"But she said you read it all."

"Good God, no. Sweetheart, I didn't survive having two teenage daughters by going snooping through your private thoughts. If I found a diary, and I did from time to time, I kept it closed."

I looked at him in wonder. I didn't understand how two such polar opposites as he and my mom could be so content after thirty-five years of marriage, yet here they were. Somehow they worked.

"Thanks, Dad."

"You'll make it right. I believe in you."

I let out a choked sound. "And if they fire me tomorrow, can I come home?"

"Absolutely not. I barely survived you and your mother living under the same roof the first time around. If something happens, we'll figure out how to help you get by."

I came as close as I had to smiling since before Alex kissed me, and I wrapped my arms around his waist in a tight hug. He hugged me back, then peeled my arms off. "Enough of that," he said firmly. "I don't want to get in trouble for fraternizing with the enemy. The lions might eat me, too, and then where would we be?"

"Eddie?" my mother's voice called down from upstairs. "Who was at the door?"

He nudged me forward and retreated into his study.

"It's me, Mom."

She appeared at the top of the stairs. "Well. You've got some nerve—"

"Actually, I need to talk to Jake and Madison first." She looked at me, taken aback. "I'm making amends in the order of who I offended most to least, and they outrank you."

She opened her mouth to respond, but snapped it shut again and crossed her arms. Then she tilted her head and nodded a single time.

"We're in the kitchen," Jake's voice rang out.

I looked back up at my mother. "Don't worry, you're next on my list." She huffed and went back to her room.

I went past the stairs and into the kitchen. Jake and Madison were at the table. Madison had her hands wrapped around a cup of tea and Jake had a beer, even though it was still pretty early in the day. Madison's eyes were red and puffy.

"Hey," I said. "Can I talk to you guys?"

Jake raised an eyebrow. Madison didn't look at me, but she nodded. I pulled out a seat at the table.

"I want to apologize to both of you, but especially to Madison."

"Hey—" Jake started to say.

I turned to him. "You and I both know you couldn't care less what I wrote in a blog unless it hurt her feelings."

He leaned back in his seat. "Continue."

"Madison, I'm really sorry. You were the most blameless of any of the five brides, and if I'd had a decent bone in my body, I would have left you out of the whole thing and just said I was in four weddings."

"That's not better," Jake said.

"I know. The blog shouldn't have existed in the first place."

"No, you idiot, it shouldn't have. But you should have taken the time to get to know Mads if you were going to post about her."

I looked from him to Madison. "I'm sorry, I'm lost here."

"She's not upset that you included her—she's upset that you had absolutely nothing to say about her because you never made any effort at all to get to know her."

I threw my hands up, exasperated. "Maybe if you ever let her speak for herself, that wouldn't have been a problem!"

Madison's eyes scrunched up like she was in pain, but she put a hand over Jake's, stopping him from responding.

"You're—a little scary," she said haltingly. "And I'm shy. But you . . ." She trailed off.

"I'm—scary?"

"Not scary, exactly. But intimidating, I guess."

"Me?"

She nodded. "The first time Jake brought me here to meet all of you, the whole dynamic changed the second you walked into the house."

I shook my head. "I don't know what you mean."

"I do," Jake said. "Am I allowed to talk yet?"

"Have I ever been able to stop you before?"

"Lily, you take up all of the oxygen in the room."

"What is that supposed to mean?"

"It means, as soon as you walk in, it's the Lily show. 'Lily is so successful.' 'Why isn't Lily married yet?' 'Lily was interviewed in the *New York Times* again.' 'Lily was on the news last week.' At the risk of sounding like Jan Brady, well—you get it."

"I'm the PR face of the foundation, that's the only reason newspapers ever quote me. It's not because I did anything. And I was on TV literally once."

"Twice. And Mom still hasn't shut up about it."

"How is that my fault?"

"It's not. But you flip your hair and bask in it, and that doesn't leave room for anyone else to exist."

I didn't know what to say.

"Look," Jake said. "You're my sister. And I love you, even though you're a totally self-absorbed asshole. But you haven't once tried to have a real conversation with Mads. Literally not once."

I began to object, then stopped myself and turned to Madison. Even if I didn't agree with everything Jake said, he wasn't wrong about that. "I'm sorry. I'd like to try again. If I can."

She nodded. "I'd like that."

"Maybe—" I dug for an idea. "Maybe email would be a good start? It might be a little less daunting?" I looked to Jake. "And there's no oxygen to use up in an email."

He rolled his eyes. "I'm going to be hearing about that one for the next fifty years, aren't I?"

"Probably." I turned back to Madison. "Would that work? I'd offer to take you to lunch, but you live kind of far away and all."

"Email sounds good." She started to say something else, then stopped herself.

"Please just say it," I said. "I promise I don't bite, no matter what Jake tells you."

He held up a wrist, which, admittedly, did have a bite scar from me. Madison smiled finally, apparently knowing the story.

"I liked the blog." I shook my head, but she continued. "The part about our wedding—about your grandmother—maybe it was because I know her, but I laughed so hard."

"As much as I hate to give you credit for anything right now, it's true," Jake said. "I came running in to see what she was laughing about because she had been so upset when the whole thing broke."

"I have a feeling she's going to kill me over that."

"If she runs you over with her car, it's fifty-fifty whether it was intentional or not. Did you see the mailbox?"

"No?"

"Exactly. She hit it yesterday and it's gone."

Madison started to giggle, and that was enough to make me laugh, though whether from the strain of it all or from the lack of mailbox, I didn't know.

CHAPTER THIRTY-SEVEN

"Oh, it's my turn now?" my mother asked wryly when I walked into her bedroom. She was sitting in one of the club chairs in the sitting room area. I sank down wearily in the other and disloyally wished for a mother who would comfort me instead of needing comfort herself.

"To be fair, you're further down the list, but I'm letting you line jump because Caryn isn't answering my calls."

"Everything is a joke to you, isn't it?"

"Not everything."

"You wouldn't know it from the way you're willing to treat people. This is why you're still single, you know."

I flinched. She wasn't going to make this easy—but then again, when did she ever? "Mom, I'm struggling here. I could use some support, not a lecture about how it's time for me to get married."

"I have never lectured you to get married."

"Fine—hinted, begged, implored, whatever terminology you want to use. But marrying just anyone isn't going to make me happy. And I'm not going to have those grandkids you want if I'm not happy."

"I obviously never meant for you to marry someone who didn't make you happy. But maybe your standards are too high. You think your father is the perfect man? Don't answer that. You probably do." She crossed her arms. "It's not easy for me, you know. You all act like he's the second coming, and me? I'm just your shrew of a mother."

I pressed a finger to my forehead between my eyebrows, struggling with what to say and what not to say. "Mom, how do you think all those little jabs about how at least *one* of your daughters was getting married felt? Or comparing my weight with Amy's? Or telling me that I should be using these weddings as an opportunity to find a guy?"

She crossed her arms. "I never compared your weight with Amy's." Of course that was the one thing she heard.

I took a deep breath. "Mom, I feel like nothing I do is good enough if I'm not living your exact life. And I can't do that."

"What's so wrong with my life?"

"Nothing. But it's not mine."

"Yours doesn't sound so great when you spend your time saying horrible things about your mother on some blog."

The blog wasn't about you, Mom, rose up in my throat and tried to come out of my mouth, but I blocked it. Because that was the bigger problem here, wasn't it? The weddings weren't about me, but I made everything about me with the blog. And I didn't grow to be that way in a vacuum.

"I painted a caricature in broad strokes," I said finally. "You—and Grandma for that matter—worked best as humorous foils to my narrator—kind of like a Falstaff character—"

"English, please." The irony was completely lost on her.

"I used the two of you for comic relief rather than creating an accurate portrayal."

"And do you see how hurtful that is?"

I exhaled heavily. "I do."

She seemed mildly satisfied with that, then moved down her mental checklist to the next of my sins. "And your poor sister, to even imply such a thing about her at her bachelorette party—"

"Amy and I talked before I came over here."

"Well, she didn't tell me that. When I talked to her this morning, she said she never wanted to speak to you again." Amy didn't come by her flair for the dramatic in a vacuum either.

"We had a heart-to-heart and I apologized. She accepted it."

"Are you still in her wedding then?"

"Yes."

She sniffed. "I suppose you're going to tell me that the whole thing about that groomsman was a caricature too?"

I looked down. I was too tired to lie about any of it. "No. That happened."

"Didn't I raise you better than that? To have some self-respect?"

"Mom, I'm thirty-two, not sixteen. I made a decision—albeit a terrible one—but I'm not the first thirty-something to have sex. You had two of your three kids by my age."

"I was married!"

"You used to love *Sex and the City*, so please spare me your outrage about sleeping with someone without a ring. I made a really bad decision, and I'm paying the price for it in spades."

"Thank God you didn't sleep with the other groomsman too. At least there's that."

I felt my face screwing up as I fought to keep from crying, but there was no stopping it. "Mom, you have to stop. You *have* to. You're all over me all the time and it's too much. I can't be you. I can't be Amy. All I can be is me. And I'm sorry me isn't enough for you, but it's all I am."

She was stunned into silence and I hung my head. I don't know what I expected her to say. It wasn't like she was going to change. I didn't think she was capable of it at that point. She was who she was, just like I had said about myself.

But the silence was more than I could bear and the truth started pouring out of me. "I wish I could be the person you want me to be and be married with kids already, but I don't wish it for me at all. I wish it for you. Because even though *I* like who I am, I wish I could make you happy."

She still hadn't spoken, and I went back to the last thing she had said. "And no, I didn't sleep with Alex. I—I love him. He's—he's my best friend. And he said I'm his. And I ruined it all. So please, Mom, please, please, *please*, don't make this about what I did to *you*."

I got up to try to leave, but she put a hand on my arm, stopping me, her face stricken. "You—love—him?"

My shoulders dropped and I nodded. I hadn't even let myself think that word. But it came out on its own, and there was no way to shove it back into Pandora's box.

Her entire countenance changed—this was right in her wheelhouse, after all. And I, unlike Amy, never allowed her to share in my romantic mishaps. She rose and wrapped her arms around me. "Oh, Lily."

It was the comfort that I wanted, but a heavy price to pay to get it. My aunt, siblings, and grandmother would all know the details of the Alex situation, probably heavily embellished with additional details that had never happened, by the time I was halfway down the street on my way home, no matter how she might swear never to tell a soul. But it wasn't like Alex would be my date to Amy's wedding anymore—if that had been the case, this would have been its own new disaster.

"It doesn't matter," I said, when I was able to stop my eyes from overflowing. "It's over now."

"Who is this person talking to me? Not my daughter, who never gives up until she gets her way. No, he'll come around."

It was the first time in my memory that my mother had offered praise of my tenacity instead of bemoaning my stubbornness. If Jake and Amy were to be believed, she talked me up constantly when I wasn't around. To my face, however, an interaction with her always left me feeling like I had been pecked at by a small but ferocious bird, who knew exactly where my weakest spots were. With love, of course, and the desire to make me better. But it still left me with the sensation that if I drank a glass of water after seeing her, it would come pouring out of the holes she had left like a sieve. So this—this was new territory. And a tiny ray of hope bolstered me.

But I shook my head. That was a pipe dream. Squaring your shoulders and vowing that you would get the guy back might work for Scarlett O'Hara, but real life didn't work that way. "No. I messed up too much."

"Nonsense. Even if he said that, he didn't mean it."

"He made it pretty clear he's done with me."

The corners of her mouth rose into a frighteningly determined grin, her eyes lighting at the challenge. "Isn't he a groomsman in Megan's wedding?" I nodded. "And aren't you giving a speech at that wedding?"

I looked away. "I don't know anymore."

"What did Megan say?"

"I haven't talked to her yet."

"Lily! She's been your friend for how many years?"

I looked back up, bemused. "And you wanted your apology before Madison's?"

She waved a hand in the air. "You have to talk to Megan."

"I'm going to." It was too complicated to explain why I wasn't ready yet.

"Good. Then you can use your speech to win him back." She kept talking, pacing as she formulated her plan of how I would convince Alex to love me back, and I watched her. This strange, indomitable woman whose body I came from. She would never understand defeat—I didn't think it was even in her vocabulary—any more than she would understand why using my maid of honor speech (if I was still giving one) to win Alex back would only prove to everyone, including Alex, that I had learned nothing.

Instead of arguing, I nodded, thanked her, and kissed her on the cheek when I rose to leave. She grabbed me in a tight hug and whispered in my ear, "They conquer who believe they can." My mother was a paradox to the last—make a Shakespeare reference and she told you to speak English, yet here she was, whispering a quote from a two-thousand-years-dead philosopher. And if I mentioned Virgil, she would respond, "Who? I saw that on a pillow at Home Goods."

She would never acknowledge the rest of what I said. It would have confused her own sense of self. But this was enough for now.

CHAPTER THIRTY-EIGHT

I still couldn't bring myself to call Megan, so I called my grandmother from my parents' driveway.

"It's Lily," I said.

"Doesn't ring a bell. Apparently I only call my eldest granddaughter Joan."

"Can I come over?"

"Why? Do you need more material? Should I invite my mah-jongg club over too so you can write about them?"

"Please, Grandma?"

"Suit yourself."

But despite the attitude over the phone, her front door was open behind the screen door when I arrived, as it always was when I was expected.

"Grandma?" I called as I came in.

"In the kitchen, Joan." I didn't correct her. "Are you hungry? I made a cake." She was sitting at the table, reading glasses on the bridge of her nose, the newspaper in front of her.

I started to refuse, then realized I was famished and said I would love a slice. She stood, but I told her I would get it, and I cut one for each of us, then brought them over on two tea plates.

"I'm really sorry, Grandma."

"For what, darling?"

I was genuinely confused—did she not remember? That happened sometimes with her, but my mother always assured us it was just old age, not Alzheimer's—the same way she didn't ever remember our names. Or was she being difficult and planning to extract a more detailed apology by playing dumb?

"For—the blog."

"You got stuck in a bog?"

"Blog. The—the thing I wrote?"

"Oh, the Google thing your mother sent me?"

"I—uh—yeah, probably."

"It was very nice. But I don't understand what a blog is."

"It's a—oh God, how do I explain it? It's kind of like a place where you can publish the stuff you write for people to read on the internet?"

"Like the Facebook?"

"No—not exactly—I mean—" How to explain it to a woman who called the internet "the Google" and who insisted, when she had me make her a Facebook page, that I use a picture of her from when she was a dozen years younger than I was now because she looked too old in all the others? "Yes, it's like Facebook. But for longer stuff that you write."

"In my day, we wrote letters."

I debated explaining that this was much more public, but that wouldn't help my cause any. "Um. Yeah. But I wanted to apologize for what I wrote."

"Why's that?"

"Because I wasn't very nice in it."

"It sounds like those girls owe you apologies, not the other way around."

"I meant for the parts about you."

She tilted her head at me. "I don't follow."

"I shouldn't have made fun of you."

"Who made fun? You wrote what Louise and I did."

"But it wasn't nice."

"You keep saying that—who cares if it's nice if it's true?"

"I—" This wasn't going how I expected it to at all. "Mom said you were mad at me."

She waved a hand in the air. "Your mother says a lot of things. How I raised such an uptight daughter, I will never understand."

"You're not mad?"

"Honey, at my age, who has time to be mad about things like that?" She took a bite of cake and gestured for me to do the same. "Is that why you came over?"

"I—well—yeah."

"You could come visit without thinking I'm mad or that you need to babysit me on an airplane, you know." I tried to remember the last time I had been to her house other than picking her up and dropping her back home for the Mexico trip. I had seen her, of course, at my mother's house and when she came dress shopping. But the last time I came by just for a visit was well before people started getting engaged. Which meant it had been at least a year. And given her age, the opportunities to spend time with her were getting more and more limited by the day.

"You're right," I nodded. "You're really not mad?"

"Did you kill anyone?"

"No."

"Steal anything?"

"No."

"Then no. I'll be a little miffed if you don't finish that piece of cake though." I took a bite, feeling somewhat lighter. "Your mother sounded pretty upset, but I don't put much stock in that. Raises my blood pressure too much. I just take my hearing aids out when she starts going on."

"Why did you act like you were mad over the phone then?"

She winked at me. "It got you to come visit, didn't it?" I mentally kicked myself again. But one of my grandmother's best qualities was that she genuinely didn't hold grudges. Yes, she might say anything and everything that popped into her head, no matter how inappropriate, but once she had said it, she was done. My weekends might be booked solid for the next month (or might not be, depending on how my friends took my apologies), but I promised myself I would be better about coming to see Grandma as soon as the weddings were done. "But you seem upset. Explain to me why this blog thing is such a big deal."

"A lot of people saw it. And I didn't have my name on it, so I didn't think anyone would know it was me, but then people figured it out."

"Well of course it was you! Who else is in five weddings at once?"

"Yeah. I didn't think that through so well."

"Why are you friends with those girls anyway? It doesn't seem like you like them very much."

"I do—well—normally. The weddings have kind of spun out of control."

"I don't understand you all with weddings. In my day, the mother planned everything. Your sisters were your bridesmaids and that was that."

"Can you imagine if Mom planned Amy's wedding?"

"Oh God no, your mother has terrible taste. She didn't get that from me either." I looked around and suppressed a grin. My grandmother still had brightly colored fruit-themed wallpaper from the seventies in her kitchen and had almost enough kitschy knickknacks to qualify as a hoarder.

She patted my hand on the table. "It'll all blow over, dear. Nothing lasts forever. Well, except herpes." My eyes widened in horror, but she didn't notice. "Do you like the cake? It's a new recipe."

CHAPTER
THIRTY-NINE

I still didn't want to talk to Megan when I got home, but I knew it was time.

Before I pushed the button on my phone to call her, though, I turned to the next page of the notepad with my apology list and bulleted out some things I needed to say.

"Talk," she said when I called.

"Hello to you too."

"Seriously, Lily, what the hell?"

"Well," I said haltingly. "You were the one who told me to write a book about my ridiculous life."

"Okay. Call me back when you're ready to be serious. I don't have time for this right now."

I sighed. "What do you want me to say?"

"Uh, that you're sorry? That'd be a great start."

"I'm sorry." I paused. "But—"

"Everything before the 'but' is bullshit."

I didn't respond immediately. "I'm not ready to apologize without a 'but' yet."

"Are you kidding me?"

"No. I need to say a few things before I can apologize. If you don't want to listen, then we don't have to talk yet."

She was quiet so long I thought she might have hung up. "Fine. Talk."

"Okay." I picked up my list.

"Don't tell me you made a list to talk to me."

She knew me too well. "I did. I don't want to mess up."

"It's me, Lily."

"Yeah. I know. That's why it's important." She didn't respond. "Okay. I love you to death. I need to say that. I know you're rolling your eyes right now, but I wanted to start with that. Number two: I didn't actually think you'd mind the blog."

"I—"

"Wait, please, let me finish, okay?" She stopped. "Number three: It really hurt my feelings when you said you wanted me to wear the minimizing bra to your wedding too. You're my best friend, and I always thought you were the one person who loved me exactly as I was, and that sucked. A lot. Number four: I couldn't believe you told me to re-dye my hair for your wedding. I don't even want this stupid hair color, but why are you making me change how I look?" I took a deep breath.

"Can I talk now?"

"No. I have one more and it's the big one."

"Okay."

"You killed me when you said I couldn't date Alex."

"I didn't say you couldn't—"

"You did though. You said I didn't do relationships so I needed to not mess around with Tim's friends. And that wasn't fair. Because it wasn't messing around with Alex. It was—well, it doesn't matter now because he doesn't want to be with me anymore. But it was real."

She was quiet. "Now can I respond?"

"Yeah."

"Look at the Alex thing from my point of view for a minute. The night of my engagement party, you—"

"I know."

"And then Alex went around telling everyone that you and he—"

"I know that too."

"And then you said Alex was saying that because Justin was trying to sleep with you. And it just looked like you were creating a lot of drama for no reason."

"I think I'm done creating drama for a while."

"I think that blog says otherwise."

"I deleted it. It's gone."

"Nothing is ever gone. That Buzzfeed post is still a thing."

"It's Buzzfeed, Megs. Name one Buzzfeed thing you remember from before this. Other than a quiz about which type of French fry you are."

Neither of us said anything for a long time. "You don't have to wear the bra. Or change your hair," she said finally.

"Well I do have to wear the bra now, because the dress won't fit if I don't and it's too late to get it re-tailored. But thank you. And I already have the appointment to re-dye my hair."

"I actually kind of like it how it is. It's subtle. And I don't want to make you do anything you don't want to do."

"It's not me though."

There was another silence. We had never had an awkward pause in twenty-five years of friendship before this conversation.

"Do you want to be with Alex?"

"It's a moot point now."

"I'm not taking the blame for that. You did that yourself."

"I know." Pause. "I'm sorry, Megs."

"No more 'buts'?"

"No."

"Okay then."

"That's all?"

"I'm still annoyed. That isn't going to go away overnight. But you're my best friend. What am I going to do? Kick you out of my wed—oh shit, are other people kicking you out of their weddings?"

"I don't know. Amy isn't. Sharon said she's got to think about it. Caryn isn't talking to me yet."

"Isn't Caryn's this weekend?"

"Yeah."

"She's got to be flipping out right now. She's so worried about appearances, and if she cuts you out, everyone will know why."

"It would probably be a relief if she did. I wouldn't have to face her coven of bridesmaids."

"They're totally doing incantations about you right now."

"I know."

"Which way do you think Sharon will go?"

"I don't know."

"Are you going to be in trouble at work?"

"I assume I'll find out tomorrow."

Megan went quiet again. "Lil—why didn't you tell me you actually liked Alex?"

I closed my eyes. "I think I was in denial. If I didn't admit it to myself, I couldn't get hurt."

"How'd that work out?" I didn't respond and she didn't press it. "Let me know what happens tomorrow?" I told her I would. "Your maid of honor speech better be amazing, now that I've seen your writing."

"Ha. I'll get right on that. I may have two of the next three weekends free."

"Good. You can help me finish favors."

I smiled faintly.

"I still love you, you know. Even though this was a horrible friend move."

"I love you too. Even if I suck at showing it." I started to say goodbye, then realized I had forgotten about Tim's sister's threat to not be in the wedding if I was. "Wait, what about Claire?"

"She's all talk. There's no way she'd miss the chance to snub you at the wedding."

"Great. Something to look forward to." I hesitated. "I know I don't have any right to ask this, but you won't make me walk down the aisle with Alex, right?"

"It would be a fitting punishment."

"Megan, please."

"You're not. You're with the best man. You're all at the same table at the reception though. It'd look weird if I had one bridesmaid somewhere else."

"Okay, that's fine. I just—I can't walk down the aisle with him. And I know this is what you were trying to avoid, and I'm sorry, but I can't—"

"How many times have you said those words today? 'I'm sorry.'"

"More than I think I have in my entire life."

"Have a glass of wine and get some sleep. It sounds like tomorrow might be a rough one too."

I agreed and we said good night.

~

I had one last apology to send that night. I was lying in bed, where I always texted him before I went to sleep. I opened the conversation with

Alex, then typed the same two words that I had been saying all day. No buts. Just, I'm sorry.

The three dots appeared to show he was typing, then disappeared. They didn't reappear.

I turned my phone facedown and cried, one more time, knowing it was really and truly over.

CHAPTER FORTY

Caryn still hadn't returned my messages by the time I stopped crying and settled in to try to sleep Monday night. But on the plus side, I hadn't gotten any emails indicating I would be fired in the morning, so I would take the victory there.

They don't give you advance warning on that anymore, Becca texted when I told her that was the good news. Prevents workplace shootings and all.

"Thanks, Bec," I said out loud. Great.

I tossed and turned, unable to get comfortable. And God, how I missed Alex. I hadn't realized how much I would miss talking to him before I went to bed at night. He would have known how to make me feel better.

When I woke up Tuesday morning, I looked in the mirror. The eyelash extensions just highlighted how red my eyes were, so I dug through the bathroom drawer for some unexpired eye drops and eventually found a bottle that still had a month left. I couldn't walk into my own execution looking like I was high. My eyes were still glassy after the drops, but at least they were a more normal color.

I rushed out the door and hopped on the Metro. As I passed Starbucks, I looked longingly at it, but decided not to stop. There wouldn't be anything from Alex, and I couldn't be late today. Coffee in the break room would be good enough.

My keycard to enter the building still worked, which was a good sign. I went upstairs and put my bag at my desk. Caryn's office was down the hall, light spilling from it to indicate she was there. Tomorrow was her last day until after her honeymoon; she was taking Thursday and Friday off to finish wedding preparations, then would be gone the following ten days.

I squared my shoulders and walked toward the rectangle of light. I had realized, as I failed to sleep the previous night, that there was no chance I was still in Caryn's wedding. That was why she hadn't returned my call. And that was fine, but assuming I wasn't fired—which was a pretty big assumption—working here would be a lot harder if Caryn couldn't forgive me.

"Hey," I said, coming around the doorframe. I didn't sit down.

Caryn didn't look up from her computer. "Martin wants to see you at nine thirty," she said brusquely. Martin was the head of the entire foundation. This was bad.

"Oh. Is he—am I fired?"

"I don't know and I don't really care."

"Caryn—I—"

She finally looked up. "I, I, I, I, I. That's all it ever is with you, isn't it?"

"I—"

"Don't even say it! Do you even know how many times I've had to cover for you? To make excuses? To remind you about things that you should know how to do by now? Everything is about you all the time. But this? This was about me. And that wasn't okay, was it?"

I opened my mouth, but she cut me off again. "I don't have time for this right now. I have to get everything ready for while I'm gone, and I don't know if you'll even still be here to do any of the work while I'm in Fiji."

"Can I come back later?" My voice was meek. I understood this was part of my penance—letting them have their say about my flaws. And so far, none of them had been wrong.

"If you still work here? Fine."

I crept back to my office, listening to the clock on the wall tick out its seconds, each tick bringing the hands closer to the time I would learn my fate, each tick echoing louder, like something Edgar Allan Poe created. *Tick. Tick. Tick.* I couldn't pretend to work. My mouth was dry and I took a sip from my water bottle. *Tick. Tick. Tick.* I finally stood on my desk and removed the clock from the wall, prying the battery out of the back with a pen.

I glanced at my phone. It was 9:22. Ugh.

At 9:26, I left my office and went to Martin's, where I knocked quietly on the open door.

"Lily," he said, glancing up at me, then at the clock on the wall. He swiveled his chair away from his computer toward the desk, where there were two seats across from him. "Come on in. Close the door behind you, if you don't mind?"

I swallowed heavily and did as I was told.

"It sounds like you've been busy."

"Yes."

"I got a call from the *Washington Post* yesterday. At home. Which was a little awkward, because normally I would direct them to talk to you."

I nodded, not trusting myself to speak.

"I didn't know what they were talking about, so they had to explain the whole thing to me. Then I googled it and saw the Buzzfeed story."

I felt my cheeks turning red. Martin was in his sixties. He wore a white beard, as all scientists seemed to—the old joke at the foundation was that you couldn't win a Nobel Prize if you didn't have a beard, but Martin had directed the staff to stop saying that because it wasn't inclusive. He was a strong advocate for women in the sciences, and sexism was unequivocally not tolerated on his watch. But I still cringed at the idea of someone who, were he to don a red hat and coat, would look like Santa Claus reading about my sleeping with Justin while blackout drunk.

"I'm sorry," I said, for what felt like the five billionth time in the last twenty-four hours. The words were starting to sound like I was mispronouncing them from semantic satiation.

Martin looked a little surprised. "Why are you sorry?"

"I—I worked on it on foundation time and that's how they found me. And now the whole foundation is associated with this and—"

The corners of his mouth turned up slightly and I trailed off, confused.

"Have you checked the analytics for the website today?"

"I—no—I haven't." My shoulders slumped. I clearly had not done any work yet, which couldn't help my case.

He turned back to his computer and clicked a few buttons. Then he picked up a remote control and turned on the monitor on the wall, which mirrored his computer screen. A side button on the remote triggered a laser pointer, which he used to point out the number.

"Admittedly, I don't look at our analytics every day—that's your job, after all—but that seems pretty high to me."

It was nearly ten times the typical traffic to the foundation's home page.

"Granted, a lot of that traffic then clicked through to our staff pages to find you, but many people did stay to look at our mission statement and some of our research projects."

I didn't know what to say. He seemed—well—almost pleased.

He leaned back in his chair and stroked his beard. "The reporter wanted to know if you had been fired." He looked at me as if waiting for a reaction and stopped talking.

"Am I?" My voice shook.

"How long have you worked here, Lily?"

"It'll be eleven years in August."

He nodded. "And how many people have you seen me fire?"

I couldn't think of any, but that didn't mean there weren't any. People came and went, and I didn't always ask for particulars. "I don't know."

The corners of his mouth twitched again. "I'm not exactly Donald Trump. I've never fired anyone."

Relief started to trickle down my back like perspiration. I might not be out of the woods yet, but I wasn't losing my job today.

"What did you tell the reporter?"

"The truth. I told her you've been here about a decade and that we don't keep strict nine-to-five hours. I've seen you eating lunch at your desk for most of this year, and if you choose to do personal projects during that break time, you're perfectly within your rights to do so. She didn't seem to think there was much of a story if you weren't being fired. Pity though. All publicity is good publicity and all that."

My mouth was open. "Are you saying it's *good* that this happened?"

"Not for you, obviously. And Caryn didn't look too happy. I assume she's Bride A? But from where I'm standing, you just brought us a bunch of free press."

This wasn't even remotely how I expected the conversation to go. "We won't lose any funding?"

He chuckled. "Over a Buzzfeed article about a blog? No. I think we'll manage to stay afloat."

"Thank you, sir."

"Don't thank me yet. That's not why I called you in today."

"It's not?"

"Well, the blog is. But you still have your job. If you want it."

"If I want it?"

"I read it—before you took it down. You're a talented writer."

I flushed, remembering the snarkiness, the description of my drunken grandmother naked in a hot tub, the graphic depiction of squeezing myself into the foundation garments that Caryn demanded I wear, the Alex and Justin debacle. Not exactly what I wanted Santa Boss knowing about my personal life.

"Thank you," I mumbled.

"Lily, I need to ask—why are you still here?" I looked up, surprised. Was he telling me to go back to my office? "Eleven years is an awfully long time to spend on something you're not passionate about."

Was he firing me after all?

"Look, you can work here as long as you want to," he continued. "I'm not going to push you out. You're great at explaining things in a way that lets non-scientists understand what we're doing. But part of my job is to help people reach their potential, because when people are comfortable enough to experiment, that's when amazing discoveries happen. And Lily, you're hiding here."

My breathing was shallow, and I was suddenly terrified that I was going to cry again. "I think you need a plan," he said. "What do you want to be doing? Because I don't think writing press releases about neutrinos is it."

He stopped, and I was clearly expected to formulate some kind of response. But I didn't know what to say. I had just been laid bare by someone I thought hardly knew my name. I spent so much time creeping past his office so he wouldn't realize how often I was late for work, only for him to tell the *Washington Post*, of all things, that our hours were flexible. For him to read such intimate details of my life and somehow see through those escapades to recognize that this job was a screen I hid behind so that I wouldn't risk failure with my own writing. Because of course young Lily hadn't lain in bed at night with a flashlight scribbling in a diary about her future career as a public relations officer for a scientific organization. I had always wanted to write. But to actually write and put that work out into the world for people to read and reject? Yes, it was what I wanted and the blog had helped me realize that, but—

"I want to write," I said quietly. "But—" I stopped.

"But?" he asked gently.

"I'm scared," I whispered, not even realizing that it was true until I said it.

"Of course you are. It's terrifying to create something that's never existed before. But like every good scientist learns, trial and error is the only way to discovery."

I shook my head. "I'm not a scientist though."

He smiled kindly. "Oh yes you are."

～

After leaving his office ten minutes later, I walked back to mine in a daze. The plan we had concocted was that I had a year. A year to keep doing what I was doing, but also to figure out what I wanted to be doing. To start writing. To experiment. And if I hadn't figured it out at the end of that year—well, we would cross that bridge if and when we came to it. Martin was confident I would be back in his office in well under a year to tell him I had found my passion project. "And if it doesn't pay the bills immediately," he grinned, "I get the feeling you're not exactly using a hundred percent of your brain writing press releases. You can moonlight."

I was terrified. But maybe, just maybe, I hadn't lost everything after all.

CHAPTER
FORTY-ONE

I waited until lunchtime to go back to Caryn. I didn't doubt that she was busy, but at least now, with my future at the foundation safe, I could offer to help lighten that load somewhat.

"You're still here then?" she asked coolly when I came back to her office. She had a green smoothie with a straw in it on her desk, which I assumed was her lunch. Ever skinny, she looked positively gaunt now, which I knew was the product of hard work for her wedding, not my betrayal.

"I am. Can I sit?"

She glanced up at her clock. "I'll give you five minutes."

"I'm sorry."

She looked at me blankly. "Great. Are you done?"

I looked back at her, the fringe of the Kewpie-doll eyelashes that she made me get dancing at the top of my vision. For a moment, I debated letting this one go. Caryn hadn't been much of a friend this year, had she? I mean, it was ridiculous that I'd had to change my hair, my lashes, and my body shape for the sake of her pictures. Not to mention, I had spent more money on her wedding than the others combined, between the minimizing bra, Spanx, dress, shoes, eyelashes, keratin hair treatment, and the horror show of her shower and bachelorette party, and she showed no sign of even knowing that was a hardship for me.

And I didn't know how to make her understand that I was happier just being who I was, metaphorical warts and all, because Caryn's whole life was an exercise in image.

I pictured my someday wedding, ignoring the fact that the groom now looked like Alex instead of a faceless mannequin in a tuxedo. Who did I see there with me? Megan, Amy, Sharon, Becca, and Caryn, of course. Did I care that they were a mismatched bunch? Absolutely not. Did I even care if they wore matching dresses? Not in the slightest. But that didn't mean I was right and Caryn was wrong, nor did it mean that Caryn was right and I was wrong. We just wanted different things.

"No," I said. "I handled this badly."

"That's an understatement."

"I should have said no earlier in the process."

"No to what?" Caryn's voice was defensive.

"To the things that made me feel like the blog was an appropriate response." She started to cut me off, but I continued. "It wasn't an appropriate response. The appropriate response would have been to say no when we went past my comfort level. I don't want to wear a minimizing bra, or lose weight, or wear these things on my eyelashes, or have this blonde, straight hair."

Caryn narrowed her eyes. "That's the worst apology I've ever heard."

"I don't mean I should have said I wouldn't do them. I mean I should have said I couldn't be in your wedding."

She rubbed her forehead angrily. "What are you trying to do to me right now? It's too late to find someone who will fit into your dress, and my pictures will look off-balance if I don't have an even number of bridesmaids and groomsmen."

"I don't mean right now. I'll do whatever you want right now. I mean earlier, when there was time to figure it out. Caryn, I spent over three thousand dollars on your wedding alone, and I'm in four others. I don't have that kind of money."

"That's just what weddings cost."

"It's not, actually. I mean, it might be for some people, but it isn't in my world. And I should have told you I was in over my head before it got to the point where I started resenting you."

Her lips had tightened into an almost invisible line, but she didn't say anything, so I kept going.

"Look, I love you. I do. And I took the passive-aggressive route here, which was me being a horrible person and an even worse friend. And for that, I am very sorry. I'm even more sorry that I repeated things you said in confidence about the other bridesmaids, because that was worse than anything I said about you in the blog. I understand if you want nothing to do with me anymore for that. And like I said, I'll do whatever you want me to about the wedding. If you want me there, I'll be there in my minimizing bra, and I'll wear my makeup however you tell me, and I'll smile for pictures and keep my mouth shut. If you want me nowhere near it, I'll respect that too." I stopped talking.

"But?" she asked.

"No buts. 'Everything before the but is bullshit,' isn't that how the saying goes? Well, I already said what I needed to say. Tell me what you want me to do about this weekend and that's what I'll do."

"And after that?"

I hesitated. "I want to write. My own writing. Martin and I talked and he said he's giving me a year to figure out what I want to do. So worst-case scenario, we be polite in the halls until then. If that's what you want."

"What do you want?"

"I'm going to leave the ball in your court on this one."

Caryn looked unsure. "I don't know if we can rebuild our trust. You told the whole world things that I told you in confidence."

I nodded. "It would take a lot of work. On both sides. But I'm willing to try if you want to."

Her eyebrows contracted slightly. If not for the Botox, her forehead might have furrowed, but that was no longer a possibility. "Maybe you were right about the lash extensions. You look like an anime character with how round your eyes already are."

My mouth curled into a hint of a smile. It was said without malice—a Caryn way of saying I looked better the way I normally was. "I can take them out. I've got the baby oil in my purse ready to go."

"Don't you dare before the wedding. After all of this, those pictures better be flawless."

"Make sure I get a copy of the one where Caroline is trying to stab me with a lobster fork."

"There's a decent chance that actually happens."

I grinned. "As long as she stabs somewhere covered by the dress, I'll be fine. She can't penetrate all of that shapewear. I'm practically bulletproof."

Caryn shook her head and almost smiled. "I don't *actually* hate you anymore. I guess that's something."

"I don't want to trash you on the internet anymore. So we're making progress."

She looked up at the clock. "You're out of time. I'll see you on Friday for the rehearsal dinner. Don't be late to that. Or Saturday."

"I won't."

"And you're on your own with the other girls."

I imagined that to look something like the Salem witch trials, only in purple evening gowns instead of puritanical dresses, but I kept that observation to myself. Instead, I told Caryn to let me know if there was anything I could do to help while she was gone.

She said she would let me know and reminded me, with a pointed look at my peeling red nail polish, that I was supposed to wear either nude nail polish or a French manicure for Saturday. I assured her that I was waiting until Thursday to get them done, so they would be fresh for the weekend.

I didn't quite breathe a sigh of relief, as part of me had hoped I wouldn't have to face the wicked bridesmaids of the west again. But if our friendship could survive this, there wasn't much that could end it.

CHAPTER FORTY-TWO

I wasn't late, but I was still the last of the bridesmaids to arrive at Caryn's rehearsal. They stared at me with what I assumed was unmitigated hatred under their frozen faces.

Then, as if cued by some dog whistle I couldn't hear, they all turned their heads and proceeded to ignore me for the rest of the evening. Caryn's grandmother and one of her uncles were the only two people who spoke to me all night.

Which was probably for the best.

I kept to myself the following day, as we gathered at the salon for hair and makeup. I was glad we weren't in a hotel suite getting ready, like we would be for Sharon's and Megan's weddings. There was room to hide at the salon.

My phone vibrated as I waited my turn to have my makeup airbrushed on. I grabbed for it, instinctively thinking it was Alex before remembering it wouldn't be.

Good luck. It was from Megan.

Thanks. It's pretty awkward.

You deserve awkward.

I know.

You gonna trip that Caroline chick?

I smiled. Probably the other way around. I'm on my best behavior.

If she attacks you, try not to let her get your face. I don't want you looking like Freddy Krueger at my wedding.

I sent a thumbs-up emoji, then looked up to see Caroline watching me through narrowed eyes. I put the phone away and stared straight ahead.

We left the salon in a limo. I sat a little ways apart, just trying to be invisible. Not that it mattered; the other bridesmaids were pretending I wasn't there anyway. When we arrived at the historic manor house overlooking the Potomac River, we all got into our dresses while the photographer took some bathrobe shots of Caryn, and then it was time to get her into her dress.

I went silently to the rest of the girls to help.

"We don't need you," Caroline hissed. "You're only here at all because it was too late to get anyone who could fit into your dress."

I recoiled as if she had slapped me.

No one said anything.

Eventually, I looked to Caryn. "Do you want me to not be in the pictures for this? I can make myself scarce."

She opened her mouth to speak, then closed it again. I remembered how happy Madison had looked on her wedding day, and I felt a wave of crushing guilt. It was my fault Caryn looked miserable today. *What have I done?*

Then she surprised me.

She turned her head to Caroline. "Can you, for once in your life, just stop? I told Lily I want her here. It's not your call. If you don't like it, you can leave."

Caroline opened her mouth in shock and started to protest, but Caryn cut her off, leaving her standing there looking like a fish. "Look, I read Lily's blog. And while I didn't like that she did that, I'm glad I found out what you did to her about the shower. Do you know she didn't even tell me? Because she knew you would spin it. So please just stop, help get me in my dress, and smile like you're happy for me."

In a huff, Caroline turned on her heel and went to the bathroom, and Dana shot me a quick, tight smile. I looked at Caryn, my eyes wide. "Thank you," I mouthed. She squeezed my shoulder in response, then plastered a radiant smile on her face. "Come on. Dress time."

~

Caroline pulled herself together and pretended nothing had happened once we had Caryn's dress on her and it was time for the ceremony. Caryn looked picture-perfect, like she had stepped out of the pages of a magazine, and every detail of the wedding felt like a fairy tale. I couldn't begin to imagine what the event cost, but between her stepfather and Greg, I didn't think anyone was counting pennies.

I hung out by the bar for much of the evening, but I nursed the same two glasses of champagne all night. Martin asked me to dance because his wife made eye contact with me and then nudged him. But I returned to the bar after the song was over.

"Mind if I join you?" a male voice asked. I looked over. His name was Finn and he was one of Greg's groomsmen. He had the kind of Boston accent that made him sound like a Kennedy.

I gave a half smile. "It's a free wedding."

He chuckled. "Free is a relative term at these things. But sure." He tilted his head at me as he leaned against the bar. "You're the scandalous one? Lily?"

"That's me."

"World's worst bridesmaid?"

"According to Buzzfeed."

He took a sip of his drink and smiled. "You don't seem so bad."

"Looks can be deceiving."

"Clearly. Because you look beautiful."

I made a disbelieving face. "You mean DC Barbie isn't your type?" I bit the inside of my cheek hard. I was supposed to be being good.

He laughed heartily. "No, it's not. I like my women real."

I turned to actually look at him. He was ridiculously handsome, as all the men in Caryn's set were, with a full, thick head of hair and an impeccably cut tuxedo. Maybe he *was* a Kennedy. "It's Finn, isn't it?" He nodded. "What do you do, Finn?"

"Investment banking." He cocked his head. "You?"

"PR. Same company as Caryn."

"I have a feeling she won't be working much longer."

"Yeah. I know."

"How about you?" I looked at him quizzically. I wasn't exactly marrying rich and quitting my job anytime soon. "How are you going to spin this whole publicity thing?"

"Huh?"

"You've got some buzz going right now. You should use it. Find a way to make it profitable."

"What does an investment banker know about that?"

He grinned. "My parents are in publishing. I cut my teeth on this stuff."

The wheels were turning in my head. How much easier would my life be if I went for this guy? Money, parents in publishing, a straight nose and strong chin that would guarantee genetically superior offspring. I pictured a whirlwind courtship and a house in the Hamptons.

But I didn't own my whole heart anymore, even if the person currently in possession of it didn't want it. Rebounds were for the old Lily—this one wanted to do right by people. And herself. And feigning interest in someone else, no matter how great he looked on paper, was a recipe for disaster.

"It's a good idea," I said finally. "I'll keep that in mind." I set the champagne glass down on the bar. "I think I'm going to head out."

He was surprised. "I was about to ask if you wanted to dance."

I shook my head. "Thank you, but no."

"What about the cake? And the bouquet?"

"I don't want either," I said over my shoulder as I walked away. "But it was nice to meet you."

CHAPTER
FORTY-THREE

I peeled off the purple dress, minimizing bra, and Spanx as soon as I got home, and then took a deeper breath than I had been capable of for the past several hours. I twisted my ridiculously straight hair into a messy bun to get it off of my neck and went to the kitchen to pour myself a well-earned glass of wine.

Becca must have come by the apartment while I was at the wedding because my mail was on the counter. I paid my bills online, so I was terrible about checking the mail. I took the stack to the trash can and flipped through it over the open bin, dropping the junk as I went until one letter stopped me.

My name and address were written on the envelope in familiar handwriting. Curious, I took it to the sofa and opened it.

Lily,
Maybe I'm a coward for writing you a letter instead of calling, but I didn't want this to be a conversation.
I would love to say that I'm strong enough to for-give you and move on, but I'm not. You violated my

trust, and you said unforgivable things about my mom. She may not be perfect, but she's my mom. And the lack of respect that you showed her . . . there's no coming back from that.

I also can't forgive you for the fact that after thirteen years of thinking you were my friend, those things you said in the blog were how you actually saw me. Do you even know how to be someone's friend? I thought I knew the answer to that, but apparently I was very, very wrong.

So this is me cancelling your invitation to my wedding.

I hope you can find a way to be happy, Lily. I won't say you deserve it after this, but I hope you find it anyway.

Please don't contact me again.

Sincerely,

Sharon

I set the letter on the coffee table with a shaking hand and leaned back against the sofa, a tear trickling out of the corner of my eye and snaking its way down my face before I wiped it away.

I deserved every word of that. To be fair, I deserved it from more than just Sharon. If anything, I had gotten off way too easily by only completely destroying two friendships. But knowing it was my fault didn't make it hurt any less.

～

I couldn't fall asleep, even after a glass of wine and some truly mindless television. I debated texting Becca, but I didn't want to bring her down. Not now, when she was finally so happy. I had been a crappy enough friend to everyone else already. I would have to downgrade to a smaller apartment when she decided to make it official with Will—I couldn't afford this on my own, and I didn't know anyone else single whom I could room with. Not that I could imagine anyone choosing to room with me after seeing how I had just publicly treated my closest friends.

For a split second, I regretted blowing Finn off, but that regret faded immediately into vague relief. He wouldn't have solved anything.

I sat up.

Or had he already?

"How are you going to spin this whole publicity thing?" he had asked. *"Find a way to make it profitable."*

Profitable.

I jumped out of bed and grabbed my laptop. In my haste to erase the blog, I hadn't considered the fact that I was generating money from it. What happened when I went viral? With the blog gone, I couldn't access my advertising stats, but I logged into my bank account, not daring to breathe while the page loaded.

There was an advertising deposit in my account for almost fifteen thousand dollars.

Oh. My. God.

I had goose bumps and could feel my whole spine tingling. Was it too late to get the blog back? What had I done?

I shut the laptop and closed my eyes. No. My friends and family mattered more than the money.

But the wheels were turning furiously in my head. *Bridesmania* was gone, but I could start a new site. I had enough notoriety right now that people would read it. And the new blog would have my name on it for full accountability.

I reopened my laptop and started writing.

Well, that didn't go as planned. Not that I really had an endgame in mind, but getting outed by Buzzfeed definitely wasn't what I expected.

That's right. My name is Lily Weiss, and I'm THAT bridesmaid.

I feel like I should probably start this post by writing, Bart Simpson–style on a chalkboard, that I will not anonymously trash my loved ones on the internet anymore until I can't feel my wrist. But I have already prostrated myself at the altar of my loved ones' forgiveness, and all, save two, have decided to give me a second chance at being a better human being.

I've learned a lot in the last few weeks, mostly about myself. Which, I suppose, makes sense. Because despite what I said in it, the blog wasn't about the brides and their exaggerated horror movie–esque behavior. It was about me—especially the mean parts. Every horrible thing that I said about them showed an even uglier side of myself. I see that now.

So why was I so blind before?

In the middle of all five weddings, I began to feel like I didn't matter. As if the fact that I had feelings had gotten lost in the shuffle. And the blog was a way to feel like some small fraction of my life was, in fact, still about me.

331

It was petty, and immature, and it cost me two people whom I still love very much.

So to everyone I hurt, please know that I am sorry, and I will work as hard as I can for as long as it takes to earn your love and trust back.

But I also learned that I miss writing. I was a journalism major in college and was going to save the world. But somewhere along the way, I took the easy way out and forgot that I ever wanted to do that in the first place.

I'm no longer under the impression that I'm going to save the world. But the explosive popularity of the blog told me that maybe, just maybe, I have something to say that people want to read.

Or you all just love snark and drama. Sickos.

But the blog *was* me, even if it was the worst side of me. So I want to see if I can re-create the same kind of energy while being held accountable for what I write.

Welcome to the new blog. Come for the public flogging of the world's worst bridesmaid. Stay for the real life.

I skimmed what I wrote. I had no clue what I was actually going to write about moving forward. But it was a way to dip my toes into the water and see if I could really do this. If nothing else, Martin would be proud.

I went to WordPress and clicked the "Create New Blog" button. It asked for a title. I wanted something with my name. *Bridesmania* had been all about trying to hide my identity so I could post with impunity. This had to tell the world who I was.

The phrase "consider the lily" came to mind. I googled it. *Oops.* It came from a Bible verse. *Well,* I thought, *it's still cute.* I typed Considering Lily as the name of the blog and looked at it. It felt like it fit with the whole idea of trying to find who I wanted to be. And when I flipped the verb into a participle, it wasn't quite biblical. I decided that I liked it.

With that set, I wrote a brief bio, then linked to my public social media accounts.

I stared at the "add title" line above my first post. I thought for a moment, then typed, For the Love of Friends. But I hesitated before hitting "Publish." If I was going to do this, I had to do it well. There were stakes now. Granted, there had been stakes last time, I just hadn't known it.

I closed my eyes and crossed my fingers, then hit "Publish." *Here goes nothing,* I thought.

~

I couldn't fall asleep. It didn't help that I was checking the stats on the new blog every three seconds since posting it to my Facebook, Twitter, and Instagram accounts, but it was the money keeping me awake. What was I going to do with the money?

Quit the foundation. Write full time, a voice in my head whispered. *Then buy shoes.*

It was an appealing idea. But that large of an amount in such a short time was a fluke and I knew it. The new blog might not generate enough to live on. Besides, I'd be writing about my life, not other people. Was I interesting enough to make real money?

And more importantly, the halo-wearing side of my conscience told me I couldn't keep what I had earned off writing about my friends. I tried to ignore that voice, but it was no use.

Finally, I decided on a compromise I could live with. I logged back into my bank account and paid off my credit card. Then I divided the remaining amount by five and Venmoed that sum to each of the five brides with the same message: Please accept your share of the blog profits as a wedding gift. I love you, and I'm sorry.

If anyone protested, I would tell them that if they didn't accept it, I would use it to buy them the tackiest, custom-made, non-returnable wedding gift that I could find. No one could argue with that.

With my conscience thus cleared, I finally drifted off to sleep.

CHAPTER
FORTY-FOUR

I spent the next two weeks in quiet penance. I did a lot of Caryn's job during the day, then I went to my parents' house and helped my mother make favors for Amy's wedding three nights in a row after work. The day of Sharon's wedding, I went with Amy for her final dress fitting and then spent the evening packing gift bags for out-of-town guests.

"What else can I do?" I asked.

Amy and my mother exchanged looks. "I think it's under control," Amy said.

"What about table arrangements?"

Amy shrugged. "They've been done for weeks now."

"Boutonnieres for the groomsmen?"

"Ordered. The best man is picking them up the morning of the wedding."

"There has to be something."

"There isn't," my mother said gently. Our relationship had undergone a definite shift since I had confided in her about Alex. There was a little less of an edge, and I didn't feel as attacked. I no longer felt annoyed when I saw her pop up on my caller ID. I didn't know if it was her or me or both, but whatever had caused the change, I hoped it lasted. "You've been a huge help this week though."

"Have gifts started coming in? I could help with thank-you notes."

Amy laughed. "Go home, Lily."

It was eight o'clock, but still light outside. Between Caryn being on her honeymoon, Sharon no longer my friend, Becca never around, Megan preparing for her wedding, and Alex wanting nothing to do with me, I found filling the hours to be a daunting task.

But I stuck to my word and emailed Madison, and we began a—halting at first—correspondence. She was well-read—much more so than my brother, who didn't see the point in reading if there was a movie—and she got literary references that traveled far over his head. By the fourth or fifth email, I discovered that, once she warmed up, she was actually pretty funny. She may not have been the extrovert that I was, but we were a lot more alike than I would have imagined, which made me feel more connected to my brother as well. I started texting him a couple of times a week. True, our correspondence consisted primarily of memes, but it was something.

I wrote more blog posts, also haltingly at first. I talked about Finn in one, not by name of course, and about why I decided being a trophy wife wasn't for me. That one generated a little buzz online, even though half of the comments called me crazy for not chasing the easy life. I responded to every comment—from home, or my cell phone if I was at work. This one would never touch the FST computers. Even knowing that Martin didn't object, *I* wanted to be professional this time.

I didn't talk about Alex. Or say anything negative about any of the brides. But I did write a post about my newfound respect for my sister-in-law. I planned to email it to her, not knowing if she was reading the new blog, but she commented on it before I did, thanking me. Or maybe it was a Russian bot, pretending to be her. Who knows? The internet is a dark and creepy place, after all.

~

Finally, it was Amy's wedding day. I hugged her moments before it was time for me to walk down the aisle. "I'm happy for you," I whispered, meaning it.

Her eyes glimmered and she elbowed me. "Don't you make me cry right now."

"Okay. But I love you, little sis."

She dabbed at her eyes. "I love you too, you big jerk."

~

I sat between Madison and my grandmother at the reception. "Joanie, when is it your turn?" my grandmother asked me. I looked at Madison and rolled my eyes. She smiled.

"I don't know."

"Well hurry up. I'm not going to live forever, you know."

"That's not morbid at a wedding or anything."

"Oh, I'll be at yours. You mark my words. I don't care if your mother has to dig me up and tie me to a chair. I'll be there."

Madison and I exchanged another look. "I'll get right on it, Grandma."

She leaned over to me and whispered, which without her hearing aids was still a volume that could be heard from three tables over, "I read that new blog thing of yours. You should call that banker. There's nothing wrong with being a trophy wife!"

"Grandma!"

"Since when do you read blogs?" Jake asked.

"I saw it on the Facebook Google. You think I don't know how all that works, but at least Joanie is posting interesting stuff. No one wants to see a picture of every meal you eat, Jake."

Madison let out a yelp of laughter and I collapsed giggling onto her shoulder.

"When did you two get so close?" he asked us, his arms crossed grumpily.

I put an arm around Madison. "I love my new sister. Best thing you ever did. I'm actually glad now that Mom and Dad *didn't* trade you for a dog when I was in fifth grade and made that poster about why they should."

"I expect an apology for that in the next blog post," he said.

"Don't hold your breath." I turned to Madison. "Let's grab Amy and get some sister shots in the photo booth."

"Definitely."

Amy was standing by a table, talking with some of our mother's cousins. "Sorry," I said, grabbing her arm. "We need to borrow the bride."

"Thank you," Amy sighed as we pulled her away. "Who were those people?"

I laughed. "You're the worst."

"You're one to talk!"

I started to sputter a response, but Madison interrupted. "Think they'll let us cut the line for the photo booth because we have the bride?" Amy and I exchanged a look. "What?"

"You follow rules," Amy said.

"That's *so* cute." I put an arm around her waist. "Don't worry, we'll have you corrupted in no time."

"Outta the way," Amy said to the waiting guests as she dug through the prop box and began loading us up with boas and signs. "Bridal party, coming through!"

~

After we spent way too long making silly faces and posing for pictures, Amy bounded off to find Tyler, and Jake came to pull Madison onto the dance floor. I went back to our table, but my parents soon joined the dancers and my grandmother went to talk to her nieces and nephews at another table, leaving me alone at ours.

I watched the dancing from my seat, leaning an elbow on the table and propping my chin in my hand. *If this were a movie,* I thought, *Alex would come up behind me and ask me to dance. And I'd look at him in shock and ask what he was doing here, and he would tell me Amy invited him after all.*

Unable to stop myself, I glanced longingly at the door to the mansion's ballroom. No one was coming.

A couple of songs later, my dad approached me at the table. "Come on. It's time to dance with your dad."

I rose and took his arm, and he led me out to the dance floor. "You doing any better?" he asked.

"Just one more wedding left to go after tonight."

"That's not what I meant."

I sighed. "Yeah. I'll be okay."

"I know you *will* be. You always land on your feet. Doesn't mean you're okay now."

I thought for a minute. "I *am* okay, I guess."

"Your mother said you were a huge help getting everything ready for the wedding."

"It was the least I could do. I still need to make it up to everyone."

He fixed me with a hard look. "Just be sure you're making time to take care of yourself too."

"I will, Dad."

He kissed my forehead. "And remember that your mother and I love you. No matter what Jake says."

I smiled. "It's not too late to trade him in for a dog."

I was rewarded with a wink. "I'm still working on your mother."

CHAPTER
FORTY-FIVE

And then there was one.

Alex didn't look at me during the rehearsal. I tried to catch his eye, but when it became apparent he wasn't going to look, I took that as a clear sign that trying to talk to him would be futile.

Megan and Tim were both semi-practicing Catholics, so the ceremony would be held at Megan's family's church, with the reception following at a swanky hotel in DC that boasted a spectacular view of the National Mall. Megan's mother didn't quite make eye contact with me either, which I recognized as evidence she had read the blog and disapproved of my sexual proclivities while drunk. And apparently even the priest was a Buzzfeed reader, because when he explained the communion to the wedding party, he made a point of saying that only Catholics were to take the communion. "If you aren't Catholic, or are and aren't pure enough to take communion at this time"—he looked pointedly at me—"you will simply bow your head."

I considered chiming in that I wasn't Catholic, so my religion was the issue, not my purity, but I kept my mouth shut and glowered silently at the floor instead.

~

I wanted to be deliriously happy for Megan. Isn't that how you feel on your best friend's wedding day? But the priest's comment at the rehearsal had knocked me for a loop. It meant *everyone* at the wedding—and on Megan's side, that included people I had known for most of my life—had read the blog and knew what I had done. And even worse, it didn't take a rocket scientist to figure out which groomsman was creepy and which one was avoiding me like the plague, so not only had I humiliated myself, but Alex was probably suffering too.

But for Megan, I put on my cheeriest smile and faked it. Even when I said good morning to Claire and she turned her head the other way, I didn't let my face show what I felt.

Megan knew though. She put a hand on my arm while the stylist curled my now semi-permanently-straightened hair around the barrel of an iron, and I looked up to see pity reflected in her eyes. "You look beautiful," I told her.

She leaned in close and whispered in my ear, "You can do this."

I nodded, not quite trusting myself to talk, and swallowed hard. "I don't matter today."

"You always matter, Lil. And I'm sorry I ever made you feel otherwise." She saw that I was struggling to maintain the cheerful front and switched gears. "You ready to get strapped into that bra?"

"I'm burning that thing after today."

"How very retro." She took my hand and squeezed it.

~

Mark was the best man, so I was paired opposite him at the altar. Alex was two people behind, with Justin standing directly behind him. I couldn't look at Alex without seeing Justin looking back at me, so I tried to focus on Megan instead, which was where I should be looking anyway. But I kept gazing back, willing him to look at me too. To offer some hope of forgiveness.

He didn't.

When the ceremony was over, Mark smiled genuinely at me as he offered his arm, and I took it, reminding myself to smile for the pictures. The last thing I wanted was to look sad in Megan's wedding album.

We toasted the couple in the limo on the way to the hotel, posed this way and that for the photographer, and finally it was time for the reception. I refused the champagne that the waiters kept pouring though; I needed a clear head for my speech.

The bandleader gestured to Mark and he went to the bandstand to begin his toast. I looked around, frantic; Alex hadn't taken his seat at our table yet. I spotted him leaning against the bar as Mark began to talk. I just needed to know where he was—even if it was so I could *not* look at him during mine.

I would love to say that I paid attention to Mark's speech, but I didn't. Instead, I ran through mine in my head. When everyone around me raised a glass, I did the same, and then it was my turn. The bandleader introduced me, and the band played a snippet of the song "Notorious" as I rose to take the microphone. I spun to give Megan a look. She threw her head back and laughed.

I left my notecards at my seat. I had the whole thing memorized, so they would just be a distraction. Mark handed me the microphone, and the bandleader gestured to the band to cut the song.

"Well, that was probably an appropriate introduction," I began, veering off course. There was some laughter.

"I've known Megan since we were seven years old. The day we became friends, in fact, she smacked another girl in the face with a Snoopy lunch box for telling the entire bus that I had a crush on Ricky Wilson." More laughter.

"Everyone needs a friend who will beat someone else in the head with a lunch box for you, and Megan has always been mine. Of course, I'm sure there are more than a couple of you here tonight who would like to hit me with a lunch box, and not out of friendship. In fact, there's a whole second reception line after dinner so everyone I've wronged can take turns slapping me with a Snoopy lunch box." Much heartier laughter. Claire caught my eye as one of the few people not laughing. She sat stone-faced, her arms crossed. If I had actually brought a lunch box, she would be racing to be first in line.

"Learning to share Megan has been hard, but Tim has been particularly gracious about it. And I couldn't wish for a better husband for my wife—oh sorry, did you not know about that? Megan and I have a pact that we're going to marry each other if either of us is still single at forty, so by my calculations, you've got just over seven years until I take her back." Less laughter at that one, but still a decent amount.

"In all seriousness, though, it's been inspiring to watch how happy you have made Megan. I've been with her through so much, but I've never seen her light up the way she does with you. And there's no one else in the world I could share her with so freely.

"Megan and Tim, may you always be this happy. May you share the joys of this world together always, and may your lives be as full of wonder and bliss as you both are today. I love you so much." I raised my glass and the crowd followed as I felt tears well up in my eyes.

"To Megan and Tim." The room echoed my sentiment, and I returned to my seat. I glanced around the table—Alex was still at the bar, so I couldn't gauge his reaction.

I picked up a glass of champagne that the waiter had filled while I was speaking. I could drink now at least—just not to the point where I did anything stupid.

Alex slid into his seat at the table, across from me, once the salads were in place. He mostly talked to Claire's husband, Alan, but finally, over the main course, he glanced in my direction.

I froze. Part of me wanted to shout how I felt across the table. Part of me wanted to crawl under the table and hide.

He held my gaze for what felt like several minutes, making non-committal responses to Alan until he eventually looked away.

It was something though. And enough to give me a quick sense of hope.

Megan and Tim were invited to the dance floor by the bandleader, and we all watched from the darkened room as they did their choreographed routine in the spotlight. As they twirled around the floor, I sat there trying to work up my courage. When the bandleader invited the rest of the guests to join them on the dance floor, I saw Mark turn to me from the corner of my eye, but I got up and ran around the table to Alex.

"Can we talk?" I asked.

"Now?"

"Yes. Or I'll lose my nerve."

He sighed, but he pushed his chair back from the table and stood, offering me his hand. I looked at him in surprise. "It'll look bad if we leave the room. It will be better if we dance." I nodded and took his hand, then followed him onto the dance floor.

We stayed near the fringe, where the music was quieter, his arm loose around my waist. He remained silent.

"Please say something," I said finally.

"You were the one who wanted to talk."

I nodded and took a deep breath. "I miss you. So much." He didn't respond. "I—know what I did was awful, but—you were married before. It's not like either of us has a clean slate."

He started. "You're comparing me being *divorced* to you sleeping with Justin? And you think that's why I'm mad at you?"

"Isn't it?"

"Well—yes. You could have had me—at any time—and you picked *him* of all people?"

Sara Goodman Confino

"I didn't know I could have had you. I didn't *want* him. I was drunk and stupid and—" I trailed off.

He looked at me in disbelief, but took a moment to respond. "I'm more upset you didn't tell me. I wouldn't have cared—well, I would have *cared*, but I could have gotten over it if you had told me. But you decided it was a death sentence without giving me the chance to make my own decision and then told the whole world about it instead."

"I—Megan told me I couldn't—after Justin—"

"And *that* was why we couldn't be together? If Megan told you to jump off a bridge, would you do it?"

"Probably, yes."

"Fine," he said, steering me toward the center of the dance floor. "Let's ask her."

"If I should jump off a bridge?" He fixed me with a withering look.

When we reached the newlyweds, Megan had her cheek against Tim's, but Alex got us close enough for her to hear. He called her name and she opened her eyes. "Can I date Lily?"

"Do you *want* to?" she asked. Tim turned to look at us.

"I didn't say that. I'm just asking if you care."

"It's your funeral," she said with a shrug.

I gave her a dirty look. She smiled wickedly and blew me a kiss, then pressed her cheek back to Tim's.

We made our way back to the edge of the dance floor. "See why it's not smart to make assumptions about how other people are going to react?" he asked.

"I'm sorry. I should have told you—I should have told you so much earlier and let you decide if you still liked me."

"When did it happen?"

"What?"

"When did you sleep with him?"

"Why? What does it matter now?"

"Do you want me to try to move past this?"

346

With all my heart, I thought. "Yes."

"Then I get to know when it happened so I can decide if I can actually get past it or not. If it was the night of Amy's party, I'm out of here."

"You can't think that I—from you to *him*?"

His face was still stony. "You tell me."

I looked into his eyes plaintively, but he wasn't budging. "I don't even remember it," I confessed finally. "It was the night of Megan and Tim's engagement party, and I had just gotten the call from my sister that she was engaged too, and I got so drunk and I—well, the next thing I remember was waking up in the hotel room next to him."

Alex dropped his hand from my waist and stepped back. He stared at me in disbelief. "It was before I really knew you," I said. "But that's why I couldn't do that to Megan even though I wanted to—when you kissed me that night, I—I think I knew all along how I felt, but I didn't want to admit it because I couldn't do that after—after—"

"This isn't happening."

"I know you said you tried to keep him away from me that night, but I don't remember. And I know it doesn't speak well of me that I would get that drunk and do *that* with *him*—"

"You didn't."

"I—what?"

He started to respond and then it was too much for him. He doubled over, hands on his thighs, laughing too hard to speak. When he finally caught his breath, he put an arm back around my waist, pulling me in close.

"You didn't sleep with Justin, you fool."

"What do you mean?"

"You stole *my* shirt."

"I—what? No. Justin said it was him at the housewarming." I pulled back, not understanding.

"Really? What did he say?"

347

"He—he said I owed him—for skipping out without saying goodbye—"

"You skipped out without saying goodbye when you came up to me and begged me to keep him away from you."

"But—he said I owed him for the shirt."

"You spilled a glass of red wine all over him."

"I—what?"

"Lily, he was all over you. You were clearly drunk and I asked if you were okay. You said you were too drunk to drive home and he wouldn't leave you alone. You really don't remember any of this?"

Now that he was saying it, I could picture the arm that I was leaning on at the hotel's check-in desk as being attached to Alex. "You got us a room," I said quietly.

"I offered to drive you home, but you said you couldn't leave your car. And you were wasted and not making a whole lot of sense."

I held a hand to my face. "Does that mean I—that we—?"

"Is that what you think of me? No!"

"But I woke up and my clothes were on the floor."

"*You* took them off. I looked away. Mostly. You said you couldn't breathe in your dress and your bra was uncomfortable."

I tried to remember. "But you were naked too—"

"I slept in my boxers."

"And we didn't—?" He shook his head. I couldn't make eye contact. I was mortified.

"How did you think I was Justin?"

"I couldn't see his—your—face—and I told Megan I didn't want to know who it was. And then Justin said that, and I thought—oh my God, I'm so stupid." I thought back to Megan's housewarming party, where Alex was so sweet on the porch. To the notes at Starbucks. The way he dropped everything to come help me at Amy's bachelorette and then the fact that I published something so wrong when there had never been anything standing between us at all. Nothing except my own idiocy.

"But—you read the blog. I said it happened at the engagement party in the blog."

He shook his head. "I read the Buzzfeed article and most recent blog post. Then I was too mad to go back and read the rest. And then by the time I was ready to, you had deleted it."

I stared at him. "I don't know what to say. Alex, I'm so—" He cut off my apology with a kiss.

"Megan-sanctioned this time," he said, a teasing glint in his eye.

"Who?" I asked, a tear slipping past my lash extensions, despite the smile on my face. His hand cupped my cheek, and he brushed the tear away with his thumb. He leaned forward to kiss me again, and I wanted nothing more in the world than to hold him and never let him go. I kissed him lightly, then whispered, "But we shouldn't do this."

"You'd better be kidding." His arm was tight around my waist.

"Here," I laughed. "We shouldn't do this *here*. At the wedding."

He smiled and kissed my cheek gently, and I felt a wave of desire wash over me. "I missed you too," he said. I wrapped my arms tightly around his neck and we stayed like that for a long time, swaying slightly with the music, but mostly just hugging each other as close as we could.

∼

As the night began to wind down, I excused myself to go to the bathroom. Megan was in there, touching up her lipstick in the mirror. "I see everyone got a happy ending today," she said to my reflection.

I sat on the ottoman next to her. "How could you not tell me?"

She shrugged. "I was sworn to secrecy, as you may recall. I figured if you two didn't work it out tonight, I'd tell you then."

"But these past few weeks I—"

She turned to face me. "I told you I wasn't going to get over the blog overnight. And you got off pretty easily if you ask me, so I was okay with you suffering a little. I feel better now."

"If I didn't love you . . ." I shook my head.

"But you do," she said sweetly. "You gave a whole speech about that tonight. And I love you too."

"So I actually have your approval?"

She hugged me. "Be happy. You deserve it." She let me go and turned to head back to the reception, then stopped in the doorway. "Should I throw the bouquet right to you, or would that just be awkward?"

I laughed. "Aren't I the only single girl here?"

"My cousin Maggie is too."

"Isn't your cousin Maggie twelve?"

"Hey, do you want the bouquet or not?"

I nodded. After she left, I looked in the mirror and almost didn't recognize the girl in front of me—but not because of the makeup or hair this time. Had I ever looked this happy? I winked at my reflection and went to pee. Alex was waiting for me.

EPILOGUE

Neither of us had driven to the hotel to get ready that morning, so we took an Uber to my apartment, me sitting in the middle seat to be closer to him, our fingers intertwined.

"We wasted so much time," I said, shaking my head. "Because I was too dumb to face up to what I thought I did."

He brought my fingers to his lips and kissed them. "We only wasted this last month. I wasn't ready for anything real when we met."

I thought about the girl who crept out of the hotel room in a stolen shirt and shook my head at the memory. "No. I don't think I was either."

"And now?"

I took his arm and put it around my shoulder, snuggling in against him. He kissed the top of my head.

When the Uber pulled up outside of my building, there was no discussion. We both got out and walked quickly to the elevator, still holding hands. Once safely alone inside, we kissed again, my back against the bar, my arms around his neck. He had to tell me that we should get out when we reached my floor; I was too wrapped up in him to realize the door had opened.

He kissed down the side of my neck, an arm around my waist as I fumbled with my key and kicked off my shoes as we fell in the door, pulling his tie off at the same time.

"Lily!" I jumped a mile at Becca's voice.

Now? I thought. *Of all times, now?* Alex pulled away and straightened up, running a quick hand through his hair.

She rose off the sofa, where Will still sat, two glasses and a bottle of champagne on the coffee table in front of them. She came toward me with her left hand extended.

"Will proposed!"

I smiled reflexively. "That's great, Bec! I'm so happy for you both!"

She beamed back at Will, happily. "I can't even believe it—you'll be my bridesmaid, won't you?"

"Of course," I said as Alex started to laugh behind me. "But starting tomorrow. Tonight, I have other plans."

ACKNOWLEDGMENTS

This book spent a very long time percolating before it actually made its way onto the page, and it would not be in your hands today without the help of my incredible support network.

First, I want to thank my superhero of an agent, Rachel Beck, along with the whole team at Liza Dawson Associates. You and I found each other at a time when I had almost given up hope that I would ever succeed as a writer, and I can never thank you enough for what you have given me. The fact that we both held off going into labor until this deal went through and then had our babies on the same day is just icing on the cake. I love and appreciate you.

To my editor, Alicia Clancy, thank you for seeing the potential in this story and in me. You made my dream become a reality, and it's a much stronger work thanks to your insight. I can't wait to work with you on the next one!

Thank you to the whole team at Lake Union Publishing for believing in me enough to publish not only this book, but a second one as well. I couldn't ask for a better experience.

Thank you to my developmental editor, Holly Ingraham, for tightening the weak spots and helping me round out Lily's character. I absolutely love the finished product thanks to you.

Thank you to my husband, Nick, and our two sons, Jacob and Max. Nick, writing this with a toddler would not have been possible without your support and absolute belief in my ability to make a career out of my passion. Not to mention giving me the time to get my edits done while eight months pregnant in a pandemic and then with a newborn. Thank you for always knowing that I would succeed, even when I didn't. Thank you to Jacob and Max, for keeping me company and providing the best distractions ever. (And thank you to Rosie and Sandy, our schnauzers, because Nick told me I needed to thank them for cuddling me and for not blocking too much of my laptop while I was writing.) I love you all very much.

Thank you to my parents, Jordan and Carole Goodman, who cultivated my love of both reading and writing practically from birth. Mom, you have always been my first reader, and I appreciate your insight and endless support. This book would not exist without you. (And no, Lily's mom isn't based on you!) Dad, thank you for the socially distanced, pandemic headshot and for always keeping my technology working (and recovering missing pages when that technology goes awry). Who would have thought that mini laptop you gave me to type my stories on when I was a kid would lead to this?

Thank you to my brother, Adam, and sister-in-law, Nicole Goodman. Seeing my early works on your shelf, three thousand miles away, made me feel loved and supported every time I've come to visit. I love you, Cam and Luke, so very much.

Thank you to my grandmother, Charlotte Chansky—you may have behaved better than Lily's grandmother in Mexico, but you were her inspiration. Your love of storytelling shaped so much of my childhood and my voice as a writer. And how Bert would have kvelled.

Thank you, Aunt Dolly and Uncle Marvin Band, for always loving and believing in me—so much, in fact, that you accidentally spilled the beans about my book deal before I did. But, at your age—I'll stop there.

Thank you to Uncle Mike, Aunt Stephanie Abbuhl, and Andrew, Peter, and Ben Chansky, for providing my very favorite writing spot. Mike, you may be a pain, but every time I see my books on the shelves in Avalon, I know it's (mostly) for show.

Thank you to my cousins, Allison Band, Andy Levine, Ian and Kim Band, and Mindy and Alan Nagler, for being some of my loudest cheerleaders. Your genuine excitement when good things happen means the world to me.

Thank you to Mark Kamins, for your unconditional love and support. I wish your parents were here to see this.

Thank you to Kevin Keegan, the best of teachers, mentors, and friends. I could write a whole book about the difference you have made in my life (actually, I kind of did) and it would not be enough. I hope you laugh as you read this, without anyone needing to hit a concierge bell.

Thank you, Jennifer Lucina, for being my friend, my sounding board, my life coach, and my friend—I said friend twice because it's amazing that you're still here after everything we've been through. I couldn't have told this story without you (and your wedding—sorry!), and I love you so, so much.

Thank you, Rachel Friedman, for keeping me sane during the writing of this book, both by being a free therapist and by making me laugh when I felt like I was drowning. I'm so lucky to have you in my life.

Thank you, Sonya Shpilyuk, for keeping me grounded, whether at work, at home, or both during a pandemic. You're my absolute favorite weirdo and I adore you.

Thank you to Jan Guttman, Georgia Zucker, Christen Dimmick, Joye Young Saxon, Chris Smith, Katie Crockett, Sarah Elbeshbishi, and Jade Pinkowitz for the many years of support, friendship, and, of course, coffee.

Thank you to the Confino family.

Thank you to everyone who supported my self-published works and blogs throughout the years. You made me believe that I could actually do this.

And finally, thank you to Uncle Jules, for giving me a typewriter when I was eight years old and telling me I should be a writer. I hope I've made you proud.

ABOUT THE AUTHOR

Photo © 2020 Jordan Goodman

Sara Goodman Confino teaches high school English and journalism in Montgomery County, Maryland, where she lives with her husband, two sons, and two miniature schnauzers, Rosie and Sandy. When she's not writing or working out, she can be found on the beach or at a Bruce Springsteen show, sometimes even dancing onstage. For more information visit www.saraconfino.com.